A Portrait in Time

A Novel

by

Charles J. Schneider

Published
by
Brighton Publishing LLC
435 N. Harris Drive
Mesa, AZ 85203

A PORTRAIT IN TIME

A NOVEL

BY

CHARLES J. SCHNEIDER

PUBLISHED
BY
BRIGHTON PUBLISHING LLC
435 N. HARRIS DRIVE
CHANDLER, AZ 85203
WWW.BRIGHTONPUBLISHING.COM

ISBN 13: 978-1-62183-150-1
ISBN 10: 1-621-83150-7

PRINTED IN THE UNITED STATES OF AMERICA

FIRST EDITION

COVER DESIGN: TOM RODRIGUEZ

Dedication

In memory of my father,
a man who always knew how to tell a good story.
Charles M. Schneider
(12/22/1928-12/15/2008)

Acknowledgements

Thank you, Dessi, for injecting logic and common sense into a story that otherwise would have been anything but believable. Without you, this piece of fiction would have never made it past its first draft. Thank you, also, for your expert computer and graphic arts skills, which brought realism to all of my memos, announcements, and newspaper clippings found between the chapters.

Thanks to my children, Rachelle, Christian, and Luke, who generously gave up more than just a little bit of their own time with me for almost three years, so that I could have the time to devote to creating this book.

A world of thanks goes to my first editor, Bill Thompson, who recognized some potential in my first concept draft and taught me to "just tell the damn story." I am grateful also for the additional editing provided by the incomparable Brighton Publishing team, and for the support and guidance provided to me by Brighton's Acquisition Editor, Don McGuire.

Finally, I am indebted to my literary agent, Anita Melograna (aka 'Merlin') of Crosswind Agency, who mentored me during the editing process and made the realization and publication of this novel possible.

"Beauty, like truth, is relative to the time when one lives and to the individual who can grasp it..."

~ Gustave Courbet

"A painting requires a little mystery, some vagueness, and some fantasy. When you always make your meaning perfectly plain you end up boring people."

~ Edgar Degas

Chapter One

She had mailed the letter herself, just this morning, waiting in line patiently behind a dozen other patrons until it was finally her turn to count out the correct combination of hard-earned coins and place them with a metallic jingle into the outstretched palm of the clerk behind the counter. He stamped it in red, making the posting date official: *31 May, 1877*; and although there was nothing more she could do, now that her message was out of her hands and in someone else's instead, she lingered for just a moment longer, simply to ensure that her envelope ended up on the right pile of letters, which it did—tossed on the top with five or six others underneath it, all of them addressed to foreign destinations, places she would never see but could only imagine. It would probably take three or four weeks for her carefully worded request to reach him in Switzerland; when he finally did receive it, she felt certain he wouldn't fail her. She was pleading not for herself but for their son, after all, so how could he possibly refuse?

He had his own financial difficulties to deal with, she was well aware; but she had figured out a way, and when he read her suggestion, he would see it too. Time, she feared, was running short, since his health was failing him, and if she didn't obtain the promise of his assistance now, it might be too late—and very soon. She had countless square and rectangular solutions to her monetary dilemma stockpiled in her *appartement*, most of them safely stacked from floor to ceiling along one wall of her tiny bedroom. She had hung a handful of her favorite paintings on the cracked and dirty plaster so she could admire them whenever she pleased. Nobody wanted them, because of what they were and who had created them, but maybe in the right hands that curse could be lifted. It might work—she hoped it would—but it would have to come from him, not her. She prayed that her words would move him to action.

She lived alone, but tonight she had company. This man would do, to pass the time, in this life of hers that seemed more and more difficult with each passing day. She modeled for unknown artists now, for a fraction of the fee her nude posings would have earned her before. This one had insisted that his money should buy him more than just the right to paint the smooth curves of her perfect body, but she really didn't mind. He was attractive and eager, and she would get as much—if not more—pleasure than he would from tonight's culmination of their weeklong business transaction. For six, long, afternoon sessions she had modeled, patient and unmoving on a couch in his chilly basement studio, her skin on one side itchy from lying exposed on a tattered wool blanket day after day; and now, still breathless, she lay reasonably satisfied beside him, having just exchanged the carnal portion of their agreed-upon terms.

It would be nice to have a warm body sleeping beside her for a change, a luxury that had been denied her most nights since the hasty departure of Edmond's father, a bag in each hand and a sack containing some personal items over his shoulder, running from government creditors and worse, the rumors following him out the door and into the carriage waiting for him at the curbside that icy night in February when he had escaped into lonely anonymity. She had to move out of the house where she had lived so comfortably as his model and mistress when the authorities had come to confiscate his assets. She'd been given just enough time to honor his last-minute request and load the unsellable remains of his life's work into a horse-drawn cart for safekeeping in her new living quarters.

Now, all she could afford was this one-room hovel, its ceiling one and the same with the house's musty rafters, sparsely furnished with only a squeaky cot in one corner and a wooden table with two chairs boasting splintered seats in the other, her chamber pot wedged between the rusty sink and the sputtering gas stove that she used for cooking year round and as a heating source in the winter. This was no place for a little boy, so Edmond had gone to live with her mother, an arrangement that she had come to accept as an expedient necessity. She saw him only one or two Sundays a month, when she would take him for an afternoon walk, more often than not in Place Pigalle, where he would stare wide-eyed at the scantily dressed dancers reporting for their shifts at one disreputable nightclub or another, their colorful costumes giving the impression of a flamboyant opulence that both she and her Edmond wished they could share. She would daydream as they passed the storefronts, imagining herself in a feather-fringed dress or a ruffled petticoat, as she gripped Edmond's hand tightly so he wouldn't get lost in the crowds or run out into the street, right into the path of some rich man's hansom cab.

She and her night's entertainment had finished a bottle of wine together beforehand, but now they switched to absinthe. Their flesh-on-flesh exertion had made her skin tacky and flushed, so she reached over him on the small cot to open the squat and narrow window in the third-floor attic room that the owner of the house on Butte Montmartre had converted hastily into a source of extra income. Her breasts pressed enticingly against his muscular chest, one arm propped on an elbow while the other jiggled the window upward, careful not to extend the jagged crack that had started in one corner of the yellowing pane.

He helped her by wedging a rectangular block of wood under the bottom of the window frame, their mutual effort allowing a meager draft of late spring air into the cluttered bedroom. He pulled her on top of him after. His dark, shoulder-length hair was tied back, its waves buried somewhere in her pillow, while hers, quite a bit longer, fell over her face and onto his with a gentle sweep of soft brunette fragrance.

"Where did you get it?" she asked, sipping the semi-illicit liquor from her glass, already stained red from a few glasses of wine. The absinthe, considered by most to be more of a drug than an alcoholic beverage, had already started to have its desired effect. She was more than a little bit tipsy to start with, and the slightly bitter burn of the hallucinogenic mixture in her throat began to seep into her bloodstream, fogging her vision and causing her to feel detached and disoriented. "It seems stronger than what I've had before," she managed to say, her words sounding far-off and distant, like they belonged to someone else, not to her at all. She became intensely intrigued, just for a moment, with her shadow on the wall, wavering in the candlelight with a movement all its own, belonging to her, of course, yet not at all.

"My friend Caroline knows someone who makes it," he answered, pouring her more from a flask at the bedside. "Rumor has it they added laudanum to this batch. It makes it more potent."

She could tell he was right. She knew she was lying on top of him, but it felt much more like she was floating, on a boat on the Seine or far out in the ocean somewhere. Vaguely, she felt him enter her again; and although it felt nice, something else was happening, something that wasn't quite right. All of a sudden her skin burned as if she was some kind of a living fire, generating a cloud of heat that blew in from somewhere deep inside and emanated outward, a backdraft ignited by God knows what, the absinthe and the laudanum perhaps?

In a moment, she imagined that the circle of heat that was one and the same with her feverish body would consume them, how could it not? It would leave a sizzling hole where they now lay, pulling her, the man, and even the painting hanging on the wall above their heads into a white void of nothingness. An absurd thought, she concluded; but that's when she saw it, horrified—a swirling vortex, opening in the wall, or perhaps the painting, leading to white nothingness. A hallucination? It seemed too real. A dream? She could only pray.

Hot, empty, swirling, pulling, it was taking her now…taking him, taking *them*. She floated upward, into the air, just for a moment—or so it seemed—but then, she was moving forward, quick and instant, although it seemed to happen in excruciatingly slow motion. This couldn't be real, but she knew it was. *Mon Dieu, help me!* She tried to resist, but she couldn't; she screamed, but no one heard. She saw the panic in his eyes, a fleeting gaze—and she felt it too. They were slipping—no, plummeting—forward, falling and tumbling and burning into terror, falling, falling, falling, into the white light of a scorching sun, so brilliant that it threatened to blind her, and so white that she had to close her eyes.

And when she did, that's when it all turned utterly and completely black.

The full moon posed in the night sky high above, while far below the sculpted outline of Musée d'Orsay reclined in the pre-midnight quiet of the Left Bank.

The interior of the museum could easily be seen through the line of glass doors, lights turned low, a solitary security guard visible at his post in front of a curved array of video monitors to the right in the front lobby. Behind him the metal, wire, and plastic of high-tech electronics hummed through the partly open door of a control room. The lobby lay quiet now, but in the morning there would be lines of people directed to the left, where a new day's shift of smiling ticketing agents would be ready for them behind the mahogany counters. Three million patrons a year would enter through those doors and wait patiently in the roped-off, back-and-forth queue until they were handed their time-stamped admissions ticket that would gain them entry to two levels of exhibit rooms to choose from, spread out in front of them over more than a full city block.

The guard was young, his skin still blemished from the recent memory of adolescence, his hair cut short and stylishly spiked in front, his expression serious, concentrating on the screens in front of him in a focused attempt at performing the night watch perfectly. This was his first real job, and although he had been assigned after-hours duty before, the weekly rotations that began two months ago when he was first hired had resulted in only two previous midnight shifts. He was trained to examine each of the four video monitors one by one, each screen divided into six digital panels, until he had thoroughly inspected all twenty-four views of the museum's interior. It was a tedious routine, but he was determined to follow the protocol.

Every hour, he would leave his post at the front desk to make his rounds, as he did now. He always began by descending a dozen stairs that led from the lobby to the sunken level of the refurbished nineteenth-century train station, a chiseled marble channel narrowed by four massive blocks of hollowed stone, two on either side, each containing exhibit rooms vaguely reminiscent of Egyptian tombs. All of these lower-level salons were devoted to permanent collections of sculptures, furniture, decorative arts, and photographs. He checked them with a quick sweep of his flashlight, just to make sure that each priceless piece was still there; and when this task was complete, he doubled back to the lobby side of the lower-level recess, to climb one of the side stairways of swirled marble that led back to the ground floor on the right side—his usual routine.

The two first-floor hallways were actually balconies, extending from one far end of the museum to the other in parallel symmetry, with the edges opening over waist-high lips of granite into the vast space of the immense structure, above and below, that had echoed years ago with the whistle and screech of steam engines. The smooth stone roofs of the sunken-level exhibit rooms ingeniously doubled as the floors for the ground-level catwalks, two imposing rectangles of polished rock on each side connected in the middle by a narrower walkway and, at the far end, by a wide flat platform, home to a small sampling of the museum's collection of Rodin sculptures as well as a double service elevator that led to the museum basement. The main complex of galleries could be accessed on both sides through one of the evenly spaced doors carved into the arching iron and steel wall of the former Gare d'Orsay, each of them leading into a connecting labyrinth of exhibit halls. On this side, he could enter the permanent Impressionist painting collection; on the other, across the dimly lit chasm of the renovated train station, he would ensure that the paintings displayed in the special exhibit rooms were safe and secure.

Tonight was no different than any other night on the catwalk. He took a moment to look and listen, confirming the eerily peaceful silence that stretched ahead of him as well as above, below, and across. Satisfied that he was alone, he walked through the nearest archway to gain entry into the Impressionist galleries, starting with the rooms devoted to Cezanne, Van Gogh, Pissarro, and Gauguin, moving on to double-check the multi-million dollar collection of Monet's water lilies and Degas' ballerinas. He patrolled past Lautrecs, Renoirs, and the works of artists he had never even heard of, eventually picking his way through the miniature forest of sculptures at the far end of the museum, maneuvering carefully through the Rodin plantings and passing the elevators on the wide platform that connected the two catwalks.

The rooms on the left were a maze that had confused him at first, but now he knew where each doorway would lead. The first three archways offered entry to a zigzagging series of connected galleries, the wood-tiled floors of one room starting where the other ended. The fourth doorway led through a straight line of medium-sized exhibit rooms to an eventual dead end for patrons, although a private exit door positioned in the corner of the last room provided access to a long hallway of administrative offices stretching along the full length of the museum on the left side. The final two doorways, closest to the front of the museum, provided entry to a single gallery with a high, vaulted ceiling—the place where Musée d'Orsay's largest acquisitions were always displayed.

He walked quickly through the first labyrinth of galleries, eager to reach the special exhibit of Courbet and Degas nudes (not yet open to the public) that the museum staff had been busily assembling behind door number four over the past month. The chief of d'Orsay security had emphasized the importance of diligent hourly patrols of the priceless pairings, especially after the exhibit's coordinator, Susanne Bruante, had taken his boss aside to verify that the security team understood the value of the extraordinary exhibit. He had overheard their conversation at his post last week, stationed like a sentry in the front lobby, his ears tuned in to this particular interaction. Mlle. Bruante was, after all, the most desirable single woman on the entire museum staff.

She was gorgeous, perhaps in her late thirties, although she didn't look it. She had actually smiled at him on her way to meet with Chief Varton, her perfume and her dark hair trailing over her shoulders. He had watched the sway of her hips from behind, how the smooth lines of her tight skirt seemed to caress her curves with an obscene intimacy. Rumor had it she was sleeping with the museum director, but this didn't stop him from hoping.

"Please make sure your night guard pays special attention to the special exhibit," he had heard her say. "All the pieces are connected to individual alarms that will trigger with the slightest movement; still, I want to be sure this unique assembly of paintings will be a security priority."

"Don't worry, Mademoiselle Bruante," the chief had replied, "your exhibit will be monitored closely. I'll make sure the night shift is alerted."

The guard stopped for a moment when he entered the first gallery, the largest of the series of six, his flashlight still necessary to brighten the details of the paintings since the recessed lighting was dim and sleepy. They were all nudes, some of them surprisingly explicit, especially the solitary Courbet hanging on the far wall. It was called *The Origin of the World* and was the centerpiece, he had been informed, of the special exhibit.

He moved on, stopping briefly in front of another painting, one for which he could easily imagine the sexy assistant director posing with the exact same stance and the identical seductive expression on her face—in the place of the alluring, nineteenth-century brunette whom Courbet had chosen for this particular depiction of a nude lying outdoors on a picnic blanket. It was probably just his infatuation with the beguiling Susanne Bruante, but tonight, he thought he could actually see a physical resemblance between the model in the painting and the primary object, these days, of his erotic daydreams and fantasies. He shook off the idea, moving on through the other rooms, the click of his polished, regulation-grade shoes on the laminated wood floors the only sound for miles, it seemed. Reaching the dead end marked by a sign on the door that read "No entry, staff only," he doubled back. Finishing there, he completed his rounds with a cursory inspection of the large, high-ceilinged acquisition gallery.

When he sat back down in his chair behind the video monitors, he looked at his watch: *June 1, 2011, 12:40 a.m.*, his digital wristwatch announced—right on schedule, he confirmed, enormously pleased with his own efficiency. All was quiet, just as it should be. He snapped open a can of Coke, its exhaled hiss of carbonation echoing his own satisfied sigh. Now it was time again for another look at the video feed.

As he started from the left, moving slowly, panel by panel, to the right (just as he had been trained), he thought that it was going to be a very long night indeed. Nothing ever happened on the midnight shift.

And tonight, he concluded with a yawn, would be no exception.

~

The walls on all four sides were covered with paintings depicting nudes, and she had absolutely no idea where she was or how she had gotten there. Her head pounded, her arms ached, her legs burned, and her body was drenched with her own slick, glistening perspiration. Looking down at herself, she startled, dumbfounded and confused. *No clothes—I am not wearing any clothes!* All she saw was skin, moist and completely exposed. She was naked.

She closed her eyes for a moment, feeling her panic build while she tried unsuccessfully to orient herself. Blank. It was all completely and utterly blank. How could she possibly have no memory of anything? Where did she live? *Blank.* Where had she been a year, a week, a day, or even an hour ago? *Blank.* Who was she? *Blank.* Had she even existed before this moment in time? If so, she simply could not remember.

She pressed both hands against her forehead, which she found was sticky with blood, and willed herself to concentrate. *Think, Nicole. Think!*

Nicole. The name, an identity, offered itself as an uninvited but warmly welcomed clue. Could she be Nicole? She had to be—why else would that name come to mind, so suddenly, so spontaneously, and so naturally? *Is my name Nicole?* The name seemed familiar, but did that mean it was actually hers? "Nicole. I am Nicole," she said aloud, trying the name on for size with her most convincing voice and deciding, finally, that it did seem to fit. But knowing her own name did very little to awaken the mystery of her identity, so, with fresh determination, she opened her eyes to examine herself and her surroundings.

She was lying in a shadowy corner, huddled against a wall. Her breasts, throbbing bright red, looked as if they had just been forcefully squeezed through a tight space, and her legs appeared to be the chafed and bruised victims of a painfully recent trauma. Her state of undress matched the theme of the vaguely familiar artwork surrounding her on all four sides, except that the nudity in the paintings seemed joyful and magnificent, while hers felt soiled and tainted. She sat up, with her back against the wall, and wiped a mixture of sweat and blood from her eyes, wincing as her hand brushed a small but painful gash on her forehead. Had she been thrown forcefully into this dark corner, resulting in a head wound and this memory loss? Blood was still oozing, just barely, from the cut above her eyebrow, wandering wet and insidious down her cheek, a drop or two falling onto the floor before she could inhibit the bleeding with the pressure of her palm.

Slowly she lifted herself onto her knees with a groan, pulling her injured frame into a standing position, her back against the wall. It seemed to be nighttime, because the room was lit by candlelight. Or was it? A soft yellow glow came from the evenly spaced recesses where the walls met the ceiling, but it didn't flicker or appear to radiate from a lamp or a torch. She had never seen anything like it, or anything quite like the room she stood in.

She touched the wall behind her with her fingertips, wondering how in the world they had been able to make the plaster so smooth and so perfect. Her bare feet stood on polished wood floors, the thin, knot-free planks resting perfectly next to each other, so close that the minuscule gaps between them were barely perceptible. Except for the paintings hanging on the walls, the expansive space was completely empty, with no furniture anywhere to be found, which could only mean one thing: the room was a showplace. Some venues, or at least their names, came suddenly to her mind: *the Salon of Paris*, *the Salon of Those Refused*, and *the Cooperative and Anonymous Association of Impressionist Painters*. Deep in her subconscious, she knew that these were all events that would take place in rooms like these, where familiar artists would show their latest efforts. Their faces blurred, in her mind's eye, beyond the limits of her injured recollection, in a past that she couldn't quite remember. The concept felt right, though, so it simply had to be.

She felt suddenly dizzy. A clammy flush barely preceded a violent wave of nausea that pulled her back down onto the cold, hard floor, onto her knees. Her stomach was empty, but she still felt better when she had finished retching—and that's when she saw him, lying directly against the wall just three or four meters away from her.

How had she missed him before, when he must have been right there? Reason one: it had taken her eyes a few minutes to focus and adjust to the semi-darkness of the dimly lit room. Reason two: she had been too preoccupied with her own predicament to process anything but the very basics about her surroundings. Reason three: his body was partly concealed, as hers had been, in the shadows. Reason four: she had examined the room just a moment before from a standing position; but now, on her hands and knees, he was positioned directly in front of her line of vision. And finally, she hadn't seen him because he wasn't moving, and the reason was obvious.

He was dead.

She crawled on her hands and knees toward his body and saw that he lay naked and bruised, face up on the floor. He was partially tilted with his right shoulder against the wall, his ghostly white skin marred by the purple and blue stains of numerous contusions and bruises. His long, dark hair was matted with blood; his face, elusively familiar, still showed the vestiges of an appealing appearance, despite traumatic disfigurement to his mouth and nose. Did she know him? It felt like she did, but she couldn't quite place him. Then she recognized his eyes, which stared up at her with a lifeless intensity, so unlike the memory that flashed by—much too fast for her to stop and examine it—of those same eyes telling her, "Yes, that's what I want," when she had slid him, hard and urgent, deep inside her. Had she known him that way? She could feel him, almost, his body on top of hers, and then hers on top of his, in some past that seemed close yet so far, far away.

His lifeless body looked grotesquely limp, as if all of his bones had been broken, perhaps even shattered. She noticed with horror the rag-doll positioning of his left leg, bent unnaturally backwards and hidden almost completely under his body, while his right leg crossed over his pelvis. His muscular chest, flattened as if from some heavy weight or pressure, sloped downward from an abdomen that was now bloated and distended. His head, angled in keeping with the downward slope of his shoulders, had been turned by gravity to the left, causing some blood that had pooled in his mouth to trickle from the corner of his purple, lifeless lips onto the floor where he lay, joining a larger puddle of the same red liquid that seemed to be coming out of his horribly compressed skull.

Who, or what, had done this to him? It looked like his body had been crushed, but cleanly, the mechanism failing somehow to produce a single laceration, slice, or gash on his pale skin. Horrified, Nicole retreated, still on her hands and knees, desperate to avoid the creeping edge of the bloody lake that had formed around his head. She turned away to retch again, her second wave of nausea fueled by the sickening appearance of a dead man she felt certain she knew. Who was he? How had he died? And what in the world was she doing here with him?

The second wave of nausea passed, but she still felt dizzy. Using the wall for support, she pulled herself up to her feet, and that's when her shoulder nudged the corner of one of the paintings, a quarter of an inch at most. That was more than enough to trigger the alarm. In an instant, she was surrounded, in all directions, by the chaotic blare of sirens and a blinding light that obliterated the shadows that had concealed her. She clapped her hands over her ears; she had never heard anything so maddeningly loud. It must mean that someone would discover her here at any moment, and then what would happen to her? She did not know whether she was innocent or guilty, but when she was discovered here, naked and confused, standing in the corner just a short distance from a bloody and traumatized corpse, they might assume she was the murderer. And quite frankly, who was to say they were not correct? Even if they asked her to explain herself, she would not be able to do this, and they would take her to prison, where she would linger in misery and squalor, awaiting a trial she could never win. She could not stay here and be found. She must run, but the question was—where?

The room where she stood seemed to be connected to others on either side, but she couldn't evaluate her options for escape from the far corner. She sprinted across the floor, stopping at a visual vantage point, where she could easily see that turning left would lead her through six or seven other gallery rooms, all of them displaying nude paintings. That escape route might or might not lead her to a dead end, where she could very well find herself cornered—a rabbit trapped at the end of a blind hole. If she turned right, she would be able to exit through an entryway three times the size of the opposite ones, into a hallway that looked over an expansive open area. If she chose this way, she would risk full exposure to anyone entering the painting gallery in response to the alarm. She would have to choose the lesser of two evils. Right, or left?

Right, she quickly decided, venturing cautiously but rapidly out of the exhibit room, where the sound of the alarm answered itself in hectic reverberation off the ceiling and walls of a cavern made of glass, stone, and steel. *What is this place?* Stunned, she stood frozen on an open hallway that stretched like a catwalk along a massive, cylindrical, cathedral-like space: the magnificent interior of a building that stretched lengthwise to encompass at least a full city block and soared upward to a dizzying height. The marble-tiled hallway looked down on similar floors below; above, an expansive steel meshwork formed an arch that, in turn, supported a ceiling constructed entirely of windowed glass, curving upward and across in an aerial semi-circle. She looked to her left, where a gigantic clock was centered on the lower end of a wall that was partitioned by an iron grid into fifty or sixty windows. This couldn't possibly be the exhibit hall for one of the *salons*. It looked more like a train station—but where in God's name were all the trains?

The sound of a commotion to her right jolted her back to her predicament. A quick glance toward the other end of the station revealed a group of uniformed men who had almost reached the top of a broad stairway that began at the bottom of the submerged grand hall and ended at the far side of the ground-level hallway where she stood. A second group of gendarmes filed in from the front lobby; in less than a minute, they would all be on her. Perhaps they had not yet seen her—but just as this fleeting thought came to her, one of them pointed in her direction.

With a pounding heart, Nicole turned on her heel, running as fast as she could back into the larger gallery and through the opposite door into another room, then another, and another, passing pairing after pairing of painted nudes (had she seen them before?), one after the other after the other. She could hear her pursuers behind her, the click of their heels on the marble catwalk growing louder as they approached closer and closer. She had to find a way out. She prayed to God that she was not heading toward a dead end.

In the last room now, she stopped short. At first, she thought there was no way out, but then she noticed the door in the far corner. The sign read, *"Pas de Sortie, Seule le Personelle."* If it was locked, she was finished, but if it wasn't, she might still be able to get away. She rushed across the room, prayed under her breath for a miracle, and turned the handle. The door pushed open. *"Merci,"* she whispered.

On the other side, she stood at one end of a seemingly endless hallway that spanned the entire length of the long building. She had gained a brief reprieve, but she didn't have much time. They knew she had come this way; in a few moments they would burst through the door that she had just closed but could not lock. They would apprehend her with grim, unspeaking faces.

She looked up and down the hallway, quickly processing her options. She could either flee by way of the stairs, which led down directly in front of her, presumably to a basement, or sprint down the corridor, which was lined with smaller doors that led to unknown rooms, to reach a door at the far end that might lead outside, to freedom. If she took the stairs, she would remain trapped inside the building, and they would eventually find her. If she fled outdoors, with a little luck she might escape. She made a speedy decision.

The marble floor felt cold against her bare feet as she sped past the doors in the hallway in her race against time. She looked back at the halfway point as she ran, noticing no pursuers—yet. She could see the door clearly now, and the sign above it that said Exit—closer, closer, and closer she drew; twenty meters, ten meters, one meter…*there*.

She stood against the wall for a moment, panting, to catch her breath. The wide metal door would open, she thought, if she pushed on a steel bar that spanned its entire width; but before she rushed blindly into the unknown, she would take a second to evaluate what was on the other side. She peered through an adjacent window and confirmed that the door would in fact lead her outdoors, down a squat metal stairway and into a short alleyway between the older and newer portions of the building, and then onto a wide street surrounded by tall buildings and the glittering lights of a huge and vibrant city at nighttime. It seemed perfect. This was her way out, to freedom.

Or was it? Was this really where she ought to go? *Think about it, Nicole*. She became acutely aware of the goose bumps covering her skin, produced by the chill air on her naked flesh. Naked—she had forgotten she was naked. Her nudity would draw unwanted attention to herself, like a target, out there, where the search party's re-doubled efforts would find her shivering in an alley or surrounded by curious onlookers. She would be apprehended in a heartbeat because she wasn't wearing any clothing. She needed to rethink her plan, quickly. There was no time for hesitation.

She threw open the exit door, which caused yet another alarm to sound, just as she had hoped. She doubled back, trying one door after another down the long hallway—two, three, and then four, all locked—until finally she found one that was unlocked. Slipping inside, she closed the door quietly behind her at the very same moment that she heard the commotion of pursuit entering from the gallery at the other end of the hallway. Crouching against the near wall, breathless and feeling the pounding of her own heart, she listened as what sounded like a dozen heavy footsteps ran past her unlocked door toward the clanging shriek of the exit door.

"She must have escaped through this exit to the outside," one of them said. "She isn't wearing any clothing—she won't get very far like that. Alert all units on the left bank, and order them to find and apprehend a naked brunette."

Back and forth footsteps in the corridor indicated that his lackeys were efficiently mobilizing additional gendarmes for an outside search party, just as she had hoped. Nicole breathed a sigh of relief into the silence surrounding her. The alarms were no longer sounding, turned off no doubt as the hunt for her continued outdoors. All was quiet, as she hid in someone's office, waiting for…what?

For the executioner to release the rope and drop the guillotine blade—that's what.

Chapter Two

It didn't take Detective Michèle Crossier long to pull on a pair of jeans, leg by leg, and slip on a t-shirt. Yes, the phone call a few minutes ago from her connection at police dispatch had gotten her out of her comfortable bed, interrupting a dream that had just started to involve nudity and quite a bit more, with an imagined partner, no less, whose physical appearance in retrospect closely resembled the man whose voice, on the other end of the phone line, had just given her a most useful tip.

Her contact had done exactly as she had instructed—namely, to notify her immediately if any promising cases came up, regardless of the time, day or night. She would take him out for a nice lunch or even dinner, plus perhaps an added extra, as a special 'thank you' for giving her this perfect opportunity to kick start her new position. If she played her cards right, this would be her first meaningful assignment since her long-awaited transfer from fraud to homicide, and she simply must be on top of her game. If she could only make it to the crime scene before the *Inspecteur en chef* got there—or better yet before any of the other detectives arrived—she just might have a fighting chance of being assigned the lead on a case that couldn't be anything less than high profile.

As she drove, she thought about what her contact, the dispatch officer with sky-blue eyes and a year-round tan, had told her. It couldn't be more perfect: a crushed and lifeless body, found at a grisly crime scene located within one of the world's most famous museums; a beautiful and completely naked witness (or perpetrator?), her shadowy image captured on videotape immediately before her escape out a side door and into the city; and a once-in-a-lifetime chance to prove herself to a demanding but unquestionably jaded chief. Granted, Xavier Deschamps was a lame duck, retiring in only three short weeks after serving for more than thirty-five years on the Paris police force. But if she started out on the right foot with the infamous chief inspector, her efforts would pave the road to success in this, her life's dream.

As she thought more about it, working with Deschamps like this, so close to his impending departure, couldn't be more perfect. He was a man with an impeccable reputation, whose opinion and decisions still carried a significant amount of weight in Parisian law enforcement and political circles. Rumor had it that his long years of service had made him weary and more than ready to cash it all in and relax for the rest of his days on a beach in St. Tropez. If she could just persuade him to give her control over a case in which he could never become fully involved, Michèle would be calling the shots and taking all the well-deserved credit, making a name for herself before her career in homicide had really even started.

Deschamps' replacement, currently the head of Internal Affairs, had been selected months ago, shortly after Deschamps had announced his retirement. The new chief was a woman—another plus in Michèle's book. All of these elements combined to create the perfect storm, delivering her a case that would never truly be Deschamps' to close, but one that Michèle Crossier vowed to make her own.

I want this, she thought as she unlocked her Peugeot and slid behind the wheel, *and this time, I'm damn well going to get it.*

As she approached the museum, making the turn down Rue de Lille, two police vehicles sped past her going in the opposite direction, sirens blaring, part of the efficient and quickly mobilized search. They would find her shortly—or perhaps they already had. The woman should be easy enough to spot and apprehend: a fugitive whose nudity would stick out like a sore thumb in a city that never slept; a suspect whose attention-grabbing state of undress would prevent her from inconspicuously joining the handful of pedestrians still out at midnight, walking back to their hotels or to the closest Metro stop; a disrobed individual wanted for questioning in this disturbing incident at Musée d'Orsay; a woman who was guilty at least of breaking and entering, if not more, given her incriminating proximity to the dead body lying at this very moment in the main gallery.

It was 1:30 a.m. when she pulled up in front of d'Orsay, alongside a line of police cars. The wide stone plaza in front of the museum entrance was swarming with uniformed officers, but just as she had hoped, she was the first detective to arrive. She gained entry with her badge, pushing her way through the front entrance detail and entering the lobby.

"Where's the body?" she asked authoritatively, her question

(along with a persuasive strong arm) enlisting a uniformed escort who obediently led her across the lobby and over to the left, onto a catwalk completely open on the right side.

As they walked, she glanced over her shoulder at the massive central lobby of the former Gare d'Orsay, the impressive Beaux-Arts train depot built between 1898 and 1900, finished just in time for the turn-of-the-century *Exposition Universelle*. Much of the original architecture had been preserved in the conversion of the station into a museum, including floors of marble and walls of granite and brick that reached upward on either side to support a complex grid of iron fingers cradling a ceiling constructed entirely of glass. They stopped in front of the special exhibit galleries.

"In there, detective," the gendarme said, pointing into a high-ceilinged room on whose walls hung numerous pairings of nudes painted by Degas and Courbet. Michèle had read with interest about the controversial exhibit and had actually planned on visiting it, but as a patron of the arts rather than a police investigator.

"Thank you, officer," she said. "Please inform me when the chief inspector arrives." She ducked underneath a band of yellow crime scene tape to enter the gallery, which was crowded with forensics personnel. She made a beeline for the body, where she found the medical examiner and three assistants finishing their preliminary examination of the corpse.

"You must be Crossier," the ME said, barely looking up at her. He and another gloved member of his team were taking samples from the body's genital area. "Deschamps told me about you."

His comment required no reply. In all likelihood, Deschamps had mentioned her for one reason and one reason only: she was a young and very attractive blonde. But this didn't bother Michèle, not in the least. She had learned long ago that her good looks could be used to her advantage, providing her with opportunities that other, less comely women would envy. She might be handed this assignment because of her sex appeal, but it was her intellectual abilities that would wow them in the end and earn her the respect she deserved.

She looked down at the body and immediately felt sick. The man's limbs were twisted, their positioning limp and unnatural—behind, across, and under his body, like a malleable bag of flesh without a skeleton. Had his bones been crushed? It looked like it, and by the same mechanism, no doubt, that had caused the collapse of his well-muscled ribcage and the partial implosion of the lower half of his skull and jaw. The crime scene investigators had pulled him away from a pool of his own blood.

A red stain marking the spot where the body must have been lying against the wall, directly beneath the pairing of a Courbet nude called *La Bacchante* and a Degas called *Reclining Nude*, the one model's positioning in the first appearing identical to the other model's posing in the second. Two forensics assistants were busy collecting thorough samples from the floor in the corner, where a separate and smaller area appeared to be speckled with a few drops of blood—somebody else's?—that by now had dried.

The medical examiner must have seen the expression on her face. "Wish you were back in the fraud division, detective?" he asked with a grin, standing up while peeling off his medical gloves. He tossed the soiled latex into a plastic bag on the floor and stuck out his hand. "I am Pascal Bernier."

Michèle managed to put on her best poker face. She would have to get used to blood and guts, and there was no time like the present to make that happen. "I know who you are," she replied with a pleasant smile and a firm handshake. She decided to play it with confidence, giving him the impression that she had already won the assignment. "Could you give me the details of what you've learned so far?"

"Shouldn't we wait for Deschamps?" he asked, his head cocked slightly to one side.

She waved the idea away. "There's no time to waste. Knowing Deschamps, he'll want me to brief him right away when he comes. So, what have you found?" Would Pascale Bernier buy it? If she were lucky, her nonchalance would guide him into full disclosure.

He pointed at the body. "This is what we've found. What do you think, inspector?"

It had worked, but now he was testing her. *Well, I'm up to the challenge.* She studied the grotesque body with a critical eye this time. "It looks as though the victim died of some sort of bizarre crush injury."

"Indeed. Very perceptive," he answered with raised brows and barely disguised sarcasm.

Michèle was not someone who could be that easily intimidated. "Whatever did this to him would have been large and cumbersome, an industrial piece of machinery perhaps," she continued, without missing a beat. "The natural conclusion would be to assume he wasn't killed here.

But look at this place. If he was killed elsewhere and then relocated to this spot, then why in the world is there so much blood on the floor?"

Pascale shrugged. "The perpetrators could have used a portable piece of equipment, dumping him here immediately after the deed was done, and then pushing or pulling the murder weapon away."

"Perhaps," she replied, "but if so, why aren't there scratches on the floor?"

"A modern piece of equipment on wheels wouldn't necessarily leave any marks."

She looked around the gallery, thinking as she did so about the irony of it all. How bizarre that their investigation involved an unclothed victim and a naked suspect in a case whose drama had unfolded in an art gallery depicting nineteenth-century nudes. Some of the paintings were quite explicit, even by modern standards, especially the only unpaired masterpiece, which was located directly across the room from the murder victim—a blatantly erotic depiction of the female anatomy painted by Gustave Courbet, titled *The Origin of the World.*

"Have you found the victim's clothes?" she asked.

Pascale shook his head. "We haven't."

"That means they either brought him here naked, or they took his clothes with them," she said, almost to herself, the wheels of her logical mind turning. It would have taken two or three people to dump him here. If the woman was a perpetrator rather than a witness or a second victim, she couldn't have done this alone. "What have you concluded about his injuries?" she asked, meeting Bernier's gaze. Now it was her turn to test him.

"He was crushed by an external force," he replied simply. "Something blunt, like a vice."

"How about an industrial trash compressor?" Michèle couldn't think of anything else large enough to crush a human being. "Maybe he was thrown into a garbage truck?"

He shook his head. "I don't think so. We haven't identified any foreign material embedded in his skin, so whatever crushed him left no obvious trace residue on the surface of his body. We'll have to perform a more thorough analysis in the morgue."

"Do you think the woman who was here with him earlier this evening could have done this to him alone?" Michèle knew there was no way that could have happened, but the question had to be asked.

"I seriously doubt it. His injuries are much too extensive for that, and crush injuries using, let's say, a baseball bat always leave impressions and disruptions, like lacerations or excoriations, on the skin. But I can't find any."

Michèle squatted next to the body to inspect it more closely. "You're right," she commented. "Except for bruising, there are no marks, cuts, or scrapes at all. What caused all of this bleeding?"

"Exposure of arteries in the skull and scalp," he replied. He pointed to a spot on the victim's head where it looked like the skin had been ripped off by the force of the trauma that had killed him. "You can see an example of it, right there. The scalp vessels are completely exposed, under that flap of skin."

"Would the type of head trauma he sustained keep on bleeding, after that fact?" Michèle had already drawn the tentative conclusion that the victim had been killed elsewhere and then carefully transported here, perhaps wrapped in a canvas or a blanket, while his injuries were still fresh.

"For a while, at least as long as the victim is alive; but once the heart stops, coagulation begins almost immediately."

Michèle stood, perplexed, and brushed a loose strand of hair away from her forehead. Her thoughts were interrupted when the gendarme who had escorted her to the crime scene leaned over the restricted access tape and poked his head into the gallery.

"He's here, Mademoiselle," he announced. "The chief inspector wants you to meet him in the video surveillance room."

"I'll check in with you tomorrow morning," she told Pascale, assuming the role of detective-in-charge that she felt confident she would win in just a few minutes from her chief. She handed the ME her card. "Call me tonight if your autopsy reveals anything surprising."

She followed her escort down the stairs to the main lobby. "What kind of mood is he in?" she asked.

"He's not happy," the officer said. "Good luck." He left her standing in front of the security desk and stepped back into his position near the front door with two other guards.

She shrugged. Luck was for people who didn't have the ability or the know-how to get what they wanted because they deserved it. She definitely had the talent, and she knew how to use it. She could handle him, no problem.

It would be a piece of cake.

Nicole sat on the floor inside the office, wondering what she should do next. One thing seemed certain: whoever worked here would find her in the morning and turn her in without asking any questions, so although she might be safe now, this refuge was, at best, only temporary. *You need a plan, Nicole. Think, Mlle. Bruante, think!*

Bruante…was Bruante her last name? Just as the name Nicole had come to her spontaneously in the gallery, a quiet voice inside her whispered, “Bruante,” as if it was sharing a long-held and precious secret. *Nicole Bruante.* It sounded right, so it must be so. It was as simple as that.

Was her memory returning? Hardly; she realized, however, that some fragments of recollection were beginning to hover tauntingly out of reach, in the perimeter of her subconscious. Images began to creep out of the shadows and into the dim but strengthening spotlight of her conscious mind. She could almost see the house now, squeezed between two others on a steep hillside street that wound its way up and around, finally leading to a white-domed church. The images came first, but now she knew the words as well. *Sacré Cœur. Montmartre. Paris.* The house belonged to someone else, but her presentiment told her that she lived there, in a tiny attic apartment without a permanent companion. Yes, men occasionally came to call, and some of them would even share her bed for a night or two, but she couldn’t quite see their faces. There was an artist as well, and a little boy, but both of them were remnants, she sensed, of a forgotten happiness that had long since soured. Who were they, and where did they fit in this confusing puzzle of a past that she couldn’t quite piece together?

Enough. Now it was time for action. She locked the door, careful to do so quietly so no one would hear. The room was dark, but the light from a full moon shone through the window. As her eyes adjusted, she took note of a desk littered with stacks of papers, a chair, some bookcases, the shadowy rectangular outlines of framed pictures hanging on the walls, a couch, and a coat rack. This certainly was an office, belonging to someone important whose job involved the paintings in this confusing place—this gallery—where they were displayed. In this room, the very serious business of planning the exhibits, acquiring the artwork, and balancing the complicated financial ledger might fall on the person who sat behind that very desk during working hours. Whoever he was, Nicole needed to make sure he didn't find her waiting like a scared rabbit in his place of business, come the morning.

The coat rack, and the piece of clothing hanging on it, would be her first destination. Afraid that if she stood, someone might notice her shadow through the frosted glass of the half-window in the office door, she crawled on hands and knees instead to reach her objective. It was an overcoat, hanging on the rack just as if it had been placed there specifically for her. Unbelievably, there was more. She could definitely use the pair of boots that the owner of the office had left, along with the hat, and maybe even the umbrella. She would have to time it right, though. She just might be able to escape from the building before morning, her nudity hidden under a tightly buttoned coat, her feet no longer bare, and her face along with the telltale evidence of trauma on her forehead partly shadowed under a hat, stylishly tilted forward, strolling among other city dwellers with her umbrella shading her from the glare of the rising sun or the imminent threat of a thunderstorm. It would be risky, but did she really have a choice? She couldn't stay here, where her discovery in the morning was nearly guaranteed; now that she had some clothes, her escape to the outside presented itself as the most logical choice.

She sat with her back against the wall, determined not to sleep despite her exhaustion. All of her muscles ached, and the wound on her forehead, small but nevertheless painful, had opened up again during her heart-pounding race down the hallway. Nicole pressed her palm against the gash, just as she had before, to prevent the fresh trickle of blood from flowing into her eyes, pushing down with a wince and applying pressure for what seemed like forever. Finally, the bleeding stopped; and she felt utterly exhausted.

It would feel so wonderful to stretch out on the couch and rest, but she willed herself to resist the temptation. If she gave in, she might very well sleep past daylight, losing her opportunity to sneak out before the office's resident came in. By now, a chill had settled on her like a sudden frost, so she pulled the overcoat from its hanger, clutching it to her chest to cover her naked bosom. As she did so, she smelled a fragrance—roses and lemon perhaps—coming from the fabric. Suddenly she realized that the coat belonged to a woman, not a man. She reached for the boots, holding them up out of the shadows and into a shaft of moonlight. *Heels;*

these have heels! They must belong to a woman, too. Chance had strangely led her into a hiding place where a woman's coat and boots were waiting to aid her in her escape.

Then it occurred to her: how could this office possibly belong to a woman? Women were employed, for the most part, as domestics, barmaids, or consorts, if their circumstances required them to work at all, but she had heard of women who were actually pursuing an education and a career. More than likely, though, the male museum administrator had entertained a mistress or a prostitute right there on his couch. After they had finished, the woman had probably left in a rush, leaving some of her things either accidentally or intentionally on his coat rack. Nicole grew even more curious to find out more about the person who had discarded her coat and boots in Nicole's temporary refuge.

She would start with the pictures hanging on the opposite wall. She crawled across the floor again, making her way to the couch and kneeling on it to examine the hanging frames. Although the room was dark, there was just enough light for her to recognize that the frames contained photographs. Family and individual portraits, taken in the new and fashionable photography studios, were becoming quite popular these days—among those who had the money to purchase them. She selected two of the largest photographs, lifting them carefully from their hooks on the wall and taking them down so she could inspect them in better light, directly underneath the window.

The hard floor, barely cushioned by a thin carpet, made for an unforgiving journey on bruised and aching knees, but with some stifled grimaces, Nicole eventually made her way from the couch to the window. She pushed the chair aside, making room for herself between the desk, which faced the doorway, and her light source. She held the first framed picture under the window, tilting it toward the moonlight. Her first try caught the reflection of the moon in the glass. The glare was surprisingly bright, completely obscuring the photograph displayed underneath. After several hit-and-miss alterations of the angle, she finally got it right—and what she saw made her gasp. The colors were so *vivid.* In all the photographs she could remember, the tones always ranged from black to white…but colors? *Never!* Could her memory lapse be so severe that she would forget something as spectacular as colors in a photograph?

She closed her eyes for a moment, trying to think back, grasping for *any* recollection, however vague, of photographs that she might have seen in her recently forgotten past. Hadn't she even posed for a photographic portrait once? Yes, she remembered now. She saw herself, in her mind's eye, standing next to a bicycle—not her own, but simply a prop in a photographer's studio, a long, long time ago. She had been ten or eleven years old at the time. Her dress was colored a soft lilac, her dark hair was tied back with a blue ribbon, her shoes were a polished and lush violet, and the bicycle sparkled a bright and striking red. A full week later, after the photo was processed, she could barely contain her excitement as she peered over her mother's shoulder to see what the image looked like on paper. She remembered the thrill, followed by the crash of disappointment, as if it was yesterday. She had expected to see blues, purples, and reds, but to her surprise, all of the bright and brilliant colors—her dress, the shoes, her hair ribbon, and the bicycle—had been replaced with shades of dull and shabby grey.

She shook her head. "No colors," she whispered. "There were no colors in that portrait. I am not crazy."

She opened her eyes again. Colors or no colors, the photograph she held in her hand would tell a story about the person who came to this office day after day. It might depict a family member or, if she were lucky enough to have stumbled into an office belonging to someone with a generous ego, it might show the resident himself, larger than life, basking in self-centered glory.

In both photographs, Nicole gazed at a man and a woman. The man in the first one—large, round, and robust—had been photographed at the exact moment an award or plaque of some kind was being transferred from his hands to the woman's.

The man in the second photo was thin and well past middle aged, with a full head of unkempt grey hair and a closely trimmed salt-and-pepper beard. He had his arm draped around a woman's shoulder, giving the distinct impression of a closeness that could only mean that he was a relative—her father, or an uncle perhaps. The two men couldn't be more different from each other, but the woman in each of the two photos was, without a question or a doubt, one and the same.

Nicole peered closely at the woman to whom this office must belong and whose features looked startlingly familiar. "Impossible," she murmured. "How could this be?" She recognized the mouth, the lips, and the smile; the hazel eyes; the dark hair; the line of the jaw, and the delicate nose. "It's me," she exclaimed, in a voice that sounded much louder than she had intended.

The woman looked just like her.

Could she actually be the woman in the photograph? If she were, it would explain a lot. Maybe she worked here; maybe the man now lying dead in the gallery had attacked her, battered her, and possibly even raped her before meeting his untimely death. Had she killed him somehow? If so, it wouldn't be surprising if her memories of such a horrifying experience had been wiped clean, as if someone had swiped a clean towel over a busy chalk board. She needed to find a name. There had to be a name, somewhere in this office.

She stood, distracted and unconcerned for the time being about casting her shadow on the door's frosted glass window, and started rifling, frenzied, through the papers on the desk. Any of them would do, as long as it had the woman's name on it. She grabbed a piece of paper, then another, and then another, until she finally found one that had what she was looking for, and when she saw it, she had to stifle a cry of disbelief. *Susanne Bruante—the woman's name was Susanne Bruante!* Did that mean that she, too, was Susanne Bruante, and not Nicole?

If she and the woman in the photograph were one-and-the-same person, then why had the name Nicole come to her spontaneously in the gallery? Her memory was muddled, after all, so she couldn't place much stock in the thoughts that had occurred when she first awoke from her state of unconsciousness. Then again, Bruante had obviously been correct, so why not Nicole? A rush of other possibilities came quickly to mind. Perhaps she was the woman's sister, or a cousin, or a niece? She looked at the photographs again, carefully studying the lines of Susanne's face, the shape of her smile, the tapering curve of her neck, the swell of her breasts, the contour of her waist and hips, the way she stood, and the implied gesture of her hands. The resemblance was striking, but by no means identical. *Am I Susanne Bruante, or Nicole?* She set the photographs on the floor and leaned against the wall for a moment to think. It didn't take long for her to decide—there was only one way to find out.

She stood, reaching over the neat pile of papers on the desk to retrieve a small stack of opened mail; then she sat back down again, out of sight, directly under the office window. Most of the letters were addressed to Susanne Bruante, Assistant Director of Acquisitions and Special Exhibits at a place called Musée d'Orsay; but near the bottom she found one that wasn't. *Susanne Bruante, 14 Avenue Georges V, Nombre 3B, Paris France,* the envelope read. It was her home address—

it had to be—and that's exactly where Nicole would be heading next.

And soon, she thought. It might not be safe to wait until daylight. The gendarmes had seen her standing on the catwalk, and who's to say they hadn't recognized her? If she really were Susanne Bruante, or even a nearly identical lookalike, where would they search next for her when the policemen out there came back inside, empty-handed? Right here, in the assistant director's own office, of course. Suddenly Nicole's cozy sanctuary didn't seem quite as safe as it had pretended to be, just five short minutes ago.

She would wait a bit longer, but not too long. Her timing must be perfect. If she left before the searchers gave up outside, they would apprehend her shortly after her exit from the building; if she waited until the police re-grouped indoors, they would either discover her hiding here, or detain her in the hallway as she tried to make her way out the exit door and down the stairway to the street below. Her window of opportunity might be very slim indeed.

She crawled back to the couch, hastily replaced the photographs on the walls, crept over to the coat rack again, and dressed in the overcoat, boots, and hat. Then she sat against the wall, umbrella in hand, to wait—not too long, but just long enough.

She prayed that her intuition would tell her when the time was right.

Chapter Three

Michèle Crossier navigated around a semicircle of monitors surrounding a broad, unmanned desk where the museum's night security officer usually sat. The chair was empty, but two museum officials were conferencing in the back room directly behind security central, with Chief Inspector Deschamps in the center.

One look at Deschamps, and she knew the gendarme wasn't exaggerating. The chief inspector was not happy—not in the least. Early in his career, he might have actually looked forward to the occasional phone call in the middle of the night, but not now. She could well imagine that, after thirty-five years, dragging himself out of his warm bed in the dead of night to investigate a gruesome murder was no longer his idea of fun. Just three weeks until his well-deserved retirement, the last thing he needed was a new challenge, and Michèle was more than willing to unburden him from that responsibility.

As soon as he saw her, Deschamps pushed aside his entourage and met her on the other side of the control room's entryway. "Since you were the first one here, you're in the hot seat," he growled, as if he was handing out a punishment rather than a reward.

Perfect, she thought, *the case is mine.*

"Forensics are just finishing up in the main gallery," she said, her tone firm and self-assured. She decided not to waste any time and dove head-on into the circumstances. "The victim is a naked male who appears to be in his early thirties. He died of extensive crush injuries most likely caused by an industrial machine of some sort, possibly a portable one. Bernier believes that more than one perpetrator was involved, which means that either our naked woman had accomplices, or she's a victim herself and not the murderer."

"Have any of our units found this naked woman yet?"

"I don't think so, sir. I've been here for more than thirty minutes, and I'm unaware of a single update from any of the patrolling units." In truth, no one would have felt compelled to report this information to her, unless she had been officially given the lead. Now was definitely the time to seal the deal. "Of course, I don't have the required clearance to check on those updates, but if you decide to give me that authority, inspector, you won't regret it."

He thought for a moment but didn't hesitate for long. "You were the first detective to arrive on the scene, so I'll put you in charge, but here are my conditions: First, don't think for a second that because I'm retiring in three weeks I'll let you off the leash for your first major homicide case. You'll be reporting to me directly on this one. And second, you'll be acting lead, for now. I want to see what you can do before making the assignment official."

"Thank you, sir. I won't disappoint you."

"You'd better not. Now, let's get back to the naked woman. Where is she?" Deschamps cocked an eyebrow at her, as if she were hiding the woman in her back pocket.

"It's like she disappeared into thin air. She escaped through the side door of the east wing not more than thirty seconds before our uniforms reached the same spot, pursuing closely behind her. She must have had a car waiting for her outside; otherwise, they would have apprehended her immediately. That door opens directly onto a six-step metal stairway and into a short alley that leads in one direction only—out to the street."

Apparently he wasn't happy with her answer; the thunderstorm of his frown bore down on his tensing brows. "How many units do we have combing the 7th Arrondisement?" he asked, referring to one of Paris's twenty administrative districts.

"More than twenty," she said, quoting the information her helpful blue-eyed friend had given her over the phone more than an hour before.

"Double that number," he said. "We have to find that woman. Do we have any surveillance footage from the outside of the building? Maybe we can identify the car she left in."

Michèle shook her head. "There are cameras in every gallery, but unfortunately none outside."

"Damn it," he muttered. "She'll be impossible to find now, without an ID of her car."

"We still don't know for sure that she isn't on foot. There are plenty of side streets around here, and she might have slipped unseen down one of them."

"This area is very well lit, so if she isn't driving, she should be very easy to spot. Make sure we have officers on foot as well as in vehicles."

"Understood, inspector."

"The mayor will want answers, and quickly." He bit his lower lip; she had noticed it was a nervous habit with him. This case was already getting to him. "A dead body found in one of Paris's premier tourist destinations will make the front page of more than just *Le Figaro*; and this type of publicity won't be good for business."

She heard him curse under his breath as he turned back to re-enter the control room, but he seemed to regain his composure as he rejoined the two Musée d'Orsay officials. Michèle followed closely at his heels.

"This is Inspector Michèle Crossier," Deschamps said. "I've put her in charge of the investigation."

One of the d'Orsay men, an overweight, balding man who looked to be in his mid-fifties, extended his hand to greet her. "I'm Hubert Varton, the head of d'Orsay security." His handshake was firm and reassuring. "We were just about to show the chief inspector the video surveillance footage from the special exhibit gallery."

"In a moment, Monsieur Varton." Michèle kept her tone pleasant but authoritative. If she was the acting detective in charge, she intended to do more than just play the role. "Would you mind if I take a minute to question your after-hours team first? It might help us to know if your night guards noticed anything at all unusual this evening."

"Certainly, mademoiselle."

"*Inspector,* monsieur," she said, determined to draw attention to her authority.

Varton blushed a faint shade of red. "My apologies. I was just saying, Mademoiselle Inspector, that we have only one officer on duty at night. This is Gerard Monteuse. I'm sure he'd be happy to answer all of your questions." The other man, thin and with blemished skin that gave away his youth, nodded to acknowledge that he was the night guard in question.

Michèle furrowed her brow. "Do you mean to tell me that you have *one* security officer on site at night? This museum is very large, Monsieur Varton, and it contains countless pieces of priceless artwork."

"We have found this coverage to be more than adequate," Varton replied. "As you are well aware, we have a direct phone line to your precinct headquarters. Our night guard has only to pick up the phone if anything looks suspicious, *et voilà!* We have twenty gendarmes knocking on our front door within minutes to assist us. Tonight's experience can attest to the efficiency of our system."

She nodded. It made sense, really, for Musée d'Orsay to preserve some of its endowment by relying on public law enforcement to back up its private security. She turned her attention to the young security guard, who was staring at her as if he had never seen such a thing as a female detective. "Did you notice anything suspicious this evening, Monsieur Monteuse?"

He shook his head. "Everything was quiet. I have four monitors with six panels on each to watch, and I was looking at panel six on screen four when the alarms began to sound. I called the police immediately."

"Did you see anyone coming or going on any of the other video monitors?"

"All the action happened on screen one, panel six," he said. "I didn't notice anything unusual on any of the other panels."

"Do you make museum rounds?"

"Yes, every hour." He had a note of defensiveness in his voice. "The place was completely quiet all night."

"So, nothing seemed out of the ordinary right before the incident occurred, when you made your last walk-through?"

"Nothing. I started my rounds at eleven forty-five and finished them at precisely twelve forty. Everything was fine."

"Thank you, monsieur. Now," she said, turning to address Varton, "can we review the video feed?"

Varton pushed a button to start the recorded footage and the group, which included Chief Inspector Deschamps, arranged themselves around the monitor. The special exhibit room was monitored in a panoramic fashion by a camera that moved slowly in a sweeping arc from the far right to the far left and back again, in two-minute cycles. The footage began at the painting by Courbet that Michèle had noted before, the explicit piece titled *The Origin of the World*. Then it panned to the left, ending at the Degas and Courbet pairing under which the dead body had been found, after which it slowly returned to the erotic masterpiece.

Everything looked quiet and peaceful, until midway through the second sweep. Michèle spotted a vague flash of light passing across the screen, moving quickly from right to left—like the blur of a quickly moving object.

"What was that?" she asked.

"I'm not sure," Varton said. "It could simply be a reflection or a glitch in the tape."

Doubtful. "It looked like some kind of movement," she said. She would wait to say more, though, until she saw additional footage. The camera panned slowly to the left; and suddenly, there they were, the dead man lying parallel to the wall and the naked woman lying huddled in the shadowy corner, a few meters away from the man.

"Where in hell's name did they come from?" Deschamps asked. Michèle wondered the same thing. That side of the room had been completely empty, just sixty seconds before; but now, as if they had materialized out of thin air, two bodies lay on the floor—one dead and one alive. Sixty seconds wasn't nearly enough time for the woman to have killed the man. If both had been dumped there, the perpetrator had acted incredibly fast, fleeing the scene at the very same moment, virtually, that he or she had arrived, leaving behind a mystery without a trace of a clue.

The camera started to move away, panning slowly to the other side of the room, and in so doing, revealed nothing unusual or disturbed in its repetitive back-and-forth journey.

"That flash of light was movement," Michèle repeated, convinced now that it was. It made sense, and it would explain how the dead man and the woman had arrived so suddenly in the room.

"What, exactly, do you think was moving?" Deschamps asked.

"Maybe the two bodies, being propelled somehow from one side of the room to the other."

"Possibly," Deschamps said, sounding distracted. He was focused now on the video, watching as the camera moved back to the left side of the room, capturing the dead body and the naked woman once again. Then, after a few seconds, he pointed at the monitor screen. "Stop the tape."

Varton pushed a button, freezing the replay. Just a moment before, the woman had risen to her feet; but then, after glancing over at the dead body, she had collapsed to the floor again, retching into the corner. When she had finished, she turned her head. Although her features were still enveloped in shadow, Michèle understood immediately why Deschamps had ordered Varton to freeze-frame the action here. This was the best view, by far, that they had had of the woman's face.

"Do you recognize her, Monsieur Varton?" Michèle said. "Does she look familiar?"

Varton leaned in closer to the screen, studying the woman's face intently.

"You know her, don't you?" she exclaimed, hoping that he actually did.

He nodded, slowly at first but then more vigorously. "Seeing this footage for the second time now, I definitely recognize an uncanny resemblance."

"To whom? Look closely—could she be a museum employee, perhaps?"

"It's Susanne Bruante," the young security guard said, sounding surprised. "It looks just like her."

"Who's Susanne Bruante?" Michèle asked. "Does she work at d'Orsay?"

Varton nodded. "She's the assistant director in charge of acquisitions and special exhibits."

"Do you agree with your night guard, Monsieur Varton?" Deschamps asked.

The director of d'Orsay security nodded again. "Gerard is correct. The woman on the videotape looks exactly like Susanne Bruante."

Michèle glanced over at Deschamps and suspected from the look in his eyes that the same thought had just occurred to both of them. "Monsieur Varton, we are finished here. The chief inspector and I would like you to take us to Susanne Bruante's office."

~

Susanne Bruante woke up abruptly to the insistent buzzing of her door monitor. She glanced at her clock. *Two forty-five in the morning—who in the world would ring my doorbell at this ungodly hour?*

Maybe it was René, although she couldn't imagine why he would feel compelled to bother her at her apartment. A few hours earlier they had spent an amazing evening together in a hotel room not far from Musée d'Orsay, their rendezvous explained away to René's unsuspecting wife as an unavoidable late night of work at the museum, a last-minute scramble to complete an important project before a mandatory morning deadline. Unless they had been discovered, René had no business on the other side of her front door; and even if his bags had been packed by an outraged wife and then thrown out into the street with the thud of finality, there was no way Susanne would let him in. Their affair, to her, had evolved, essentially, into a business transaction, and as such it should stay right where it belonged—namely, at work, or in a hotel room every now and then, but not in her apartment.

She didn't love him—never had and never would. Even from the very start, he was a mediocre distraction, a casual amusement, a temporary stopgap between countless failed relationships, and an eternally grateful recipient of her sexual acquiescence, an essential component of their relationship that she would never let him forget. One good turn deserves another, as they say, and she quickly learned that sleeping with the director was an investment that could yield some very high returns.

Not only that, but the thrill of the tease, and the excitement of seduction, were simply too much fun. She loved the exposure; loved the attention he paid to her body; and loved the effect that her nudity always had on him, every time they met for a roll in the hay. The way he looked at her with undisguised lust reminded her of the days when she would model, nude, for an art class or some amateur painter, her curves immortalized for hundreds of eyes to see when the drawings or paintings of her naked magnificence were exhibited in the university's fine arts show, or at some regional art festival. What a picture-perfect way to live forever, as a perpetually youthful model whose unchanging and unaltered image was captured on canvas for posterity's benefit. The true artist's model was someone Susanne had always envied. Perhaps in another life, she would live that fantasy.

But the benefits of Susanne's periodic physical liaisons with René were hardly one sided. She surmised that, for her director, she represented a young and beautiful boost to his middle-aged ego—a dangerous and invigorating contrast to his stagnant thirty-year marriage to a "boring and overly conventional" spouse. He had no intention of leaving his wife for Susanne, thank God, because even if he did, she would never consider marrying him. The only reason she hadn't broken it off by now, truth be told, was because of his position as Musée d'Orsay's executive director. She might be on top in the bedroom, but in the workplace their positions were painfully reversed. There was no conceivable way she could dump her boss.

The honest truth be told, Susanne had painted herself into a corner, although she would never outwardly acknowledge her mistake. One day, if her relationship with René eventually ended, she ran the risk of losing more than just her special privileges. Regardless of who dumped whom, she would be the ex-girlfriend, a constant reminder to René of his infidelity and a veritable thorn in his side that he would feel compelled, she felt certain, to remove. She might very well find herself transferred to some back office at Versailles—or worse yet, to someplace provincial like Lyon. He would call it a promotion, of course, the irrevocable scribble of his signature on the bottom of the transfer papers sending her away, problem solved once and for all.

That just wouldn't do. Susanne had other plans, and she kept telling herself that if she played her cards right, it would all work out. Musée d'Orsay was her life; someday, she would be the executive director—or at least, this was her plan. If she could keep René close for just a little longer, he would get his hoped-for appointment to the Ministry of Culture, and Susanne, being at the right place (naked in his bed) at the right time (whenever he wanted her), would be the logical choice for him to recommend as his replacement. It was perfect, really. And so she diligently met him when he wanted her, even on short notice, biding her time and waiting until the moment when he would get his, and she would get hers.

"Goodnight, Susanne," he had said with a satisfied smile when they had parted earlier. "Celeste will be away in two weeks, to visit her mother. May I see you again then?"

"You'll see me tomorrow, at the museum," she had said, teasing him.

"You know what I mean," he had said with a pout.

"Of course, René!" She had laughed flirtatiously. "You know I am yours—wherever, whenever, and however you please." It never hurt to play the pliable whore, a role that should have made her feel cheap, but it didn't. Her accommodation invariably bred his accommodation, so it was in her best interest to nurture the charade with more than just a flavoring of submissiveness.

“Good,” he had said, believing, she knew, that her remark was sincere. He was such an easy dupe. “See you tomorrow, then. We need to talk about the Degas and Courbet pairing exhibit.”

“We’ve already talked about it.” She had felt her blood start to simmer. “What more is there to say?”

“You know how I feel about the negative publicity. I’m not so sure I’m willing to stick my neck out there with yours at the opening reception next Saturday.”

“We’ve already discussed this. It’s my presentation, not yours; and I’ve already told you that I’m willing to take full responsibility for any repercussions.”

“Calm down,” he had said, trying to embrace her again. “You’re so sexy when you’re angry.”

She had pushed him away gently, trying to suppress her indignation and shift her gears into a diplomatic mode. “Look, René—I have some new evidence that I think will convince the staunchest critics.”

She had definitely piqued his interest. “What evidence?”

“You’ll see. I’ll be using it in my presentation next Saturday.”

He had rubbed his chin, the gesture he always used when his wheels were turning. “If this new information is so persuasive, why haven’t you shared it with me?”

The truth was, she didn’t fully trust René. Technically, she should have given the letter to him, as her director, but instead she had submitted it directly to the National Archives for analysis of the materials and the handwriting first, in order to confirm its validity. Henri, her uncle, had found it papered over, attached with adhesive to the back of the canvas of the unsigned and unfinished painting that he was restoring in his home workshop for d’Orsay. Henri had agreed, with a little gentle and logical coercion, to let her handle the historic find instead of turning it over to the museum’s executive director. Why shouldn’t it be her? Henri had found the letter in a museum acquisition; and she was, after all, the assistant director in charge of d’Orsay’s artistic purchases and procurements. It was true that René might feel slighted by the intentional bypass, maybe even angered; but all would be forgiven, she felt certain, when he eventually heard the startling results that she would present next week on opening night.

So why had she not shared it with him? "Because your curiosity works to my advantage," she had finally answered, opening the hotel room door to let him out. With feigned playfulness, she added, "You'll have to wait to hear my lecture to find out, which means that you wouldn't dare cancel me, isn't that right?"

He shrugged. "All right, then. The opening reception will take place as planned, but don't expect me, or the museum, to whole-heartedly endorse your heretical fantasies."

Whatever, she had thought, as long as she was allowed to share her insights to a roomful of critics and benefactors next Saturday. Even though her theory, in her not-so-humble opinion, was brilliant, the evidence contained in the letter, although circumstantial, would go a long way toward validating her argument.

"See you tomorrow, René," she had said, not at all unpleasantly, swallowing her pride and closing the hotel door gently behind him as he left, instead of slamming it like she wished she could. She tried to convince herself that she didn't truly need him, yet clearly she did. One thing was for certain: he had given her the forum she needed to argue with her critics and prove that she was right, so she had better tread lightly, at least until after opening night.

The door monitor buzzed again, interrupting Susanne's rapid-fire recollections. Whoever was seeking entry downstairs kept buzzing, repeatedly and insistently. It was obvious they would not go away until she answered.

"I'm coming, I'm coming," she muttered under her breath, throwing off her comforter and sliding, sleek and naked, out of her sheets. She stretched, leisurely slipping on a sheer peignoir, arm by arm. She was in no particular rush; her after-hours caller would just have to wait. Unhurried, she walked on bare feet across the spacious master bedroom, large enough to accommodate two seven-drawer dressers, an armoire, a loveseat, and two chairs. Unintentionally picking up speed, she was in the hallway now, the polished wood floors cool and smooth on the soles of her feet. To her immediate left, she passed a closed door behind which was a guest room that she used as a resource library and study; and then, more than halfway to the other end already, she moved beyond another guest room on the right, its door partly opened. Her hallway also served as a full-length gallery displaying, on both sides, her own exquisite black-and-white photographs, conceived as her final project before completing her exchange year of college in the United

States. She admired them, as she usually did—her favorite series of male and female nudes—out of the corner of her eye until she finally entered into a sizable front foyer offered access to the dining room and adjoining kitchen, and the threshold leading to her living room to the right.

Her apartment was a contemporary flat on the top floor of a three-story former family mansion in the exclusive Georges V district. The renovation had resulted in six separate condominiums accessed via a central stairway—one apartment on each side of the stairs, on each of the three floors—and guarded by an electronic call panel. There was no concierge.

Her entry door lay straight ahead, leading out into the central stairway, flanked by a newly installed, high-tech audiovisual sentry positioned on the wall to the right, and a line of polished bronze hooks for coats and hats to the left. She pushed a button, and the monitor flashed on to the remote display of a face belonging to a very attractive blonde with her hair pulled neatly and professionally back. The fact that the woman was surrounded by a background of blue uniforms and silver badges could only mean trouble.

"How can I help you?" Susanne asked warily, holding down another button in order to activate the audio.

"Mademoiselle Bruante?" the blonde woman said.

"Yes, I'm Susanne Bruante. It's very late, officer. Is there something wrong?"

"We're sorry to trouble you. Please forgive the intrusion, but we were hoping to question you about this evening," the blonde said, her face an unsmiling harbinger of something serious.

"About this evening?" Susanne's mind raced to put two and two together. Had something happened to René? When he had left the hotel room first, leaving her behind for their usual sequenced departure so that no one would see them together, he had seemed just fine.

"We realize the hour is quite inconvenient, Mademoiselle Bruante, but if you would agree to come down to the station with us, it would make it so much easier to take your statement."

"What in the world do you think I've done?" she asked, her surprise verging on panic. Had something terrible happened to René after she had left the hotel, and was she a suspect because they had been seen together? It would be truly ironic if her carefully planned affair ended up backfiring, landing her in jail rather than in the museum director's swivel chair—a criminal sentence substituted for the professional promotion she had hoped to eventually gain by sleeping with her boss.

"We think you might be able to give us some insight into tonight's incident, that's all."

"Whatever happened, I don't know anything about it. Can't we talk here?"

"It would be much better for us if you came down to headquarters. It won't take long."

They obviously considered her a person of interest in whatever had just occurred at the museum. Susanne quickly decided that inviting the police into her apartment was reckless—correction, it was downright stupid. Of course she had nothing to hide, but God knows what they were looking for and what they were after. Let them get a search warrant if they wanted, but keeping the Trojan horse outside, on her doorstep, was far better than letting trouble in; and going down to the station rather than opening her door and asking for problems was a much safer strategy.

"Give me a moment," she said. "I'll be down in just a minute; I'll have to get dressed."

"Take your time, Mademoiselle Bruante. We'll be waiting right here for you when you come out."

Susanne had no doubt in her mind, whatsoever, that they would.

Chapter Four

Susanne returned to her bedroom, slipped on a designer dress and a pair of perfectly matched pumps, and tossed her keys into her shoulder bag. *I may as well look fashionable for the police lineup.* A moment later, she descended the two flights of stairs to emerge at the building's entrance, where she was greeted by the unsmiling faces of one female detective and three uniformed gendarmes.

"This must be serious," Susanne said, gesturing at the gendarmes. "I'm neither armed nor dangerous, officers, so I don't think this kind of welcoming party is even remotely necessary."

"Our apologies—we didn't know who or what we would find when we got here, so we came prepared for the worst." The blonde held out her hand. "I'm Inspector Michèle Crossier, with the Police Judiciare. I'm in charge of this case."

The Police Judiciare? Everyone knew that the PJ, more commonly called "The 36," handled homicide cases. Had René been murdered? If he had, there was only one reason they had come to collect her. They must think she had killed him.

"Does it involve René?" she blurted out, without thinking. Immediately, she knew that she had said too much. This business definitely spelled trouble for her, if she had been the last person to see the executive director of Musée d'Orsay alive.

"Who's René?" Michèle asked, gazing back at Susanne with an inquisitive yet knowing look.

Now I've done it, Susanne thought. Maybe René wasn't the victim after all; or maybe he was, and the astute detective was just playing her. She had best remain quiet from now on, until she learned more about what had actually happened at the museum.

"Just a friend," Susanne responded, almost under her breath. She decided to try a re-direct. "Can we get this over with quickly? I have a very long day of work ahead of me, since we're about to open a new exhibit."

"I don't think you'll be going to work today," Crossier said, her tone noticeably less polite now than it had been just a moment ago. "Musée d'Orsay is a crime scene, Mademoiselle Bruante, and it will be at least a few days before it's open again to employees or the public."

A crime scene attended by the homicide division could only mean one thing. As the two policemen escorted her, one on each arm, into the back seat of a police car, Susanne concluded that, number one, someone had been murdered—maybe René, maybe not—and number two, the police considered Susanne to be the prime suspect.

They rode in silence for a little while. "Where are you taking me?" Susanne finally asked, just to confirm what she already knew.

"Thirty-six Quai des Orfèvres," Crossier replied from the front seat.

Just as Susanne had suspected, she would be questioned at the regional headquarters of the Police Judiciaire of Paris, commonly known as the DRPJ. Without traffic, the trip to the criminal investigation division of the Police Nationale didn't take long at all. It was 3:35 a.m. when the police car pulled up to the curb in front of the historic nineteenth-century building. She had never been inside the five-storied Napoleonic structure, the impressive granite home to more than two thousand detectives and gendarmes, all of them dedicated to solving the most serious and complicated felonies, ranging from sexual assaults to drug trafficking, kidnapping, monetary fraud, and of course homicide. Well, now it was her chance to take an intimate, too-close-for-comfort tour.

They escorted her through the front doors and into a two-storied lobby that could easily be mistaken for the entrance to a museum. Crossier led the way across a polished marble floor, showing her badge to an officer sitting behind a security desk who obviously recognized her and nodded her through. They stopped in front of a grouping of elevators, rather than continuing on through the hallway to a room that Susanne could see, through windowed double-doors, was bustling with activity. The sign above the door said "Processing."

"So, we're not going in there?" Susanne said, her tone light.

"Not yet," Crossier said with unsmiling seriousness.

They took the elevator to the fourth floor, where the doors opened into a small lobby, manned by yet another gendarme who was sitting behind a smaller desk. The wall behind him offered Susanne the greeting she had expected: "Major Criminal Division, Homicide," it read. After another unnecessary flash of her badge, Crossier led the way through an automatic door that opened into a room full of desks, some of which were occupied. "You guys work late," Susanne said. Crossier didn't bother to acknowledge the comment.

They led her to the back, where Crossier motioned her into a dimly lit room. The detective followed Susanne in, closing the door behind them. A distinguished-looking man with a silver goatee, his head mostly bald and the rest shaved close, stood up from his seat at the conference table as soon as the women entered, the gentlemanly deference seeming contrived rather than sincere. Although he was probably in his early sixties, he was dressed more like a much younger man, entirely in black, right down to the tips of his impeccable Italian shoes. His trim and tall build helped to exude a robust air of no-nonsense authority.

"This is Susanne Bruante," Crossier announced in a matter-of-fact tone, giving the man in black a knowing look. "She wonders if a friend of hers named René was involved in the incident."

The older man nodded acknowledgement. "Have a seat, Mademoiselle Bruante," he offered, indicating with his hand a chair positioned directly across from him at the table. "I'm Chief Inspector Xavier Deschamps. Can I get you something to drink—mineral water, or an espresso, perhaps?" Once again, Susanne felt as though he was trying to disarm her with insincere politeness. His smooth hospitality didn't deceive her.

"No thank you, Monsieur L'Inspecteur," she replied as she calmly took the seat across the table from him. "Why have you dragged me out of bed at three o'clock in the morning? Do I need to call my attorney?"

"That all depends on whether you're innocent or guilty." As Deschamps spoke, Crossier took the seat next to him. It was now most obviously two against one, and the odds did not seem to favor Susanne.

"Innocent or guilty of what crime?" she countered, knowing without even hearing his reply that the answer would be murder. "I have the right to know what you're accusing me of."

He took a pack of cigarettes from his breast pocket. "Do you mind if I smoke?" he asked.

"It's late, and I'm tired," Susanne replied with annoyance, quickly losing her patience as he lit up. "Could we please get on with the questioning? What, exactly, am I being charged with?"

"Nothing, yet," Crossier answered, picking up where Deschamps had left off. "Could you tell us where you were this evening at approximately twelve-forty-five a.m.?"

"In a hotel room with my lover. Why?" Susanne answered their first volley in this game of cat and mouse without hesitating, more comfortable now with the concept of defiance, given the fact that she clearly had an alibi at the hour the crime was committed.

The detective and the chief inspector exchanged skeptical glances. "Are you sure about that?" Crossier asked.

"Absolutely certain." Susanne crossed her arms and glared across the table at her interrogators.

"That's funny," Crossier explained, "because a certain museum surveillance recording that documented tonight's occurrence in the special exhibit galleries would argue differently."

"What in the world are you talking about?"

"Both the night guard and chief of d'Orsay security identified the woman on that footage as you, fleeing the crime scene and leaving a grotesquely murdered body behind. Do you still claim you were elsewhere?"

"Of course," Susanne answered, indignant. "It must have been someone who looked like me. There's no other explanation." She looked Crossier right in the eye. "Who was murdered—do you know the victim's identity?" She prayed that it wasn't René, because if it was, she no longer had an alibi.

Crossier and Deschamps exchanged glances again, this time with uncertainty. "We haven't been able to identify the person yet, because the injuries were so extensive," explained Crossier. "You—or your lookalike—escaped out one of the side doors after hiding in your museum office."

"You searched my office? Don't you need a search warrant to do that?"

"Your office at Musée d'Orsay is public property," Deschamps said with a shrug. "Monsieur Varton let us in with the museum master key."

"So tell me then, what did you find?" Susanne asked,

bracing for the worst.

"Well, let's see," Crossier said. "We found some evidence suggesting that you had been there and left."

"And how, may I ask, would you know that?"

"Because of the blood."

"I have no idea what you're talking about."

"We found fresh blood in your office," Deschamps said. "Some drops on the carpet right next to your coat rack, and smears on the wall next to two framed photographs. One of the pictures was hanging off kilter, and there were bloody fingerprints on the corner of the glass as well."

What in the world was going on here? Susanne hadn't been anywhere near her office at 12:45 a.m. In fact, that was just around the time when she and René had started their final round, with her on top for the grand finale. "I wasn't in my office tonight," Susanne declared. "Whomever you saw on that videotape must have hidden in there."

"How, might I ask, could someone have gotten in without a key?"

"That would be easy. You see, I never lock the door to my office." It was true, she didn't. What was the point, really? All of the night personnel had a master key, so anyone who wanted or needed to get in would, whether the door was locked or not. Why make it unnecessarily difficult for the cleaning crew? She would always take important documents home with her in her briefcase, or else lock them in her desk drawer, which was accessible only with a tiny key that she kept in a side pocket of her purse.

Deschamps nodded, taking another drag on his cigarette. "Well, we'll see. Let's get back to your alibi. Who exactly were you with last night?"

René wouldn't like it, but she had no choice. "The executive director of Musée d'Orsay, René Lauren." Was he still alive, or was he the d'Orsay victim, transported by now from the crime scene and lying on an autopsy table at the Paris morgue with the medical examiner bent over his dead body with scalpel in hand? She needed René alive, not dead, as her alibi. Without him, she would be in serious trouble.

"The executive director is your lover?' Michèle asked, raising her eyebrows slightly. She pushed a pad of paper and a pen across the table toward Susanne.

"He's married, so please be discreet when you call him." Susanne scribbled a phone number on the piece of paper and pushed the notepad back across the table. How would he react to receiving a phone call like this from the police in the middle of the night? Not well, Susanne felt sure; but if he was alive, he had probably been awakened already, informed no doubt—perhaps even in person, by museum security, or the police, or both—about the horrifying incident at his museum.

The scene she imagined in her mind actually made her laugh to herself. René was a nervous adulterer, always looking over his shoulder and covering his tracks with an alias, a pre-paid cell phone, and cash rather than credit card transactions. God forbid that his wife should ever find out about his secret trysts with a younger and much more attractive woman. She was a jealous spouse, and René was a weak and timid cheater, who would never stand up and take responsibility for his allegedly justified infidelity.

She could see him now, startled out of a sound sleep as his secret cell phone called to him from the pocket of his pants, which she imagined he had hastily removed and folded neatly on the bedroom lounge chair before slipping quietly under the covers next to his unsuspecting wife. The pre-paid mobile was the only personal number Rene would ever agree to give Susanne, and now his compulsive attention to discretion would come back to bite him. She smiled to herself, she couldn't help it, as she envisioned René stumbling over his own feet in an unsuccessful attempt to retrieve the source of his marital destruction before the incessant ringing woke up the unsuspecting Celeste, who would be snoring on the other side of their king-sized bed.

"Uh, René Lauren here," she imagined him stuttering.

"Who is it, dear?" his wife might say, raising herself up on one elbow and squinting into the darkness. "I don't recognize that ringtone—did you change it?"

"It's the police," he would say, taking the call out into the hallway so his wife wouldn't overhear. "There's been a murder at d'Orsay," he would stammer, if he didn't know already; but Susanne wondered whether an explanation like that would fly, especially if his jealous wife crept quietly out of bed to listen to his conversation, ear to the door, as he gave his replies in a quiet voice just a few feet away. It depended, really, on what he would say to the insistent detective on the other end of the line, after all. "Thank you for informing me, officer," sounded just fine, but, "Yes, I was with Susanne Bruante at *Le Meridien Etoile*, stepping out on my wife from ten p.m. until one-thirty a.m." definitely did not.

Michèle ripped the piece of paper off the pad, and stood up. "Thank you, I'll call him now." She gazed at Susanne with a slightly condescending smile. "And don't worry, mademoiselle. I'll be discreet."

A moment later, Susanne sat alone with Deschamps, who eyed her up and down, his face a mask that was difficult to interpret. What was he thinking? Maybe that she had in fact been with René at the time of the murder, but at the museum rather than in a hotel room? "I didn't murder him," Susanne said, "if that's what you're thinking. When he left the hotel room at one a.m. right before me, he was just fine."

"We'll get to the bottom of it," he said. "We always do."

She felt sure they would. This Inspector Deschamps, so cool and collected, seemed like the type of seasoned detective who always got his man, or woman. But Crossier, all business and the epitome, it seemed, of efficiency, seemed a bit young for a homicide detective and probably had yet to prove herself. A major case like this one would be the perfect opportunity for a woman like her to show her stuff, and even make a name for herself, perhaps at any cost. The drive to succeed and climb the ladder would motivate Crossier to get to the bottom of things all right, but Susanne would have to swim fast in order to avoid getting inadvertently caught in the indiscriminate dredge of the lake bottom.

Who in the world was the victim at d'Orsay, and who was the lookalike who had somehow stumbled into her unlocked office, leaving traces of someone's blood on the carpet, wall, and photographs? This whole thing, bizarre and surreal, was troubling; but even more important, so very inconvenient. The museum wouldn't open again for days, and that meant her much-awaited presentation on the opening day of the Courbet and Degas pairings exhibit would probably be delayed as well.

The door opened, and Crossier entered. She answered Deschamps' questioning gaze with an affirmative nod. "He's alive, all right," she confirmed, addressing her chief. "I just spoke with him on the phone, and he confirms your story," she continued, redirecting her comments to Susanne. "He agreed to come in first thing in the morning to give a sworn statement that corroborates his whereabouts, and yours, from ten p.m. until one a.m. at *Le Meridien Etoile*. I guess you're off the hook—at least for now."

If Deschamps felt any disappointment, he didn't show it. "You're free to go," he said, looking past her and gesturing subtly with a finger to someone who stood on the other side of the interrogation room window, "but there is one more thing, if you would be so kind."

"What is it?" Susanne stood and reached for her purse.

"Would you mind giving us a DNA sample and a set of fingerprints? Just to confirm that you weren't the one who left the bloodstains in your office, of course." The technician to whom he had signaled a moment earlier came into the room with a portable kit.

Susanne considered for a moment and then decided, why not? It would definitely go better for her if she remained cooperative. "No problem—in fact, I'd be more than happy to cooperate."

An hour later, Susanne Bruante stepped out of the police station and onto the curb, sliding into the back seat of the cab that the police had called for her. It had been a long day and an even longer night. She would be very glad to get home.

Nicole stood, finally, outside a building that displayed a bronze plaque that read *14 Avenue Georges V*. It had taken her long enough to get here, not because there was any great distance between Musée d'Orsay and Susanne Bruante's apartment, but because of the stealth that had been required for her to travel on foot, furtive and vigilant, to at last reach her destination, a full two hours after she had escaped from the museum.

It also didn't help that she had been overwhelmed by her surroundings, at first. It seemed that she had forgotten the very world that she lived in, or so it seemed when she found herself faced with noisy vehicles of painted iron and steel that rolled down the streets of their own accord, and colorful lights at every corner that seemed to give instructions to the passing traffic. She didn't remember any of these things; but no matter, she quickly concluded. Since her survival depended on rapid adaptation, she couldn't waste her precious time trying to sort out the unique idiosyncrasies of her special brand of amnesia. She must focus on a plan rather than squander her energy on things she could not change.

Observation and intuition had served her well. Peering out of the office window a few hours before, she had had a clear view of the street, including the entrance to the museum, almost half a block from where she was hiding. After a while, she could see the flashing lights and the uniformed men congregating there. This was her cue; it was time. If the gendarmes who had been searching for her out there were coming back inside, their next stop would be this office, and she had to be sure she wasn't in it when they kicked the door down.

Gripping the umbrella like a weapon, she cracked open the door, double checking to make sure that she had pushed the metal button on the office side of the doorknob back in, so that the door would remain locked after she left. If the gendarmes didn't have the key, maybe locking the door would slow them down, buying her more time to put some distance between herself and her pursuers. She poked her head out, just a little bit. The hallway, dark and quiet now, would soon be teeming with police, so now was her chance.

She slipped out into the open and closed the door as soundlessly as possible, hearing a soft but definite click as it locked behind her. She moved cautiously toward the exit, her steps muted, careful to suppress the echoing tap of her heeled boots on marble. She wanted to run, but she didn't, telling herself that patience was her friend and panic the enemy. Finally she reached the exit door. Would it alarm again when she opened it? That would bring them on her for sure. Should she try to find another way out? That would be much too risky, she hastily concluded. *I just need to get out of here, now.*

She took in a breath, preparing herself for the door's triggered siren to give away her location, leading to a frantic chase that would last maybe a block or two, a taste of freedom that would inevitably end in her capture, she feared. *I have no choice.* She put her hand on the metal bar that she had pushed before, expecting resistance; instead she found it lax and spent, resting flush against the door. It hadn't been reset, she realized, which meant that she could slip out quietly. Luck, so far, was on her side.

One gentle push, met with easy silence, and she was out, a solitary figure in a hat and coat, stepping carefully down the metal stairs until she reached the bottom. She crept alongside the building, hiding in the shadow of a short alley until she reached a shield of bushes, steeling her courage for the next step. The lights, the activity, and the danger threatened from down the street, so she would walk the other way, her leisurely midnight stroll offering a quiet escape that she hoped no one would notice. *There's no need to run, just take it slow and easy.*

The street was clear, so she took a deep breath in and struck out into the open. One block, two blocks, three blocks, then ten, she walked without looking back, praying that no one had noticed her and that she was not being followed. A handful of pedestrians passed her going in the opposite direction, but none of them made eye contact, and none of them seemed the least bit interested in the woman disguised in beige, the collar of her overcoat turned up around her neck and the floral-trimmed fedora pulled down low over her hair and brow. Soon enough, she had left the commotion far behind; far enough, she finally decided, that it might be safe to rest. She sidestepped into a dark alley, nestled between a tavern with its lights still on, and a closed café, the interior dark and sleeping. She crouched in the shadows with her heart racing, catching her breath and willing herself to stay calm so she could concentrate on the next step. *So far, so good,* she thought, surprised that her improvised agenda had actually worked. *Not bad for an amateur*.

The city bore no resemblance to the Paris she remembered, in her mind's eye. All of the buildings were gigantic, many of them soaring into the sky for miles it seemed, and the streets were cluttered with unmoving parked vehicles, the same ones that she had seen passing her in motion, some of them moving fast enough to rustle the bottom of her overcoat with their swirling, smokeless breeze. Hadn't there been carriages drawn by horses in her Paris? She thought so, but maybe this recollection wasn't a memory but a bizarre dream instead, a confabulation resulting from the trauma of her head injury.

What should she do now? She fingered the envelope she had taken from Susanne Bruante's office sitting at the bottom of her overcoat pocket, wondering how far it was to 14 Avenue Georges V and whether she should head north or south, east or west—a futile question, at the moment, since she lacked the most fundamental reference point to even determine these directions. She didn't know central Paris very well. Montmartre was her home, and without a map to guide her she was truly lost. She would have to stop a pedestrian, she had no choice; and so she walked to the end of the alley and watched for a reasonable candidate.

The street was deserted, and she thought it unlikely that anyone except drunks or vagabonds would be wandering the street at this time of night. She noticed an inn or tavern that appeared to be open, but she couldn't risk the public visibility by going inside, since there might be dozens of patrons still waiting for closing time and the last call for absinthe or a final glass of Marc. She waited outside; after fifteen minutes or so, the door swung open, and two men in their early twenties stumbled out, arm-in-arm in a show of masculine affection that could only result from ingesting an excessive amount of alcohol. One of them laughed as the other finished a confused and slurred story about a barmaid and what she might look like naked.

They started crossing the street, so Nicole followed. It couldn't be more perfect. They were men, so she might be able to use her feminine charms to divert suspicion, and they were clearly intoxicated, enough so that they might not think it odd for a woman to be out and asking for assistance in the middle of the night. She pulled the hat down over her eyebrow on one side to cover the cut on her forehead, while at the same time unbuttoning the top of her overcoat to expose the swell of her breasts, hoping they wouldn't notice the telltale signs of her recent trauma if she dangled a subtle enticement. When they stopped at the intersection to argue about which way they should go, she approached them from behind and sidled up beside them.

"Good evening, gentlemen," she said, smiling. "You both seem very happy tonight."

They gave each other a knowing look. She knew exactly what they had in mind, and she would play along until she got the information she needed from them.

"We could be happier," one said. "Would you care to join us?"

"Perhaps." She dug into her pocket and pulled out the envelope with Susanne's address printed on it. "Could you tell me first, please, how I might arrive at this address from here? I am scheduled to meet a friend there; but afterward, I would be pleased to come back and meet you."

They both nodded with enthusiasm. "We live right around the corner," the first one said, leaning close enough for her to smell the yeasty aroma of red wine on his breath. "Your friend can wait. Why don't you join us now?"

"I am afraid not. He would be angry if I missed our appointment." She winked, with a tilted head and a smile. "When I am finished, I will come right back. Now, what about this address? Is it possible for me to walk to 14 Avenue Georges V, or must I take a carriage?"

She could have kicked herself. What had she said? Those weren't carriages parked along the street; they must have another name. Now, the two men would suspect that she really didn't belong here. They looked at each other for a moment and then exploded simultaneously in a fit of laughter. "I get it," the first one said, wiping the tears from his eyes. "It's theme night, and the guy on Avenue Georges V asked for the nineteenth century. Will you do the can-can for him after you lose the coat?"

"Something like that," she replied, relieved. "I can dance for you, too; but directions first, if you please."

"It's not far," the second one explained, eyeing her up and down with undisguised desire. "Walk ten more blocks down this street, then turn left on Avenue Georges V and follow it up the hill. Number 14 should be five or six blocks from the intersection. The buildings are well marked."

"Thank you."

The closest one tried to put his arms around her and steal a kiss, but she backed up a step to avoid the embrace.

"Not now, messieurs; but I will be back, I promise." Then she turned and ran, as fast as she could, crossing the intersection diagonally to the other side of the street, and she didn't stop.

"Wait," she heard one of them call after her. "You didn't write down our address!"

They didn't try to follow her, but she kept running anyway, leaving three blocks behind her before she finally stopped to catch her breath. After that, she made the rest of her journey slowly, sliding into an alley or pulling her hat down whenever she saw someone coming, until she finally found herself standing in front of Number 14.

What next? Either she would find Susanne here or she would not; and if she didn't, she would need to entertain the serious possibility that Nicole and Susanne Bruante were one-and-the-same person. So, nervous yet curious, she climbed the half-dozen granite stairs that led to the landing, trying the handle of the entry door and finding it locked. She wasn't at all surprised, but still, she had hoped for easy entry.

She peered inside, confirming what she already knew from the address on the envelope—namely, that 14 Avenue Georges V was not a single-family residence. The entryway led to stairs, flanked on either side at the bottom by two separate doorways that obviously belonged to two different apartments on the ground level. She glanced up at three stories of windows, quickly determining that the same arrangement applied to floors two and three, which added up to six apartments; and sure enough, six names were listed on a gold-plated panel to the right of the front door, each one with a number and a letter assigned to it, and each one with its own polished call button.

This is very expensive, she thought. *Far above my means.* She flashed back to the image in her mind of the little apartment on Butte Montmartre, with its cracking plaster walls, rusty metal sink, squeaky cot, and creaky wooden stairs, in such desperate need of repair. *I cannot be Susanne,* she insisted to herself; *I would remember living in a place like this.* The shiny plaque confirmed that Number 3B belonged to Susanne Bruante, just as the address on the envelope had claimed; and the call button promised to wake her.

Nicole pushed it once, then twice; waited and waited; and then pushed it again, and again. Nothing—she wasn't at home. *Does that mean that I am not home too?* she wondered.

So here Nicole stood (or was her name really Susanne?) on the landing of 14 Avenue Georges V, without a plan. She had counted on finding Susanne Bruante at this address, on the other side of this door—her cousin perhaps, or better yet her sister, groggy and irritated from being awakened from a peaceful sleep by the insistent buzzer. Instead, Nicole had been greeted with silence, which could mean only one thing: if Susanne wasn't home at this hour, it was probably because she was somewhere else—namely, standing right here, on this very landing.

What should she do now? If she was Susanne Bruante and not Nicole, and if she were recognized at the museum while she was being chased, where would the police decide to search next, after coming up empty handed at Susanne's workplace? It seemed obvious that they would make a beeline to her place of residence; and here she was, standing like a sitting duck in front of what appeared to be her own apartment, just waiting for the gendarmes to round the corner and detain her, exactly as common sense would predict.

So where should she go now? For the short term, staying here was not an option; but long term? She had no clue. She had no money, no clothes, and no identity. Without these basics, how could she possibly survive? *Stop feeling sorry for yourself,* she thought. There would be plenty of time for that later, crouched at the far end of another alley somewhere, far away from the next stop in law enforcement's logical search for Susanne Bruante.

Nicole turned to leave, and that's when the yellow carriage with the word *TAXI* displayed on its roof pulled up on the curb. A woman, stylishly dressed in a slim-fitting embroidered dress and matching shoes, got out, handed the driver some money, and turned to climb the landing stairs. She was holding something up to her ear, talking into it as she walked. "Of course I gave them his name," she was saying, her voice edgy. “They would have arrested me if I hadn’t produced an alibi.” As she reached the landing, the woman glanced suspiciously at Nicole, who was standing off to the side next to the front doorway.

She looks familiar, Nicole thought at once, rapidly processing the resemblance and realizing where she had seen that face before. She found herself standing face-to-face with the woman pictured in the photographs that she had examined earlier in the museum office, undoubtedly the very same Susanne Bruante; and the face that frowned back at her with undisguised annoyance looked very much, without an argument, like Nicole’s own reflection in a mirror.

Nicole pulled down her hat again to hide the gash on her forehead, unintentionally obscuring the top half of her face as well. “I am looking for Susanne Bruante,” she said, trying to buy some time while she figured out the best way to handle her visibly irritated lookalike. “Do you know her?”

“I’ll call you back in a minute,” Susanne said in a low voice to the object in her hand, which she took from her ear and slid into a side pocket of her handbag. “Who’s asking?” she answered, addressing Nicole in a none-too-patient tone of voice.

Nicole had one chance, and she made an instantaneous decision. It was probably true, after all, so why shouldn’t she just go ahead and take the leap? She removed her hat, so that Susanne would have an unobstructed view of the family resemblance.

“You should recognize me,” she declared with a smile. “I am your sister.”

Chapter Five

Henri Bruante put his phone down on the workbench, right next to the open case containing some of his more delicate instruments. Many of the paintings he was hired to restore had foreign material imbedded on the surface, usually from careless storage practices, and *Nude Reclining* was no exception. God knows how some of the dirt and residue, not to mention the strange fibers, ended up in this one; and it was taking significantly longer than he had expected, even with the miniature forceps, pick, brushes, and tweezers, to examine the surface and remove the debris without damaging, or even chipping off, the paint.

He had been working on this orphaned painting for at least eight weeks now. This project, like most of his others, required patience and painstaking attentiveness, both characteristics that he had learned to foster over the past four decades while he had worked as an art conserver and restorer. Immediately after d'Orsay had agreed to have him labor on *Nude Reclining,* and as soon as he had transported it safely to his home workshop, he had applied a layer of facing tissue to the surface in order to hold any loose pigment to areas where the canvas was torn or buckled. He had then taken the oil-on-canvas nude off its cracked and splintered stretcher, laying it face down on the lining table; discovering, then, that the back had been papered over, a not-uncommon practice that normally wouldn't have made a difference in the process of re-lining. He had almost missed it, but luckily the uneven discoloration had formed the discreet outline of the letter, folded over twice, and hidden ingeniously a very long time ago between the canvas and the paper. Susanne had taken the letter for examination by historical experts; if authenticated, his intuition that one of the French masters had in all likelihood created the anonymous nude would be confirmed.

Then it was on to the next step. After removing the paper backing and his unexpected find, it had taken him a full week to apply the heat sensitive glue, section by section, to the back of the old canvas and then roll it carefully onto a new one, already suspended on a modern frame loom. Eventually, the glue would secure the canvas, primer, and pigment as a new, completely bonded entity, but that took time.

A full week later, after the glue had dried, he had finally been able to start the tedious process of cleaning and restoring the surface, removing the facing paper bit by bit as he worked on a single three-by-three centimeter section at a time.

He used the ground floor of his home in Saint-Germain-des-Prés for business first, and pleasure second. Like most art restorers, he was good at what he did because of his own intrinsic talent: oil painting, to be exact, his understanding of the medium lending itself to a profession that began after art school and was still going strong. Although it seemed like just yesterday, it would be forty-one years this year since he had opened his home business right after college, removing all but the load bearing walls on the bottom floor of his newly purchased city home so that he could devote the majority of the demolished-then-refurbished space to *Bruante Art Restoration Incorporated*, his pride and joy.

Since he had also set aside the back end of the enormous room for his none-too-shabby artistic efforts, he found himself, from the start, spending most of his time downstairs in the wide-open and spacious studio, equipped with fluorescent warehouse-style lighting and concrete floors, stained over the years with splashes of white, green, and black from almost daily paint, solvent, and detergent spills. His living quarters up above were modest and slightly cramped, but he didn't care. The three rooms on the main floor, including one that had been converted into a kitchen and a dining room combined, were more than adequate for him to take his meals and to entertain the rare visitor; while in the top room, on the third level, he would take his nightly rest, sleeping six hours at the most, always up before the crack of dawn, answering the call of his workshop below, where he would routinely get started with a cup of coffee while the rest of Paris slept.

He didn't need much space, since he had never married and hardly ever had any visitors, except of course for an occasional nephew or niece, or now and then a lady caller. He spent most of his time either in his workshop or on jobs that required on-site attention—jobs like the one he had recently contracted with d'Orsay to complete.

Certain pieces were either too valuable or just too large and too heavy to be taken out—or, as it happened every so often, the restoration of a piece of artwork might require special equipment that Henri simply didn't have at his home workshop in Saint-Germain-des-Prés. Case in point: the Rodin sculpture in bronze, his d'Orsay in-museum project.

This particular piece, about three-quarters of the height of an average-sized man, weighed much too much to transport off the premises; more importantly, Henri needed access to the high-pressure submersion tank in the museum basement to restore it properly. And so, for the past four weeks, he had worked on the Rodin for three or four hours each day at d'Orsay, always in the afternoons, and on *Nude Reclining* and a handful of other private jobs at his home, first thing every morning, until just after lunch.

Always an insanely early riser, he had already started where he had left off the day before when his cell phone rang just before 5:00 a.m. He had *Nude Reclining* secured on one of his oversized easels so that he could inspect some of the more problematic areas with a rolling spotlight mounted on top of an optical magnifier, its focus repositioned just a moment ago on the model's hair, brushed in with bold strokes by the artist to cover the rounded top of her left shoulder and the front edge of her arm, and the discreetly sensuous beauty mark on her left cheek. The caller ID told him that his niece was on the line, so he took it after the first ring.

"It's early for you," he spoke into the receiver, turning off the heat-generating examination light to give the century-and-a-half-old paint a breather. He backed up a step, admiring the unsigned and unfinished cast-off again for just a moment—a beautiful brunette (who just so happened to bear an uncanny resemblance to the person he was speaking to right now on the phone), posing on the sketched-in outline of a couch, her nude, perfect body partly reclining backward, leaning on an outstretched arm. He heard Susanne take a deep breath in. Her calls were frequent, since he and his niece were close, by her standards at least; and he knew immediately from the tone of her greeting that he was in for an earful. She usually had some kind of drama to discuss with him, but he hadn't expected this.

"There's been a murder at d'Orsay, and I'll give you one guess who was just dragged into police headquarters for questioning as a suspect." If she had expected him to actually offer a conjecture, he had missed his chance. "They still think I killed him," she continued, "even with my alibi. The blood won't match, though. It's not mine, thank God."

"Slow down," he said, navigating around the end of the custom-made table that occupied the central space of his studio and extended from one side of the room to the other. The table, if it had been used for a banquet instead of as the cluttered home for all of Henri's tools, supplies, and restorations-in-progress, easily could have seated twenty. "Could you start over, my dear? You're talking a mile a minute."

He could hear her take in another breath and then let it out slowly. "Okay. Sorry, *Ton-ton*." She occasionally used the traditional French diminutive for uncle that harkened back to their abbreviated relationship when she had been a little girl, but only when she really needed something. His niece was definitely a woman who could take care of herself, and she would never come right out and ask for help, but he knew her well enough by now to understand the implied meaning in this word choice.

Susanne, who was actually his great niece, was his nephew Didier's only legitimate child; and Susanne's childhood, from an emotional if not from a financial standpoint, had not been an easy one. The divorce had been anything but amicable, and her mentally ill mother—bipolar, with a touch of undiagnosed but inarguable psychosis—did everything in her power to keep the six-year-old Susanne away from her father, as well as anyone else who carried the Bruante name. Strong-willed and difficult to brainwash, Susanne didn't believe her mother's ranting accusations. At age sixteen, she took the matter into her own hands and embarked on a secret search for her father.

It hadn't taken her long to find him. He was still living in Paris, not even two kilometers from the house where he had endured co-habitation with her mother until he simply couldn't stand it any longer. A general internist with a busy practice and a kind and gentle demeanor, Didier Bruante was nothing like the monster that her mother had described. Although Susanne had struggled to understand his passive acceptance of the father–daughter estrangement her mother had produced, their two meetings went a long way toward reviving an affiliation that should have been permanently damaged by a decade of heartbreak.

It was ironic, really, that he had died just as Susanne's hope for rediscovering their relationship had started to come alive. He was walking to meet her for lunch, no less, immediately after making his teaching rounds at the hospital on a cold and frigid Saturday afternoon. The hit-and-run accident had killed him instantly, leaving behind a sizable estate that he had willed to Susanne as his sole heir, the money a poor substitute for an absent father, not even forty, who had now been taken from her for good.

A few years later, liberated by her mother's death from a stroke at an early age, Susanne reconnected with Henri too. *Cher Ton-ton*, she used to call him, when she was only four or five, in the days before her mother had isolated her from everyone who had been even remotely associated with Didier Bruante. Having no children of his own, Henri had adopted Susanne in spirit, hoping she might be the daughter he had never had; but Susanne was far too emotionally damaged to let anyone come that close to her.

Henri had watched sadly as Susanne moved from one relationship to another, always running before the roots of a romantic attachment could take hold, long before there could be any risk of being committed to anyone long term. It was painful for Henri to watch; yet oddly enough, Susanne seemed perfectly happy with her loveless existence, interspersed every now and then with a short-lived and superficial affair—a life that had become unhealthily focused, to the point of obsession, on her profession and career.

"Explain, now, about this murder," he said, reaching for the cup of coffee, already growing cold, that he had left on the table when he had begun his workday almost an hour ago.

"They came knocking on my door at a quarter to three. All I know is that they found the victim in the special exhibit gallery. The surveillance cameras got a pretty decent view of the woman who was with him. She tripped one of the painting alarms before she ran off."

"Let me get this straight. The man is dead, and the woman—"

"Apparently looks a lot like me," Susanne finished.

He hesitated, but decided he had to ask. With Susanne, anything was possible. "The woman they saw on the videotape, Susanne, didn't happen to look like you for a reason, did she?"

"Please, Henri," she said. "I have an alibi."

"Well, that's a relief. Who?"

"René Lauren."

"The executive director of d'Orsay?" He couldn't keep track of her fly-by-night affairs, and he had long since stopped asking. "He's married, Susanne!"

"It's nothing serious, just a pragmatic little affair that I hope will pay off for me big time, in the end." He heard her rifle through her change purse. "Hold on a second, I have to pay the cab driver." After a brief, muffled conversation, he heard her open and close the taxi door.

"Did you give the police his name?" Henri knew René Lauren. D'Orsay's executive director would be none too pleased to have his dirty laundry exposed for everyone to see.

"Of course I gave them his name," she replied, picking up the conversation where they had left off. "They would have arrested me if I couldn't produce an alibi."

He heard some noise in a background, a woman's voice perhaps. "I'll call you back in a minute," Susanne said in a low tone; a second later, the call disconnected.

He set his cell phone on the table next to his open leather tool pouch. Should he just wait here for it to ring again? Unlikely. Susanne hadn't asked for his help, but there was no question in his mind that she needed it.

He picked up the phone again and slid it into his front pocket. He carefully covered *Nude Reclining* with a sheet, just to make sure that no one could spot it from one of the windows. One could never be too careful. How fortuitous that he had seen the piece, part of a bulk acquisition by d'Orsay toward the end of last year from a bankruptcy auction, gathering dust in the storage room behind the sculpture renovation workshop in the museum basement. And how lucky for him that the acquisitions department, with Susanne's nod, had approved his request to take it off the premises and restore it, free of charge, his special pro bono project that had started out as a whim but had turned out to represent a major historical find. He had more than enough evidence, now, even without the letter, to conclude that his suspicions about the mysterious painting were true. If his conclusions were valid, *Nude Reclining* was probably worth millions.

After grabbing a light jacket, he set the security alarm by punching in a series of numbers and then stepped outside and triple locked the front door. He peered through the captain's window to the right of the entryway, just to double check. Satisfied that *Nude Reclining* was safe and sound, he put his hands in his jacket pockets and began the forty-minute walk across town to Avenue Georges V.

~

Susanne's first impulse was to keep on walking, leaving a locked door between her and the ongoing insanity. She had had her fill of crazy, starting with René in the early morning hours and ending just a little while ago with the police; now she had to deal with this woman, who was clearly out of her mind. Susanne stepped toward the security entrance, hand in her purse, groping through the contents until she finally found her key card. One swipe in front of the sensor would do it, and then she would be safe.

"Look at me," the woman insisted, grabbing Susanne's arm to stop her. A moment ago, Susanne had been unable to make out the woman's features, obscured in the pre-dawn darkness; now, from this angle, the streetlight was shining directly on her face. She could see her, all right—and the hat, a unique, floral-trimmed fedora, available only by special order. The woman had her hat, not to mention her coat and boots—and her face.

"You're the woman from the museum, the one the police are looking for!" Susanne declared. One simple phone call and Susanne's problems would be solved. She reached in her purse, this time for her phone.

"Wait." The woman was in front of her now, blocking her planned escape route into the haven of the secured building. She clutched Susanne's arm, her grip somehow resolute but also imploring at the same time. "Please," she said, and their eyes locked—identical shades of hazel, Susanne couldn't help but notice. "My name is Nicole Bruante. I think I am your sister."

The woman's manner of speaking was formal, proper, verging on ceremonial. Odd, how she used the antiquated pronouns—for instance, *vous* instead of *tu.* No one did that anymore. There was something very wrong with this picture, and also something very wrong with the woman standing in it, who claimed to be her sister.

"I think not. I don't have a sister," Susanne said, indignant; but as she stood, face-to-face with this woman who could very well pass for her twin, she began to wonder.

"It is a long story," the woman said, looking furtively over Susanne's shoulder as if she were being pursued. "We should talk about it upstairs."

"I'm not so sure I want to harbor a fugitive." Sister or not, affiliating herself with a murder suspect was simply not on Susanne's agenda.

The woman stepped closer to Susanne. "I think it would be best for everyone involved if you let me in," she said, her voice steady but her speech rapid, giving the distinct impression of controlled desperation.

"And why is that?"

"Because I am very confused. I do not know what happened at the museum, but I think it may have involved you, somehow. If the police find me, your name will come up." The woman who claimed to be named Nicole gave Susanne a knowing look. Yes, Susanne's name would come up—because this lunatic would make sure it did. "It could go very badly for both of us," the woman continued. "Do you really want to risk it?" Her eyes widened in earnest supplication; her tone was conciliatory. "Please—I will explain everything upstairs."

Susanne took a moment to deliberate the pros and cons. She had a rock solid alibi, so anything Nicole said to the police about her wouldn't carry much weight; but still, explaining away their association, now that Nicole had made contact, might not be that easy. Susanne didn't need any more trouble with the police than she already had, and any further implication in the d'Orsay incident could create a mess that would take considerable time to mop up. For the moment, damage control was the name of the game; letting Nicole in would achieve just that.

Susanne put on her best look of concession. "All right, I'll let you in, but you have to promise to behave. Turn out your pockets, please. I need to make sure you aren't carrying a weapon."

Nicole pulled out the lining from the two front pockets of the overcoat, proving to Susanne that she wasn't armed. Susanne nodded. "Now do the same for whatever's underneath."

"There is nothing underneath. I am naked. Do you want me to show you?"

That was odd, to be sure, but Susanne wasn't one to judge too severely when it came to the lack of clothes. She had done her share of figure modeling, and she was the first to admit that she liked the feel of nothing at all between her skin and the outside world. "Keep it on," she replied. "We'll save the peep show for later."

Nicole moved aside, but then made sure she was the first to enter when the keycard tripped the electronic lock to open. "Third floor?" she called to Susanne over her shoulder as she started up the stairs.

This Nicole had chutzpah, Susanne had to give her that; but admittedly, if their roles had been reversed, Susanne would be doing the exact same thing. She couldn't help but admire the girl's audacity. "First door to the right. I'd tell you to let yourself in, but I have the key," she added sarcastically.

As she trailed a few steps behind her determined lookalike, Susanne came to the smug conclusion that nothing could be more perfect. In a moment, she would have the unsuspecting Nicole cornered in familiar home territory, and the game would be hers. It definitely worked in Susanne's favor to have Nicole continue to believe that her couched attempt at blackmail had actually worked. The longer Nicole erroneously thought that she had the upper hand, the better. This would give Susanne more time to work out the best timing for her phone call to the police. *Perfect.*

They reached the top of the stairs, and Susanne opened the door. "Make yourself at home," she said, leading Nicole to the right and into the dining room. It couldn't hurt to give the impression of hospitality, to keep Nicole's guard down; plus, befriending a crime scene eyewitness had certain advantages. Nicole would probably be able to provide some very useful information that might go a long way toward explaining the d'Orsay incident.

"I think we got off on the wrong foot. Why don't we begin with a fresh introduction?" She offered her hand. "I'm Susanne Bruante. Who, exactly, are you again?"

"I told you, I am Nicole Bruante. You and I share more than just a name, I believe. We are related, I am sure." The girl persisted in speaking her antique version of the French language. This much, at least, didn't seem contrived.

"I thought you said you were my sister?"

Nicole gazed back at Susanne defiantly. "Look at yourself in the mirror, and then take a moment to look at me. How could we be anything *but* sisters?"

Nicole had a point. Unrelated people sometimes looked the same, but to this extreme? Could they really be sisters? She didn't know much about her father's personal life, either before or after his association with her mother; theoretically, Susanne could have a multitude of half-siblings out there, just waiting to be discovered. Henri, being the self-designated family historian, would probably know. She'd call him back in a little while and find out.

"I can see the resemblance as well as you can," Susanne replied nonchalantly. She had moved from the foyer into the dining room, making a beeline for a liquor cabinet standing against the far wall. It wasn't even close to cocktail hour, but she could sure use a drink. "Would you like a drop of brandy, or a glass of wine?" This time, her offer was genuine, more or less. Susanne had nothing to lose and much to gain by appearing hospitable.

"No thank you." Nicole pulled out a chair from the dining room table and helped herself to a seat. She looked exhausted, a woman who had unquestionably been put through the wringer. Whatever had happened at the museum, even Susanne the cynic could see that Nicole had been on the receiving end, rather than the delivery end, of something terrible. Yet one could never tell; appearances were often deceptive. Lucrezia Borgia had fooled everyone too.

"How about something non-alcoholic?"

"Some water, or a *café*, would be nice."

Susanne poured herself some sherry into a wine glass and set it down in front of the seat directly across the table from Nicole. "I'll be right back," she said with a disarming smile.

Susanne pushed her way through the swinging door that led from the dining room into her kitchen, all granite and marble and equipped with the latest equipment incorporated tastefully into the floor plan. Feeling hungry herself, she decided that it couldn't hurt to offer Nicole some food. She found a fresh baguette on the bread shelf, some Brie and Camembert stacked neatly in the back of her refrigerator, and a bowl of fresh fruit, just replenished, on the center island. A moment later, she returned to the dining room with a heavily loaded tray.

Susanne sat across from Nicole and watched as the woman helped herself to the food and drink with measured restraint. She was obviously parched and most likely famished but seemed determined to disguise any sign of weakness. She picked some cheese from the tray, sliced a pear in half on the plate in front of her, and carefully poured some ice water from a pitcher into the crystal glass that Susanne had just retrieved from the china cabinet.

"You must be hungry," Susanne commented, watching Nicole's mannerly efforts with a half-smile that she managed to hide behind her glass of sherry.

"Mostly thirsty," Nicole admitted. She drank the water in gulps, despite herself. After Susanne had let her indulge herself for a while, she decided it was time to get some answers.

"So, what happened at the museum?" Susanne finally asked. In her usual fashion, she got right to the point. The time for small talk was over.

"I am not sure," Nicole answered. Susanne studied the woman's face, which no longer wore a mask of defiance. Perhaps she was ready to come clean.

"What, exactly, do you mean?"

"I think I was knocked unconscious. I do not remember anything, not even being hit in the head."

"You must remember something."

Nicole shook her head. "Nothing. It is all a complete blank."

"Let's back up, then. Where were you right before the incident?"

"I told you; I do not remember anything."

Amnesia? Possible, if she had really sustained a concussion; but more likely she was just faking it. "You know your name, though," Susanne pointed out, still the unwavering skeptic.

"True, but that is all. I have no idea where I live, what I do, or even who I am."

Was she telling the truth? She seemed sincere, but Susanne had learned, over the years, to trust no one, and she wasn't about to start now. "How did you end up here, then?" Susanne asked. If Nicole had truly lost her memory, then how in the world had she known where to look for her long lost sister? *Let's see how you answer this one.*

"When I was trying to escape from the museum, I hid in the first office I could find that was unlocked." She shrugged. "It was yours, believe it or not. I know it sounds as if I am lying, but it is true. I saw your picture on the wall and recognized the resemblance between the two of us immediately." She pulled an envelope from her pocket, tossing the evidence on the table in front of Susanne. "Here, look for yourself. I found this on your desk. Your address is on it," she explained with finality.

Susanne picked up the letter, appearing to confirm the plausibility of it all with a subtle nod of concession. She still had big-time doubts, but she would continue to string Nicole along so she wouldn't let her guard back up. The fact remained that Susanne never, *ever* locked her office door, which meant that Nicole could have very well ended up in Susanne's office by accident—a pure coincidence, plain and simple.

"What about the man?" Susanne asked, moving on to another line of questioning. She felt as if she were the detective now, and Nicole the suspect, guilty as charged.

"I knew him. The moment I gazed upon his face, I had a flashback." She looked down, embarrassed. "I think he shared my bed."

Susanne laughed; she couldn't help it. "There's no crime in that, unless you killed him afterward." *Got you, Nicole.*

She shook her head. "I did not kill him. You should have seen his body. He was crushed by something very heavy. Never could I have done such a thing."

How had Nicole gotten into the museum? What had happened to her unfortunate friend? How had she been injured and last but definitely not least, who the hell was she? Susanne would get her answers, by God, starting with the last question first. She walked over to the credenza and picked up her landline.

"What are you doing?" Nicole asked. She seemed oddly fixated on the phone, almost as if she had never seen one before.

"Calling my uncle," Susanne replied. "I have a feeling that he'll know who you are."

It only rang once before he answered. "I'm downstairs," Henri said. "Why don't you buzz me in?"

"Downstairs?" Susanne repeated, surprised.

"I thought you might need my help," he said, "so here I am."

Chapter Six

Henri waited for the click of the lock, its mechanism remotely tripped by Susanne upstairs, allowing him entry into the softly lit stairway of the condominium. He took the ten steps or so that led to the first landing, then another ten in the reverse direction to floor one, repeating it again until he reached the third floor. He didn't have to ring the bell, since Susanne was waiting for him, standing partly in the hallway, one shoulder and a leg in the door threshold to prevent them from being locked out. It looked almost as if she might not let him in.

"I have a visitor," she said immediately.

"The pragmatic affair?" he asked, wondering why she would care if he met yet another one of her easy-come, easy-go love interests.

"No. She says she's a Bruante."

Now that was unusual. In general, Susanne didn't care one iota for family, with the exception of her great uncle. Susanne had adopted Henri as a surrogate father of sorts, whether she cared to admit it or not, after Didier had died suddenly. Having been unable to cultivate a meaningful relationship with her own father, she had half-heartedly nurtured a tenuous emotional bond with her uncle. She still played her cards close to her chest, and refused to let him entirely in, but it was something. Henri was the closest thing to a father that she had ever had; by the same token, she functioned in some respects as a daughter to him. Regardless, hosting a relative would be drastically out of character for his niece, even if it weren't well before 6:00 in the morning. Had one of Susanne's cousins come to call, perhaps? They were plentiful, but he couldn't imagine any of them fraternizing with his niece at any hour.

"Are you going to let me in so I can see who it is, or do you want me to guess?"

"She was waiting for me outside when the taxi dropped me off. She's the woman the police confused with me—the suspect from the museum. Imagine Henri, she fell right into my lap. I'll be off the hook the minute I turn her in."

"Hold on, Susanne. Didn't you say she was family?"

"Yes—or at least she claims to be."

"Well if she is, you can't just throw her to the dogs." This was just so typical of Susanne. Henri had learned to overlook her selfish side, choosing to focus instead on her other qualities. She was an astute art historian and scholar, with a master's degree that had focused on the pre-Impressionist Realist movement; a skilled photographer, who had chosen to put her talent aside, for better or for worse, in order to focus on her successful career as a museum curator; a one-time figure model, a beautiful woman who had posed nude in her student days, not that long ago, as a hobby, when she probably could have made it a vocation of sorts if she had just set her mind to it; and a good person, deep down, Henri kept reminding himself. It wasn't her fault that her childhood had been emotionally troubled. Henri was, if anything, patient, and he had never given up on his complex niece. "Did she kill anyone?" he asked.

"That's hard to tell. She says she can't remember what happened—some kind of post-traumatic amnesia, she claims. I'm not sure I believe her."

"Let's go in, then, so I can see for myself. If she's a Bruante, chances are I'll recognize her."

Susanne stepped back through the doorway, and Henri followed close behind. They passed through the foyer to the right, and there she was, sitting at the dining room table with her back facing the entryway. Hearing them behind her, the woman turned her head, and then pushed the chair back abruptly to stand. The overcoat she wore did little to hide her apprehension or her injuries. The gash above her left eye had recently reopened, judging from the dried blood on her forehead and hands, and the bruises on her neck were visible above the collar, which was buttoned in front in an unsuccessful attempt to disguise the black and blue evidence of her recent trauma. He could tell immediately that she was trying to put on a brave face, but that face, at the moment, had turned a few shades paler than ashen.

"I feel so dizzy, all of a sudden," she said, trying unsuccessfully to grab the edge of the table for support. In the blink of an eye—before Henri could move—she was on the floor.

Henri ran to kneel beside her, reassuring himself with two fingers on her neck that she had a strong pulse. She hadn't hit her head on the table, thank God. "Help me move her over to the couch in the living room," he said. Susanne took the woman's feet while he lifted her off the floor with two hands hooked under her arms. They managed to half-drag, half-carry the unconscious guest through the dining room and foyer and into the living room. Once she was on the couch, Henri asked Susanne if she had a first aid kit. "This gash on her head should be cleaned up," he said, his tone more than a little bit accusatory. "Otherwise, it might get infected."

Susanne didn't argue, fetching the kit from her bathroom with sheepish obedience. "Can't you see this woman has been traumatized?" he said when she had returned. "She needs a bath, food, and a warm bed. If you're still thinking about turning her in, you can do it tomorrow."

Susanne's face blushed red. "I hadn't decided about that one way or the other, *Ton-ton*. I wanted your opinion first."

Henri took a deep breath to calm himself. Susanne had called him, after all, and she usually followed his advice when she bothered to ask for it. "Well, my opinion, since you've asked, is that we should try to avoid drawing premature conclusions. I can tell you right now, Susanne, this woman is no murderer. With all the bruising, I'd be willing to bet that she was another victim—one who barely escaped with her life."

"I don't necessarily disagree. It's just that her story sounds so outrageous. She actually thinks she's my sister, Henri. You and I both know that I don't have a sister."

"Actually, Susanne, you might." He had never told her, because she had never asked; plus, the embarrassing incident was nothing less than a family scandal. To Henri's knowledge, Didier had never even been in touch with his child, conceived when he was a minor, the result of a shocking affair with a household domestic.

Susanne looked back at him, dumbfounded. She opened her mouth to say something, but nothing came out. This was the first time that Henri had *ever* seen Susanne at a loss for words.

"Her name was Anaïs Montague," Henri explained to his speechless niece. "She was a maid, living in the servant's quarters on your grandmother's estate—a beautiful woman, in her late thirties or early forties when your father became involved with her. He was only fifteen years old."

Susanne was still in shock. "Your grandmother was furious when she found out about the pregnancy," he continued, using this rare opportunity to provide an explanation without being interrupted by his customarily mouthy niece. "My sister and Monique were roughly the same age, and her son, your father, was an underage teenager. Your grandmother made certain—with money, legal maneuvering, and more—that the scandal would remain a secret forever. She drew up the papers and had Anaïs sign a no-contact agreement—in exchange, of course, for a sinfully large sum of money."

Henri remembered that day, when Anaïs had been quietly escorted into the Mercedes that had pulled up in front of the family mansion. Henri, fourteen years younger than his sister Joelle, and only three years older than her favorite son, had really been more like a brother to his nephew Didier. Henri had known about his nephew's affair, and in truth he couldn't blame him. Anaïs would be difficult for any man to resist, at any age.

"Did he love her?" Susanne finally asked.

Henri shook his head. "I don't think so. Honestly, I don't recall any tears that day my sister had her taken away."

"What about the baby?"

Henri shrugged. "My sister had a very strong will and was very persuasive, to say the least. Anaïs and her unborn child were sent away, their memory swept under the carpet. We never heard from her again, which was my sister's intention precisely. I don't even know if the child was a boy or a girl."

Susanne regained her composure as she thought through this information. "So, Nicole could very well be my older half-sister," she said, almost to herself.

"Is her name Nicole?" Henri asked.

"That's what she said. Nicole Bruante."

Interesting. Nicole was a family name belonging to Susanne's great-great-great grandmother. "I'll do some investigating," he promised. "With a little luck, I can probably find out what happened to Anaïs and your father's illegitimate child." He nodded at Nicole, who had just started stirring. "I think it's very possible, Susanne, that you've just been reunited with your long-lost half-sister."

He saw Nicole's eyes flicker open. She abruptly raised herself up on one arm, extended backward, and then she turned her head to one side and rested it in the crook of her other outstretched arm—a maneuver that Henri guessed had something to do with an attempt to lessen a throbbing headache. It looked so familiar, he thought—the pose, and the beauty mark, positioned just so on Nicole's left cheekbone. Then, in an instant, he knew.

As he sat on the edge of the couch in Susanne's apartment, he found himself looking at a bizarre modern day replica of *Nude Reclining,* dressed in an overcoat.

Nicole sat up completely, breaking her pose; with the change in position, Henri's strange feeling of déjà vu passed. Still, there was the birthmark. How peculiar that Nicole would have exactly the same beauty mark as the model in the cast-off painting he was restoring. But this was not the only coincidence to consider. Henri had originally been drawn to *Nude Reclining* when he saw it lying in the corner of the acquisition storage room in the museum basement expressly because of the model. To put it simply, she had reminded him of Susanne. Now, one falling domino had toppled the entire line. *Nude Reclining's* model looked like Susanne; *Nude Reclining's* model looked like Nicole; Susanne and Nicole looked like each other; and all three women—two from the twenty-first century and one from the nineteenth—could easily pass for sisters.

But this was no time to ponder the irrelevant. "What happened?" Nicole asked them, rubbing her forehead. "My head is pounding."

"You passed out," Henri said. "How do you feel?"

"Dizzy."

"You need to get some rest," Susanne said.

Finally, Henri thought. With the right encouragement, Susanne usually came through. Case in point: his request to restore *Nude Reclining* for free. Susanne had agreed to argue in Henri's behalf, not because there was anything in it for her, but because the project seemed important to him. As it turned out, Susanne had gained much by facilitating her uncle's entreaty. He had found the hidden letter shortly after the piece had come to his workshop, an unexpected treasure of evidence that Susanne seemed convinced would be the pièce de résistance for her upcoming presentation for the opening of *Courbet and Degas: Nude Pairings*.

"This is my Uncle Henri, by the way," Susanne said. "He's going to help us figure out who you are."

Nicole nodded, looking Henri up and down with a critical and intelligent eye. "It is a pleasure making your acquaintance," she finally said, using the formal *vous* rather than the familiar *tu*, in a tone implying that she had made her assessment, and he had passed the test. Strange, Henri thought, that she would choose such an outdated grammatical convention. That old French linguistic standard had died out long ago; for someone of Nicole's generation, using the overly polite form of the pronoun "you" was almost unheard of.

"It's nice to meet you, too," he replied, using the familiar *tu* rather than the formal alternative. "We'll talk some more; but first, let me dress that cut of yours, and then I'm sure that Susanne would be happy to show you where the shower is, and offer you a bed in one of her guestrooms to sleep in after you're cleaned up." He gave Susanne a look that clearly transmitted the message, "Treat her nicely or else."

Susanne nodded her understanding. A few minutes later, after Henri had cared for Nicole's head wound and Susanne had shown her to the bathroom, Susanne sat down next to Henri on the couch. "So, what do you think?" she asked, keeping her voice low.

"There's no question about it. She's a Bruante, all right. She looks just like you."

"My sister?"

"Maybe." He got up and headed for the door. "Whoever she is, I intend to find out before nightfall."

"Where are you going?"

"To the Office of Public Records. Give me a few hours."

"Are you coming back?"

"Of course." And, Henri felt certain he would have some answers when he returned later.

Dr. John Noland always had a mild case of the jitters before addressing a crowd, but this time it was worse than usual. Usually, his audience consisted of scientists who could easily understand the technicalities of his theories; this time, he would be speaking to a group of popular journalists and television personalities with minimal, if any, scientific background.

He had never really been subjected to public scrutiny, but things were different now. Mathematical formulas scribbled on a blackboard and discussed with excitement amongst the scientific elite were one thing, but the actual transfer of genetically altered rodents between two distinct Time-Shells was quite another. His successes were a subject of discussion now in the trendy fringe press, the laughable exaggerations making the tabloid headlines now on a regular basis. This was his chance to set the record straight, so he had cautiously agreed to this unconventional forum, taking place immediately after his keynote lecture at the International Convention of Astrophysics in London, a televised press conference that would reach the masses on not one but two continents.

He had a script, of sorts. Questions had been distributed to the invited participants in advance, but there would still be ample opportunity for the wild card query or the off-base comment. The answers he had prepared were consciously dumbed down, with all equations and most of the mathematical and astrophysical terminology simplified to make the explanations of his experiments more accessible to the lay public. It would be tricky to pull off, to be sure; but if he could, he might be able to stifle the crazy rumors that had been propagated by the very same people who would be attending the taping.

They led him to a table in front of the crowded room and had him sit in front of a microphone. He poured himself a glass of water as they rolled a television camera through the standing-room-only crowd and into position just a few yards from the table and slightly to his left.

A London newscaster, the host of a tabloid-style morning show, got up from his seat next to John at the table and made an animated introduction while standing at a podium. He was used to hearing his degrees and credentials listed chronologically, followed by a summary of his most important achievements, but this time there was none of that. Instead, he learned that he had just made *The Sun's* top ten list of the world's most eligible American bachelors; that he would be turning forty this October, but not to mention it because he was touchy about his age; that he was not only the youngest, but also the best looking, faculty member at the University of Chicago to ever be promoted to full professor; and that he had toyed with the idea of sending himself instead of a lab rat into the future.

After a few "Jolly good shows," one or two "Smashing, old chaps," and a handful of "Bloody amazings," Tony Briggs finally finished, turning to John with a smile and an exuberant thumbs up. "You're on, mate," he said, the cockney seeping ever so slightly into his incompletely tutored accent.

What had he gotten himself into? "Thank you, Mr. Briggs," John spoke into the microphone. This was going to be interesting.

Returning to the table, the newscaster sat back in his moderator's chair as if he were about to watch a fireworks display. "First question?" He pointed to a woman with her hand raised, sitting in the front row.

"Julia Wellington, *The Daily Star.* Is it true that the old adage referring to time as a river is actually true?"

She had asked one of the scripted questions, so this one would be easy. "Yes, in fact that is true. And believe it or not, the now that you and I are currently riding in is very similar to a boat. This boat is actually a self-contained, positively charged Time-Shell, which is being pulled along a magnetic river that we call the Stream toward a negatively charged pole. The positive end of the magnet reaches backward into the past, and the negative end stretches forward in time, into the future."

He took a sip of water, which gave the female journalist sitting in the front row just enough time to ask for clarification, tongue in cheek. "You contend, then, that we're riding in a solitary bubble, floating merrily down some kind of a cosmic energy river? Next, you'll be telling us that mermaids are guiding us, and that Neptune is the oarsman."

He ignored the laughter. "This is no fairy tale," he said with a tolerant smile. "As it turns out, ours is not the only Time-Shell floating down the Stream. There are countless other Time-Shells lined up ahead of us and behind us—an infinite number of them, actually. The presence of many Time-Shells rather than just a solitary one is actually what allows the transfer of an object either into the future or into the past. We have incontestably proven their existence with our experiments."

The moderator pointed to another journalist, sitting toward the back. "Next question, please, for Dr. Noland?"

"Robert Morrow, *The Independent*. This is more of a direct follow-up," admitted the journalist, a young man dressed in denim jeans and a polo shirt. "What, exactly, is in these Time-Shells?" This one was not scripted, but it didn't matter. It dovetailed beautifully with the previous one.

"Our mathematical models and observations indicate that each Time-Shell is an exact replica of every other, existing however in a different point in time, at a different location on the Stream. Imagine billions and billions and billions of Time-Shells traveling together in single file down the Stream." He looked at his watch to enhance the drama of the example he was about to provide. "At the same moment our Time-Shell passes some imaginary signpost for this exact moment—four-seventeen p.m. on June 1st, 2011, according to my timepiece—another co-existing Time-Shell located exactly ten years ahead of us passes the marker for four-seventeen p.m. on June 1st, in the year 2021; and the one ten years behind us passes the four-seventeen p.m. marker on June 1st in 2001. If we were able to jump forward to the 2021 Time-Shell, we would find ourselves there, ten years older. Similarly, if we jumped backward into the 2001 Time-Shell, we would encounter the younger versions of ourselves from a decade before. As our Time-Shell moves ahead, so do all the others. When our Time-Shell located in 2011 eventually reaches the point on the Stream ten years from now, in 2021, the Time-Shell ten years behind us in 2001 will take its place in our current year—2011."

The moderator pointed at another member of the audience, her hand raised. "Carrie Johnson, *The Morning Star*. So how, exactly, is an object transferred from one Time-Shell to another? We're all wondering, I think, if you and H.G. Wells both use time machines." Her comment elicited some hearty laughter from the back of the room, which he ignored.

"The Stream is normally a perfectly linear electromagnetic field, with no waveform or curves at all. We can encourage connections between Time-Shells only by forcing the Stream to buckle into peaks and valleys, called Waves, which bring two Time-Shells into close approximation. So far, we have discovered only two ways to produce Waves. One method is to use a Magnetic Field Generator Plate, while the other involves the use of a naturally occurring hormone called chronotonin."

"This plate of yours sounds like the transporter pad on the *Starship Enterprise*," Ms. Johnson quipped—resulting, of course, in more laughter. This *Morning Star* reporter was a real comedian.

"Hardly," he replied, trying to keep his cool. "Our Magnetic Field Generator Plates are strictly used to study the physical properties of the Stream. Our Time-Transfer experiments on mice were conducted with no machinery whatsoever. Sorry to disappoint all of the *Star Trek* and H.G. Wells fans out there." Now it was his turn to enjoy a chuckle or two.

He knew exactly where to take this next. "There are certain

physical laws that control the pairing of Time-Shells, and whether a connection between them is made at all. First of all, when Waves are created in the Stream, Time-Shells always orient to each other with remarkable chronological symmetry. In layman's terms, this means that when a Time-Shell on the upslope of one Wave lines up with a Time-Shell on the downslope of another, it will be the exact same month, day, and time in each Time-Shell, but in different years. For instance, if it's seven-thirty a.m. on Christmas Day in 1925 in the Time-Shell on Wave One, it will be Christmas Day at seven-thirty a.m. in another year, let's say 1955, in the Time-Shell on Wave Two. Is everyone following me?"

He looked out into the audience and saw about half of the heads nodding in acknowledgement. The others were staring back at him blankly. Oh well, he would simply have to leave the slow ones behind. "Okay, then. Next, you should understand that once an initial connection is established between two Time-Shells, the same two Time-Shells will always find each other, again and again and again, whenever a geographically appropriate buckle is produced in the Stream. This process is called Recollection. And finally, last but not least, something called a Common Object must be present in both Time-Shells to function as an alignment post, of sorts, on both ends. We call the opening that forms between two Time-Shells, anchored at both ends by a Common Object, a Virtual Hole, interchangeably known as a Time-Tunnel."

"Question, on the left?" the moderator interrupted. John had admittedly gotten a little carried away with his scientific soliloquy.

"Jamie McIntosh, *The Scotsman.* What exactly do you mean by a Common Object?"

"A Common Object is something inanimate that's present in both Time-Shells. It can be anything, really—the same dresser, table, boulder, or tree, for instance, as long as it exists in repetition, as a constant variable, in Shell after Shell after Shell. In our rodent experiments, the Common Object is an antiquated penny, minted in 1926, which we place in the mouse's specially manufactured, body-sized cage. Old objects work best as a duplicated anchor on opposite ends of a Time-Tunnel."

A multitude of hands were in the air now. "Over there, on the right side," Briggs said.

"Ian Canter, *The Sun.* Could you tell us about your Time-Transfer experiments with mutant mice, minus all of the scientific jargon?"

This question was another scripted one. "Certainly. As you know, we've discovered a hormone called chronotonin that has the ability to buckle the Stream. We've created genetically engineered mice that have mutations in the chronotonin gene. These mice either have higher than normal levels of chronotonin circulating in their bloodstream, or they produce a more potent version of the hormone. Some of the mice also have a mutation in a part of the gene called the promoter region. In these mice, their chronotonin production is increased exponentially when they are exposed to certain hallucinogenic compounds. When we inject the psychotropic mixture into these mice, they produce a chronotonin halo that facilitates Wave formation in the Stream, opening a Virtual Hole, or Time-Tunnel, between Time-Shells."

"Do the animals simply disappear?" This time it was Tony Briggs asking the question. "What, exactly, do you see during this Time-Transfer?"

"Funny you should ask. The animal disappears, but not permanently. The reason for this, we think, is because of a phenomenon that we have termed the Ricochet Effect."

"Could you please explain?" Briggs said. The entire room was quiet now. Finally, he had their undivided attention.

"First, the animal produces an electromagnetic halo that won't dissipate until hours later, when the hallucinogen is out of its system. Second, the animal is trapped within its custom-made cage, which is transported with the animal through the Virtual Hole created around the penny that we place inside. If the transported mice were able to remove themselves from the cage, putting a safe amount of distance between themselves and their Common Object—the penny—we believe that the Virtual Hole would close. But since they're trapped in the cage, in such close proximity to their Common Object, their chronotonin halo keeps the Virtual Hole wide open. The result is that the mice disappear, but they return almost immediately to our Time-Shell. If we don't remove them from the cage right away, they'll keep traveling back and forth continuously, kind of like a Ping-Pong ball, until the hallucinogen finally wears off."

"Does this back and forth time travel harm them?" the moderator asked.

"Yes, it does. Let me say first that the mice with gene mutations seem to enjoy some degree of protection from the Virtual Hole, presumably from their electromagnetic chronotonin halo. They can go back and forth once or twice without too much of a problem. After three round trips, they demonstrate behaviors that are indicative of central nervous system damage, such as confusion, loss of balance, and seizures. After four round trips, they show signs of respiratory distress; and after five, they die. For the mice without a chronotonin gene mutation, the picture is quite a bit different, to say the least."

"How can mice who don't produce an excess amount of chronotonin create a Virtual Hole between Time-Shells?" the moderator asked.

"They can't, but they can be sucked into a hole as a passenger of sorts, along with the mouse that generated the connection."

"What happens to them?"

"They die instantly, probably because they don't have an electromagnetic shield around them, in contrast to our mutant rodents. We postulate that the external pressure force within a Virtual Hole must be substantial, because of how the normal mice meet their end."

"What do you mean?" the moderator asked.

"They look as though they've been squeezed by some kind of powerful vice," he explained, flashing back with a shudder to the image in his mind of the limp and lifeless rodents. Strangely, none of the mice had exhibited any external evidence of trauma, in contrast to what one might expect—no guts or extruded body fluids, and no blood, except from their compressed and exposed skulls.

The room was deathly quiet; waiting. "It's a horrible thing to see," he added. "Every single bone in their bodies has been crushed, but cleanly, by the electromagnetic force of the Stream pushing in on them—surrounding them—as they pass from one Time-Shell to another through the Virtual Hole."

Chapter Seven

Nicole woke up between sheets that felt cool and soothing against her naked skin. Susanne's hand was on her arm. "Henri's back," she was saying. "You should get up now."

Nicole's sleep had been solid and dreamless. "What time is it?" she asked.

"Four thirty in the afternoon," Susanne said. "You've been asleep all day."

The sleep had been recuperative, for her body as well as her mind. The pain from her bruises had lessened considerably, and where her thinking had felt fogged and sluggish before, her thoughts were distinctively clearer now.

Susanne had some clothing in her arms. "You can wear these," she said, putting them on the end of the bed. "I'm sure they'll fit you."

"Thank you," Nicole replied politely, feeling gratitude toward this stranger who seemed so familiar.

Susanne shrugged. "It's the least I can do. After all, you're probably my sister."

As Susanne closed the guest room door behind her, Nicole shook her head. She and Nicole were related, but they weren't sisters. Everything was coming back to her now, in more than bits and pieces, unbelievable as it all seemed. She still had no idea how she had gotten here, but she knew now that she didn't belong. Yet here she was, regardless.

She would need some time to work it all out in her mind. There were still huge gaps, and some of the memories seemed distant and vague. One thing was certain, though: she would have to play along with the sister charade. Why? Because the only thing standing between her and the gendarmes was Susanne, and the only thing preventing Susanne from giving her up was the concept of sibling fealty. It had worked so far, so why tip over the lifeboat?

She felt as if she had an advocate in Henri, regardless of Susanne's feelings. Nicole didn't quite trust Susanne, not yet, but her intuition told her that Henri was trustworthy. The brief interaction between uncle and niece told Nicole immediately that Henri was a man Susanne respected, whose opinion carried an enormous amount of weight in every aspect of his niece's life. Having Henri on her side would definitely tip the scales in the right direction. If Nicole could convince him, Susanne might eventually come over too—but not now. It would work best, she knew, if she promoted the sister–sister relationship, at least until Nicole herself figured out who she really was. No one would ever believe something so fantastic without proof, and until Nicole had some, she would hold the secret close.

She picked up the trousers that Susanne had called *des jeans*. Nicole had never worn trousers—they were for men, not women—but here, those rules apparently didn't apply. Susanne was right, they fit perfectly, and so did the lavender *chemise* that, curiously, had no sleeves or neck, leaving her arms and the upper part of her chest completely bare. She slid her bare feet into the open toed sandal-shoes that Susanne had left at the foot of her bed, and then took a moment to look at herself in the full-length mirror hanging on the back of the guestroom door, astonished by the end result. Though she remembered little of her former life, she recalled the headache of corsets, linen stays, drawers, and stockings; but not here, where people apparently didn't mind showing some skin. That suited Nicole very well. She turned from side to side, admiring her reflection, giving herself a quiet nod of approval when she noticed how the tightly fitting denim hugged her hips and showed off the lines of her shapely legs. One thing was certain: she would become quite fond of the liberating simplicity of this unfamiliar attire.

She found Susanne waiting for her in the foyer. "He's in here," she said, leading Nicole to the dining room, where Henri had laid out some papers on the table. "We'll have some food in just a few minutes. Can you wait to eat?" Susanne was cordial enough; in fact, just a trifle too cordial. Nicole was willing to wager that Susanne had been pressured by Henri to be tolerant and hospitable. Nicole, it seemed, had Henri to thank for her brief respite from pursuit, and it was Henri whom she must court in order to win Susanne's guarded confidence.

Nicole nodded. "I am fine for now," she replied. "It helped me to rest."

Henri had pulled out two chairs on one end, positioned in front of a stack of papers. He smiled at her, his face warm and somehow familiar—and then suddenly, she knew. This was a man that she felt comfortable trusting because she felt like she knew him. He looked precisely like someone she was very close to, from her previous life. Who, exactly? She couldn't quite put her finger on it yet. But with a little more time…

"Why don't both of you sit down," he said. "I'll show you what I found."

Nicole took a seat at the table on the left, and Susanne sat down next to her. Henri stood between the two women so he could point out some of his discoveries, which he proceeded to lay out in front of them. "Let's start with this birth certificate." He had taken if off the pile, placing it face down on the tabletop. As he started to turn it over, Susanne gave him a sidelong glance.

"How did you get this so quickly, Henri?"

He grinned. "I have a contact in Public Records. She had quite a thing for me, a few years back." He slid the certificate, which was now face up, right in between them; and there it was, plain as day, written neatly on the official birth record.

"My sister's name is Nicole?" Susanne asked, turning with disbelief to face the accused.

I'm not her sister, Nicole thought; *I can't be.* Yet here it was, a birth certificate that might actually be hers. She passed her hand over her forehead, as if the action would wipe the confusion from her mind. Was she going mad? This whole thing seemed completely crazy; and now, she didn't know what to think, except that her memories would not agree to just lie down and submit to the strong arm of a piece of paper.

"Now that we know something about you, Nicole, I've filled in this part of the family tree," Henri was explaining pleasantly. He took a thick stack of papers in his hand, unfolding a complicated chart that he had handwritten on more than a dozen industrial-sized sheets of white paper, attached one to the other. The final product was a complicated diagram that extended across and down to fill up the entire sixteen pieces of paper, combined together four across by four down, taking up half of the dining room table's surface area when it was finally spread out.

"Here you are, Nicole," he explained, motioning toward the bottom of the chart. "I wrote your name in the right place on the family pedigree: Nicole Bruante Montagne."

"Born on August 8, 1968," Susanne said, pointing with an index finger to the box that detailed Nicole's name and date of birth. Susanne gave Nicole a quick once-over, head to toe and back again. "That would make her forty-three. That doesn't seem even remotely possible, Henri. She barely looks twenty-five!"

"That doesn't mean a thing," Henri insisted. "Everyone in our family ages well. For instance, look at you, Susanne. How old are you now, thirty-six or thirty-seven? You know as well as I do that you could still easily pass for someone in her early twenties."

"I suppose," Susanne replied, not sounding entirely convinced. Nicole didn't blame her. She herself wasn't convinced, either.

"According to this chart," Nicole noted, finger on another box, "your niece and I have the same father." She hadn't been invited yet to call Susanne by her first name—or Henri by his, for that matter.

"That's right, Nicole. Your father, as well as Susanne's, was Didier Bruante, my nephew."

Nicole traced, with the same finger, the line from her father that led to her mother. "My mother was someone named Monique Montague? Do you know anything about her, Monsieur Bruante? I cannot remember anything about her." Her curiosity was sincere, in part; she wanted to know, because she might actually be Nicole Montagne, but she was also buying some time to inconspicuously study the family tree, with a focus on the upper portion, of course. She had a theory; if she was right, maybe she would find herself closer to the top, rather than at the bottom, of Henri's branching tree trunk.

"Please call me Henri," he said with a warm smile, as he launched into an explanation. "To answer your question about your mother, Monique was a maid in your grandmother's service; your father became, well, involved with her. You were the result." Nicole nodded, feigning interest, while her eyes climbed up Henri's hand-written ladder. Didier's mother was named Joelle; Joelle's father was called Marcel; and Marcel's father was Edmond Bruante.

Edmond—I knew an Edmond. Rather, I know an Edmond, and he is barely four years old. Can it be? Mon Dieu, it must be! If so, she also knew Edmond's mother—knew her, in fact, as well or better than she knew herself, because...

Nicole pointed at the name, a relative from nearly a century and a half ago. "Here is another Nicole," she declared, unable to prevent her voice from trembling. "Do you know anything about *this* Bruante?"

She met Henri's gaze and their eyes locked; she had the feeling that maybe the same thought had occurred to him, a fleeting suspicion that the impossible might actually be possible. Had he recognized her, perhaps, from an old photograph? The way he looked at her suggested recognition; then again, she was still confused, and admittedly prone to this type of misinterpretation. *He might not know me*, she thought, *but I certainly know him—or someone who looked exactly like him.* His kind face, those empathetic eyes, the wild grey hair, and the closely trimmed salt-and-pepper beard…she could picture him, even now, in her mind, and she knew just where to find him on the family tree, one branch above her on the papers spread out in front of her. Henri looked just like Jerome Bruante, her dear, sweet *Papa*.

Henri gazed back at her with unmistakable affinity, the only person in this strange, new world whom Nicole could trust—her father's lookalike, the bizarre result of a family's genetic heritage, passed down through the generations to end up here. "She was your great-great-great grandmother, Nicole," he said, his gaze never leaving hers. "In all likelihood, you were named after her. Although your grandmother prohibited your father from ever meeting you, she wouldn't have been able to prevent him from suggesting a name." He leaned over the pedigree, and put on his reading glasses. "This particular Nicole died young. Some kind of accident, if I recall. She had a son named Edmond," he added, pointing to the appropriate box, "born out of wedlock. The boy's father remains unnamed, a family mystery. That's why your great-great-great-grandfather's spot in this tree is empty."

"For the moment, Henri, can we focus on this particular family mystery who is sitting next to me right now?" Susanne said with impatience. "Is anything coming back to you, Nicole? You'd think that something here, a name or a date, would jog your memory."

Nicole shook her head again, trying her best to look confused. "There is nothing. It is all a blank."

Henri was busy folding up the pedigree. "There's more," he said. "I found your address and phone number, Nicole."

Nicole understood the word address—but not "phone number." She would add that phrase to her growing vocabulary list, as soon as she found out what it meant.

"Now we're getting somewhere." Susanne stood up and retrieved something from her purse that Nicole quickly deduced was a phone. Susanne had been talking into this particular phone right before their confrontation in front of the building.

"She lives just outside of Paris," Henri explained. He pulled a slip of paper from his pocket and handed it to Susanne.

"Thirty-five Rue de L'Arbre, Croissy-Sur-Seine," Susanne read. "That's not far." She glanced over at Nicole with a self-satisfied half-smile. "I could get you there in thirty-five minutes, without traffic; an hour and ten minutes, with."

"Not so fast," Henri said. "First, she doesn't have a key, remember? And second, we're not one hundred percent certain that this Nicole and that Nicole are one-and-the-same person."

"That's why I intend to call."

"What if she lives alone?"

"Then no one will answer, but if she happens to have a husband, boyfriend, or roommate living there with her, then maybe someone will."

Susanne tapped the face of the phone, which appeared to be covered with glass, and then she held the device up to her ear. *Amazing,* Nicole thought; the small, flat box that Susanne referred to as a phone apparently connected voices, somehow. Nicole knew better than to show her ignorance of these modern contrivances, so she put on her best air of casual disinterest, pretending that all of this was completely normal instead of utterly bewildering.

Susanne tapped one foot impatiently for five or six seconds while holding the device to her ear. Nicole could make out a faint ringing sound, like a doorbell, coming from the phone. Then Susanne said, "*Allo,* is Nicole Montagne there?"

Nicole heard a voice saying something in response, but she couldn't make out the words. "I see," Susanne said. "Can you tell me when you expect her to return?" Susanne nodded a couple of times, while the voice inside the box said something else. "Well, this is a rather unusual situation. Would you mind if I put you on speaker phone so my friends can talk to you, too?" The answer must have been yes, because Susanne tapped the phone again and then put it in the center of the table.

"Allo?" a voice spoke out of the phone. It was eerie, Nicole thought, this disembodied voice—like some speaking from thin air.

"Yes, we can hear you Sylvie," Susanne replied loudly. "Sylvie is

Nicole's roommate," Susanne explained in a low aside to Henri and Nicole. "Sylvie," Susanne continued, her voice just a decibel or two below a shout, "my name is Susanne Bruante, and I'm here with my uncle, Henri, and someone who claims to be my sister, Nicole. We think she might be your roommate. You see, she hit her head and claims to have complete amnesia for everything that happened before the incident. We were hoping you might be able to help us confirm her identity."

"Why don't you recognize your own sister?" the woman on the other end of the line asked, understandably cautious.

"Because I have never met her. She's my estranged half-sister."

"You said your name is Susanne Bruante?"

"That's right."

The phone was silent for a moment, while Sylvie tried to put two and two together. "Well, that makes sense, I guess. My roommate's middle name happens to be Bruante."

"Your Nicole and I are definitely sisters," Susanne replied. "That's not the issue. We need to know if the woman sitting here, at my dining room table, is actually Nicole Bruante Montagne, or an imposter instead."

Nicole didn't like the sound of that. Once Susanne discovered that *that* Nicole and *this* Nicole were two different people, it would all be over. In just a few moments, there would be nothing at all preventing Susanne from turning Nicole in.

"Do you think you can help us?" Susanne continued.

"Sure. Nicole is away on vacation, in Morocco. She won't be back until next week. I don't really see how she could be sitting there with you, when she's supposed to be someplace else."

"Do you think you'd recognize her voice?" Susanne asked.

"Probably."

Susanne turned to Nicole. "Could you say hello to your roommate, Nicole?" Susanne asked, not disguising her sarcasm.

Nicole cleared her throat. "*Allo,* Sylvie," she said loudly. "Something happened to me, I am not sure what, and I ended up naked in a museum. Does my voice sound familiar to you?"

The phone on the table didn't reply at first. "It could be you,"

Sylvie finally said, "but I can't be sure."

Susanne's face dropped. She was obviously on a mission to prove that Nicole was not who she claimed to be. "Does her voice sound familiar, or not?" she demanded.

"Kind of..."

Henri leaned over the edge of the table, speaking toward the phone. "Does your cell phone accept text photos?"

"Great idea!" Susanne exclaimed. "We can take a picture of Nicole and send it to you."

"Yes, that would work," Sylvie replied. She rattled off a number, and Henri wrote it down.

"We'll have to use my mobile to take the picture, so we have to hang up now, Sylvie," Susanne said. "Simply text message me a yes or a no, once you receive the image."

"Will do," Sylvie replied.

Text message. Text photo. Mobile—so many confusing terms! Nicole watched as Susanne grabbed her mobile—another name for a phone, apparently—from the center of the table and ended the call. "Good thinking, Henri," Susanne said. "We should have done this first."

Susanne pointed the phone at Nicole and pushed a button. Nicole heard a click, and at the same time saw a flash of light that made her see stars for a second or two. This phone was more than amazing—apparently it was a camera, too. What else could it do?

Susanne tapped the screen again several times, looking back and forth from the device to the piece of paper with the number on it that Henri had written down. "There," she said with satisfaction, "it's sent. Now, for the moment of truth."

So the phone also was a telegraph of sorts, sending telegrams with photographs! Would the answer be yes, or no? Nicole felt sure it would be no, which meant that she would have to do some fast talking in just a few seconds, in order to prevent Susanne from making another phone call—to the police this time.

A series of beeps came from the phone, which could only mean that Sylvie had telegraphed her answer. Nicole began to tremble.

"Well, well!" Susanne smiled triumphantly. "Who are you, really, Nicole? Because according to this text message from Sylvia, you're definitely not my half-sister."

"She's not?" Henri asked, his forehead wrinkled in surprise.

"*Non;* not according to Sylvie," Susanne answered, "and I think she'd recognize her own roommate. I think a phone call to the police right now is probably in order."

"Wait," Nicole and Henri both said at the same time. They looked at each other, and there it was again—a kinship that simply had to be derived from common blood.

"You can't turn her in just like that, simply because she isn't the Nicole we thought she was," Henri argued. "She could very well be, let's say, a distant cousin, for instance. Just look at her, Susanne. There's no question in my mind, she's a Bruante."

"Who, exactly, are you?" Susanne asked, her eyes narrowing to slits. "Now is your chance to come clean."

"I will tell you who I am," Nicole replied defiantly. She had never been easy to intimidate, and she wasn't about to be bullied by anyone, especially her great-great-great granddaughter. "I am Nicole Marie Bruante," she said, her tone assured and surprisingly matter-of-fact. She pointed to the pedigree, folded up in a neat stack in the center of the table. "I am the other Nicole on that family tree."

"What?" Susanne asked in disbelief. "How in the world—?"

"Don't ask me how," Nicole retorted, "but it is true."

Henri's eyes lit up. "Now that you mention it, the resemblance is striking."

"Henri," Susanne chided, "we already know that Nicole and I look alike."

"No, that's not what I meant. I'm talking about something entirely different."

Susanne opened her mouth to say something else, but Henri stopped her with his hand in the air. "I'll show you," he insisted.

And a few minutes later, all three of them were on their way to his apartment, so that he could show them.

Michèle Crossier sat in the hot seat, directly across from the chief inspector on the other side of his desk. She had gathered quite a bit of information in less than twenty-four hours. Although she couldn't help but feel proud of this accomplishment, the troubling inconsistencies were a nagging thorn in her side. Nothing added up. She already had her theories, but she couldn't prove anything—yet. With enough time, she would. This was only the beginning.

"This is the preliminary autopsy report," she said, sliding a laminated folder across the desk for Deschamps to peruse.

He picked it up and thumbed through it quickly. "Can you give me a summary?" he asked, his attention still focused on the pages in front of him. He apparently wanted her to talk while he read.

"The cause of death, as we suspected, was extensive internal injuries from crush trauma. The victim had been stripped naked before, rather than after, he was killed, due to the lack of clothing fibers on or in his skin. If he had been wearing clothes when he was crushed, embedded traces of polyester or cotton would have been recovered from the surface of the body, but the ME found nothing." She paused to take a breath.

"Go on," he said.

"Our John Doe, being completely disrobed, carried no identification, and his fingerprints and dental records have no matches in either the French or EU databases. Furthermore, he had no implanted medical devices or hardware anywhere in his body." *What a shame,* Michèle thought. Serial numbers on surgically placed health-care appliances often led to a positive identification through the patient's medical records.

Deschamps said nothing, only nodding as he flipped to the next page of the autopsy, studying Pascal Bernier's notations on page four or five while Michèle continued with the update.

"His skull was crushed, resulting in exposure of blood vessels that accounted for the pool of blood underneath his head and body. His lungs were punctured from the inside by the jagged edges of his broken ribs, his liver and spleen were ruptured, and the chest *and* abdominal cavities were filled with blood. Apparently, the inwardly directed pressure caused a tear in a blood vessel called the aorta, just at the exit point from the heart."

"In other words," Deschamps interrupted, "his heart burst from being squeezed from the outside, and he bled internally."

"Something like that," Michèle confirmed. "Honestly, it seems like more than just the heart and aorta were damaged in this victim. Bernier said that every single bone in his body was crushed. He'd never seen anything like it." She leaned forward. "But that's not the only odd thing about the victim's injuries, sir. The amount of spillage was minimal, in relation to the degree of internal trauma."

"What exactly do you mean by spillage?"

"Bodily fluids, intestinal contents—you know, that sort of thing. There was some blood, of course, resulting strictly from the skull injury, but according to Pascal there should have been some extruded visceral material if he was squeezed to death."

Deschamps closed the autopsy report and tossed it onto the desktop. "Anything else?"

"Yes, actually. Remember I said a minute ago that the ME didn't find any traces of clothing fiber embedded in the victim's skin? Well, that's not all he didn't find."

"Meaning?"

"Meaning that our victim couldn't have been crushed by something grimy—for example, a trash compactor. If he had, there would have been debris stuck to his hair and pushed into his skin. There wasn't."

"What do you make of all this, Crossier?" Deschamps asked.

She had hoped he would ask. Michèle had a theory that she was eager to get out there; she answered without hesitation. "First, our victim must have been crushed in a tightly confined space. If his body was completely surrounded by the injuring device, more or less, that might explain why the contents of his body were contained inside, rather than being expelled forcefully outward. In order to explain the lack of foreign material embedded in his skin, the machine in question would have to be easy to clean, with a surface that's amenable to decontamination after each job. I'm thinking that either a glass-like surface or stainless steel would fit the bill."

"Do you have a specific candidate for this murder weapon in mind?" He obviously knew that she did.

"Yes, in fact I do." She put another folder on the desk. "Here's a picture of it."

He opened the folder. "What is this thing?" he asked, "and how the hell did you find it?"

"Monsieur Varton, the chief of d'Orsay security, gave me the lead. I was thinking about a conversation I had with the ME at the crime scene about the victim's injuries and what might have caused them, and I decided to ask Varton about d'Orsay's industrial inventory. I asked him if the museum owned any portable or permanent, equipment—let's say for restoring or cleaning artwork—that might be large enough to accommodate a human body. He told me to check in the basement, in the art conservation workroom, and sure enough, this is what I found."

"I'll ask you again: what exactly is it?"

"It's a size-adjustable, high-pressure submersion tank, used to remove rust and corrosion from sculptures and other metal pieces of artwork." She stood and leaned over the desk, using her index finger to point out some relevant features of the piece of equipment on the image. "As you can see, it's made of reinforced stainless steel. The dimensions can be adjusted depending on the size of the item that's being cleaned."

"How?"

"By extending or shortening the component panels and locking them into place with these corner latches. You see, the interior pressure jets need to be in very close proximity to the piece that's lowered inside in order to drive adherent and ingrained particles off the metal surfaces. This baby is capable of generating some extreme inwardly directed forces, especially when the unit is sealed."

"Hm. So you're thinking the victim was stuffed inside this tank?"

"Exactly, but minus the sulphur chelation liquid. Do you see these connected rubber hoses?" She pointed again, and Deschamps nodded. "The rust removal agent is pumped into the tank after it's sealed, and the positive pressure generated by the associated air tank agitates the solution against the surface of the sculpture to remove any embedded material or corrosion. My theory is that our victim was knocked unconscious with a blunt weapon, causing a non-fatal injury that bled later, after he was moved upstairs to the gallery. He was then stripped and squeezed into the dry submersion tank. The tank was sealed; then the pressure jets were turned on.

"I spoke to Bernier about it. He agrees that the victim's crush injuries could have been caused by this method, using a machine with these capabilities. What do you think? I know it sounds kind of far-fetched, but I think it makes sense."

Deschamps scratched his chin. "Maybe. I'm not quite sure I buy it.

Why would anyone go to such trouble, especially if they've already used a blunt weapon to start the job?"

"I haven't completely worked that out yet. But what if the killer was trying to make some kind of a statement with his choice of murder weapon? If an art restorer was the victim, for instance, being killed with a piece of art restoration equipment might strike an ironically appropriate chord in a certain type of sick mind."

"All right—now we're getting somewhere." The chief inspector offered her a rare smile. "I assume you've already asked forensics to check the inside of the tank for evidence?"

"First thing this morning. I thought for sure we would recover something useful."

"But you didn't?"

"Unfortunately no; but in my mind, at least, this doesn't rule out the submersion tank as the murder weapon. What if our resourceful murderer filled the tank with submersion liquid after he removed the body? It turns out the nitric acid, benzene, and acetone that are used in the corrosion removal process have the ability to emulsify oils and disintegrate proteins. Any hair, blood, skin, or fingerprints would be obliterated with even short-term exposure to this mixture. All our perpetrator would have to do is let the chemicals sit for a while before draining them, *et voilà!* The inside of the tank would be as clean as a whistle."

"Interesting." Deschamps drummed his fingertips on the table, his gaze resting on the contents of the folder. "How about the area around the tank?"

"I've asked forensics to check for fingerprints on the outside of the tank and to comb the entire workshop for pertinent evidence. I'll contact you immediately if they find anything at all of interest."

"Speaking of forensics," he said, leaning back in his chair, "do we have anything yet on the DNA analysis?"

"It's too early to have the final results, but I pressured Bernier for something preliminary. He said they found the victim's own semen, containing viable sperm no less, on his penis."

"So, he had sex with someone shortly before he died?"

"It would appear so, and probably with the person whose pubic hair they found, dried into the semen on our victim's genitals."

Deschamps' quick mind made the obvious connection. "Does the pubic hair match the DNA sample we obtained from Susanne Bruante?"

"A quick and dirty chromosome analysis confirms that the pubic hair belongs to a woman. The full genetic analysis will take another day to run to completion, but Bernier was willing to tell me that the comparison gene sequencing, so far, suggests a high concordance, although not a match, to Susanne Bruante's DNA."

"Concordance? Do you mean to tell me the woman our victim had sex with before he was murdered isn't Susanne Bruante, but someone related to her?"

"Apparently so." It was surprising, to say the least, and not so easy to explain. "I've been promised the full report by tomorrow morning."

"So our victim's lover, it seems, is a Bruante." Deschamps frowned, as if trying to work out the different scenarios in his head. "What then are your conclusions, inspector?"

Michèle sat up straighter; this was her opportunity to impress the boss. "We should pursue Susanne Bruante's involvement further. Just because she didn't sleep with our John Doe doesn't exclude her as a suspect. Finding Bruante DNA on the body definitely implicates her, by way of family association, if nothing else. If she isn't our perpetrator, I'd be willing to bet she knows who was."

"My thoughts exactly." Deschamps nodded. "I want a surveillance team tailing Susanne Bruante—from the moment she leaves her apartment each morning until the minute she turns her lights out and goes to bed every night. I want to know where she goes, when she goes there, and who she goes with."

Michèle was one step ahead of him. "I thought you would ask for that, sir. I hope you don't mind, but I went ahead and authorized a vehicle dispatch and a personnel assignment, right before our meeting."

How would he react? She needed to be careful not to step on his toes, but at the same time she had to prove to him that she had what it took to be the lead detective on a major homicide investigation. Of course she had the authority to order surveillance on a suspect, but this was the kind of thing that usually waited for *l'inspecteur-chef's* endorsement.

"Good." He actually gave her a nod of approval. What a relief. "I want another update by lunchtime, tomorrow." He picked up his phone and started to dial out—the signal, she gathered, that their meeting was over.

She got up and headed for the doorway; before she reached it, he called after her, "Keep it up, Crossier."

"I will, sir," she called back over her shoulder. *I will.*

Chapter Eight

Susanne stood with Nicole in awkward silence, waiting for Henri to return with the box of family photographs. He was planning on using the uncluttered far end of his workshop table on the ground floor to display some selected examples.

"We can't do this upstairs," he had explained. Susanne was well aware that Henri used his dining room table on the main floor, upstairs, for many purposes, including a desk as well as a disordered filing cabinet. Piles of invoices, receipts, and other sundry paperwork were scattered and stacked here and there across the surface, to the extent that it could no longer be used for eating or entertaining, so using the workspace downstairs was really the only option.

"We might as well sit down," Susanne finally said. She took a seat in a wooden chair at the end of the extra-long table, and Nicole chose a metal stool, positioning it a good two or three spaces away. Susanne didn't trust Nicole; apparently, Nicole didn't trust Susanne, either. Maybe it was time to barter a truce.

"So you think you're a time traveler?" Susanne knew it sounded ridiculous, but this was as good a place to start as any. She braced herself for some not-so-trivial small talk.

Nicole shrugged. "I believe so. Nothing is familiar to me in this strange place, and all of my memories seem so…antiquated, compared to everything I have seen here. I can think of no other explanation."

"What do you remember?" This would be interesting, if nothing else. Susanne would give this a little more time, at least until Henri showed them the pictures, but her skepticism was poised and ready. There was only one reason she had not turned Nicole in yet, and he would be back in a minute. Henri seemed convinced that Nicole was the real thing; out of respect for her uncle and his oft-demonstrated intelligence, she would bide her time.

"A garret apartment, in Montmartre; artists—more than one; and flashbacks of a woman that must be me, posing for them in the nude.

Always in the nude…" She had a far-off look in her eyes, as if the recollection of those days brought to mind both joy and sadness, at the same time.

"Do you mean to tell me that you were a nude model?" Susanne asked, incredulous. This was really too much. It was one thing for Nicole to steal Susanne's looks, but quite another for her to start encroaching on hobbies that, at least until recently, bordered on a vocation.

"I think so," Nicole said with a sigh. "I loved the exposure, I loved the way my body looked on canvas when the paintings were finished…and I loved him."

"Who did you love?" Now that, at least, was something Susanne and Nicole did not have in common. Susanne had never truly loved anyone but herself, while Nicole apparently had.

"I loved the artist—my little Edmond's father. He had to leave, though, and I—" She took a breath in, visibly composing herself. "I could not take care of a little boy, not without money, and not without his father." A weaker person might have broken down, but this Nicole was tough, if nothing else. "He is better off without me, I think. My Edmond is with my mother, who dearly loves him and dotes on him. I—I see him when I can."

Did Susanne feel a twinge of compassion? A little stab, maybe, she had to admit. Could Nicole be telling the truth? She sounded sincere. *Careful, Susanne; it might just be a scam.* Susanne had been a nude model, too, and it seemed a very odd coincidence that she and Nicole would share the same calling. It was entirely conceivable that Nicole was attempting to gain Susanne's trust by concocting a shared interest and by drumming up Susanne's sympathy with an imaginative fairy tale about the tragic separation of a mother from her son.

"But how did you get here? A door, a window—a rabbit hole?" Susanne asked, unable to hide her tone of skepticism.

"It was a little bit like a hole." Nicole was actually serious; Susanne could see it in her face. She looked down, intently studying the surface of the table as she struggled to describe it. "The memories return slowly. I remember it was bright and swirling, empty and hot. It was a tunnel, a wind tunnel, that pulled me in—pulled us in. There was nothing I could do to resist it. It was much too strong to fight, sucking and drawing us both over the lip and into its center. I remember floating up, then rushing forward, screaming—screaming and falling, tumbling into the whiteness. And then it was dark, all dark. I thought, at first, when it started to happen, that it was just the wine. You see, the two of us had been drinking wine, and absinthe too, so my head was spinning. But it wasn't the absinthe. It was real." She looked up, her hazel eyes locking on to Susanne's with convincing intensity. "It was real," she insisted. "I am certain that it was real."

It was real. Nicole spoke those words with such conviction that even Susanne, the ultimate Doubting Thomas, imagined that her story might be true. Was it real? It couldn't be, and yet…

"I…" Susanne looked away. She had intended to say, "I'm starting to believe you," but the words just wouldn't come. Would it be so terrible to let her guard down, for once? Why did she feel as if acknowledging Nicole's story as truth, however unlikely, was a sign of weakness? Yes, she was admittedly a defensive person—overly distrustful and exceptionally vigilant, but for good reason. She had learned, through personal experience, that trust led to heartbreak, and that it was safer to simply go it alone. Even the people who were supposed to care didn't. Case in point: look at her own mother, and even her father, who had left her not once, but twice. They had both had their own interests in mind, so why shouldn't she? Being selfish was necessary, a prerequisite for survival in this cold and lonely world. This hard-won philosophy had served her well so far—why change now?

When she heard Henri's footsteps on the stairway in back, Susanne breathed a sigh of relief. His timing was perfect, saving Susanne from the need for further commentary. He was carrying a box, which he set on the table with a soft grunt. "It's heavy," he muttered.

Nicole walked around the table to stand next to Henri. "Have you seen pictures of me in there?" she asked.

"I do believe I have," he replied, acting very pleased with himself indeed. He started emptying the box of its photographs by the handful.

"They're all loose?" Susanne commented. "Ton-ton, you really should have organized them into photo albums or something, don't you think?"

"Since when do you care about the family?" he chided.

His comment was innocent, but still it stung. Susanne acknowledged the reprimand with a grimace. "Touché," she responded grudgingly, knowing deep down that Henri was right. It wasn't entirely true, though. She cared for Henri; and Henri, the last time she checked, was a relative. He was different, though. He had no agenda, unlike everyone else she had ever known, who did.

It took a good half-hour for Henri to sort through the photographs. Nicole helped; after a while, Susanne did too, although reluctantly. Finally, when they had picked out the relevant ones, Henri lifted the box containing the others out of the way and set it on the floor, arranging his samples in three neat rows in front of him on the table, with Nicole standing to his right and Susanne on his left.

The ancient photographs were no longer black and white, but aged by time to washed-out grays and faded browns. “It’s a shame these were never preserved,” Susanne said. “The images have faded in some of them, to the point that it’s difficult to make out any of the details.”

Henri nodded. “Your grandmother stored them in her attic. When she died, they were passed on to me. I think it’s too late to undo the damage. Photographs are not like paintings, you know. They can’t be restored.” He flipped over one of the photos. “Most of them aren’t even marked. My sister didn’t show much interest in our family’s history.” He gave Susanne a sidelong glance and winked. “You and Joelle had a lot in common!”

“Enough, *Ton-ton*,” she snapped, the sharpness in her tone a knee-jerk reaction to Henri’s good-natured ribbing. He gave her a pained look that said he was only joking. “I’ll help you put them in albums someday, all right?” she added hastily, the conciliatory offer her way of apologizing for her overreaction. Where had her sense of humor gone? The stress of the past few days must really be getting to her. When this was all over, she would definitely have to book herself a vacation—to someplace far, far away.

“All right.” He nodded, her apology accepted.

Nicole pointed at a little boy in one of the photos, picking it up and speaking in a tone laced with sadness and conviction. “This is Edmond,” she said. “He is my son.”

Susanne and Henri looked at each other. “Is she right?” Susanne asked. “Is that a picture of Edmond Bruante?”

Henri nodded. “Yes.” He selected another photograph that pictured the same little boy sitting on a woman’s lap, and flipped it over to display the back. “Edmund Maurice Bruante,” he read, “sitting with his *grandmère*.” He pointed to the second name, running his finger across the words and the numbers as he read. “‘Brigitte Solange DuPres

Bruante, 1876.' Someone in the family wrote the information down on this one, but it's one of the very few with this type of annotation."

"That is my mother," Nicole chimed in, without hesitating. "It was Edmond's third birthday when that photograph was taken."

"Who's this?" Henri asked, pointing to a photograph depicting a man with a closely trimmed salt-and-pepper beard and a full head of unkempt grey hair.

"My father," she replied. She gave Henri a keen look. "Does he look familiar to you?"

"Handsome, wasn't he?" He chuckled softly. "They always said I looked like him."

"Yes, very handsome," Nicole answered with a serious face, "and kind as well. He was always there to help me, especially when times got hard. He paid for my little apartment after Edmond's father left four years ago—I mean, in 1873."

Henri indicated another photograph, on the far right side. "And this beautiful woman?"

"Me, of course," Nicole laughed, her face brightening.

Susanne picked up the photograph and studied it with a critical eye. It showed "Nicole" standing in front of a studio landscape with an opened parasol balanced on one shoulder. She wore a below-the-knee dress, a ruffled shirt with a high collar buttoned in front, and lace-up boots, undoubtedly the height of fashion for the time. Of all the photos, this one seemed the clearest so far. Susanne looked back and forth, from the photograph to Nicole and back to the photograph again, making a careful comparison. Angled jaw—the same; mouth, lips, and smile—the same; auburn hair, shoulder length, even down to the cut and style—the same; body type—identical; and the birthmark on her left cheekbone—the very same.

"We look alike, do we not?" Nicole commented, in her formal way of speaking that was actually starting to sound natural to Susanne, because she was getting so accustomed to hearing it. Nicole passed behind Henri and stood next to Susanne, giving Henri the opportunity to view them side-by-side and make a comparison. "It is interesting how appearances can be passed down through the generations, do you not agree? Henri looks just like my father; and you, Susanne…"

There was no denying the similarity. Susanne tried her best to make some sense of the utterly fantastic coincidence. "I have to say, the resemblance is truly remarkable," she finally said in the most objective voice she could muster. Except for the birthmark, Susanne and Nicole could easily pass for twin sisters. Could she really be Nicole's—*what*, exactly? Great-great-great granddaughter? All of the evidence so far, unbelievable as it seemed, pointed to this bizarre conclusion; yet, Susanne would need something more than just photographs to accept the impossible.

Henri picked out three additional photographs and lined them up in front of Nicole, near the edge of the table. "Do you remember when these were taken?"

Susanne listened, her skepticism lessened but by no means dispelled, as Nicole spoke. "I was about ten years old when this photograph was taken," she said, pointing to the first one on the left. It pictured her standing next to an old-fashioned bicycle, wearing a frilly dress and with her hair tied back in a ribbon. "My mother brought me to a photographic studio to have it taken, and I remember being so very disappointed when I saw the image. I expected colors…" She motioned with her hand at the picture. "But, as you can see, everything came out in greys and blacks. I was wearing a lilac dress, and the bicycle was a bright red."

Next, Nicole pointed to the second photograph, the one in the middle. "I was fourteen or so in this one." Susanne peered over Nicole's arm at the fading image, noticing a teenager who looked a lot like herself at the same age, sitting on the edge of a large stuffed chair and posed with her legs crossed and her hands folded over one exposed knee.

Henri picked up the third one, on the right side. "How about this one?" he asked.

"It was taken when I was pregnant with Edmond," she explained. Nicole was seated on a park bench this time, another prop in some photographer's studio. Her radiant face had filled in with the extra weight of a woman eating for two, her breasts large and full, and her belly protruding and round, almost but not quite as large around as the hoop supporting the creased fabric skirt she was wearing. Susanne didn't recognize herself at all in this last one, most likely because she had never been pregnant. She would *never* look like that, she suddenly realized. Did this trouble her? Yes it did, more than just a little bit; but no matter. There were more important things to accomplish in life, after all. She was much better off without children.

"Well, Susanne?" Henri asked. "What do you think?"

What did she think? Nicole actually seemed to know the people in these photographs and could even explain when and where they were all taken. Was there some way she could have seen them before, maybe with Grand-maman in secret, a few years ago before she died? Somewhat unlikely; then again, this theory was hardly as preposterous as the alternative. "Maybe she's seen these photos somewhere before," Susanne offered.

"I have," Nicole countered, clearly indignant. She obviously knew where Susanne was going with this. "I saw them when they were taken."

Susanne ignored Nicole and addressed Henri. "Do you think Grand-maman could have been in contact with, let's say, a distant cousin or a niece—one neither of us had known about, who just happened to be named Nicole, perhaps?" Now this was a hypothesis that deserved further consideration.

"Wait!" Nicole said, her face turning red. "I am the person in all of these photos; I posed for them. I told you already how I got here!"

"I know, I know." Even with all of this evidence, the cynical side of Susanne still remained stubbornly unconvinced. "You told me already. You were pulled into some kind of 'time-tunnel' when you were drunk." She rolled her eyes. "That was how you said you got here, wasn't it?"

Nicole took a step toward Susanne, incited by her comment, but Henri stepped between them before the argument could escalate any further. "Stop," he ordered. "Calm down, both of you. I have something else to show you, Susanne. Sit down."

"But…"

"Sit, *now*!" he repeated. His face tensed. It looked like he meant business. "Please," he added, the polite entreaty, an afterthought, doing very little to take the bite out of his command.

Susanne reluctantly took a seat in the chair that Henri had pulled out for her. "You too, Nicole—but over there." Nicole walked around to the opposite side of the table and sat down. Her face was still flushed, but pink not red.

Henri went to an easel and pulled off the sheet that he had used to cover a painting. "I've nicknamed it *Nude Reclining*," he explained to Nicole. "Susanne pulled some strings, and now I'm busy restoring it."

"It is me!" Nicole exclaimed, without even a second's hesitation.

"This woman in the painting, Henri—it is me!" she repeated excitedly.

"Correction," Susanne stated. "The model looks like you. She looks like me, too, but you don't hear me claiming that I actually posed for it." Although Susanne protested, she had growing cause to wonder, and she felt herself losing ground in the two-against-one debate. *Nude Reclining* was painted in the mid to late 1870s, according to the results of Henri's materials analysis; handwriting experts at the *Archives Nationales* had confirmed, without question, that the letter Henri had uncovered, papered onto the back of the canvas, was authentic. Degas, the recipient of the written request, had undoubtedly hidden it there, behind the painting, and that meant that he, or the author of the letter, famous himself, had probably painted the unfinished masterpiece sitting on the easel in front of them.

"But look here," Henri said, pointing to the model's left cheek. "It's the same birthmark. But that's not all." He walked over to a drawer in one of his workbenches against the wall, opened it, and pulled out a small sample bottle. "I found this strange material embedded in the paint, but only in certain locations. I think I've finally figured out what it is."

"Hair," Nicole contended with certainty. "It is hair; my hair, to be exact."

"Henri?" Susanne queried.

"That's right," Henri confirmed. "I had it analyzed. It's human hair."

"And you found it painted into the picture only in places depicting hair—is that not correct, Henri?" Nicole crossed her arms and gazed across the table at Susanne with an expression that seemed to say, "I told you so."

"Yes, Nicole, that's precisely correct."

"That was his…ritual. In every one of his nude paintings of me—or any other model—my Edmond's father took some strands of hair and mixed them into the paint. He thought that if he put a real part of his subject into the picture, in just the right place, it would breathe some life into his painting."

This was incredible. Susanne's wheels began to turn at a hundred kilometers per hour. "Who was the artist?" she stammered.

"Why, Jean, of course."

"Does Jean have a last name?" Susanne threw her hands in the air.

"*Mais oui,*" Nicole replied. "Courbet. Jean Désiré Gustave Courbet."

~

It was already half past ten on the day following her strange arrival in this strange place. Nicole rode in the passenger seat, while Susanne drove. This was her second experience traveling in what Susanne and Henri had called a "car," so this time around, it seemed almost natural. On the drive to Henri's, though, Nicole had been seated in the back. In the front now, she had a better view of all the dials, buttons, and flashing lights, a truly amazing sight. She had found out that she had a knack for assimilating new information quickly, a talent that she hadn't been aware of until now. Who knows, she might even try her hand someday behind the so-called "wheel," as Susanne called it—maybe for their third trip, whenever that might be. It did not look so difficult.

Susanne had changed her tune—mostly, it seems, because of the hair that Henri had found in the painting of her, as well as Nicole's innocent reference to the artist, her lover Jean Gustave Courbet. Susanne and Henri had exchanged some words in low tones, trying to digest this newest revelation. Nicole decided to give them a few minutes. It wasn't every day that you found yourself face-to-face with a time traveler, and although this whole thing wasn't as stressful for them as it was for her, she understood that her presence here, one hundred and thirty-four years out of place, would take some getting used to.

Then there was the Courbet connection. From the back-and-forth exchange between uncle and niece, Nicole surmised that her Jean was apparently famous here—known by his middle name, Gustave, rather than his first; respected, it turns out, rather than reviled! If this fact was a surprise to Nicole, both Henri and Susanne seemed to be doubly stunned—stupefied, was more like it—to discover the identity of Nicole's unknown partner, on Henri's family tree. Now a name could actually be scribbled in that empty box on the Bruante pedigree—but not just any name. Gustave Courbet, her Jean, was the father of a group of painters in France known as the Realists, Henri had told her. Nicole had been unaware that Jean was the father of anything, except for her darling Edmond. Back there, he had been scorned by other artists; but here, he was loved and admired. What a shame he would never know about this. He would be so proud.

"I was his mistress," Nicole had explained to them after the dust had started to settle. "I was the closest thing to a wife that he ever had. I even lived with him, but he would go no further."

"That sounds familiar," Susanne quipped.

"So, you have had men like that?" Nicole asked.

"That's not what she means," Henri said quickly. "You were on the receiving end, Nicole. Susanne has always been on the delivery end. She's had some very nice boyfriends, too. What a shame they never seem to last."

"Men never do," Susanne responded elusively, after shooting Henri a look that seemed to say, "Stay out of my business; and while you're at it, keep her out of it, too."

"Oh, I see," Nicole said, taking the cue and backing out of Susanne's personal space with a quiet nod. She did see, though. Susanne was independent, stubborn, and driven. Also, she did not seem like the trusting sort. These character traits, in combination with a self-centered outlook on life, did not constitute a winning recipe for long-lasting relationships. No wonder Susanne had never settled down with anyone.

"If Nicole is really who we think she is," Susanne continued, steering the conversation back on track, "there might be a way to prove my theory. I already have the letter, but it's vague. With the hair—"

"First things first." Henri held up the bottle. "Your theory can wait. I want to have Nicole's hair analyzed and compared to these samples."

"Of course, of course." Susanne was excited now, and talking a mile a minute—mostly to herself, partly to Henri, and most definitely not to Nicole. "If Nicole's hair, and the hair from *Nude Reclining*, match, I'll concede that she came from the past. How else could her hair end up in a painting from the 1870s, unless she was actually the model? With that kind of objective evidence, how could I possibly continue to argue?"

Now it seemed that Susanne was more than eager to believe Nicole's story. What had changed, all of a sudden? Before, she would have argued black in the face of white; but now, she would have taken it at face value if Nicole had claimed she was from the moon. It had something to do with this theory of hers. Susanne was out for Susanne; suddenly, now that she had something to gain, she had turned her colors as if she were a chameleon.

"We'll have to find a way to collect some samples from the paintings in the museum," Susanne was saying. "I'll think of some excuse to get us in there, at night." She turned to Nicole. "If I showed you some paintings, do you think you'd remember where Courbet painted in your hair?"

"*Mais oui*. I remember all of Jean's paintings of me. I can show you where to look, but more often than not, his choice was obvious."

She thought back to the time she had posed, barely eighteen, for the explicit one, the painting that he called *The Origin of the World*. Jean had teased her, asking where he should place the strands of her hair. She had lifted her head, looking through her open legs to smile at him, his focus elsewhere, down there, as he painted in the dark and curly details of his banned masterpiece. She had teased him back, then rested her head again and closed her eyes. He had finished it that day and framed it the next week. Rejected, of course, by the Salon, the sensational painting never did get a proper showing. Nicole had hung it over her bed after he left, in her rooftop apartment, just to keep it close. It was always her favorite—and Jean's too, he had always claimed.

"Obvious? That's good," Susanne said, nearly salivating with eagerness. "If we get some samples from two of Courbet's paintings, and two of Degas', that should clinch it."

"You can't use evidence that you allege was obtained from a time traveler, Susanne," Henri pointed out patiently. "Everyone will think you're *folle*."

"I won't have to. We won't have to share the results of the hair analysis from Nicole and *Nude Reclining* with anyone. If the DNA report confirms that Nicole came from the past, we'll have to figure out, in private, what we should do with her, of course; but that's a problem for later, and not something that we'll need to publicize."

Nicole didn't like the sound of that—not one bit. Her guess was that Henri hadn't either, judging from the scowl on his face. Nicole was obviously a secondary concern, now that Susanne's precious theory, whatever that was, had come to the forefront. Henri sat down next to Nicole at the table—a defensive maneuver?

In the meantime, Susanne was moving ahead with her manic-sounding diatribe, seemingly oblivious to her listeners. "The important evidence will be provided by comparing the hair extracted from both the Degas and Courbet paintings, with or without the hair obtained from *Nude Reclining*. It's beautiful—I won't have to identify Nicole as the model at all! If the DNA results show that the same anonymous model posed for all of these nudes, then my theory is validated."

"But what if Courbet and Degas simply used the same model?" Henri countered, playing devil's advocate.

"Impossible" Susanne declared with a smile.

"Why?"

"Because," Susanne declared triumphantly, "Courbet's nudes, and Degas' *After the Bath* pieces, were allegedly painted in disparate centuries—thirty or even forty years apart. Proving that the same youthful model appeared in all of the paintings supports my contention that Degas couldn't have been the artist who painted those nudes. Courbet, not Degas, created them—and she was the model!" Susanne acknowledged Nicole with a nonchalant wave of her hand, as if Nicole was simply a painting herself and not a living and breathing person. "It couldn't be more perfect. I'm going to be famous."

Henri rolled his eyes. "Let's take this one step at a time," he suggested. "First things first." Henri retrieved some scissors from a kitchen drawer and then took a snippet of Nicole's hair. "My contact in the Materials Laboratory can send these off for rapid DNA testing. It shouldn't take very long at all to find out if the hair fragments are identical or different. I expect to have an answer in less than twenty-four hours."

He had kissed Nicole warmly on both cheeks, taking her hands in his. "I never thought I'd meet my great grandmother. You died long before I was born, *chérie*!"

Nicole's heart swelled, looking at this man who so closely resembled her dear Papa. "And who would have thought that my great grandson would look just like my father! I wish I could tell him all about this."

"Well, maybe you'll have that chance. You got here somehow, so maybe we can get you back the same way, *n'est-ce pas*?"

Nicole couldn't imagine how in the world they would ever be able to manage that. Her journey from the past had been triggered by who knows what—an accidental fluke, an unexplainable process that no one could possibly understand or reproduce. Or could they? Susanne apparently knew someone who might.

And that was exactly who Susanne was talking about right now, as they drove together back to the apartment on Avenue Georges V. Nicole was shaken from her reverie by Susanne's laugh. "It's funny, I just saw a clip of a press conference the other day on *France 24*, and there he was, larger than life, Dr. John Noland. We were…involved for a while in college, when I was an exchange student in the United States."

"And you think he can help me?"

"If he can't, then no one can. He's made quite a name for himself in a scientific field they call time-space quantum mechanics. From what I've read in the newspapers, your problem is right up his alley."

"Truly? In what way?"

"In exactly the way we need. In the press conference, he explained that he's actually sent mice backward and forward in time."

They were approaching an intersection just around the corner from Susanne's apartment, where the dangling light up above them had just turned from green to red. Red, Nicole had surmised by now, meant to stop, and Susanne was doing just that. She slowed the car, easing it to a halt well into the white-lined crosswalk. From this position, they could easily see Susanne's apartment, off to the left and across the street; and glancing over, Nicole noticed the same thing that Susanne obviously had.

"Police," Susanne murmured. A white car, marked with an emblem on the door and what appeared to be a colorful lantern on its roof, had pulled alongside an unmarked vehicle that was parked almost directly in front of Susanne's apartment. The drivers were talking with each other through open windows, the friendly interaction leaving no room for doubt. There were uniformed gendarmes in the unmarked vehicle as well. A moment later, the marked car pulled away and drove in the opposite direction down a side street, well before their light turned green.

"What should we do?" Nicole asked.

Susanne didn't answer; but when the light changed, she drove straight ahead rather than turning left, pulling over alongside the curb on the quiet street, three blocks down. She turned the key and shut off the engine.

"I think they've put me under surveillance," she commented. "We can't let them see you."

"So, now what shall we do?"

Susanne rummaged through her purse and pulled out a long iron key. "There's a courtyard behind my building that you can access from a walkway, located two and a half blocks behind us, on this street. You can't miss it. A street sign marks the alley—it's called *La Rue Étriqué."* She handed Nicole the key. "When you get to the end, use this to open the gate. Once you're in, keep out of sight. You should hide behind some bushes, over by the wall toward the back of the garden. I'll come down and get you later, once the police in the car outside think I'm sleeping. There's a back stairway. I'll let you in, maybe in an hour or so."

"Do not forget me, please." Nicole was only half-joking.

"No need to worry about that. After all, we're related."

Yes, that was true; nevertheless Nicole had a feeling that Susanne would turn in her own mother if there were something in it for her. Make no mistake about it, Susanne was keeping Nicole around now because it suited Susanne. Nicole's identity was now a means to an end—one that involved recognition and advancement in her career.

Well, if that prevented her from turning Nicole in, so much the better, and now there might actually be someone out there who could help Nicole return to where she truly belonged. Susanne seemed optimistic that this John Noland would know what to do. Nicole hoped that she was right. She also hoped that the nature of Susanne's past relationship with the man would not dampen his willingness to help. If what Henri had said about Susanne was true, Nicole could well imagine that a jilted ex-lover might not be very eager to drop everything and come to Susanne's aid.

Nicole stepped out of the car, watching as Susanne pulled out and drove back the other way. She waited a few minutes, to give Susanne enough time to distract the watching gendarmes with her arrival. Would they stop her after she had parked, while she was climbing the front stairs to her apartment's entrance, perhaps to ask her some more questions about the incident at the museum? In all likelihood, no, Susanne had said. She felt fairly certain that they had been dispatched to watch her comings and goings, and maybe to follow her when she decided to leave her flat again.

The street was dark and quiet, with no sign of commotion three blocks down, so Nicole clutched the key in her hand and made her own way back, the way they had come. She finally reached the cobblestoned alley—Susanne had been right, it was impossible to miss. At the end of the walkway, she turned the key in the lock and opened the gate as quietly as she could.

The bushes would provide good cover; now it was time to wait. An hour would pass quickly, especially with her eyes closed, she thought; with that, she settled in with her back to the wall, drifting a few moments later into a light sleep.

Chapter Nine

John Noland stepped away from the tour group at the famous Tower of London when his cell phone rang. He didn't want to disrupt the guide, who was gearing up to begin an explanation of the Jewel Room's history. This was John's first trip to London, and the tour of the historic medieval castle had been fascinating so far. He could see from the caller ID that his secretary was calling, so he would probably be able to take the call quickly, without missing too much of the guide's dissertation.

"Hi Janet. What's up?"

"Sorry to interrupt your vacation, but a woman by the name of Susanne Bruante just called, asking for your cell phone number. She sounded French, by the way—she had a lovely accent. Is it okay for me to give it to her?"

He almost dropped the phone. "Did you say Susanne Bruante?"

"Yes. That's the name she gave."

Stunned was the only way to describe his emotions. Susanne? Why in the world would Susanne be calling him after almost twenty years—and why now?

She had completely ignored all of his attempts to contact her by letter or by phone after she left Chicago that spring so long ago, without a single word of explanation. After a year of silence and many unanswered phone calls and letters, John had finally given up. He had eventually come to the realization that he had grossly misinterpreted their college affair as something serious. In retrospect, she had obviously viewed their relationship as a trivial source of entertainment, a fly-by-night affair that served mostly to pass the time, but was never destined, from her perspective, to amount to anything but a fling. It was painful to remember how naïve he had been back then, and how easily he had fallen hopelessly in love with her, from the very first moment he had seen her.

Was she calling to apologize? He tried to tell himself that it hardly mattered anymore; still, a word of explanation would go a long way toward closing the door that she had left wide open when she disappeared. He had long since ceased to care—or so he had thought, until he had heard her name spoken again just a moment ago by Janet on the other end of the phone line.

"Dr. Noland? Are you still there?"

"Uh…yes, I'm here."

"Well?"

"Well, what?" His mind was elsewhere—at Northwestern University in 1993, to be exact, and he had honestly forgotten what Janet had just asked him.

"I asked if it would be okay for me to give her your cell phone number."

Should he? "I'm not sure. Did she say what she wanted?"

"All right, out with it. Who is she?" Janet was a matronly woman in her early sixties who had been John's secretary for ten years now, and more often than not, she functioned more as a mother than as an administrative assistant. "If I had to guess from your reaction, I'd say that she's probably one of your most recent romantic conquests."

He sighed. She was actually just the opposite. "Hardly. She's an old love interest, and one that I haven't heard from in years." She was the one that got away, but he wasn't about to tell Janet that.

"Hm. Is it a good thing or a bad thing that you're hearing from her now?"

"That's hard to say. I guess it depends on why she decided to contact me, after almost two decades."

"Well, there's only one way to find out," Janet said. "You haven't answered me yet. Should I give her your number, or not?"

He sighed again. Now that Susanne had made the first volley, he couldn't very well refuse to return the ball. Her unexpected phone call had definitely piqued his interest. "Okay, Janet, give her my cell phone number, but tell her to wait until tonight to call me, no earlier than eight o'clock London time. I still have some sightseeing to do, and we're just getting to the most interesting part of the tour." He had to admit that it felt good to put her off. Now it was his turn to make her wait, although a measly three or four hours was nothing compared to nearly twenty years.

"I'll tell her. And good luck."

John finished his tour, but while the tour guide spoke of William the Conqueror, Edward the Confessor, Henry VIII, and Anne Boleyn, all John could think about was Susanne.

Susanne Bruante. Just hearing her name for the first time in almost two decades brought back all the memories in a nostalgic flash. He saw himself sitting at a long, oak table cluttered with books, in the hushed silence of the library reading room in late October, so long ago. He had looked up from his quantum mechanics textbook, and that's when he saw her for the first time: the gorgeous epitome of what he felt certain was an unapproachable and impossible fantasy. John Noland, shy and overly studious, had never dreamed that such a beautiful woman would ever have an interest in him, so he had resigned himself to admiring her from a distance, finding himself spending more and more time at the library, sitting in his usual seat and hoping that she would come to the reading room again—which she did, on one or two occasions. Once he thought she might even have looked his way, if only for a fleeting moment.

And so the months had passed. The fall semester ended and the winter term began; and then one day, he found himself sitting behind an easel on a cold, snowy day in early January, while he waited with the rest of his painting class for the model of the day to emerge from the back room and remove her robe. This was an evening elective for the biophysics major, who had inherited a knack for science from his father and a talented artistic eye from his mother. It was 7:00 p.m., and the clear winter sky, already speckled with stars, was visible through the domed skylight of the studio. This sitting would be one of three using the same nude subject—female this time—and he would have three short hours tonight, Wednesday night, and one week from now, on Monday again, to produce a unique interpretation of her posing, using oil on canvas.

The art studio, a vast room occupying the entire second floor of the art building's annex, was a chilly warehouse of creative clutter. One glance at the disorganized collection of metal stools, wooden easels, partly finished projects, and paraphernalia arranged in haphazard displays for various still-life drawing classes drew his attention, tonight as always, to the drastic contrast between the artistic and the scientific. The clean sterility of autoclaved test tubes arranged neatly in dust-free laboratory cabinets appealed to his analytical side, but the limitless reaches of disorder that he always discovered in his imagination whenever he picked up a paintbrush seemed to represent an essential antidote to his all-too predictable mathematical equations.

The instructor set up two portable heaters on either side of the raised platform that he had pushed against the wall in the front of the classroom. Next, he adjusted the lighting by moving a floor lamp closer; then, satisfied, he covered the rough wooden pedestal—an eight-by-four-foot rectangle standing two feet high or so—with a burgundy sheet. He completed his preparations by placing two worn couch pillows against the wall—intended, of course, to make the model more comfortable after the details of her posturing were decided. Accustomed to this routine, John and his classmates had arranged their easels in a semi-circle in front of the set-up so they would all enjoy the same view, more-or-less, of the model's pose.

It felt so primal—it always did. He was surrounded by the organic smells of pine resin distilled into turpentine, musky earth transformed into sculpting clay, flax seed pressed into oil paints, and rock and mineral pulverized into plaster and charcoal. Soon, the aroma of primordial nature would be visually enhanced by a live model, her skin and flesh exposed, her naked body harking back to some ancient sexuality. In a moment, she would be lying there, reclining on a bed of burgundy, the feminine symbol of mankind's creation and the origin, really, of the world's first beginnings, and he, of all people, would have the opportunity to brush her image—and everything it represented—onto his canvas. He looked at his watch. The sitting would begin in two or three minutes, and he was ready.

"Another nude." Paul, the student to his left, gave a short laugh. "I always have a problem with the hands—and the arms, legs, and feet," he joked.

"Your nudes are always perfect, and you know it." John and Paul had been friends since freshman orientation week; during sophomore year they had roomed together in the dorm. They saw each other less frequently now, since their majors, and their circle of friends, were so different. They shared this final art class together, knowing that soon, after graduation, they would be going their separate ways.

"I'm more of a landscape artist," Paul answered. "You're the expert in nudes, my friend—which reminds me, did anything happen between you and that cute freshman at the student center last night? She seemed to like you quite a bit."

"You mean Leslie? I'm her TA in bio, Paul. There's an exam next week, and she had some questions, that's all."

Paul shook his head. “You’re blind, man. She likes you, and she’s a knock-out.”

John waved away the comment. “My interests lie elsewhere.”

“Do you mean the brunette from the library you keep talking about?” He laughed. “I’m skeptical, John. I think you’ve made her up just to get me off your back. I don’t think she exists.”

John shrugged. “Oh, she exists all right. She’s beautiful, and I think I’m in love with her.”

“That’s ridiculous. You won’t even talk to her!”

“I’ll talk to her; it’s just taking me a while to get up the nerve.”

“Three months?”

“I just don’t want to rush in too quickly and ruin everything.” What he didn’t want to ruin, he kept telling himself, was the image of the perfect woman he had constructed of her in his mind, but this was just an excuse. It was better to live miserably with false hope than to live even more miserably with the disappointment of rejection.

Paul was just about to give John another earful of well-intentioned but useless advice when the instructor started talking. “You will have three sittings to complete your painting. Ms. Bruante, we’re ready for you now.”

The model emerged from the side room, and his heart stopped—not because she strode confidently to the front without even bothering to tie her bathrobe, her unabashed exhibition of frontal nudity a heart-pounding paradigm of female perfection; not because her naked body was utterly stunning; and not because she was the most beautiful woman he had ever seen; but because he actually knew her.

When John’s jaw dropped, Paul noticed. “What’s wrong, man?”

“It’s her. I can’t believe this.” John kept his voice low, not wanting Susanne to hear.

“What do you mean, ‘It’s her’?”

“It’s her—the model—she’s the girl from the library!”

Paul laughed.

“What’s so funny?”

“Well, you certainly have good taste. She’s a beauty, all right. If I knew Susanne was your love interest, I would have introduced you months ago."

"What—you mean you actually know her?"

"Sure I do. She's an exchange student in the art department, from Paris. A sophomore, I think."

"You will tell my pose now, me for us, professor?" Susanne asked, her accent exotic and her English endearingly broken.

"I think we'll paint you reclining tonight, Ms. Bruante." The professor offered his outstretched hand to indicate that she should lie on the platform he had so meticulously prepared for her a moment earlier.

With a nod, she let the bathrobe slip to the floor, gracefully stepping, completely and gloriously exposed, onto the slightly raised pallet—the most compelling "nude, reclining" that John could ever imagine; the epitome, he quickly concluded, of artistic and human perfection. How his hand shook when he held the charcoal pencil in his trembling fingers to trace and shadow her oval face, those elegant cheekbones, the rounded fullness of her breasts, and the smooth curve of her waist and hips. The moment was exquisite—she was exquisite, a goddess for his hand to worship as it filled in what his eyes could hardly believe he was seeing. She was his unreachable and unapproachable ideal—yet here she was, not even ten feet away from him. It was nothing less than a miracle. Fate had smiled on him, and now was his opportunity to smile back—but he had only three nights to do it.

He was painting now, and she was his world. He wondered what it would feel like to touch the strands of soft auburn hair that fell on her delicate shoulders or to explore the greens and browns of her warm and complicated eyes, or to kiss her smoldering red lips and feel the universe spin out of control around him. One hour, two hours, then three—their time was up, but she promised to return.

The second night, he worked on her limbs—arms, hands, and fingers positioned just so, thighs and calves smooth and pale, leading to the high arch of two delicate feet and ten perfect toes. How many lovers had those arms and legs embraced with passion and tenderness? How many hearts had been hers, and how many hearts had she broken? Would she, or could she, ever give herself to a man like him? His work completed for the night, he had left the studio with an aching heart. Now he would have to wait until Monday to see her again—five long days and five sleepless nights. How would he survive?

Monday, the night of her final sitting, came at last; with it, he vowed to approach her and make the impossible possible. Some shadowing here, a lighter tone there—a perfect body complete. Now the burgundy, the final touches under and all around. How he wished that he could be that backdrop, touching her, awed and reverent, in those places that heaven had made so perfectly—that only the lucky chosen few had been given the nod from the goddess herself to caress and adore.

Then, suddenly, their eyes locked—her hazel spark connecting, for a moment, with his imploring blue. Her lips parted in what he imagined to be a silent offer, and then she smiled, she actually smiled! His heart stopped. *This can't possibly be true!* It was a dream, but someone else's, not his—it couldn't be his. How had he gotten here, in this place where he definitely didn't belong?

It doesn't matter how you arrived here, her eyes seemed to say; *you're here, and I'm very glad you are.*

"Amazing, Mr. Noland." Yes, she was; but that's not what the instructor, who was standing behind John's left shoulder, was referring to. "Your nudes are amazing, and this one is no exception. She's turned out quite well. You realize, of course, that this hobby of yours could easily become a career." The professor was already on to his next critique, but his interruption broke the spell. John tried to make eye contact again, but Susanne's gaze was occupied elsewhere. Was she flirting with Chad now, who was sitting two chairs over from John? His heart dropped. He should have known—this was Chad's dream, not his. It all made sense, really; this girl was way out of his league—a much better match for Mr. GQ, of course. He should have known…

The clock on the wall said 10:00; their time was up. A moment later Susanne was excused with a grateful "thank you" from the professor. She stood, stretching out the cramps with both arms in the air, intentionally seductive, it seemed, her breasts firm and her nipples hardened from the chill in the air—and something more? She no longer bothered to cover up with the bathrobe, which she had left behind in the dressing room for sitting two and sitting three, so she had nothing to gather. As she had for the past two nights, she took her time getting off of the platform, and John fully expected her to wander, as per her usual nightly routine, between the easels on her way back to her dressing room, over there and to the right, exactly as she had before…but she didn't.

What was she doing? She was actually coming this way—her straight-shot slightly angled that way, toward Chad, maybe? John's muscled classmate with the chiseled jaw was blatantly eyeing her up and down as he gathered his art supplies, just two easels down and to the right. It looked at first as if she would accept the implied invitation of his lurid stare; but no, for some reason she changed her mind and her trajectory. She was walking straight ahead, walking this way—definitely walking this way, there was no doubt about it—directly toward John!

Now, sleek and naked, she veered dangerously closer—so close he could smell her skin, her perfume, and even her sex. She slowed down, stepping around his supplies, but toward him, not away, her body turning to face him as she sidestepped between his paint box and his easel…and him.

She smiled again, right there beside him, seductively close, lingering for just a moment. *"Excusez-moi,"* she whispered, meeting his eye but then looking down again; and then, she was gone.

Had he detected the spark of attraction in that look? Yes, definitely yes; and now, as she disappeared into the changing room, she actually looked back for a moment over her shoulder, at him. Maybe it was his dream, instead of Chad's, after all; and so, in a split second, it was settled. He would try to approach her because fate, after all, demanded it now—but if he didn't hurry, he would miss the opportunity.

He finished gathering his supplies quickly—no, frantically. When she emerged, dressed in jeans and a V-neck sweater, he timed his exit perfectly to ensure that he would be a step or two behind her on the stairway leading down to the lobby. He rushed to catch up with her, and was just about to offer her an awkward compliment when she abruptly stopped and turned. He barely had time to stop, almost losing his balance as he grabbed the stairway railing. Now, he found himself standing only inches away from her, on the same stair no less, face-to-face and eye-to-eye.

Her eyes: what color were her eyes? Hazel, amber, ochre, russet—all of these combined and blended into some kind of magical kaleidoscope of browns. And now, up close, he suddenly noticed the greens, too—delicate slivers of olive, emerald, clover, and teal that shimmered in the flickering fluorescence of the annex stairwell.

"I am beautiful statue with no clothes on, no?" she asked, unashamed—no, proud—of her willingness to expose herself to a roomful of students, most of whom she interacted with on a regular basis and would have to face in class the next day. Actually, she seemed to delight in the shock factor, smiling mischievously as she waited for his response to her self-commentary. He was taken aback that she would draw attention to her nudity with such nonchalance in their first interaction.

Although he wanted to, he wasn't sure if complimenting her stunning body was the most appropriate response, so he decided to choose the middle ground. "Yes, you were a perfect statue. I'm not sure how you can hold a pose for that long without moving. It's very…impressive."

She smiled knowingly and handed him a scrap of paper. *"Telephoné mois, demain; et je poserais pour toi encore, mais en privé, d'accord?"* she said. Then, before he could stop her, she was gone.

Foreign language was another one of his many talents. He spoke French fluently, along with a little German and a spattering of Russian, but he didn't need to use his linguistic skills to translate what she undoubtedly had in mind. "Call me tomorrow, and I will pose again for you, but in private, okay?" she had said; but she intended to give him a hands-on experience with his nude subject this time, he felt certain, judging from the look she had given him, combined with her tone of voice. He couldn't believe it. She was the sexiest woman he had ever seen, and for some unclear reason she had picked him.

Alone then, he had sat on the stair as the last few stragglers from the dismissed art class passed by, unfolding the slip of paper on which she had written her phone number. Now, twenty years later and alone again, he sat in the corner of the Dickens-style English pub, in the heart of London, and ordered a Guinness to accompany his shepherd's pie. He looked at his watch—8:00.

He laid his cell phone on the table, pretending not to care that the screen remained dark and quiet. She might not call until 9:00, or 10:00; she might not call at all. It didn't really matter, he told himself; but deep down, he knew it did. The stout tasted bitter, just like his memories; but he had resolved to do his best and let bygones be bygones. It was healthier that way.

What would she say, and how would he react to hearing her voice? Every scenario made him feel nervous. It made no logical sense. He was over her—wasn't he? Maybe so; but why, then, did the thought of talking to her make him break out in a cold sweat? He made a concerted effort to relax. When, and if, the screen turned bright, he would be ready. After all, he had the upper hand, now, not her.

She was reaching out to him; so if he played it cool, it would all work out. Wouldn't it?

It would. Maybe if he kept repeating it in his mind, it would.

Chapter Ten

It was just past 8:00, almost time to call him. Susanne sat in her office, considering how best to persuade John Noland to drop whatever he was doing in London and come to Paris to help her. She could claim that she had never forgotten him and that she regretted the way she had dropped him years ago, but that would be a lie. The physical aspect of their campus romance had been mutually satisfying, but the emotional investment in the affair had been truly one-sided. She had been perfectly satisfied with the concept of their involvement as being nothing but a superficial fling and had had no desire whatsoever to move their relationship into the realm of serious commitment.

Had she led him on? Not intentionally; but after the fact, she later recognized that her failure to openly define her casual intentions had led him to think otherwise. She wanted sex without the endless discussions of love and obligation, and he was the perfect solution, at least on the surface—attractive, quiet, and reserved, insecure and inexperienced, and so easy to distract with a kiss and a promise that they would talk about it later. How could she have predicted that he would fall so terribly hard for her?

Well, that was his problem in the end, not hers; so she had left without even leaving a note, never feeling a single twinge of guilt as she tossed his unopened letters into the trash and deleted his piteous voicemails without even a second thought for his feelings. He'd get over her; he'd have to.

She couldn't offer him her heart, then or now, but what about her body? He had taken it once—correction, over and over again—for a full semester, but admittedly under false pretenses. The concept of *l'affaire* was foreign to him, and their intimacy was a sacred promise, clear and final. He was so naïve, assuming that physical closeness automatically translated into something more. Admittedly, she had never told him otherwise, and her reticence, unfortunately, he had misinterpreted as some kind of silent affirmation. In the few messages she'd read, he had moved from puzzlement to betrayal, and she wouldn't be at all surprised if now, after almost two decades, he still felt used.

No, she firmly decided; unless he was still the same green and trusting John Noland from 1993, she would never be able to lure him to Paris with the promise of sex or as an old love newly discovered. There was only one way to get him here, and that was by appealing to his mind. Could he resist the opportunity to see the embodiment of his life's work in a real live person instead of a lab rat? Susanne had watched the press conference on YouTube and had Googled his experiments and theories, so she knew he couldn't pass up this once-in-a-lifetime chance to see his sci-fi brand of science at work.

And Nicole was the real thing—Susanne was certain about that now, thanks to the positive match between the hair extracted from *Nude Reclining* and the snippet of Nicole's hair. Henri's contact had been true to his word, turning around the DNA analysis, as promised, in less than a day. It was fascinating, really; but more than just a little bit bizarre. Her great-great-great grandmother was actually her houseguest, hiding like a fugitive at this very moment in Susanne's apartment.

John would come—she felt certain he would—because her strange guest was living proof of his theory. After all, hosting a time traveler was certainly not an everyday occurrence.

Nicole's fortuitous arrival would be a career-maker for Susanne, as well. Once they obtained the samples from the Courbet and Degas nudes, Susanne Bruante's name would be on everyone's lips, her hypothesis the guaranteed talk of the art history world. It would be tricky getting them without obtaining the proper authorization, but there was no other choice. Why? Because she just couldn't risk bringing her executive director into her confidence. René was a man cut from the same cloth as she was, out for himself and likely to take the credit and all the accolades, once he learned that her thesis was in fact true.

They would collect the samples, she had decided, tomorrow night, after her presentation at d'Orsay was over and when all of the attendees had left. Susanne would stay in the museum, pretending to work well into the morning hours, as she often did—perhaps going so far as to actually spend the night on her office couch, her occasional practice anyway, especially when the backlog of paperwork started to pile up. She would let Henri and Nicole in the back way, and then the bizarre vandalism would begin.

The night guards, for the most part, were young and gullible, so chances were good that a particularly suggestible security officer would be on duty tomorrow night. Why would he question an assistant director? She would tell him, "Dr. Leclercq and his associate have just arrived from Belgium. They will be collecting samples from some of our paintings for an international project, so could you please turn off the motion detectors in the special exhibit gallery?"

Yes, it was perfect. The video monitors were on the same circuit, so they would be able to get what they needed without being watched—no muss, no fuss. Henri and Nicole would leave the same way they came in, and that would be that, their caper executed. If the results came back as expected, Susanne's fame and fortune would quickly follow. It was a shame, of course, that she wouldn't have the results in time for the opening of the Courbet and Degas exhibit tomorrow, but it didn't really matter. Her presentation was convincing and eloquent, even without the additional evidence, and Susanne could always announce her findings later, in a well-advertised press conference that would leave them cheering.

Amazingly, Nicole's story matched perfectly with Susanne's hypothesis. Was Susanne shocked? Not at all. She had known, all along, that her theory about Courbet and Degas was true—how could it not be? It's not like she had made it up. And so this coincidental and timely validation hardly came as a surprise.

Nicole had mailed Courbet a letter, the very same morning of her disappearance, pleading with him to help her financially, for the sake of their son Edmond. Courbet himself was destitute, but Nicole had all of his nudes, some of them hanging on the walls of her attic apartment, the rest of them piled up along the wall—unsellable pieces, due to Courbet's overly explicit style, his notoriety in the artistic community, and his banishment, literally and figuratively, from conventional Parisian society. Courbet had then written his own letter, addressed to his friend and former pupil, Edgar Degas—undoubtedly the direct result of Nicole's earlier correspondence, presenting Courbet's proposed solution to his mistress's monetary dilemma.

"Do what you must do," Courbet had written in the letter that Henri had discovered, papered onto the back of *Nude, Reclining*, "and use whatever means you have at your disposal to help my poor young son."

"Whatever means" referred, of course, to the stash of paintings Nicole had taken for safekeeping into her Montmartre apartment. Courbet had named no names, intending to maintain Nicole's anonymity, given the fact that she had been the model for what many considered pornography. Courbet had given Degas an address, however, specified in the letter and matching exactly with the street and number confirmed now, by Nicole, as her mother's residence.

"The paintings must have been moved there," Nicole had commented quietly, realizing, at the same time that Susanne had, that she must have died shortly after mailing her letter, killed in some kind of accident. Degas had retrieved them at her mother's house; the rest was history.

Degas had sold the paintings, one by one over the course of a decade or more, beginning in the late 1880's, passing them off as his own—his impeccable reputation as one of the fathers of Impressionism the catalyst for acceptance rather than rejection of the erotic masterpieces. The sale of the extensive collection would have been lucrative, to say the least; and Degas, of course, would have given all of the proceeds to Edmond, following Courbet's instructions to the letter and honoring his dying teacher's last request.

Nicole had been ecstatic to hear Susanne explain this. "I knew he would help us," she had said quietly, tears starting to pool in the corners of her eyes. "He loved Edmond, he always did. Now I don't have to worry about my little boy."

Edmond had made out just fine, Susanne thought. The money that had come to him directly from the sale of his father's (and Susanne's great-great-great grandfather's) cache of nudes had made a very respectable inheritance indeed.

And what about *Nude Reclining*? This piece, in its unfinished state, was not in saleable condition, and that's probably why Degas chose it as the unlikely hiding place for Courbet's letter. Perhaps he had intended to give both of them to Edmond, two gifts posing as one—the token heirloom, the sole remaining legacy of Edmond's father, an inherited piece of artwork containing a hidden secret that Edmond had obviously never received. Had Degas died before he had had a chance to give his surreptitious ward the gift? That explanation seemed most likely, since the painting was purchased by d'Orsay in a bulk estate sale acquisition, one of the many assorted possessions of a distant Degas relation.

How serendipitous that the painting had caught Henri's eye, due to the uncanny resemblance of the model to Susanne. Life, as it turned out, was full of unlikely happenstances. One of them, among others, come to think of it, was having a scientist as an ex-boyfriend—and one who, by pure coincidence, happened to have a special interest, and a special expertise, in time travel.

She must, in just a moment or two, call this ex-boyfriend and time travel expert of hers. How would he react to hearing her voice? He had loved her so, and she couldn't help but wonder if he still did. She thought back to that day in early January, when she had posed nude for a figure painting class in college, surrounded by a semi-circle of admirers, including John, who had sat busily recreating her sensuous curves with oil on canvas behind their easels. She had undressed for each of the three sessions in the side room, stripping off her sweater, slipping out of her jeans, and removing her bra and panties, folding them neatly on the metal chair in the changing room. That first night, she had used the bathrobe, kind of—untied, falling open in front, her breasts and the rest of her full-frontal splendor exposed and out there, the enticing appetizer to the whole thing, baring it all just a few minutes later when she acknowledged the professor's signal and let the covering slide off her shoulders, caressing the small of her back and more as it slipped noiselessly to the floor.

After that, she always left the bathrobe behind, hanging untouched on the hook behind the door. Why in the world would she cover up after showing her stuff for a full three hours for the roomful of artsy and (she was more than willing to accept) desire-filled voyeurs? Truth be told, she was proud of her body and actually savored every single second that she could show it off naked. To be honest, though, it wasn't just the liberating exposure that thrilled her so. It was the way they all looked at her, with lust in their eyes and sex on their minds that truly excited her. It was the ultimate tease, really; she alone was in the driver's seat. Who would she pick out of the crowd this time?

It was always someone different, but on that day, after the final sitting for this particular three-night pose, she had narrowed it down to two candidates: John, and another student, a muscular guy with a chiseled jaw who had the look of someone who thought he was God's gift to women. She was intrigued by John, who sat there so quietly handsome, a man who seemed completely oblivious to his own sex appeal. When he had locked eyes with her toward the end of the session, it was decided, then and there: it would be him.

She remembered timing her exit perfectly, allowing him to follow her closely down the stairs. Then, at just the right moment, she had turned to face him, confronting him with her warm smile and a blatant invitation in French, accompanied by her phone number scribbled on a piece of paper. It hadn't taken him long—he had called her the next night on the dormitory pay phone, and they had agreed to meet at 8:00 on Thursday, at the café across from the Fine Arts Center.

She had found him sitting quietly at the table by the fire, sketching, of all things—a way to calm his nerves, perhaps, since she could see from across the room that he was nervous. She shook the cold and a few flakes of snow from her hair, pulling the gloves from her hands and easing herself into the chair to sit across from him at the table. The conversation was stiff, at first, but after a while, he started to relax. As they talked, she took off her sweater, which she didn't need due to the heat from the fire, slipping it over her head, feeling much more comfortable now in a scant turquoise t-shirt that hugged her bra-less chest tightly, with just a few millimeters of fabric covering the growing hardness of her nipples. In her book at least, less was always better than more, when it came to clothing; and that night, she fully expected to undress later with her new conquest, under the sheets.

He had picked up the sketchpad and his charcoal pencil again, looking across the table at her and then down at the paper, back and forth and back and forth, as they continued to talk.

"What are you drawing?" she finally had asked. They could actually speak French, since he was fluent.

"You, of course," he had replied with a smile.

"Can I see it?"

"Not now."

"Later?"

"Maybe someday."

Later, when she had put on her sweater and gloves again, he had politely offered her an escort. She had accepted of course, since it was all in the plan. A few blocks later he had stood with her outside the dormitory doors. He had hesitated, but not her—not even for a second. The air was cold, but her kiss was warm, and as the snowflakes fell urgently down around them, she actually felt him fall, instantly and abruptly, in love with her. She could have stopped it then, knowing full well that she would eventually dump him, but she didn't.

She had asked him up to her room, undressing when they got there with natural ease, just as she had for the art class. She coaxed him out of his jeans and t-shirt, pulling him under the warmth of double blankets, where her body, for that night and many thereafter, was a canvas that he traced with the brush of his fingertips and painted with the touch of his lips. He had wept that night, when their lovemaking was finished, yet another signal that she was playing with fire. How could she have known that she was his first real relationship? Oh well. What was done was done.

She picked up her phone. Her watch read 8:25; she had waited long enough. It was time to call.

It rang once, then twice, and he answered.

“Hello, John,” she said, and she was surprised to hear her voice shaking. “This is Susanne.”

When their conversation came to an end, John put his cell phone back in his jacket pocket. He had already paid the restaurant bill including tip with his credit card during the phone call, but he dug out a few extra pound notes and set them on the table as he got up to go. The pub wasn’t that busy, but he had tied up his table in the corner for an extra thirty minutes while he had talked with Susanne. He nodded to the bartender as he walked out the door.

In the end, he had agreed to go to Paris. Was this a wise decision? Probably not, but the lure of a potential scientific anomaly, materializing for some reason right on Susanne’s doorstep, was too much for him to resist. Did he actually believe Susanne’s wild contention that she was hosting her great-great-great grandmother at this very minute in her apartment in central Paris? Not completely; then again, the evidence that she had just presented to him did sound convincing.

Did he question Susanne’s sincerity when she offered a cursory apology for what had happened between them eighteen years ago in college? Absolutely. Susanne was out for herself and no one else. Their half-hour discussion had focused almost exclusively on her family problem, with hardly a mention of their heated but embarrassingly one-sided affair at Northwestern. If she had felt even a smidgeon of remorse, he would have heard more than one attempt to apologize. Instead, she had sounded more like an attorney trying to convince a jury to give her a favorable ruling. The call was all business, make no mistake, but maybe it was better that way.

Had she even been fleetingly faithful to him, during the three-and-a-half months they had dated? After she disappeared from his life—an unexpected turn of events that had taken him completely off-guard—he had realized, in retrospect that he had merely been a diversion the entire time. He had devoted himself, heart and soul, to her, and she had repaid him by sidestepping the issue of commitment and ignoring his repeated attempts to have her clarify how she really felt about him. Her avoidance of a frank discussion, in his mind, was indirectly deceitful, and there was no question that she had led him on, perhaps even from the very beginning.

How many times had he called her up, wanting to get together on this night or that night, only to have her pretend that she had work to do in the photography studio, or plans with her endless list of female and male friends? She would usually offer him another day as a consolation, and when they finally got together, she was sweeter than ever, and even more passionate in their intimacy than the time before. To him, the sex was more than just entertainment—it really meant something. The problem, he later decided, was that he had assumed that she viewed their periodic overnight encounters in the same way. Would it have been that difficult for her to be honest with him from the beginning? If he had known that a casual relationship was all she cared to pursue from the very start, he might have been able to adjust to a non-exclusive type of arrangement; then again, maybe not. He simply wasn't made that way, and knowing that the sex meant nothing to her would have been difficult for him to come to terms with.

It was just a week before his graduation when he discovered that she had gone. He hadn't seen her for a few days, so he had decided to pay her a visit that night, unannounced, to see if she might be interested in grabbing a bite to eat. To his surprise, he had found the door of her dorm room standing wide open. All of Susanne's personal belongings had been removed.

"Where's Susanne?" he had asked the neighbor from two doors down, an attractive redhead named Claire who was wrapped in a towel, heading back to her room from the bathroom at the end of the hallway.

She had given John a look of pity. "Didn't she tell you?"

"Tell me what?"

"That's so typical of her."

"But where is she?" he had asked, already knowing the answer and feeling as if his world had just collapsed.

"Back in Paris." Claire had touched John lightly on the arm. "You're much too good for her, John. You're better off without her, in my opinion."

Claire was right, of course, but it still hurt—not for just a day, a week, or even a month. He had pined over her for more than a year, finally giving up when all of his letters and phone calls were answered with stony silence from across the Atlantic.

He had been such a different person then, insecure to the point of being self-demeaning, and overly reliant on his impression of what other people thought of him. Her rejection of him had only worsened his low self-esteem, for a time. It had taken years to dig himself out of that hole, and it was only his successful scientific career that managed to rebuild his self-confidence. He could hardly recognize the man he had been in 1993. Today's John Noland could easily handle Susanne Bruante, he told himself, and maybe this trip to Paris was exactly what he needed to finally clear her skeleton out of his closet. Closure was what he needed, and closure was what he would get.

Closure, and the opportunity, perhaps, to study a human time travel subject. Susanne's explanation, at first, had been very hard to follow. It didn't help that her manic accounting of the sequence of events, just a little while ago over the phone, had jumped from one day to another, completely out of chronological order. Finally, after some pointed questioning, he thought he had her story straight.

As he walked back to his hotel from the pub, he thought with analytical excitement about the woman named Nicole, the one Susanne claimed was her great-great-great grandmother. If she had truly been transported through a Virtual Hole from one Time-Shell to another, Nicole would represent living proof that his concepts related to the time-space continuum were not just the wild imaginings of a mad scientist. He suspected the connection between Nicole's time and his own had been flanked on both ends by a Common Object, present in both 2011 and 1877.

When he had asked Susanne about this, she had felt certain that the Common Object in question simply had to be the painting, Courbet's erotic masterpiece titled *The Origin of the World*. The painting had hung on the wall, above Nicole's bed, in the past; and it was hanging right now, in the present, in the exhibit room at Musée d'Orsay, where Nicole had magically appeared, along with a very dead body, just five days ago.

How had the Virtual Hole opened? Why had Nicole survived the trip, whereas her nighttime companion had not? Was there a way to get her back? These were all questions that would need to be answered, but in person, not from far away.

In person. Those words gave him reason to pause, just as Susanne's comment had. They weren't talking about a lab rat here, but a person. "She'll be your crowning achievement," Susanne had said, in her most persuasive tone of voice. "The ultimate human experiment. You'll be famous."

He had felt uncomfortable when she had said that, and now he knew why. It was one thing sending a mouse back and forth through a Virtual Hole, but quite another to contemplate doing the same thing to a person. Ethically speaking, he was treading on shaky ground here, but it went far beyond that. Susanne, with her usual flair and with one offhand remark, had reduced Nicole from someone meaningful to a simple object. He was better than that; or at least he hoped he was. He didn't need fame, he already had it. Whatever happened when he got to Paris, he pledged to himself that he would do the right thing, and do it with kindness and compassion.

He hadn't even met this Nicole, but already he felt a certain protective affinity toward her. One thing was certain: Susanne was anything but an advocate for the poor young woman. Would Nicole be timid, or intrepid; confused, or assured; frightened, or calm? Would she be the vulnerable damsel in distress? If so, would he be her white knight, or her black? If he could somehow return her to the past, would she welcome that return, or oppose it? How did she feel, what would she say, and what would she want?

And how would he feel? Would his compassion rule him, or his science? What would she look like, and would he feel drawn to her? She looked like Susanne, according to Susanne herself, but did the resemblance go beyond simple outward physical appearance? It would be best for everyone involved if emotions didn't muddy the waters; if the objective didn't become confused with the subjective; and if what was meant to be, and should be, didn't evolve into what he, or Susanne, or even Nicole, wanted.

His mind was racing; he had to slow it down. *First things first,* he thought. *You need to get there before you start worrying about the ifs and maybes.*

He turned the corner and walked the final half block to his hotel, pushing through the revolving doors and making his way across the polished floor of the lobby to the reception counter.

"Good evening, Dr. Noland." The attractive hotel clerk's accent was easy enough for him to identify by now, after being in the UK for almost a week, as Northern English—maybe even Welsh. Everyone at the hotel knew him, even if he didn't know them, since he was a celebrity of sorts. "How may I assist you this evening, sir?"

He could think of a few things, but he wasn't the type of man to put himself out there like that. He would spend the rest of the night alone—unless, of course, she made the first move. "I'll be checking out the day after tomorrow," he announced.

She looked up his reservation in the computer. "That's five days early. Hasn't everything here been quite to your liking?" she asked with a pretty pout. "Perhaps we just didn't show you the right kind of hospitality?" There might have been a twinkle in her eye, but he couldn't be quite sure.

"Everything has been just fine, Carys," he replied, reading her nametag. "I need to leave on a business matter. Could someone get me a schedule for the Chunnel train to Paris?"

"I can do that for you, Dr. Noland—straight away." She looked across the counter at him, right into his eyes. "Would you care to have me hand-deliver it personally to your room, in a little while? I'll be off my shift soon, and it would be no bother at all for me to get it to you, on my way out."

"That would be lovely, Carys." He tried to look interested. "How wonderfully accommodating of you, really." It seemed that he would be doing "casual" again tonight, the usual routine. How apropos, he thought, a little sadly. Susanne had taught him well, and tonight's little adventure would serve as a bittersweet reminder that the lessons she had taught him had lasted a lifetime.

"The pleasure, I think, will be all mine." And his as well, she implied, as she flashed him a mischievous smile. "We can't have you leaving London, after all, with anything but the fondest of memories."

John had no trouble whatsoever imagining the fond memories she was referring to. His life was full of this kind of memories. What a shame, really, that thanks to Susanne he could not really think back on any others.

Chapter Eleven

Michèle Crossier stood in back of the gallery, waiting for Susanne's presentation to start. She had gained access with her badge, presenting it in lieu of a ticket and hoping that in plain clothes she would blend in with the crowd, just as if she were another inconspicuous art critic or journalist.

To Michèle's surprise, there was hardly a crowd to blend in with. The turnout was meager at best, and Michèle thought she knew why. Anyone who was anyone in the art world did not take Susanne's thesis seriously, and they were voting with their feet. The paintings themselves would draw the crowds starting tomorrow morning, but not Susanne's attempt to explain her outlandish claim that Courbet painted the Degas *After the Bath* nudes.

Michèle had been in this same room just six nights before, surveying the crime scene and pondering the how, what, and where of a dead body with Bernier, the medical examiner. It seemed strange that they would still hold the program here, where a murder had just been committed not even a week ago; then again life, and business, must go on. The d'Orsay was not about to cancel an exhibit that promised to keep the cash registers ringing.

Deciding that she might as well make herself comfortable, Michèle decided to take a seat in the back row, against the far wall and underneath a painting by Courbet titled *Le Sommeil*. As audiovisual personnel busied themselves with the set-up of a laptop, screen, and projector at the front, Michèle took a moment to study the notorious nude couple hanging behind her. The brunette, peacefully asleep, lay with her right leg draped over her female partner, while her left leg was gently wedged in between the blonde woman's legs. The blonde's left hand rested intimately on the brunette's leg, while her head was pillowed cozily on her lover's near breast. Both of the women's faces drew in the viewer, their peacefully content expressions intimating a physical encounter that, now ended, had resulted in this satisfied post-coital slumber.

But was it really the look of universal contentment that seemed so familiar to Michèle? No, it was something more. The brunette's face itself reminded Michèle of someone; she didn't realize exactly who, until that someone walked in through the main archway, accompanied by a tall man with combed-over hair who just had to be the museum's executive director.

Michèle looked back and forth, from the model in the painting to Susanne Bruante, and back again. Odd that the brunette pictured in the Courbet nude really did seem to resemble Susanne. Was Michèle's mind just playing tricks on her? Susanne and Courbet's model shared the same shoulder-length auburn hair; identical full and perfect lips; indistinguishable twin noses, both of them slightly upturned; and matching cheekbones, high and prominent. The only difference was the well-placed birthmark, on the model's left cheek. Otherwise, the woman who was about to take her place behind the podium could have easily passed for a replica of Courbet's model.

Ridiculous. The case was definitely getting to her. It was Susanne Bruante in the videotape, Susanne Bruante at the podium, and now Susanne Bruante in the painting? Michèle would need a long vacation, after this case was solved, or a good psychiatrist...or both.

Michèle watched as Susanne glanced out into the nearly nonexistent audience, surveying the attendants; after two or three seconds, Susanne's gaze rested on Michèle. The look in her eyes said that she recognized the policewoman immediately, but that it didn't matter to her one way or the other that Michèle was stalking her. The woman was cool, verging on arrogant. Anyone else would have felt intimidated to have the police shadowing her, but not this one. Every morning, she waved flirtatiously to the men on the surveillance detail as she left her apartment, and when she reached her destination—getting out of her car one shapely, bare leg at a time—she would wink and smile at them again as she passed their parking spot two or three cars behind, intentionally teasing them with the sway of her hips on five-inch heels. It was unbelievable, but it didn't really matter; Michèle's professional sights were about to be focused elsewhere. She had just a few more questions for Susanne that she'd cover when she cornered the assistant director after her opening remarks, and then she'd be prepared to bring Henri Bruante in for questioning in the morning.

She saw Susanne whisper something deferentially to her companion, in a manner almost but not quite obsequious. There was no question about it: he was the executive director, René Lauren—Susanne's boss, lover, and alibi all rolled into one, a three-for-one special. He should have been disappointed with the poor attendance, but if he was, he certainly didn't give that impression. He smiled pleasantly in response to whatever Susanne had just told him and then took his seat in the front row.

Now that Michèle thought about it, though, the director's reaction to a close-to-empty room made perfect sense. Susanne's contention that Degas had committed fraud by passing off Courbet's paintings as his own was a viewpoint that brought with it bad rather than good publicity for d'Orsay, and it would be in the museum's best interests to distance itself from its assistant director's crazy beliefs. Having most of the invitees turn out as no-shows was probably a big relief to Lauren, whose museum relied, in part, on public support and benefactor donations for its financial viability. Having only a handful of journalists in the audience tonight was the perfect way to limit the number of scathing reviews in tomorrow morning's newspapers. In fact, Michèle wouldn't be at all surprised if Lauren had actually engineered tonight's poor turnout.

Susanne stepped up to the podium, testing the microphone with a gentle series of taps with her index finger. Michèle found it interesting that Lauren had not even bothered to introduce his assistant director.

"Welcome," she said. "I'm glad those of you who are here tonight were able to make it." She didn't seem to be bothered by the poor turnout either, almost giving the impression that today was just a prelude to something bigger, yet to come. "I'm Susanne Bruante, assistant director in charge of acquisitions and special exhibits and the creative architect of *Degas and Courbet: Nude Pairings*. Our apologies for canceling the original date for this preview, but you're all aware of the unfortunate reason for the last-minute rescheduling. The doors to my fascinating exhibit will open to the public tomorrow morning, but tonight, you'll be able to peruse our seven galleries devoted to the conceptual theme I'll be discussing with you, without having to fight the crowds."

One thing was certain; there were no crowds here tonight to fight. Michèle settled herself in as Susanne continued. "It has taken quite some time and energy to acquire or borrow the paintings that you see hanging on the walls of these rooms tonight. Each pairing display has been designed to illustrate the concept of this exhibit: namely, that Courbet actually painted all of these nudes. After you hear me out, I'm certain that you'll agree."

Michèle looked around, quickly counting the heads and comparing the result to the number of chairs in the room, most of them empty. Fourteen attendees, versus ninety spots, and some of the people there, probably four or five, were almost certainly museum officials. Susanne would not be making much of an impact by convincing this gathering that her theory wasn't rubbish.

"Gustave Courbet is best known as a landscape artist," Susanne said, "but his nudes, rather than his pastoral scenes, arguably represent his most enduring legacy. In accordance with historical precedent, an artist's most controversial paintings usually make the most lasting impression; in Courbet's case, one cannot emphasize enough the accuracy of this observation. A mere handful of his nude paintings—all of them considered scandalous by nineteenth-century standards, and some of them regarded as provocative, still—have become the most memorable works in his vast collection of over five hundred artistic renderings."

She stopped a moment to take a sip of water, and then she gestured to her right, instructing the audience to turn their attention to a solitary painting hanging on the far wall of the gallery. "Consider, as a case in point, *The Origin of the World*—a piece of artwork that is unique in its conception as well as its historical isolation. This painting was banned from exhibition for over fifty years due to its explicit portrayal of a woman's genital area.

"Other examples include *Two Nude Women* and *Le Sommeil*, both exceptionally controversial because they overtly suggested an intimate relationship between the female models; *Woman in White Stockings*, criticized by the moral majority when it was initially shown because of the openly lascivious expression on the model's face, as well as the shocking posturing of her legs; and *Le Bacchante*, shunned by the conservative members of the Parisian Salon because Courbet's depiction of the sleeping woman suggested, to many, the recuperative slumber after a drunken sexual encounter that had taken place outdoors. Even his masterpiece—*The Artist's Studio, a Real Allegory*—was rejected when Courbet submitted it for display at the Exposition Universelle, on the pretext that the canvas was too large. In reality, this piece was rebuffed because of the sexual innuendo inferred from the close proximity of the nude model to the painter in the scene. Courbet was forced to exhibit this piece, along with forty of his other paintings, in his own gallery, since no one else would show them.

"Courbet had an obvious interest in the sensual side of the human form, and he had a true talent for depicting the nude subject. We have managed to gather all of his nude paintings in these rooms, and what strikes me is that there are only seventeen of them. How odd that only seventeen paintings out of his immense assortment of conceived images are nudes. Why would he stop at seventeen, when he had already defied the accepted conventions of his time by pushing the barriers of the nude premise? Well, he didn't. My contention is that he painted many more, as I'll show you."

She turned on the projector, synced to a small laptop that was opened on the podium in front of her, and the light flashed on to display a pairing: a Courbet nude on the left, and a Degas on the right. "Compare, if you will, Courbet's *La Bacchante* to Degas' *After the Bath, Reclining Nude*—identical poses, identical bodies, identical faces…identical models. How could this be, when a time span of more than thirty years separates one painting from the other? Because Degas didn't paint any of these nudes; Courbet did."

Susanne advanced the slideshow to show pairing after pairing, slowly so that the audience could study the striking physical similarity between the dark-haired models depicted in each. Occasionally, Susanne would stop and read the names of the paintings and offer some brief commentary. "Courbet: *Woman with White Stockings*, and Degas: *After the Bath, Woman With a Towel*—please note, if you will, the identical posturing of the legs, the matching props, and the irrefutable duplication of body and face in the one compared to the other." Then, five slides later, "Courbet: *Le Sommeil*, focus please on the brunette; and Degas: *After the Bath, Woman Lying Supine*. How could these not be the same models?"

Finally, the pairings had all been shown—a projected summary of the entire exhibit, Susanne said. "Convincing, isn't it?" she remarked, more to herself than to the handful of listeners in her audience. "It certainly is," she replied, responding to her own question, "but pure conjecture, I admit. Without evidence to support it, my theory is simply…a theory. You ask for proof? Well, here it is."

Michèle sat up a little bit in her seat. *Now this might be interesting*. Susanne had projected a letter, larger than life, on the screen to her right.

"This letter was discovered accidentally by a d'Orsay art restorer, papered into the back of an unsigned and unfinished nineteenth-century painting that he has nicknamed *Nude Reclining*." Susanne glanced over at the executive director, sitting directly in front of her in the first row of the audience, with a look that seemed both apologetic and triumphant. "I had this letter analyzed by materials and handwriting experts at the National Archives. They have confirmed, beyond a doubt, that this letter, written by Gustave Courbet on 16 July 1877 and sent to his friend and former student Edgar Degas, is authentic."

Had Susanne hidden the existence of the letter from Lauren, even going so far as to have it analyzed and authenticated without his approval? The smug look on her face suggested that this was in fact what she had done. Michèle was not at all surprised. This woman had nerve.

"Now, for a brief history lesson. Courbet fled Paris in 1873 to La Tour-de-Pielz, Switzerland, in order to avoid paying the staggering monetary penalty—323,091 francs and 68 centimes—imposed on him for taking down and destroying the Vendôme Column in 1871. Previously, he had been sentenced to serve six months in prison for the leadership role he had played in organizing this political vandalism; and after his release, he found himself destitute and unable to pay the fine. By the time he wrote this letter in 1877, his health was failing due to liver cirrhosis, caused, no doubt, by his excessive drinking."

Susanne advanced to the next frame by tapping a key on her laptop screen. She had prepared a slide-set, carefully reproducing the Courbet letter piecemeal. She began to read it for the audience.

> *My dear Edgar, I am exiled and destitute, but God has decided that these punishments are not enough. My skin has turned a sickening shade of yellow, and I spend hours upon hours sleeping due to the fatigue. I have started to have stomach pains, and I fear the end may be drawing near.*
>
> *I lie awake at night with worry for my son, born four years ago as the result of a long-term love affair with my favorite model, the one I used for nearly all of my sensational nudes. She has died, unexpectedly; and I am likely to join her soon. I implore you to help her boy...my son; and to use whatever means you may have at your disposal to raise him up above the financial troubles that now surround him.*

She paused for a moment to address the audience. "You may be surprised to hear that Courbet had a son. True, he never married, and historical records have never indicated that he fathered any children, but this wouldn't be the first time a man sired a child in secret." She advanced to the next slide. "This is the last one, and it gives us the biggest hint yet.

I have no money, and my only earthly possessions have been taken for safekeeping by my son's grandmother, stored at this very moment at her home at 45 Rue Saint-Vincent, Montmartre. They are valueless in their present state, but perhaps in your hands, they will serve the intended purpose. You have my unrestricted blessing to do what you must with my legacy, in order to keep my son in comfort.

Susanne's complacent smile said that she was very pleased with herself, indeed. "So, there you have it," she said, beaming. "By the time Courbet was exiled, Degas was a well-known and successful artist, so it seems logical that Courbet would call on his old friend for financial help.

"But his pride prevented him from asking for money outright. Instead, Courbet gave Degas permission to sell his nudes, passing them off as Degas' own. The proceeds from this good-intentioned fraud would be used as a kind of trust fund for Courbet's son, his inheritance paid out slowly over the years. Degas, of course, would have had to encourage the impression that he was actually painting the nudes, rather than just picking them out of storage in his own basement or attic, one after the other after the other. So, he might exhibit two or three a year, selling them afterward—but slowly, not quickly. This may have gone on for twenty years or more, which corresponds exactly with the flurry of *After the Bath* exhibitions in the 1890s."

At this point, Lauren leaned forward, motioning to her with his hand to finish things up, and quickly. If Michèle had to wager a guess, she'd bet the house that Susanne's executive director still viewed his girlfriend's theory as pure conjecture, despite the so-called evidence that Susanne had just presented from the letter.

Michèle would have to agree with Susanne's boss. From Michèle's own trained investigator's perspective, Susanne simply didn't have what was truly necessary for an open and shut case. Courbet's letter didn't specify the paintings as the personal property in question, and he only implied that Degas could sell whatever it was that his son's grandmother had been holding in her house, for safekeeping. Yes, he had used the word *legacy*, but that could mean anything. Susanne was taking a giant leap, and Michèle would be surprised if many people, in this room or elsewhere, would be willing to risk it and jump along with her.

Susanne nodded, surprisingly agreeable to Lauren's hook-and-pull attempt to remove her from the stage. She had probably presented everything she had planned to; eliminating the opportunity for questions and answers did, after all, work to Susanne's advantage. If anyone listening tonight had an objection or a complaint, indirectly suppressing open criticism by preventing the opportunity for an open discussion was actually an ingenious plan.

"I guess we're out of time," Susanne announced, "so I won't be able to take any questions. Please enjoy some light hors d'oeuvres in the lobby, after you've taken a few minutes to view the exhibit."

And that was that. Susanne quickly packed up her laptop and started toward the doorway that led out onto the marble catwalk overlooking the sunken ground level of d'Orsay. Michèle was on her, though. The slippery assistant director wouldn't be able to escape that easily.

"Mademoiselle Bruante," Michèle called after her. "Could I have just a few moments of your time?"

Susanne pivoted on her heel. "Why certainly, inspector. Walk with me?" she suggested, her tone actually amiable.

Of course Michèle would walk with her. She could be as pleasant as the next person and would even match Susanne's fabricated sweetness. Walking, running, or sitting, Michèle was determined to get her woman.

Or man, as the case may be. Michèle had a theory of her own; if her evolving hypothesis panned out, the man in question went by the name of Henri Bruante.

Chapter Twelve

Crossier walked with Susanne—down the catwalk, around the corner, and through the set of double doors off to the right side of the lobby that led to the back hallway of administrative offices. "What can I help you with?" Susanne asked the detective, as they stopped outside her office door.

"I need some information about your uncle, Henri Bruante. Before that, though, I wanted to tell you that the DNA evidence has essentially eliminated you as a suspect."

"Of course it has," Susanne replied, with just a hint of condescension. "I wasn't there, remember?"

"Yes, I remember," Crossier said. "I just thought you'd be curious about the results."

"As long as they exonerate me, that's all I really need to know."

"I suppose; then again, the DNA analysis uncovered something very interesting that involves you, indirectly."

Curiosity killed the cat, but this feline had eight lives left to go. "You've got me wondering now, inspector. Do you want me to guess, or are you going to tell me?"

"I'll tell you. The DNA results absolve you, but they implicate another Bruante."

Another Bruante? Crossier had just mentioned Henri a moment ago, but he hadn't been at the crime scene either. Nicole had, though; in all likelihood, then, this other Bruante to whom Crossier was alluding would be Nicole. "Who, exactly?" Susanne asked, feigning ignorance as she opened her office door part way, turning around and blocking the detective's entrance with her body.

"Why don't you let me into your office? We can talk about it inside."

Should she let her in? There was really no reason to be obstinate, except for the pure thrill of it, so with a shrug she stepped aside. "I'll give you five minutes," she answered, pleasant as could be. "Fair?"

"Fair." Crossier nodded and stepped past Susanne. "May I sit?"

"Don't make yourself too comfortable. I have quite a bit of work to do, on our next special exhibit." Susanne might as well feed the queen bee, and the information would trickle down to the workers. "The papers have been piling up, literally." She pointed to her desk, in order to prove it. "You should tell the guys parked outside that they might as well settle in. I'll be sleeping here tonight."

Crossier didn't react—not even a hint of surprise. Perfect. Once the surveillance detail got the word, they would let their guard down, maybe even catch a few winks out there themselves. With the diversion of Susanne's flawlessly placed misinformation, the last thing they would be focused on would be her activities inside the museum.

Inspector Crossier sat on the couch, crossing one bare leg over the other. She was dressed in a knee-length skirt that actually showed some skin—right up Susanne's alley. This policewoman was certainly attractive, with shoulder-length hair, unbleached and naturally blonde, startling green eyes, and measurements that even Susanne might envy. Well, almost. Susanne definitely had her beat in the chest department.

She and Michèle Crossier probably had a lot more than good looks in common. Susanne didn't need to be a psychic to know that Michèle was career driven, just as she was; and, given the ring-less finger, she had probably sacrificed her personal life, just as Susanne had, in order to succeed at her job. Had Michèle ever been married? Unlikely, was Susanne's guess. A husband would just get in the way, and so would children, for that matter. This had always been Susanne's viewpoint, and Michèle seemed the type of person who would share in that philosophy, one hundred percent.

"You were about to fill me in on family matters, weren't you?" Susanne reminded her.

"Yes, I was. We found a pubic hair on our victim's genitals, and it doesn't belong to the dead man. Our theory is that he had sexual relations with someone right before he died, and that person left something behind."

A hair, again? It seemed that the best theories these days involved hair, in one form or another. "It wasn't mine, we both know that. So, whose hair was it?" Susanne knew exactly whose hair it was, of course. The time tunnel had pulled Nicole and her bedmate in, killing the man and sparing Nicole, for some reason. The hair was Nicole's, because she was the person who had had sex with the victim right before he died.

"Luckily, the hair had been pulled out by its roots," Crossier explained, "consistent with the type of mechanical influence one would expect during intercourse. This means that we had the follicle with attached skin, freshly torn from our victim's partner from the friction of their lovemaking, to work with. A hair fiber alone can only provide mitochondrial DNA for testing; but a hair follicle is quite a different story. Our CSI lab ran a complete chromosome analysis on the hair follicle, and on your DNA. Guess what we found."

"I'm not in the mood for guessing games, inspector. I give up. What did you find?"

Crossier ignored the edgy comment. "We found high DNA concordance between your sample and the hair sample, but not a complete match. Someone related to you slept with the victim right before he died. Do you have any idea who that might be?"

Susanne would continue to play dumb. "You mentioned my Uncle Henri a few minutes ago. I honestly didn't think he was gay, but these days you never can tell." She tried to put on her best contemplative face. "It's true he never married…"

"We'll get to Henri in a moment," Crossier stated. "Our victim's lover was a woman, not a man. Chromosomes don't lie."

Susanne shrugged. "I'm afraid I can't help you. I don't know the victim, and I have no idea who might have slept with him before he had his unfortunate accident."

"I realize we're talking about your family, Mademoiselle Bruante, and blood is thicker than water. I also know that your instinct is to protect your own; but your relative, whoever she is, might be in danger. If you want to protect her, then give me her name. I don't think she's the perpetrator, but another victim. All I want to do is try to help her."

Maybe so, but the chances were slim that a twenty-first-century homicide detective would be able to help a nineteenth-century time traveler. That's what ex-boyfriend scientists were for, and that's exactly who would be arriving tomorrow morning on the Chunnel train from London. The only way Michèle Crossier could possibly help would be to get her nose out of Susanne's business, but Susanne couldn't see that happening anytime soon.

Or could she? It dawned on her that there just might be a way to put Crossier's nose onto a completely different scent. Susanne couldn't give up Nicole, but she could suggest some alternatives that would steer the inspector out of Susanne and Nicole Bruante territory and right down a blind alley.

Susanne sat next to Michèle on the couch, playing the unwilling conspirator. "Look, I honestly don't know anything about this horrible business, but I have some ideas. My father's half-brother, Uncle Jacques, had a drug and alcohol problem. He got into some trouble with the law, and my grandmother disinherited him. I'm not in contact with my cousins, but none of them ever amounted to much. You could start there, perhaps."

Michèle had her cell phone in her hand and touched the Notes icon. "Can you give me some names and addresses?"

"Names, yes; addresses, no. My grandmother, the family matriarch, was hard and unyielding; when she was done with someone, she was done. When she disinherited my uncle, my cousins—three boys and a girl—were black listed too."

"I'd like to speak to the girl."

Susanne nodded knowingly. "I think that's a very good place to start. Her name is Claudine Bignon." She spelled it. "The last I heard, she was working in Pigalle, I think as a dancer." She shook her head. "It's a shame, really. My Uncle Henri is in touch with her every so often, now that my grandmother has passed away. He says she's very pretty. She could probably do much more with her good looks than what she's doing now."

Crossier typed the name in her phone, the look on her face unmistakably satisfied. Susanne felt satisfied too. What a stroke of genius, planting the Claudine Bignon lead! This was Susanne's best idea yet, and it would result in a protracted wild goose chase that would waste many days of police time, eventually leaving Crossier empty-handed.

The inspector put her phone down on the couch between them. "Thank you, I'll find her. Now, speaking of your uncle Henri—"

"Yes, what about him?"

"He's an art restorer, isn't he?"

"Yes."

"With a home workshop?"

"Yes."

"But he works as a private contractor at various museums in greater Paris, isn't that true?"

"Of course." Susanne knew that Crossier knew all of this already; she was just playing the role of hard-nosed investigator. "Let's just get straight to the point. My uncle is employed often by d'Orsay as an on-site art conserver. He's on a job there now, in fact."

"I know he is," Crossier said. "At the moment, he's working on a Rodin sculpture, in fact."

Susanne nodded. She wasn't quite sure where Crossier was going with this.

"Do you know if Henri is romantically involved with anyone?"

"You'll have to ask him."

"I intend to. I just thought that if his sexual leanings were slightly off-center, if you know what I mean, he might not be as open to discussing it as you might be."

"If you're asking if he's straight or gay, I would have to say straight. He's had too many lady friends to count over the years."

"But he never married?"

"Maybe he just never found the right woman to settle down with."

"Or maybe he has a secret life, and all the female companions are just a cover?"

Susanne shrugged, putting on a face that she hoped would be interpreted as noncommittal. Henri was straight as an arrow, but if Inspector Crossier left tonight with more questions than answers, all the better.

Susanne quickly tried to envision Michèle's thought process. Henri, as a d'Orsay employee, would have access to the museum and its equipment; as a Bruante, familial association alone would link him to the incident in the gallery. Susanne tried to think like Crossier. If the victim's sexual partner was a Bruante too, how was she connected to Henri? More importantly, how was the victim connected to Henri? Were Henri and the dead man lovers, the murder a crime of passion that resulted from the victim's infidelity with another Bruante? Or, had Henri killed a rapist, his act of violence meant to protect and defend a niece or a cousin?

Actually, it was hilarious. The police were trying to fit a square peg into a round hole. This was no murder, but rather an unfortunate accident that resulted from a fatal journey through a time tunnel, of all things! Crossier and her associates at the 36 were trying to solve a crime that never occurred. *Good,* Susanne thought. The longer they spun their wheels, the more time she would have to figure out what to do with Nicole, and the more time John Noland would have to determine whether he would actually be able to send her back to where she belonged.

"As far as a secret life goes, anything is possible," Susanne finally replied. "You'll have to ask Henri, though. I can only give you educated guesses; he'll be able to give you the facts." She looked at her watch. "It's getting late, and I have some work to do. Are we finished now?"

Crossier picked up her phone, smiling pleasantly as she stood up. "Thank you for the information, Mademoiselle Bruante. You've been quite helpful."

Susanne couldn't be fooled that easily. The police might be following some other leads, but Susanne wasn't completely off their radar screen. She had to be careful where she stepped; there were landmines out there, still.

"Anytime, inspector," Susanne replied, smiling back at the detective just as pleasantly. "Have a good night."

It had gone very well, all things considered—both the presentation and the unexpected visit from Inspector Crossier. Granted, her opening remarks tonight had been made to only a handful of listeners, but that really didn't matter. Soon Henri and Nicole would arrive, and the three of them would take samples from the paintings. Those results would be the clincher, trumping all of the circumstantial evidence that had been the crux of her argument until now. It would be those results that would make her famous. The press conference that she imagined in her mind would be an once-in-a-lifetime, standing-room-only event, in contrast to tonight's meagerly attended prelude to the real thing. She could almost taste the victory, and it made her mouth water.

Sitting down at her desk, she glanced at her watch. It was 9:30 p.m. She had two hours to kill until Henri and Nicole's pre-arranged arrival time. Henri would text her, and she would let them in through the service entrance. Then the fun would begin.

Well, she might as well make use of her time. She did have

another exhibit to plan—that much was true; so she pulled a pile of paperwork from the other side of the desktop toward her, and got started.

Soon, very soon, her theory would be confirmed with the irrefutable certainty of DNA analysis. She could taste the victory again, and it was truly delicious.

Henri waited with Nicole for Susanne to answer his text message by letting them in. The taxi had dropped them off in the back, no questions asked, and just as Susanne had instructed, they had followed the down-sloping concrete driveway all the way to the bottom. They had found themselves in front of an industrial-sized garage door, locked and secured of course, which Susanne had explained led into the museum's basement acquisition warehouse. On the far right, a steel door without an outdoor handle would open momentarily from the inside, as soon as Susanne made her way from upstairs via the service elevator in response to his text.

Henri had his bag, which contained all of the equipment he would need to collect the hair samples from the paintings. It wouldn't take that long, as long as Nicole pointed out exactly where in each picture he should concentrate on carefully teasing out one single fiber from paint that had aged for a century and a half. It would be meticulous work, requiring caution and patience to extract a single hair, or portion of one, without damaging the surface of the painting. Henri could do it; he had the experience and the know-how to do the job right—as long as he knew precisely where to look.

"I will show you," Nicole had promised. "I remember, do not worry."

It was funny to hear the formality of her language—the old-fashioned grammar and the antiquated syntax, all of it sounding so out of place coming from someone so young, but born so long ago. Henri had to keep reminding himself that Nicole had lived in another time, where the conventions of the nineteenth century had left its indelible mark on her speech and mannerisms. Otherwise, in Susanne's clothes—the designer jeans and the trendy Express t-shirt with "Oolala!" written across the front—Nicole seemed completely modern in her appearance. The clothing fit her perfectly, in a way that went well beyond the matching size. They suited her somehow, much more than the long dresses and the buttoned boots that she had worn in the fading family portraits they had looked at together just the other day. Henri almost had the feeling that she belonged here, rather than there. Perhaps she did.

Nicole's way of thinking, too, was anything but antiquated. You might say that she had left everything pre-Belle Époch behind her, except that she had probably never held to those conservative beliefs to begin with. Was she a woman ahead of her time, independent and self-assured, uninhibited and unconcerned with other people's opinions of her? Undoubtedly—and now she had become the literal materialization of this aphorism. Somehow she had ended up here, exactly one hundred and thirty-four years after her time, and she seemed anything but out of place.

"Posing was my life," she had told him on the ride from Susanne's condo to d'Orsay. Henri had hired a taxi, picking her up right in front of the little alley that led to the courtyard behind Susanne's apartment building. Although the surveillance car had followed Susanne to work and had not returned, they had all thought it best for Nicole to use the back way for all of her comings and goings, just to be certain that no one saw her. Henri had watched her put the small ring of extra keys that she was holding into a shoulder purse that Susanne had given her, as she pulled the taxi door closed behind her and slid in beside Henri in the back seat.

"How was it viewed, in those days?" he had asked, referring of course to the nude modeling.

She had shrugged. "It was not something usual for a woman to do. People were shocked by it, including my mother, but I did not care. I love posing naked—it is so very natural." She had paused for a moment to think. "The feeling it gives me is hard to explain. It is freedom and rebellion; it is daring and boldness; it is me standing up to everything that is timid and little-minded, and saying to them that I am beautiful and proud, and that I am not going to hide it. I am not afraid to show people who I truly am, Henri, and posing nude is my way of doing just that. It is beautiful, I think."

It was beautiful—and she was beautiful, there was no argument there. The paintings of her had captured both her beautiful image and her spirit with a permanence that would represent her legacy. Courbet had brushed some oil onto canvas after canvas after canvas, transforming something inanimate into something that pulsed with life. His renderings of Nicole's perfect body had essentially made her immortal, her essence captured in time forever. It was, and she was, a thing of beauty.

"Did you only model for Courbet?" Henri had asked, curious.

"Mostly, especially when I lived with him. But there were some others."

"Whom, for instance?"

"I posed for Édouard Manet a few times and for Pierre Renoir, and Henri Latour. Mary Cassatt painted me nude, too, right before she returned to America."

"Did you ever pose for Degas?"

She shook her head and laughed. "*Mais non!* He was interested in painting dancers, not nudes. I do not think he even liked women."

It was mind boggling to think that all of Degas' *After the Bath* nudes were not really his. Susanne was actually right about that; now she would have her proof. The revelation would shake up the art world, make no mistake—the truth delivered by an artist's model, the woman who stood next to Henri in the shadows of a dimly lit delivery alley at this very moment, an inadvertent time traveler whose identity would always remain anonymous.

Whether Nicole stayed in the present or returned to the past, her story could never be made public. It was simply too fantastic for the average person to accept. Henri could see the media frenzy now, led by the paparazzi, with accompanying headlines such as, "Nude Time Traveler Exposed," and "Sexy Artist's Model Poses Naked—Any Day, Any Time." Henri didn't know much about Susanne's scientist friend, who would be arriving tomorrow to help them, but one thing seemed clear—he would not let this John Noland turn Nicole into the equivalent of a circus freak. If Nicole needed protection, Henri would provide it.

He truly liked her. She was levelheaded, thoughtful, intelligent, and kind—a strong woman, but totally selfless, unlike someone else he knew. Funny, how the genes for physical appearance had been passed down through the generations, from Nicole to Susanne, without even a hint of dilution, yet Nicole's personality traits had ended up elsewhere, entirely—except for the exhibitionist ones, of course. Susanne had loved the nude pose as much, or maybe even more, than Nicole had. They both had it in their blood.

Finally the door opened and Susanne motioned them in. It was dark inside, but Susanne held a flashlight in her hand. "This way," she instructed them, and in a moment they stepped into a triple-sized elevator with padded walls, designed for moving equipment and heavy pieces of artwork such as sculptures from the warehouse and art restoration workshop downstairs into the museum exhibit areas upstairs. Susanne pressed the button that would take them to the ground-floor level, and the elevator lurched upward. A moment later, it opened onto a granite balcony that connected two catwalks on either side, used by the museum to display a number of Rodin sculptures, stone and bronze alike. Directly below them, they could look over the sunken expanse of the museum's belowground exhibit space that eventually ended in a wide stairway leading to the front lobby on the opposite end, flanked by two similar stairways leading up to the left and right end of the catwalks respectively. At this location, they were well out of the night guard's earshot and view.

They had worked it all out beforehand. Nicole stepped off the elevator, leaning against the wall off to one side, patiently prepared to wait. After all, it simply wouldn't do to have her seen side-by-side with her double. Henri followed Susanne, zigzagging through the Rodin display and onto the walkway on the left side, walking behind her as she led him into the front lobby for the fictitious introduction. "This one will be easy to convince," Susanne explained to Henri in a low voice. "He has the hots for me."

Didn't they all? Susanne walked with an exaggerated feminine sway over to the security module, her body language hinting at the promise of reward if the guard sitting behind the desk would simply agree to let them collect their samples.

The night officer, a heavyset fellow in his early forties with a scraggly beard and a very thick neck, looked up curiously from his monitors and put out his cigarette in an ashtray that was already overflowing with stubs. He was not at all surprised to see Susanne, since she had signed the late-stay register earlier, but he hadn't expected her to have a companion.

"Who is this?" he asked suspiciously.

"Good evening to you too, Pierre," she responded pleasantly.

He lit up another cigarette, without a word. To Henri, he didn't look as pliable as Susanne had claimed.

"This is François Leclercq, one of our conservators," Susanne continued, ignoring Pierre's silence. "He's an art historian from Brussels, who has been engaged by the EU Endowment for the Arts to collect materials samples from various paintings."

Pierre looked Henri up and down, as if he were trying to confirm the name by matching it with his appearance. He didn't look convinced. "François Leclercq?"

"Yes," Susanne said, "his team will be studying the composition of various oil paints used by the great Masters from different eras. He needs samples from some of our Courbet and Degas pieces."

"And why, exactly, does he have to collect these samples in the middle of the night?" It didn't seem like he was buying it.

"Monsieur Leclercq has a long day scheduled tomorrow at the Louvre," Susanne explained. "If he can squeeze us in tonight, then he'll be able to catch tomorrow evening's flight to Madrid. He's on a very tight schedule, you see."

"No one told me about this, Mademoiselle Bruante. I'm not sure I can let him in without the proper authorization."

"I am authorizing it," she declared firmly, while at the same time adjusting her low-cut blouse in order to draw Pierre's attention elsewhere. Interesting, how she was able to combine the insinuation of seduction with the unquestionable assertion of professional authority. Leave it to Susanne to invent a whole new blend of persuasion.

Pierre's eyes flicked downward at her cleavage and then up again. Susanne's strategy was having the desired effect. "This was all arranged at the last minute," she added, her tone bordering now on apologetic. "Monsieur Le Director has approved it, take my word; and I'll be personally supervising Monsieur Leclercq's interaction with our paintings."

Pierre hesitated for a few more seconds, but then nodded his agreement. Henri could actually see the lust in his eyes. "I suppose it makes more sense to collect the specimens at night, anyway," he said, visibly distracted by Susanne's assets. "That way, Monsieur Leclercq won't interfere with our patrons during daytime business hours."

"Exactly!" She leaned over the edge of the desk on her outstretched arms, giving Pierre an even better view of her partly exposed bust. He seemed convinced already, so now she was just playing with him—the ever-desired Susanne Bruante, every man's fantasy (at least in her own mind), and every bit the penultimate tease. Henri sighed. She would never change.

"Where will you be collecting the samples?" Pierre asked. "I'll have to turn off the motion sensors and the video surveillance cameras wherever you'll be working. They're on the same circuit."

"We'll confine the collection procedure to the large special exhibit gallery," Susanne replied. "All the paintings Monsieur Leclercq needs to work on can be found there."

"How much time will you need?" Pierre directed his question to Henri this time.

"It's tedious work," Henri explained, "but I think three hours will suffice. Maybe less."

Pierre consulted his monitors, touched a few icons on his computer screen, and then looked up. His expression was hard to read. Yes, he seemed duped by Susanne's performance, but another part of him was probably feeling conflicted. Henri would be tampering, after all, with paintings worth millions and millions of euros each, and it was Pierre's job to prevent d'Orsay's collection of masterpieces from being damaged, disrupted, or stolen. Who wouldn't feel uneasy about this whole thing?

Henri crossed his fingers, praying that he would be able to get what they needed, safely and quickly, without being arrested. All he needed was one fragment of hair from each of four paintings. How difficult could that be? Difficult enough, he thought; he would have to be very careful not to damage the surfaces of the masterpieces in the collection process.

"Thank you, Pierre. I'll escort Dr. Leclercq to the galleries so he can get started." She winked at him. "When we're finished, I'll come back and visit with you—all right?"

Did Pierre actually hope to get more from the beautiful assistant director than just some additional idle chitchat later, when she came back to visit? Maybe; but Henri still saw some doubt on the man's face as they left the lobby and headed for the special exhibit gallery, by way of the Rodin sculpture platform.

"That went well," Susanne said as they walked down the catwalk, on their way to collect Nicole.

Whatever you say, Henri thought. All he knew was that he had better get the collection done quickly, before someone caught him red-handed. Tampering with property belonging to La République Française was a federal offense and would probably result in years of jail time for both Susanne and Henri, if they were found out.

Their plan was to have Nicole quickly identify the right places for Henri to focus on, and then to get her out of the museum and back to Susanne's apartment by taxi. The guard made his rounds every hour, Susanne had said, and it would be very difficult to explain why a Susanne lookalike was helping Dr. Leclercq with his materials collection. Nicole had the keys to Susanne's back door, so it was just a matter of taking the taxi back to *La Rue Étriqué*, the alley that led to Susanne's courtyard entrance, in another ten or fifteen minutes. With a generous pre-payment, the cabbie had agreed to return at 12:15 sharp to the same drop-off location in back of the museum, to pick up Nicole and drive her back home.

Susanne led the way to the Courbet and Degas pairing exhibit, with Henri and Nicole in tow. When they got to the main exhibit gallery, Nicole brushed past both of them, making a beeline to *The Origin of the World*.

"That's the painting I have hanging over my bed," she declared. "It's my favorite."

"It's you, I presume?" Susanne asked, a quite unnecessary request for confirmation. Did Henri detect a hint of jealousy in Susanne's voice? His niece stood examining the painting, her arms crossed in a pose that could only be described as defensive. He knew her so well that he could virtually read her mind: *I could have done that, and so much better,* he could almost hear her say. Susanne had modeled nude, of course; but never for anyone really famous. It probably bothered her more than just a little bit that she had been outdone by her distant relative.

"*Mais oui*," Nicole replied. "I am that woman." She pointed to the upper right-hand corner of the dark, intimate triangle that formed the central focus of the painting. "Here, Henri," she indicated, without even the hint of a blush. "Jean brushed in my hair right here."

Henri reached into his bag and withdrew a small notebook that he had packed for this express purpose. He quickly sketched the landmarks between Nicole's legs and made a careful notation with a series of Xs to guide him in the upcoming collection process. "Okay, I've got it." He breathed a quiet sigh of relief. The painting was so realistic that he felt a little uncomfortable examining Nicole's genital area while she stood by watching, so he was glad to get this one out of the way. The next three pieces were bound to be much less explicit, in comparison, and much easier to work with for that reason, even with Nicole looking on.

Henri turned to Susanne. "Which other Courbet would you like me to sample?"

"How about *Woman With a Parrot*," Susanne suggested, looking over at Nicole again with her eyes narrowed, as if she doubted their visitor had actually posed for this one too, despite the similarity in physical appearance between the image and the real person. She pointed at the painting, which was hanging on the opposite wall, close to the archway that separated the first room from the second.

Nicole walked over to the painting, crossing her arms as she analyzed it with a somewhat nostalgic eye. She hadn't seemed to notice that Susanne was showing subtle signs of model-envy. "Jean painted me in this one right after we did *Le Sommeil*," Nicole said. "It was a very difficult pose to hold."

It must have been, Henri thought as he studied the image. Nicole's left arm was positioned straight up in the air, holding a stuffed bird. After only ten or fifteen minutes like that, her limb would have most certainly fallen asleep.

"Lying with Jeannette in the other painting was so much easier." Nicole was referring, of course, to *Le Sommeil*, the painting that pictured her entwined with a female lover, happily asleep with an after-the-fact look of satisfied contentment. "So much easier," she repeated with a lusty grin, "and so much more fun." That was more information than Henri needed to know, but it still made him smile. Nicole's open-mindedness undeniably belonged here, in 2011, rather than in 1877.

"He put your hair in the hair," Henri commented, "but where, exactly? There's so much of it in this painting." He made another rough sketch in his book, while Nicole pointed to a wave of locks that flowed along the nearest edge of the white-sheeted covering on her cot.

"Right in here," she said. He made the notation.

"How about the Degas nudes?" he asked Susanne.

"Correction," she replied, her tone discernibly snippy. "They're all Courbet's nudes, remember?"

He believed it, too, but they needed the proof. "This will confirm it," he said. "Nicole, which of these paintings of a woman washing in the toilette are you?"

It sounded ridiculous for him to phrase it like that. She smiled. "All of them," she said. "I modeled for every single painting in this room."

"Could you just pick two, Nicole?" Susanne asked, actually rolling her eyes. Henri had picked up on her desire to move past the moment, since she wasn't the center of attention—the quicker, the better, so the focus could be re-directed on Susanne Bruante and her critical agenda. It was all about Susanne, as usual—always had been, and always would be.

"Certainly." Nicole went to stand between two *After the Bath* paintings. One of them depicted her reclining seductively on her back, arms behind her head on a white bath towel; the other showed her from the back, kneeling on a chaise lounge and toweling herself off from a most provocative angle. Henri sketched an outline of one, and then the other, waiting to mark his Xs.

"On the left side of this one; and to the top and just over to the right, on this one," Nicole indicated, without hesitating for even a second. There was no question in Henri's mind that the model in the paintings was Nicole. After his contact in the DNA laboratory had a chance to run a test on these samples, they would know it for sure.

"All set?" Susanne asked, tapping her foot impatiently.

"All set." He stepped back to *The Origin of the World*, where he had left his collection bag. It was time to get started.

It was also time to get Nicole out, before the guard started his rounds. "Come on, Nicole," Susanne said, obviously thinking the same thing. "The taxi should be out there by now. We need to make you disappear."

Disappear was right. Susanne didn't need Nicole anymore, now that she had served her purpose. Susanne's first step would be to get Nicole out of this place; her second would be to get her out of this time.

How ironic, really, that Susanne would choose that particular word—disappear. Henri watched a bit sadly as Susanne led Nicole out of the gallery. The poor girl had disappeared, not by choice, from a distant time and place. If Susanne eventually had her way, Nicole would disappear again, leaving this world to go—where? It seemed doubtful that Susanne's scientist friend would be able to guarantee a round-trip ticket back to Nicole's old life. Even if he could, was that really the right place for her? Where did Nicole truly belong? And now that she was here, what did fate intend for her? Henri sighed. Philosophy had never been his strong point, so he would just have to leave that to the experts.

But was John Noland the right kind of expert? Perhaps he was; then again, perhaps he wasn't. Time would tell, very shortly—tomorrow, in fact. When the expert arrived tomorrow, they would know.

Chapter Thirteen

Susanne stood silently against the wall, around the corner from the security desk, listening intently to Pierre's conversation on the phone.

She had thought the soft echoes, muted by the great distance between where she had been standing outside the service elevator and the lobby on the other side of the museum, were from his voice, but she couldn't quite be sure. She had sent Nicole off in the waiting taxi and had been poised to turn to the right after exiting the elevator, intending to rejoin Henri in the main exhibit gallery, where he was busy at that very moment at the delicate task of extracting a single hair from four separate century-and-a-half old paintings. But then, she had heard what sounded suspiciously like a voice in the lobby. The sound, undeniably real and not imagined, had caused her to stop dead in her tracks.

It was one voice, not two, thank God. At least Pierre wasn't conversing with a gendarme. It was so easy for d'Orsay security to summon one, with a simple push of a button and a few words of concern or panic over the direct phone line to the nearest Paris police outpost, located half a block down the street. As she had listened from across the sleeping expanse of the darkened museum, she had no doubt now that he was talking on the phone, but the question had plagued her: to whom?

She had sweet-talked Pierre into allowing the sample collection; perhaps he had realized that she would never really sleep with him. She could kick herself. Having come to his senses, recognizing that he had been duped, he had probably decided to call Hubert Varton, the head of d'Orsay security—or worse yet, René. She had realized very quickly that she must get closer to find out.

She had slipped off her heels and had turned left, not right, and then she had run as quickly (and as silently) as she could, until she finally had ended up here, where she could hear Pierre's conversation as clearly as if she were standing right next to him. Needless to say, she didn't like what she was hearing—not one bit.

"That's exactly what I thought," he was saying to whomever he had on the other end of the phone line. "What do you want me to do now, Monsieur Varton?"

Just as Susanne had feared, Pierre was speaking to the head of d'Orsay security. She waited nervously through a moment of silence, while Pierre listened to whatever was being said to him. "Yes, that makes perfect sense," he finally said. "Are you sure don't want me to call the police while you do that?"

Police! That was the last thing they needed now. She would have to think fast, if Pierre was planning on calling in reinforcements. It looked as if they were in serious trouble, and she had only herself to blame. She should have given Pierre more than just a little cleavage, and then maybe she wouldn't have been faced with this major crisis.

"Yes, sir," Pierre was saying. "I'll hold off on that, until you've spoken to the executive director. I'll wait for your call back."

Susanne breathed a sigh of relief, although she would have to work fast in order to make this brief reprieve a permanent one. She had told the guard that René had given her authorization to take the samples; now all she had to do was to make that lie into the truth. If she could just get to René first, before Varton did, she would convince him to give her his endorsement, after the fact. There would be a price to pay for his approval—a steep and risky price, potentially—but she truly had no other choice. Bringing René partly into her confidence was the only way to avoid being arrested and thrown into prison for tampering with state property. These paintings were a national treasure; the courts would not look kindly on what they would almost certainly view as a sophisticated twist on an international vandalism offense.

Her cell phone was in her purse, already programmed to reach René on his pre-paid device, the one they always used to make arrangements for their clandestine rendezvous. She couldn't make the call here, where Pierre would be certain to hear. She turned and raced back along the catwalk, taking one of the entryways midway to the other end into the labyrinth of galleries to the right side, running past Degas ballerinas and Monet water lilies in the first and second rooms, then Morisot portraits and Valadon still-life paintings in the third, until she finally found herself in the far back corner of the museum, in a room devoted entirely to Van Gogh landscapes and Lautrec nineteenth-century poster art.

She paused and caught her breath. Now that she was in a spot where Pierre could not hear her, she made the call, waiting impatiently for the director to pick up, tapping the ball of her foot on the cool veneered wood. The line rang once, twice, three times, four times. “Pick it up, René,” she pleaded under her breath. Getting his voicemail was simply not an option.

“Hello,” he finally answered, his voice hushed. She imagined him, once again, sleeping next to his average-looking wife when his cell phone startled him awake. Seeing Susanne’s name on the caller ID, he would have rushed out into the hallway, taking the call secretly, as he always did on the rare occasions when she called him after hours. “What is it, Susanne?” His voice sounded edgy and irritated. “Celeste will find out about us for sure, if these late-night phone calls don’t stop.” Last week, it had been the police calling him at 1:00 in the morning, but now it was her, waking him at an ungodly hour with a phone call that had nothing whatsoever to do with their relationship. This time, it was all business.

“You’ll be getting a call in a moment from Hubert Varton.” She decided to launch right into it, since her timing was undoubtedly right down to the wire; and sure enough, as soon as she said it, she heard the shrill ring of René’s house phone in the background. “That’s him now, René. Tell him, please, that you’ll call him back.”

“Why?”

“I’ll explain it to you as soon as you get rid of Varton. Do it, René. I promise, you won’t regret it.”

“Okay, okay; hold on a second.” He sounded annoyed, but she would be able to appease him in a moment with her offer of partnership.

She waited, while he walked down his house stairs to the ground floor to answer the phone. “Lauren, here,” she heard him answer a few seconds later, his voice muffled by distance but still audible. “Yes, yes; I have her on the other line right now.” Then, after a momentary delay, during which time he was undoubtedly listening to Varton hanging her out to dry, she heard him say that he’d call the head of d’Orsay security back in a minute.

“What in the world are you up to?” he asked her, picking up their call again. “Hubert says you’re in the museum with some kind of international art historian who wants to collect samples from some of our paintings. I didn’t authorize this, Susanne.”

She could hear him seething through the phone line. Had she gone too far this time, not only by undermining René's authority, but also by placing four valuable pieces of artwork at serious risk of being damaged? Admittedly, her judgment had been colored by the promise of professional accomplishment and validation, but that hardly meant that she had made the wrong call by deciding to go behind René's back for the sample collection. "Wrong" was a word that simply was not in her vocabulary. The problem here, to put it simply, was that she had been caught. That was her mistake—nothing more, nothing less.

But there was no point in lingering in the past. Now was the time to fix things, and she intended to do just that. "Remember my uncle, the art restorer?"

"Of course I remember him. Thanks to him, you had some additional circumstantial evidence to present tonight, in support of your crazy theory. That letter was a historic find, I'll admit; but it adds nothing incontrovertible to back your thesis."

"I know that. But he found something else in *Nude Reclining,* René—something that I think will interest you greatly."

"What?" She could hear his skepticism; in a minute, he would change his tune.

"During my uncle's analysis of the painting, he noticed some organic material embedded in the paint."

"What kind of organic material?"

"Hair."

"Did I hear you correctly? I thought you just said hair."

"I did. He found human hair, integrated with the paint. It was blended into the image, in a location corresponding to the model's hair in the picture."

"That's very interesting, but I fail to see the relevance. Unless you enlighten me, you and your uncle will find yourself serving time for destruction of national property."

That was cold, especially considering that she was his mistress; but then again, they were long overdue for another hotel room marathon. With all the commotion, she had been shirking her duties. She'd have to remedy that, and fast. "I'd miss our little get-togethers in prison—which reminds me, we haven't had a conjugal visit in way too long. How about tomorrow morning, early?" It would be Saturday, and he often worked at the office for part of the day anyway. His wife would never suspect that he had checked into a hotel room instead for a little physical therapy. A few hours of hard encouragement would go a long way toward softening him up.

There was a pause, and she knew she had him. "Yes, that would work. But back to this business with the hair—"

"All right, listen carefully. You know I'm convinced that Courbet painted *Nude Reclining*, and you heard why in my lecture tonight. I now have reason to believe that maybe Courbet mixed his model's hair into his paint in all of his paintings, as a kind of signature, if you will. With this theory in mind, I brought Henri to the museum last week," she lied, "and had him examine some of the Courbet and Degas paintings in the special exhibit; and guess what?" She didn't wait for him to answer. "There's hair in all of them, René."

His wheels were already turning. "So your uncle is collecting hair samples?"

"Exactly. René, this is the proof that I've been waiting for all these years. If the DNA analysis confirms that the hair imbedded in the paint matches, then the balance weighing in on my theory will definitely be tipped over to the 'no question about it' side. Think about it. We have an authenticated letter, written by Courbet, that sets up the plan; we have identical-appearing brunette models depicted in paintings allegedly created thirty or forty years apart; and now, if all goes well, we will have DNA evidence that the brunette in all of those paintings is the same person. This new discovery will tie it all together, and the conclusion will be obvious—namely, that Courbet, not Degas, painted the *After the Bath* nudes."

"Hm. That is interesting." There was a moment of silence on the other end of the line. The logic of it all was starting to sink in; she had him.

"You should have run this by me first," he finally said, his tone showing signs of changing from severely threatening to increasingly indulgent.

"Yes, I know I should have, and I regret that now. I just didn't want to risk another moment's delay, so I thought I'd just get the samples, quick and dirty, and we'd be done with it."

"A team of restorers working in a closely controlled setting should have handled a job like this. This was incredibly irresponsible of you, Susanne. You've placed these paintings at risk of sustaining surface damage from an inappropriately executed collection procedure."

"Look," she countered, "none of the paintings will be damaged. All we need is a single hair—even a fragment of a hair will do—to prove our theory. Henri is an experienced restorer. He knows what he's doing. It will be okay, I promise."

"It had better be."

He needed something more to clinch the deal. She knew what she had to do; she had no choice but to offer a gold-plated carrot. "Once we get the samples and have the DNA analyzed, we can share the recognition. We'll be equal partners in this. Deal?" If she knew René like she thought she knew him, he would turn a blind eye to her unconventional retrieval methods if she offered him an alliance. A discovery like this was a once-in-a-lifetime opportunity to advance his career and make a name for himself. He wouldn't turn her down.

She didn't have to wait long for his answer. "Deal."

It was settled, then, but there would surely be conditions. First, he would let her handle the DNA analysis. Why? Because he would want to steer far, far away from any direct involvement in the matter, at least until it became clear that he would have something to gain from the results.

"How long will it take for the DNA testing to be completed?" he asked.

His predictability was laughable, really. "Forty-eight hours, at the most. My uncle has a contact."

"Good." What would come next? The after-the-fact authorization, of course, signed and sealed, but with the date falsified. He would store it away, waiting until later to file it through the proper channels, after he made certain that the paintings weren't damaged and that the DNA testing had hit it big. "I'll swing by the office first thing tomorrow and get all the paperwork together for you to sign," he said. "We can take care of it in the hotel room."

She hung up the phone with a smile. It felt good to always end up on top—her favorite, and usual, position. It felt very, very good indeed.

~

The taxi dropped Nicole off right where she had started just two hours before, back in the little alley that led to the courtyard directly behind Susanne's apartment building. The driver, a man who was not unattractive, had been outwardly flirtatious, and she felt flattered. He had even asked for her phone number and whether he could call her on her mobile sometime, but she said she didn't have one. He didn't believe her, and she quickly realized that he assumed her preposterous excuse was meant to spare him the embarrassment of rejection.

"Everyone has a phone," he insisted as she got out of the cab with a smile and a thank you. She didn't answer him; it was just too complicated to explain. Besides, it would be best to minimize unnecessary contact with other people during her limited time in this place. Forming emotional connections was simply out of the question, since she was just a temporary visitor in this here and now.

She liked it here, though—loved it, really, was more like it. Everything was so convenient and so incredibly comfortable. These vehicles they called autos, for instance, transported people to distant places in no time, and luxuriously. Carriage rides were always so bumpy and slow, and the odors were often overwhelming.

Susanne and Henri had no idea how lucky they were. It wasn't just the modern transportation that made it so wonderful to live here; it was all the devices that made it so easy to do much, much more than simply exist. Her life had been extremely difficult in 1877, although she hadn't known that when she was there. It always took a comparison to point out how perfect or deficient something was, and the contrast between then-versus-now was as extreme as night versus day. How strange that now she had been given the rare opportunity to compare them yet here she was. Who would have thought that she would be able to take a peek into the future?

It was more than a peek, of course. Now that she had experienced life here, it would be very difficult to leave—assuming that leaving was even possible. But did she have any choice in the matter, really? Even the most simple-minded individual could understand that transporting someone from the past into the future might drastically change what was meant to be. Nicole's absence from where she was supposed to live her life, there in the past, as well as her presence in a place where she shouldn't be, here in the future, could both alter events in a way that would unquestionably have important repercussions for other people around her, or even for society as a whole.

Granted, she wasn't someone important like Jean Courbet; but being common instead of famous did not necessarily make her a less valuable individual, at least to the people whose lives she had touched. Or would touch.

Take Edmond, for instance. She had already been absent from her son's life for more than a week, and she was starting to imagine, in nightmare-like vividness, more than just a few time-altering scenarios that might have already resulted from this deprivation. Granted, she only saw him every two weeks, but what if he was ill? Or what if missing their usual Sunday afternoon walk had placed him in harm's way? She was his mother, and he was her baby; she was expected to be there, right by his side to protect him. But she wasn't. She would go back there, if she could, for Edmond's sake; she had to, didn't she? Of course she did. That's what mothers did, after all.

It had been a long day, and she was tired. The entire city was asleep, it seemed, and that's where she would be in a little while, too. She slid the old-fashioned brass key into the garden gate, turned it halfway to the right, and swung the grated iron door inward. She stepped carefully onto stone fitted into stone, the path somewhat difficult to see in the darkness, taking a diagonal route across the courtyard directly to the back door, over to the right. She had a key for that, too: a small, flat one that fit into both the dead bolt and the doorknob locks. When she was inside, she took the side stairs up two flights, using the last key on the ring to let herself into Susanne's apartment.

She felt at home here, even though she could clearly see through Susanne's ulterior motives for letting her stay. Nicole liked the little guestroom, her home away from home, with the walk-in closet stocked by Susanne with a variety of clothes that fit Nicole perfectly and were right in line with her newly discovered sense of style.

She also liked the bed, large enough for two but intended for one, with an enormous, thick mattress that was so much better than the feather matting she was used to—that thin rectangle of stingily stuffed fabric that did little to soften the wooden slats of her cot underneath her. She couldn't wait to climb into that bed right now, naked and exhausted, pulling the sheets and blankets around her for the sound and dreamless sleep she sorely needed in preparation for the next day. She would meet John Noland when he arrived tomorrow, an experience that she predicted would be lengthy as well as stressful.

She made her way down the hallway, her first stop the bathroom, to the left, where she pulled off her t-shirt, arms crossed at the bottom lifting it smoothly up and off. Her breasts, barely covered before under the thin cotton fabric, were naked, and the cold air turned her nipples hard. Her body was more than ready for the warm, steamy wetness of a hot shower. She pulled off her jeans and panties and stepped into the extravagant cascade of clean water, yet another modern convenience, closing her eyes and soaking her hair with the dripping caress of the pulsing stream. Her nudity, soaped and slick, trickled in sensuous, slippery rivulets until it was rinsed clean.

A white terry-cloth bathrobe doubled as a towel, and by the time she moved into the bedroom, her body was dry. Bathrobe off, she lay it on the foot of the bed, and in she crept, between cool sheets and into the warm and inviting summons of double blankets. She settled in, her head on the pillow; in a matter of seconds, she fell fast asleep.

Her hope for a dreamless sleep did not come true, though.

Nicole followed a winding street as it led from the top of *Butte Montmartre*, down and down toward the bottom of a hill. It was Sunday; in just a little while, she would see her Edmond. She had sent word to her mother that today they should meet in Place Pigalle, rather than in her attic room, in contrast to their usual routine. It was a very warm day, unseasonably so—much too hot to visit with Edmond in the stifling heat of her third-floor garret.

It would feel so nice on a day like this to sit on the edge of the fountain while Edmond played with the gift Nicole had bought him. She imagined how his eyes would grow wide when he unwrapped the little wooden boat, and how he would laugh, pushing it along with happy splashes in the cool water of Pigalle fountain.

It would be nice to see her little boy. She missed him, but the arrangement she had worked out with her mother was really for the best, at least for now. Although her parents didn't have much, they had more—much more, by far—than she had. Thank God for her father's generosity and her mother's love. Without them, she would probably be out on the street. And Edmond? She didn't even want to think about it.

It was slightly after 2:00, approaching the peak of the day's heat, and she felt it. She wore her summer dress with the bare minimum of undergarments, but it was still too much for such a warm day. How she wanted to strip it all off and toss the clothes aside, as she had done the week before last for that young artist, the one who had expected more than just a nude posing for his money, which she had willingly given. He had been handsome enough, a decent distraction for one night; plus, there was the wine—and the promise of absinthe, which in the end he had not delivered.

She tugged at her collar, moist with perspiration already, though she was only halfway down the hill. What a shame that the convention of clothing, intended to warm the body in cold weather, had somehow been carried over into the summer months. Nudity would be so much better, in the face of such heat; but, oh well—who was she to question the rules that people had imposed upon themselves?

Down and down she walked, until finally the street opened into the bustling expanse of Pigalle. She turned right and passed by a nightclub that featured the latest Parisian rage: the gaudy burlesque. A dancer rushed in front of her, late perhaps for her upcoming shift, dressed in a red skirt that showed a shocking amount of leg. Nicole laughed to herself. She herself routinely showed that much leg, and much more, whenever she went to her job. She imagined, with a smile, how she would shake up the place, if ever they hired her as one of their cabaret girls. She was no dancer, though; that was the problem. Her talent lay in showing excess skin, not in moving it.

She saw the fountain now, across the way and on the other side of *La Place*; and between Nicole and this destination, she had horses, and carriages, and pedestrians to contend with, too many to count. Edmond loved the bustle of activity down here, and that was yet another reason why she had chosen Pigalle rather than the *La Butte* for today's visit. She had sent her mother the message that they should meet here at 2:00, and it was well past that hour by now. Nicole shaded the sun from her eyes with her hand, searching for them across the busy courtyard; and then she saw them. She would just wait for this carriage to pass, and then she would cross.

Edmond saw her too—he was waving his arms, and probably calling her name. She couldn't hear him, of course, but she imagined his little voice, screaming "*Maman, Maman*" as he tugged at his grandmother's arm and tried to free himself from her grip. The carriage passed, one of many. Nicole would have to hurry if she wanted to make it across before this next one—black, large, and ornate, trimmed with silver, being pulled at a fast clip by not one but two horses. The driver sat on top, dressed in a tailcoat and hat. This one belonged to someone wealthy.

She rushed ahead, waving to Edmond as she ran. He jumped up and down, tugging again at his grandmother's arm, pulling against her—

and then, he was free. He took off, running ahead well out of his grandmother's reach. Now Nicole could really hear his little voice, shrill and excited, as he ran toward her—right into the path of the approaching hansom cab.

Nicole's mother tried to react, but it was much too late. A group of people had inadvertently blocked her way, and Edmond had easily left her far behind, by the side of the fountain. Nicole realized with horror that in a moment, the two horses pulling the shining carriage behind them would trample her little baby. They barreled forward, eight battering, hammering hooves—trotting at full speed. The driver saw the danger at the same time Nicole did, and although he pulled back on the reins frantically, he would be unable to stop the horses in time to save her child.

Nicole sprinted forward, reaching Edmond at the same moment the horses did—reaching for him, touching the cloth of his shirt, grabbing his little arm, pulling him away with her eyes closed tightly against the dust that swirled in a choking cloud around her. She had him—or did she? She felt him next to her, against her, behind her—thrown by her last effort out of harm's way; unless, of course, she had failed. She would never know. She had paid a price for her mother's duty—a deadly, deathly price.

"Nicole!" she thought she heard her mother scream. "Nicole—"

The horses were on her, heavy hooves and whinnying screams and blood-soaked iron. Where was Edmond? Was he under her, or beside her—or behind her? *Oh God, make him be behind me!* Her face was on the ground, her body was in the dirt, and her soul seemed to be floating upward. Her body felt like someone else's, and at that split second—during that fateful moment of impact, right before it all went black—she felt as if her eyes were looking forward and backward, up and down, out and in, all at the same time. She was reversed and inversed—her location in the here and now, and the there and now, a reflection of a bizarre rearrangement caused by her journey through the time tunnel that had landed her far, far ahead of herself, so that her near future in 1877, as seen from 2011, had now become her distant past.

This was nothing imagined, no bedtime reverie—no dream, no fantasy, no invented illusion. She had just seen her own death. This was a memory, and it was real.

Nicole awoke with a start.

It was real…

Chapter Fourteen

Henri had accomplished a lot, and just in the nick of time. Right after Susanne's close call with d'Orsay's security team, and while she kept him company in the main exhibit gallery during his tedious task of hair extraction, Susanne had warned him. She had told him to expect that the police would probably bring him in for questioning today—and she was right.

Thank God Inspecteur Michèle Crossier hadn't been waiting for him outside his residence at 3:00 a.m., at the very moment when he had returned, exhausted, from the museum. She hadn't even been there at 7:45, as he slipped out his side door, feeling refreshed after almost five hours of sleep. He had intended to drop off the sample to his contact from the DNA lab as quickly as possible, only to find that with one phone call from his turmoil-attracting niece, his simple one-item errand list had just been doubled.

It had taken him hours to find the information Susanne had requested him to search out. Now he had it, folded neatly in his jacket pocket, copied just a little while ago from digital media files at the comprehensive newspaper archives of *Le Bibliothèque Nationale de France*. Would Crossier be there now, waiting to take him in for questioning? Henri rounded the corner onto *Rue du Bac*, and sure enough, there she was, the steadfast Inspector Crossier, waiting patiently in front of the business entrance to his home workshop, just as Susanne had predicted.

A lot had happened during the twelve-plus hours since he had extracted the first hair from the first of the four paintings at d'Orsay, beginning just after midnight. As he walked the final block toward his front porch, where Crossier stood by the door waiting for him, he thought back on the events of the day, starting with his post-midnight conversation with Susanne, in the special exhibit room at the museum. She had made herself comfortable, sitting on the floor with her back to the wall, next to where Henri was working.

"Inspector Michèle Crossier paid me a visit tonight, right after my exhibit lecture," Susanne had informed him, after filling him in on her conversation with René. He finished collecting a hair sample from the first of the four paintings, the one titled *The Origin of the World*.

"Are you still a suspect?" Henri had asked.

"Apparently not," she had replied, "but you are."

She had described her chat with the inspector, including the detective's interest in Henri's restoration work on the Rodin sculpture, on site at d'Orsay, as well as her inquiries regarding his sexual preferences. "She wanted to know if you were involved with anyone."

The detective's curiosity about Henri's romantic leanings had made him laugh, but her queries about his work at d'Orsay didn't. Because he had never married, many people made assumptions, and that didn't bother him one bit. He had never concerned himself with what people thought of him; in fact, it was kind of fun to be the source of speculation. He was happily heterosexual, enjoying an occasional interlude here and there in private, while the rumors circulated in public. Maybe he should have settled down—but why? He just couldn't be bothered with the work and time involved in maintaining a committed relationship. In that respect, he and Susanne were on the same page.

"Does she think the victim was my gay lover?"

"Probably, at first; not now. The pubic hair they found on the man's genitals was a woman's, not a man's, so at least your first name has been cleared."

"What exactly do you mean by that?"

"Our last name continues to be dragged through the mud, it seems. The DNA analysis of this particular hair shows that it belongs to someone with a high, but not completely matching, genetic concordance with mine."

"A female Bruante?"

"Nicole's hair, of course. She and her friend did the deed, and she left behind a little something that belonged to her in the process. The police don't know about Nicole, though; and we don't want them to." Susanne had smiled mischievously. "So, I decided to feed Crossier a false lead."

"What would that be?" Henri had no idea what to expect. With Susanne, it could be anything.

"She asked me if I had any questionable relatives. Well, it turns out I do. I gave her Claudine's name."

His mouth had fallen open. "Claudine? Why would you involve that poor girl? She's had a tough enough life already, as things stand." Sometimes, the extent of Susanne's insensitivity was mind-boggling. Claudine was his nephew Jacque's only daughter, an attractive young woman who had paid the price for her father's disinheritance. Forced to strike out on her own long before she turned twenty, she had found a dingy apartment in Pigalle and decided to use the only asset she had to survive—namely, her body. Now, she made a close-to-decent living doing some very indecent things, but she didn't seem to mind.

"I like stripping," she had told Henri once. "The exposure is so thrilling." When it really came down to it, though, how much different was that kind of nudity, compared to Susanne's kind, or Nicole's? The exhibitionist gene definitely ran strong in the Bruante line, passed down through the generations to express itself in more than just one of Nicole's female descendants.

Susanne had waved away Henri's concern. "Look, *Ton-ton*, this case the police think they're investigating isn't a case at all. There's no foul play involved, and no one is guilty of any crime. The time tunnel killed Nicole's little playmate—not Claudine, or me, or you. None of us will be arrested, because the police won't be able to find one shred of evidence to convict us, because all of us are innocent."

"But—"

"Relax, Henri. All that will happen to Claudine is the exact same thing that has already happened to me, and is more than likely to happen to you in the morning. She'll be questioned, then they'll take her DNA sample, and then, that will be that. When the results come back again showing genetic concordance but no match, the police will be left scratching their heads, and Claudine will be allowed to continue dancing around her pole, every night if she wants, to her heart's content."

It wouldn't pay to argue with her. Yes, nothing would come out of all this, but there was considerable stress involved in being the focus of a police investigation. Henri could certainly handle it; but he wasn't so sure about Claudine. He would try to reach her in the morning, to warn her.

Unless, of course, he was otherwise indisposed, being grilled himself by the police. Why in the world would they be interested in his on-site work at the museum?

"Would you like to hear what I think?" Susanne had asked, after he had voiced his puzzlement. "You work with some heavy pieces of stone and metal sculpture-art down in d'Orsay's basement. Maybe they think you crushed the victim with a Rodin sculpture."

That didn't quite add up. From Nicole's description of the dead man's injuries, the police would never make that kind of assumption. "Maybe a granite block that weighs a half-metric ton or so could cause damage like that, but not the metal Rodin piece that I'm working on right now." Crossier's team would have made a thorough search of the restoration workshop, failing to find anything heavy enough down there to flatten a person to death. "The Inspector must have something else in mind."

Susanne had shrugged. "I guess you'll find out soon enough. You'll probably find the good inspector waiting for you in front of your house, as soon as you get back this morning."

She hadn't been waiting there at 3:00 a.m., thankfully; and after catching five hours of sleep, there had been no sign of her, or anyone else from the 36. Perhaps they had decided to question Claudine first? Henri had tried to call her, getting voicemail, not once but twice; decided he would try again later; and then headed out, exiting from the side door to his upstairs living space, down the wooden stairs and into the well-manicured strip of greenery at the side of the building, and into the street. It had taken less than an hour to walk to his contact's house, umbrella in hand, on this cloudy Saturday morning. She had agreed to run the samples herself, even though it was the weekend, in exchange for a dinner date next week. That wouldn't be a problem. They had been off and on for as long as he could remember, and a little bit of "on" was probably long overdue in any case.

He had received the phone call from Susanne on his way back. "I'm on my way to meet René for a quickie; then it's off to the Chunnel station, to pick up our travel consultant."

Would John Noland really have a way to send Nicole back? To Henri, it seemed doubtful; but maybe that was just wishful thinking on his part. Nicole seemed happy here, so why risk her life by attempting the unthinkable? If she stayed, though, where would she live, and what would she do? Henri had already been thinking about that and had even started to make some preliminary plans. Nicole couldn't stay with Susanne on a permanent basis—that was simply out of the question, the reasons far too many to count; but she could stay with him.

Henri worked on the ground level of his house; did his living on the *premier étage*; and slept under the rafters, on the *deuxième étage*. He could move his bedroom down to one of his guestrooms on the first level, giving the attic space to Nicole, creating a temporary garret apartment for her that would probably remind her of her previous living quarters in Montmartre—but a much more comfortable version of it, of course. He could take her under his wing, find her a job, screen her dates—his great grandmother, transformed no less by a fluke of time into the daughter he had never had. It was nice to think about that, but very troubling to think about sending her away. One thing for sure, there was no such thing as a time machine, which meant that this visit from Susanne's ex-boyfriend would probably—hopefully—be a bust.

"I'm a little bit worried about Nicole," Susanne was saying to him over the phone line. "She was pretty agitated when I got in this morning."

"She wasn't sleeping?"

"She had been; and that's the problem. She had a dream that woke her up."

A nightmare? He had them too, sometimes. "A little shot of brandy is my home remedy for that," he said.

"Mine too, and it helped some. This dream of hers, though—it seemed real."

"They always do," he replied.

"You don't understand. She thinks it was a memory of something that hadn't happened to her yet."

"Do you mean a premonition?"

"No, a memory. She had actually worked it all out in her mind, already. Basically, the time travel has placed her ahead of everything that happened in her life, including things that haven't occurred yet. Her entire life, as seen from this location in time, has already taken place in the past. It makes sense, in a perverted kind of way."

"I guess so."

"Henri, I need you to find an obituary."

Immediately, he knew. "Nicole dreamed of her own death?"

"She thinks so. Anything you can find out about a carriage accident that took place in Place Pigalle in the 1870s would help a lot."

He had gone to the library to make his search. He recalled Nicole Bruante's date of death from his family tree, so finding what they had expected to find hadn't been all that difficult. It was just a matter of finding the right newspapers—the ones that had been in circulation in 1877—and searching the digital records for accident reports and deaths, on or around June 13th. This was good—very good. Henri patted his coat pocket, making sure that he still had the newspaper clipping and the obituary that he had found, safely folded and tucked away.

Yes, this was very, *very* good. There was no way, now, that they could ever consider sending Nicole back—because if they did, she would die.

He smiled as he walked the last few meters, from the sidewalk onto the front porch of his house. "Good afternoon, Inspector Crossier," he said pleasantly. "How can I help you?"

Henri Bruante hadn't even looked surprised to see her. Michèle Crossier had gotten there just a few minutes earlier, standing with her arms crossed in front of his house, trying to deciding if she should linger there or return later, when she saw him approaching down *Rue du Bac* from around the corner of the street's intersection with *Saint Germain Boulevard.* Now, she waited patiently as he unlocked his door, a tedious process that involved three keys and the de-activation of a security alarm that was operated by a touch-pad located just to the right of the doorjamb. Henri often had costly artwork inside, perhaps even now, Michèle assumed, which explained the semi-paranoid behavior.

She knew exactly why she hadn't taken him off guard with her visit. His niece, Susanne Bruante, had undoubtedly warned him that the police would most likely come to call; but that was all right. The questions she had to ask him did not require the element of surprise, so it didn't really matter that he had been expecting her. The Bruante relative, Claudine Bignon, on the other hand, had been taken completely off-guard by Michèle's visit this morning—and that had been a beautiful thing, indeed. Michèle had suspected that prostitution and small-time drug trafficking might be sidelines for the attractive young stripper; and sure enough, when the half-naked Claudine had answered the door to her apartment at 7:00 a.m., she had a man in her bed that she claimed was her boyfriend. Michèle knew better than that—one glance at the look on the guy's face when Michèle had shown them her badge, plus the way he had scrambled to get dressed and excuse himself in a nervous rush, had said it all.

Prostitution was not illegal in Paris, but drug dealing was. Claudine kept looking uneasily over her shoulder at a plastic bag under her bed, probably thinking that if she had only looked in the peephole before opening the door to a Paris police officer, she could have flushed the entire stash down the toilet. Now she could only pray that the stony-faced Inspector Crossier was here on a different agenda. Michèle intended to use this hope as some very effective leverage in her upcoming interrogation.

Claudine Bruante resembled her cousin, d'Orsay's assistant director—not identical, but close enough to pass for the Susanne Bruante lookalike whose image had been captured on the grainy, shadow-plagued footage from the museum crime scene. Claudine brushed her dark hair—wild and unkempt, but in an undeniably sexy, "you caught me in bed with my legs spread" kind of way—from her hazel eyes, the typical Bruante shade, but bloodshot. Her nose was Susanne's too, but the shape of her face was more oval, less narrow. The curves of her body were more pronounced than Susanne's, narrowing inward from a generous size C bust to a very slender waist, and then out again and gently down, her hips tapering into long and shapely legs. She was pretty, even striking. What a shame Claudine Bruante-Bignon had settled for this kind of life.

Michèle stepped into the apartment, a tiny, well-kept efficiency with a pull-out bed on one wall, the sheets a tangle of sweaty passion, and a stove and sink on the other. The place was bare bones when it came to furnishings, but spotless and neat. Claudine motioned toward one of two metal kitchen chairs, thinking perhaps that offering hospitality to what she undoubtedly thought was a vice detective would divert attention from being caught red-handed. Michèle glanced knowingly at the package poking partly out from under the bed, and Claudine most definitely noticed. Good. The girl would talk if she thought that it would save her skin.

Michèle wondered how a nice girl from a good family had ended up like this, selling her body for money and probably acting as a go-between for some minor drug dealers in the red-light district. Perhaps the gig as a *putain* had started with a large tip from a stage-side admirer, given in exchange for a quick liaison in her apartment after her shift was over. The word would spread quickly in those circles, and before she knew what had happened, Claudine might have had two or three takers a week, showing up for Claudine's strip show in their business suits and ending up naked in her bed shortly after closing.

Maybe it had become too much to handle for Claudine, alone; perhaps the man who approached her unannounced as she exited the dressing room one night offering to manage the confusing stream of after-hours customers seemed so sincere, so kind, and so competent. In short order, Claudine had started making much more money working for him than she had ever made on her own—but at a dreadful price.

Michèle looked closely at Claudine, easily imagining the subservient employee being lured into increasingly dangerous liaisons, undoubtedly with the promise of outrageous monetary compensation. Little by little, perhaps, things had gotten out of hand. So many young women in Paris—not only strippers, but also students, and waitresses, and even housewives—had turned to the easy and lucrative sideline of prostitution, so why not Claudine? It made sense—complete and logical sense. Were there drugs involved? Undoubtedly. Often, the two professions went hand in hand.

Michèle, feeling certain now that the John Doe who had been murdered in the museum was Claudine's pimp—or drug supplier—had no problem picturing the scenario in her mind. Maybe Claudine had disappointed a client or missed an appointment or two, or failed to deliver an order. Maybe she had kept some of the product for herself. Her panderer had promised retribution; Claudine, having no one else to turn to, had called her uncle Henri in a panic. He would act to protect her, as any good uncle would, perhaps even resorting to extremes to do so.

But how in the world had Henri and Claudine persuaded the victim to come to the museum? Michèle hadn't quite worked that part of things out yet, but she had some theories. Had Henri, or even Susanne, given Claudine an access card, instructing her to lure the man to d'Orsay with the promise of sexual appeasement, her wildness unleashed in the soundproofed and deserted basement where she could freely seduce him without having to worry about neighbors eavesdropping on her moans and cries of contrived ecstasy?

Henri would be waiting patiently in the museum's basement, of course, hiding quietly behind the benzene tanks and heavy machinery, choosing an opportune moment to quietly approach the villain from behind with a blunt object while his niece's panderer was distracted with the temptation of Claudine's nudity, and so much more. After inflicting the fatal head injury, Claudine and Henri would have worked together to lift the body and stuff it into the pressure tank. This explanation, Michèle thought, seemed the most plausible.

But there were inconsistencies, unanswered questions, and pieces of the puzzle that simply didn't fit. Michèle's proposed basement crime scene, for instance, was devoid of blood—not even a trace. And then there was the pressure chamber, clean as a whistle on the inside, an expected consequence of the chemical wash of course; but spotless on the outside too, surprising but true. There simply was no evidence trail—nothing in the basement; nothing on the outside of the restoration tank; and, most importantly, nothing leading across the basement, out into the hallway, and up the elevator or stairs, to the gallery above.

But it wasn't just the "hows" that didn't add up; the "whys" were enigmatic, too. Why would Henri and Claudine feel compelled to crush the body in a corrosion removal pressure chamber; and more importantly, why would they even want to move the body? Why not just leave him in the pressure tank?

At this stage of the game, Michèle had more questions than answers, an impasse that she hoped to leave far behind, after today's interrogations.

Claudine had denied it all at first, beginning with the prostitution. Then, with some well-placed words by her interrogator, and another deliberate look or two under the bed, Claudine had suddenly became more talkative.

"Who's your manager?" Michèle had asked pointedly.

"There's more than one."

"Have any of them ever threatened you?"

"All the time."

Now they were getting somewhere. "Serious threats?"

She shrugged and wouldn't look Michèle in the eye. "Sometimes."

Although Claudine wouldn't name names, Michèle felt ever more certain now that this young woman was the one on the museum footage, and the dead man was one of her pimps or a drug supplier.

“Where were you on Wednesday, the first of June, between the hours of midnight and one a.m.?”

Claudine had not been working at the strip club; she denied having had a client in her bed that night, as well. Claudine had no alibi, so now all Michèle needed was the DNA evidence—the sample swab obtained from Claudine Bignon just a little while ago at the station—and she’d be golden.

Now it was time to concentrate on Henri, who had just taken the third key out of the third lock, opened the door to his workshop, and invited her in with a gracious smile. “Would you like something to drink, inspector?” he asked as he motioned her inside, the picture of composed and unruffled calm.

“No thank you.” She took a seat on a wooden chair situated at the end of a long table that obviously doubled as a workbench, and Henri pulled up a metal stool. “I had a little visit this morning with your niece,” Michèle informed him, eyeing him carefully for a reaction.

“Which one?” he asked, his expression flat.

“Claudine Bruante Bignon.” He nodded, as if he had expected that answer. “When were you last in touch with her?” Michèle continued.

“I tried to call her this morning, but got her voicemail.”

He had probably intended to give her a warning, but Claudine had been otherwise engaged. “When did you see her last?”

“About a year ago. We’re not that close.”

“Are you sure you didn’t see her in the early morning hours, on June first?”

He shook his head. “No,” he replied calmly, without even a hint of edginess. “I didn’t see her then.”

“Where were you that morning?”

“Here, at home—asleep.”

Henri Bruante had no alibi either. Today was Michèle’s lucky day, and she was hitting pay dirt. “Have you been working for d’Orsay, restoring a metal Rodin sculpture?”

“You know I have, or else you wouldn’t be asking,” he answered, his tone blasé.

"Have you used the high-pressure restoration tank in the basement lately?"

He cocked his head slightly, looking as if something had just clicked in his head. This was the first reaction that had registered on his face. Was there something about the corrosion removal chamber that had triggered it? "Yes, in fact I have," he finally answered.

"On the thirty-first of May?"

"Yes, during the day."

"Have you used it since?"

"No. With all the commotion in the museum surrounding the murder, I haven't had a chance to get back there to finish my job."

"Does anyone else know how to operate the pressure tank?"

"Certainly. The museum contracts with other restorers from time to time. They all know how to operate that kind of machinery."

"What kind of damage do you think that machine would do to a human body if it was sealed inside?"

He looked past her, his gaze focused on the wall somewhere but really inward; then he nodded to himself, almost imperceptibly. It looked as if he had just put two and two together. "If someone were to turn the positive pressure switch on after sealing the chamber, I suppose the body would be...crushed."

Crushed—her thought, exactly.

He agreed to go down to the station for fingerprinting and for DNA testing, just in case new evidence came up that might require comparison matching. Henri was the second Bruante to visit the processing area of the police station within a two-hour time span. This was not a good day for the Bruante family—but a very good day, indeed, for a certain homicide detective.

Chapter Fifteen

John Noland stood outside *Gare du Nord*, Paris's central rail station. His journey on the Eurostar Express from London had been rapid and comfortable. Although he had chosen a partially protected location to wait for his ride, he was still getting wet. The rain, which had been coming down in buckets when he first stepped outside, had slowed down substantially; still, each gust of wind sprayed him spitefully.

He looked at his wristwatch. Susanne would be here any second now, in a red BMW, she had said. As he peered into the drizzle, he thought he saw it now, approaching from the left side of the train station, cutting across *La Place Napoléon III*.

He wondered if the years had changed her physically. She had been so beautiful. Would she still be as stunning now as she had been then? Would he still feel that same attraction that he had felt for her on that first day he'd seen her at Northwestern's undergraduate library, or when she'd removed her loosely tied bathrobe as the model for the painting class his senior year, displaying her perfect body in front of a roomful of admirers? Later, when she'd chosen him and paid him all of those late-night visits during the four months while they had dated, and long after she had left him, the memories of her sexual allure had lingered, for more than a year in fact. The very thought of her had kept him awake at night, preventing him from even looking at another woman. He had been deeply in love with her, in those days, and the way she had left him without even a single word of explanation or goodbye had devastated him.

But that was then, and this was now. He was over her—or at least that was what he kept telling himself. He had a worry, more than just subconsciously, that he might relapse when he saw her, a reaction that he hoped he had the willpower to resist. He reminded himself that she had called him to enlist his help with a scientific anomaly, not to rekindle a romance that he now knew had been entirely one-sided. It might help if her beauty had faded—he hoped it had, in fact. It would be so much easier to focus on the problem at hand if he could put the old, desirable

Susanne away and replace her with a new, unappealing one.

Although it felt superficial to think that way, he knew it was true. Physical attractiveness had lured him into a painful relationship before, and, like most other men, he could easily be fooled again. He would have to keep his guard up, or else he might easily revert to the way it had been—or, more accurately, the way he had been: the young and vulnerable John.

As her car approached, he thought about how he had idolized her as the ideal woman, physically; how he had been blinded by her sex appeal. He flashed back to that night at the café, their first date. He had sketched her where she sat, across from him at the small corner table by the fireplace. She had worn a grey sweater-coat, which she quickly removed because of the heat from the fire. He knew full well what her body looked like underneath the tight turquoise t-shirt that pushed against the rounded fullness of her breasts, giving him more than just a hint of the details underneath. He had seen it all before: her splendid nudity, just a few yards away from him on the model's pallet, so close, yet so far—and so completely unreachable, then.

That night, suddenly, when they were both very young, she was actually there with him, sitting within unbelievable arms' length from him in the café—his dream come true, the wavy fingers of her rich brown hair touching on her chest and drawing attention to what the cotton barely covered, what he longed to see again. The rising steam from her mug of cocoa had reminded him of smoke: panting wisps of pale and white, breathing in and out and up and around, slender fingers against her t-shirt, transformed by charcoal on his drawing paper into lines of curling grey. Her face, her arms, and her breasts became one and the same with the fire, smoke, and steam: images sketched on paper that he had completed later.

He had truly treasured that drawing of her, which had taken on a life of its own after she had left him. She was the goddess that had inexplicably picked John Noland, a mortal, and now all that he had left to prove that she had actually come down from her pedestal to grace his earthly reality was that heavenly picture, which he still kept in the bottom of his dresser drawer.

It was strange how he worshipped those memories. He knew now that they were only memories, and he hoped he wouldn't succumb when he saw her again.

He was drawn back to the present when her car pulled up, and the passenger door opened abruptly from the inside. He got in, wet from the weather, and closed the door; delaying the inevitable just a few seconds longer, his gaze focused on the windshield and the unrelenting wipers, which mercilessly kept time against the raindrops. "It's really raining out there," he said in fluent French. Strange, how fearful he was to face her, troubled by the delicious fear that she might still be as beautiful as he remembered. He took in a deep breath to steel his nerves, pulling the seat belt across his chest at the same time, turning partway in his seat to greet her, and actually fumbling with the buckle latch.

Yes, she was still, without a doubt, incredibly beautiful; in fact the years had added, rather than detracted, from her physical attractiveness. "You haven't changed a bit," he managed to say, feeling as though his words were tripping over each other. Her beauty, at present, was enhanced by a self-awareness that she had only partly had in college. To put it simply, she was exceedingly comfortable now in her skin and probably reveled in the knowledge that her desirability was difficult, if not impossible, to match.

"And you haven't exactly lost your looks either," she teased, shaking out her hair with a sidelong glance, which he sensed was meant to test the waters between them. Yes, she was flirting; but no, it wasn't sincere. He wouldn't take the bait, because if he did, she'd reel him in and toss him away again, just as she had before.

He drew in a breath, determined not to show her that his weakness might still be her. "So, this is Paris," he said, resorting to small talk, hoping perhaps that diverting her with the trivial would save him.

"Yes, it is." She gazed over at him for a moment, sizing him up it seemed, and quickly inferring from his stony face that he had no interest whatsoever in rekindling their romance. To his great relief, she launched directly into the matter at hand. "Here's the deal, John. I need you close. If you're going to help me, there's no possible way you'll be able to do that from a distance. Cancel your hotel reservation. I have two extra rooms at my place. Nicole's in one, and you can take the other."

He started to object, but she interrupted him with a gesture, unwilling to hear anything that threatened to contradict her agenda. "Look in the rear-view mirror," she commanded. He did, and saw a blue Audi following very close behind them. "I'm being tailed. If you stay in a hotel room, they'll never believe that you're my boyfriend."

What in the world had he gotten himself into? He hadn't expected the police to be right on top of them; already the first few seconds of this crazy reunion had taken on a surreal quality. Boyfriend? This was a problem. He had come here on a scientific adventure, but it looked like she intended to draw him into a soap opera instead.

"I'm sure they snapped a photo of you as you got in, and they've already sent it in to headquarters. Their computer techs will be able to ID you with no problem. Your face has been all over the Internet lately."

"Susanne, I'm not sure this is what I signed up for." This was outrageous, actually. He felt his face turning red. "The last thing I need is trouble with the Paris police. Do you understand that this could even become a diplomatic issue?" He could see the headlines now: "American scientist arrested as an accomplice in the d'Orsay murder."

"Come on, I didn't drag you here." She turned the wheel sharply and took a corner rather too fast as she glanced in the rear-view mirror. "You knew the story, John. I told you everything on the phone the other day." She shrugged. "Go back, if you'd like. I'm not holding you captive."

He told himself to calm down. This was a once-in-a-lifetime opportunity, after all. If what Susanne had told him was actually true, a discovery of this magnitude could very likely propel his career down a path leading directly to a Nobel Prize. He pushed his anger down a level, consciously willing himself to relax.

She must have seen from the look on his face that he was weighing the pros and cons, and that the pros were winning. "If you can send Nicole back, it will be a win-win for both of us," she said. "I don't need her here anymore—she's served her purpose, and now she's just extra baggage that has to go. For you, proving that someone can travel from one time to another by actually doing it would guarantee you more than just a page in the history books. You'd be the most famous scientist the world has ever known—bigger than Einstein, even."

Then it hit him. Eighteen years had passed, but Susanne's modus operandi was still the same. Nicole was no longer useful, so Susanne would toss her away—just as she had tossed him away, after he had served his purpose. She had done this to him without feeling even a tiny bit of remorse; even now, there were no apologies. Why? In a rare moment of insight, John suddenly understood why.

Now it all made sense. Susanne would never say she was sorry, because she didn't even realize that she had done anything wrong. Susanne was the very epitome of selfishness: a person who was so completely focused on herself that she could see nothing beyond her own wants and needs. Her narcissism had made her oblivious to other people, to the extent that it never even occurred to her that she was being hurtful. He suddenly realized that there was nothing inherently malicious about Susanne—she was just incredibly self-centered, a truth that did not entirely excuse her actions but went a long way toward explaining them. Being out for herself did not necessarily make Susanne a bad person—just an egotistically unmindful one.

Well, one thing was certain—this was not his style. Yes, he would try to return this Nicole to her rightful place in time, but not just because it would make his work—his science—famous. If it was possible to send her back, he would, because having her here instead of there could drastically change the course of intended events. Imagine, for instance, if Nicole was supposed to have children that wouldn't be born now, because she was residing in the wrong Time-Shell. Or, what if she had been an integral part of some life-and-death event in 1877, but the crucial outcome was altered because she was not there to prevent it—or to cause it? If he could return her to the past, he would. He would do it for science, and for humanity; he would do it to preserve the order of things, and to ensure that what should be, would be; and if he became famous in the process, then so be it.

But these thoughts gave him reason to pause. What about Nicole? He realized again, as he had after his phone call with Susanne while he was in London, that they were talking about a human being, not a lab rat. Susanne might view Nicole as an insignificant means to an end, but John refused to subscribe to this philosophy. He hadn't even met Nicole, but that didn't really matter. She was a person, and she deserved to be treated like one.

"All right," he finally answered. "I'll stay. What's your plan?"

"Your agenda here needs to be viewed as anything but professional. Act like we're involved when we get to my place."

He could do that—a little handholding wouldn't kill him. He nodded his assent. "Okay." This charade would probably even help him gain the closure he so sorely needed. If he could touch her without feeling that old thrill, it would spell victory.

They drove on, and he used the opportunity to call the hotel on his cell phone and cancel his reservation. Finally, Susanne stopped at a light; when it turned green, she turned down a street that was marked at the intersection as Avenue Georges V.

"I think we should cut them a break. I'll introduce you when we get out," she told him.

She pulled in to a parking space on the street, directly in front of a building with three levels that he assumed was her place of residence, and cut the engine. She smiled mischievously. "This will be great fun. You get out first, and then open the door for me. That way you'll look like the perfect *petite ami*."

The rain had stopped. He got out of the car and walked on puddled pavement over to the driver's side to play his role. He opened the door; put out his hand; felt her skin on his, a distant memory suddenly revived; helped her out, her body brushing against his as she stood; and closed the door with his other hand, surprised—no, shocked—to feel her pull him toward her. Before he could resist, she was actually pressing her body against his, and then her lips. The kiss was soft, wet, and lingering. He started to feel dizzy.

But wait—was the kiss sincere? Hardly. She disengaged, and warm turned to cold in a heartbeat, the manufactured passion just a show, yet another means to an end—a meaningless ten seconds of feigned intimacy, intended to lend credence to Susanne Bruante's agenda. She hadn't changed—she would never change; and somehow, this realization felt good. She was not the one—had never been the one. Susanne was Susanne, intensely focused on her own wants and needs, then and now, the polar opposite of what John Noland wanted and needed in a partner. Claire had been right, that day in the hallway when she had broken the news to him that Susanne had left without even bothering to say goodbye. He did deserve better; he could see that now. Funny that it had taken him eighteen years and a trip to Paris on a rainy day to finally come to that realization.

"That should do it," she said, just as if the kiss had been some kind of a business transaction. She took his hand in hers, the touch of her skin on his no longer electric, leading him to the trunk where he grabbed his one suitcase, and she the other.

"Yes, that should do it," John said with a smile. He was over her, once and for all. He was free.

He followed her lead, putting the suitcase on the sidewalk and following her across the street to the blue Audi. Two red-faced gendarmes sat inside. She knocked on the glass with her knuckles, and the window came sliding down.

"*Bonjour, messieurs*," she said. "How's the Susanne Bruante duty going?" The police didn't know how to respond to the question, but it didn't seem to matter to her—she just kept on talking. "I want to introduce you to my boyfriend, Dr. John Noland. Just so you don't wonder, he'll be staying with me for a few days. You can mark him down as present on your surveillance log."

She pulled him away, one arm around his waist, and after they crossed over to the other side of the street, she drew him against her again. The second kiss was even more passionate than the first. This time, though, he didn't feel a thing—nothing. What a beautiful, beautiful moment. Magically, Susanne—actually, that would be the memory of Susanne—no longer held him. It was over; he could finally move on with his life.

He followed her up the stairs—four sets, up and back, and up and back again, the journey leading them past the first floor landing and then up to the second. Susanne opened the door to her apartment and stepped through with John and his luggage in tow, into a spacious foyer with a hallway directly ahead leading to several bedrooms and bathrooms. He saw a dining room with a kitchen hiding behind a swinging door to his right, and a living room to his left.

Susanne craned her neck forward, looking into the dining room and then the other way, into the living room. "Nicole must have gone back to sleep," she said. "She had a rough night."

"Why?" he asked.

"A nightmare—one that will probably be of great interest to you."

He gave her a quizzical look. "The interpretation of dreams isn't my specialty. You'll have to find yourself a psychologist to help you with that problem."

"No," she countered, "this dream is right up your alley. You'll see. We'll talk about it when Uncle Henri comes. I sent him on an errand to find us some proof."

What in the world was she talking about? "Proof—of what?"

"Nicole thinks the dream was a memory," she answered, in a matter-of-fact tone of voice. "Let's see what Henri comes up with." She looked at her watch, the frown on her face intimating more irritation than it did concern. "I wonder if Henri got held up, somewhere. He should have called back by now. I'll try to reach him in a few minutes."

She headed down the hall, and John followed with a shrug. He would find out what she was talking about soon enough. He would get nowhere by pushing it now.

As they approached the first room on the left, Susanne stopped for a moment and tapped on the closed door. "Nicole," she called. "Our time travel consultant is here."

John heard what sounded like rustling sheets, followed by a voice calling back from inside. "*Mon Dieu*," it said, "I did not mean to sleep again, for such a long time."

Susanne continued walking, motioning for John to follow. She opened a door to her right, just a few paces down the hall and across from Nicole's room. "You can stay in here," she said. "I think you'll be comfortable."

He was just about to enter with his two suitcases, when the door behind him opened. He turned, and his mouth fell open.

There she stood, a close-to-identical replica of Susanne, and there he stood, speechless. The resemblance was more than astounding, to the extent that he never would have believed it if he hadn't seen it with his own eyes: the rich brown hair falling across her shoulders and curling slightly to touch her angled jaw and prominent cheekbones; the hazel eyes, competing brown against green with equal intensity; the petite, slightly upturned nose; and a body, covered loosely by a terrycloth bathrobe, that he felt certain would be a duplicate of Susanne's underneath. In a flash, he recalled that night when Susanne had emerged from the dressing room at the art studio, her robe—terrycloth, also—boldly left untied, her immodest frontal nudity intended to taunt and to tease. Nicole's robe, unlike Susanne's, was tied, but in her rush to open the door, the loose knot was coming undone, resulting in this moment of accidental exposure that seemed oddly, and unbelievably, reminiscent of Susanne's identical but intentional display of nudity, that first night in the art studio.

His eyes drifted downward, he couldn't help it. When she saw where he was staring, she realized what had happened and hastily grabbed the front of the bathrobe, pulling the two halves closed, her neck flushing from alabaster to a subtle shade of pink. Nicole's discretion was obviously not a character trait that she shared with Susanne.

John couldn't help but recognize that Nicole's outward appearance might be all Susanne, above and below the neck—but what was she truly like, inside? He wondered to what extent Nicole's personality, attitudes, and viewpoints corresponded with her distant descendants'. Genetics was a funny thing, and now he found himself gawking at a full-fledged case in point, standing right here in front of him.

The moment of mutual silence had become awkward, but it still took him a few seconds to find his voice. "Nicole?" he finally inquired, in a tone that he hoped sounded both smart and professional, intended not only to diffuse the slightly embarrassing moment that the two of them had just shared, but also to recover his fumble. His deaf-and-dumb impersonation, coupled with an admittedly adolescent reaction to Nicole's inadvertent nudity, had made him look inexperienced and parochial. He was here to provide his advice and to use his skills to deliver a solution to her problem. Ogling her with a stupid schoolboy's face just wouldn't do. "I'm John," he continued, holding his hand out in greeting. "It's very nice to meet you."

"Bonjour, monsieur," she responded, with a smile that would melt an iceberg. "I am happy, too, to gain your acquaintance." She used the old formal French—the prim and proper grammar that old Madame Barrat had taught him, her chalkboard stick in hand, as John sat attentively, three days a week, in the front row of French III when he had studied the language in high school. It was funny to hear the old-fashioned styling coming from someone so young; but Nicole had, after all, come from a different time. John shouldn't have been at all surprised.

Nicole took his hand to shake it. Her touch felt familiar; as he looked down, he noticed that she had Susanne's fingers, too. He gazed into her eyes for one fleeting second, but had to look away—because half a second more, and they would have held him captive forever, just as Susanne's had eighteen years before. Would her lips feel as soft, her skin as smooth, and her hair as lush as Susanne's? He actually started to sweat. *Oh God, help me*. Was it happening all over again?

He knew himself, and this was bad. If he didn't get control of himself now, the bad would quickly turn to ugly, and it would happen all over again.

Perhaps it already had. He looked into her eyes again—he couldn't resist. He was a moth lured irresistibly into the light, despite its promise of certain death, and in an instant, he knew.

It was happening, all over again.

Chapter Sixteen

Nicole stepped out of her bathrobe, standing nude in front of the closet to sift through the clothes hanging there with one hand, trying to pick out what to wear. After a second, she pulled out a white sundress patterned with red flowers along the bottom, the blossoms climbing up ivy-like in a diagonal across the front to connect with a dense bed of colorful petals encircling the chest. She slipped it over her head, settling the straps over her shoulders and adjusting the flowered bosom just so, over her uncovered breasts. Susanne had lent her some bras and panties, but why bother? A dress like this one was meant to touch on nothing, cotton whispering directly on tingling skin, breathing a soft and secret moan of indulgence to barely hide what pushed gently outward, firm and supple beneath.

He was handsome, this John Noland—but he didn't seem to know it. His sandy hair was cut short, the style in this time for some odd reason, but the barber had left enough on the top for John to push some over to the side, the wavy strands touching on the line of his two intelligent and serious eyebrows. Men where she came from always let their hair grow, and she couldn't help but imagine John's hair that way—long, thick, and lush, pulled behind and tied against the back of his neck, perhaps with a string that she had knotted. She sighed, lost in that vision as she considered some shoes, but then decided against it. She preferred bare feet; anyway, she would not be leaving the apartment today.

Yes, this John Noland had a handsome face and a very attractive body, too. She could see the lines of his stomach, tense and firm, between the widely spaced buttons of his crisply pressed shirt, just as she could see his chest, sloping outward to broad shoulders, not overly muscled but definitely strong. She thought his neck was perfect, not too long or too short, supporting a strong and masculine jaw, full and expressive lips, a thin nose—and those eyes. They were crystal blue; and although they had met her gaze only briefly (twice, to be exact), his blue and her greenish brown had shared an undeniable moment of understanding. He was attracted to her too, she could tell—she could always tell.

Nothing would ever come of it, but it didn't hurt to dream. John had come here to help Susanne get rid of her problem, and he seemed like the type of man who always took his job seriously. Anyway, it was unrealistic to think of him as anything more than a doctor, a mechanic, or a technician; and in fact, it would be in her best interest to make sure she didn't. She wasn't normally the kind to love them and leave them (unlike Susanne), and it would be no fun to fall for someone from another time and place, just as she was getting ready to return home. There could be no relationship in this bizarre situation, when and if she was transported back to 1877. But this was all impossible, anyway. Just because she sensed the spark of attraction between them didn't mean that something would necessarily happen. If she thought with her head and not with her heart, everyone would be much better off.

She headed out into the hallway and down to the foyer, following the sounds of activity to the left. Susanne was in the dining room, setting out some food. Nicole pulled out a chair, sitting down at the far end, with her back facing the front entryway and the hallway leading to the bedrooms.

"Your old boyfriend seems very nice," Nicole said.

Susanne shrugged. "It doesn't really matter how nice he is, as long as he's able to help us."

"Was he a good lover?" It just came out, before she could stop herself. She was wicked to ask, but she simply couldn't resist—she just had to know. One thing about fantasies: the more you colored them in, the better the image turned out.

Susanne nodded, completely emotionless. "*Oui*. Let's just say that he really knew what to do, for someone so incredibly inexperienced."

That could mean one thing only. "So, you were his first?"

She nodded again. "He admitted to it, afterward. I would have never known—it came so naturally to him, somehow."

"You ended it, not him, I am sure. You must have really hurt him when you left."

"*C'est la vie*." Susanne arranged some fruit on a plate. "He got over me, so no harm done—*n'est ce pas*?"

Nicole felt certain that plenty of harm was done. Poor John. She wished she could console him, but she tried to steer her thoughts away from that particular corridor. "He is very handsome," she said quietly, almost to herself. He was good-looking, there was no denying it, and Nicole was not the sort of person to keep her thoughts to herself.

Susanne shot Nicole an unpleasant glance from across the table. "Don't get any ideas. Remember, you'll be going back soon, if all goes well."

That comment really got Nicole's hackles up. She didn't need that kind of self-serving advice from anyone, especially her egocentric great-great-great granddaughter. Nicole was more than capable of deciding about these things herself. She had half a mind to go right ahead and follow her animal instincts, just to see how Susanne would react. She wouldn't, of course—too many people would get hurt; but it felt very nice to imagine it.

"I called Henri," Susanne said, changing the subject. "He was held up with the police for a while, but he's on his way here now. He found it." She said it almost triumphantly, and Nicole's heart dropped.

She knew that her dream wasn't just a dream, but an actual memory. Now that Henri had uncovered some hard evidence that her suspicion was in fact true, it brought the horrible reality of it all abruptly out of the shadows and into the harsh light of day. What would happen now if she went back to 1877? If she returned, would she die that grim and dreadful death she had foreseen—no, remembered—in the early morning hours of a sleep that had been interrupted by the unthinkable? Or would she remember it all, when she got back, and alter the fate that awaited her, somehow, with this gift of foreknowledge? Maybe she would change the meeting place she had arranged in advance with her mother; perhaps she would cancel her visit with Edmond altogether. That way, he wouldn't run out in front of the carriage, and if he didn't need to be saved, Nicole wouldn't need to die.

There was only one problem with this hopeful scenario—namely, that Nicole might not remember that she was destined to die at Place Pigalle. If she had no memory of the impending tragedy, she would have no reason to change her plans. She reminded herself that she had been plagued with a dense amnesia when she had arrived here—a total lack of memory for everything and anything that had come before, her mind a complete blank, a condition that had lasted for two or three days, the recollections gradually coming back, but not all at once. Logic predicted that the exact same memory loss would happen when she took the difficult journey back. And what did that mean? Certain death, that's what—because Nicole would have no memories at all to warn her. She shivered. What a horrible, terrifying thought.

But failing to return could result in something much worse. What if Edmond's actions remained unaltered by Nicole's absence, and he still decided to run straight into the path of the galloping horses? What would happen to her little boy if she wasn't there to save him? Nicole could imagine it now: her mother letting go of Edmond's hand for just a split second, distracted perhaps by something transpiring on the other side of the fountain; turning just a second too late, grabbing for him unsuccessfully; running to catch him, her path blocked, as it had been before, by a crowd of passing people. Nicole envisioned her little baby, running right under the crushing hooves of the carriage horses—his face in the dirt instead of hers; his blood on the road and his screams in the air, not Nicole's; his soul rising up to see itself, down there, a trampled and unmoving body, rather than his mother's; and his life taken much too early, the wrong life in fact: his instead of hers.

"We'll need John's input on all this—you know, to tell us what it all means, and what we can do about it," Susanne said.

What it all means? It meant nothing to Susanne, that much was clear. All she cared about was her theory—the one that Nicole's coincidental appearance in Susanne's work place one hundred and thirty four years after the fact would prove, beyond the shadow of a doubt, thanks to her. It was Nicole's hair in all of those paintings; this thing they called DNA analysis would attest to that, making Susanne rich and famous—or so she said. And what would Nicole get in return? A one-way ticket back to a grisly death, that's what.

"Before I can tell you what even a small part of it means," the voice behind her said, "I'll need a lot more information." She turned, and there he was, passing behind her over to the right, changed out of his dress clothes and looking much more casual now in jeans and a deep blue t-shirt. He pulled out the chair immediately beside her and sat down, dangerously close to her—much too close.

He looked over at her, and their eyes locked again—a brief and momentary joining, yet full of meaning. He was trying to hide it, but she could see right through him. He wanted her, she could tell; she could also tell that he was fighting the feeling as hard as he could. Why? For more than one reason, she felt sure. First, he was not here for pleasure, far from it; and second, getting involved with his assignment was simply not in line with professional decorum.

But there was another reason—she could sense it. He was scared of her. Terrified, in fact, and she thought she knew why. It was her appearance that frightened him so. She looked exactly like Susanne, after all, and that would be a source of distress for John if Susanne had broken his heart so long ago. Nicole tried to imagine what it might be like for him—finding out that his time-travel project could easily pass for Susanne's twin. The first thing he might conclude is that Nicole and Susanne were interchangeable, both of them the same person inside, as well as out; and that would be enough, on its own, to give him pause. Just on principle, Nicole would have to dispel that fear—in fact, she felt determined to do so. Did it really matter what John thought of her? Of course not; but she was not Susanne, and it pained her to think that just because they looked alike, John might assume that they were alike in every way. She was her own person, more dissimilar when likened to Susanne than similar, and she would make that clear to John, if that were the last thing she did before disappearing back into the past.

The video monitor by the door buzzed. "Speaking of information, that must be Henri," Susanne said lightly. "He's here to give us some—on newsprint, he claims."

"Your uncle?" John asked.

"The very same." Susanne went to the electronic remote to push the entry button.

"He's here because he found it," Nicole murmured softly, feeling numb. In a moment she would see it, and it would all come true. It would be real.

"Found what?" John asked, addressing Nicole. He leaned toward her, very close now, putting his hand on her arm for the briefest moment, the gesture so concerned, so kind. Had his fingers trembled when he placed them, with just a hint of intimacy, on her skin? She thought they had; she was trembling too.

"The obituary," Susanne answered plainly, as if she were talking about an invitation to a garden party instead of a death notice.

"Whose obituary?" John countered.

Nicole's mouth felt dry. She looked into John's eyes again, and this time he didn't look away. Was he giving her permission? His eyes said yes, and so she put her hand on his and kept it there. It felt right.

"Mine" she whispered.

~

Susanne buzzed him in almost immediately, but Henri lingered a moment, looking out of the corner of his eye at the surveillance car that had followed him, block by block, as he had made his way on foot from the police station to Susanne's apartment.

The car, a white Mercedes, had stopped right next to a blue Audi—Susanne's tail, no doubt, both of them just idling there with the windows down as gendarme spoke to gendarme. Then, just as Henri was about to step into the building, the white car eased into reverse, the driver giving an all-clear nod to his colleague. Henri turned part way as he entered the foyer; as he did so he saw the blue car, which had pulled out of its parking space, speed past him on its way to who knows where. As he climbed the stairs to the second floor landing, Henri glanced out the front window, making a mental note of the white car's new vantage point—directly across the street from Susanne's building, parked in the blue car's previous spot.

Was it their change of shift? Maybe, but he seriously doubted that. Henri, rather than Susanne, was now the person of greater interest to the police, and Henri would bet money that later, when he left Susanne's apartment to head home, the white car would discreetly pull out and follow him, keeping a safe but hard-to-miss distance, as he walked from Avenue Georges V to his house in the Saint-Germain-des-Prés neighborhood, a good twenty blocks from here.

He wondered what type of man this John Noland would turn out to be. Henri patted his inside jacket pocket, just to ensure that he still had the photocopy of Nicole's obituary that he had carefully folded and slid inside when he had left the library. This changed everything, in Henri's opinion. Susanne seemed to think that her ex-boyfriend, a scientist with expertise and, unbelievably, experience in the field of time travel, would be able to send Nicole back to the past. But how could they possibly consider doing that now, if it would mean certain death for their misplaced ancestor? In Henri's opinion, Nicole should stay, but what would John Noland say?

There would certainly be ramifications, in a scientific sense, from keeping someone from the past living here in the present; but could it be worse than carrying out a ghastly and unjust death sentence by re-establishing the status quo? Henri would make his argument, and they would go from there. He could only pray that their time-travel consultant had a sympathetic heart as well as an astute and analytical mind.

Susanne was waiting for Henri when he reached the top of the stairs, standing in the doorway to let him in. He followed her inside, eager to meet this scientist, whom he found sitting next to his subject, Nicole, at the dining room table. John Noland—tall and slim, with sandy blonde hair and piercing blue eyes—stood up, politely extending his hand to greet Henri. It struck Henri that seeing them seated next to each other gave the impression that they were a couple—an uneasy and artificially arranged one, granted, the two of them thrown together by circumstances, the eventual outcome of their blind date anyone's guess.

"I'm Dr. John Noland," the bio-astrophysicist said, with a serious look on his face. There was something in his eyes, though, that told Henri this man had empathy. No, John Noland definitely wasn't just a robot. Henri sensed that this was a man who would take the human into consideration and factor it prominently into the equation.

"I am Henri Bruante." He shook John's hand; the man's grip was firm and confident, matching Henri's. "I'm glad you're here," he added sincerely. "I hope you can help us." Henri glanced at Nicole, whose face looked paler than it had looked the night before. She was scared. "Help Nicole, that is," he corrected himself. Because, after all, this was about Nicole, wasn't it? In Henri's mind, nothing else really mattered at this point.

"I'm not certain I can help," John said. He was honest, too. "I'll need some background information first, and then we'll see."

John Noland sat back down and touched Nicole's arm, briefly but reassuringly. Henri breathed a sigh of relief. *Thank God.* This was a man with a level, intelligent, and compassionate head on his shoulders; he had a soul. Henri couldn't help but have a good feeling about their American guest, and first impressions were, after all, his specialty.

Susanne took a seat at the head of the table. His niece was very quiet, taking it all in, it seemed. What was she thinking? It would be interesting to eventually see where Susanne stood on all of this. One thing was for sure: she wouldn't be in favor of Nicole's staying in this century. Having her twin close by would just be too weird—and, quite frankly, Susanne didn't do well with competition. Not that Nicole would directly vie with Susanne for anything in particular; but just the thought of having a double around to divert attention from the one-and-only Susanne Bruante would be enough to incite more than a little jealousy.

"Should we start with what you found at *Le Bibliothèque Nationale*?" Susanne asked. Apparently, she was planning on functioning as the moderator.

Henri pulled out the copy of the newspaper clipping, unfolded it, leaned over, and placed it face-up on John's empty plate. John took a few seconds to read it, his eyes moving back and forth, his eyebrows knitted by the time he had reached the end. Good thing this American spoke and read fluent French. It would have been difficult to work through the complexities of what lay ahead if translation had to be thrown into the mix.

"Does this date," John inquired, turning the obituary around so it faced Henri, and placing his index finger directly on the line that showed a date of 13 June 1877, "correspond with Nicole's date of death in your family records?"

Henri nodded. "Yes, it does correspond, and Nicole's dream—the one that Susanne told me about early this morning over the phone—seems to fit exactly with the story that I heard about my great-grandmother's death, too."

"Nicole's nightmare," Susanne explained, "had to do with the accident that killed my great-great-great-grandmother."

John turned to Nicole. "Would you be comfortable telling me about the dream?" he asked gently.

Nicole swallowed hard, her gaze focused on a plate of fruit right in front of her. It was clear to Henri that this would be very difficult, emotionally, for her to recount. "I was back at home," she began, her voice low, "in Montmartre, going to meet my little boy, Edmond, at Place Pigalle. He stays with my mother, you see, and I had made arrangements to meet them for a visit in the square at 2:00. I was a little bit late; he saw me from across the way, and—" She covered her face with her hands, taking a deep breath to calm herself. Henri handed her a napkin, and she dabbed the tears from her eyes.

"Go on, Nicole," John encouraged her, kindly. "It's okay."

"He was standing near the fountain, holding my mother's hand, but she let go." She paused for a few seconds, as she tried to recall. "No, that's not true—it wasn't my mother's fault. Edmond was pulling and tugging, trying to get free, and then he succeeded." She turned now, to look John right in the eyes. "I think I saved him, but I can't be sure. He ran in front of the horses, but I did too. He was in front of me, then next to me—and then maybe behind. I grabbed him by the arm, I pulled him around me, but then they were on us—on me. I remember the hooves, the blood, the dirt, the screams. And then it all went black."

"If this is what really happened in 1877," Susanne interjected, "can science explain how a person can actually remember something that hasn't happened to them yet?" She didn't sound skeptical, just curious. It seemed as though she knew John would be able to give them an answer.

John was hardly stumped. "Quite frankly, I think this phenomenon is easy to explain, given the circumstances. Think about it: from Nicole's perspective in the here and now, everything occurring prior to the year 2011 happened in the past, including events in her life that didn't physically transpire before she was sucked into the Time-Tunnel. She remembers her death on the thirteenth of June at two-twenty p.m. in 1877 because it's an incident that no longer exists ahead of her on the river of time, but behind her. By jumping ahead of herself on the Stream, her future has, in essence, become her past. Does that make sense?"

It actually did make sense, but it staggered the imagination. Now, it was time to address the dilemma that this logical distortion of the past and future had produced. "I'll leave the science to you," Henri said, "but what about the ethics? What should we do now? If you can somehow figure out how to send Nicole back to 1877, you'll be returning her to a place where she'll end up being trampled to death. We can't do that to her. I won't allow it." Henri sat back in his chair and crossed his arms, waiting for the rebuttal—which came, of course, from Susanne.

"If Nicole returns to the past, she won't necessarily die," his niece declared.

"And you've concluded this—how?" He met Susanne's gaze with an equally unwavering one.

"She'll remember," Susanne replied, as if this assertion was incontestable. "Because she'll have her memories to warn her, she'll change her plans and won't end up meeting her mother and Edmond at Place Pigalle. As a result, no one's life will be lost." She shrugged and smiled, probably thinking her victory had been won. "It's very simple, really. Nicole can return safely."

"I thought of that, too," Nicole said, "but what about my memory loss?"

Henri cocked his head, looking inquisitively at Susanne. "Yes, that's right. What about the amnesia?"

"She had amnesia because of the concussion," Susanne countered rapidly, doing her best to hide a hint of fluster. "She won't hit her head on the trip back. She'll remember, and it will be just fine." She spoke as if the very act of saying it would make it true.

"The amnesia might not have been the result of her head trauma," John said, transforming Susanne's hint of a blush into the real thing. "The mice we've sent back and forth through a Virtual Hole become confused and disoriented after one or two trips. The electromagnetic properties of the Time-Tunnel probably interact with the electrical circuitry of the brain's neurons. I'm afraid the memory loss might happen again, simply as a result of traveling through the Virtual Hole."

Susanne's lips compressed, but she didn't say a word.

"It's not only about myself." Nicole put her hand on her forehead and closed her eyes for a moment. "It's Edmond I'm worried about. I have to go back, to save him."

"But wait a minute, Nicole," Henri said. "If you're not there on that day in 1877, your mother won't have a reason to meet you at Place Pigalle, and Edmond won't have a reason to run in front of a carriage. If you stay here, Edmond will be safer than if you return."

"Not necessarily," Susanne said heatedly, sounding as if she had found her second wind. "What if Edmond and his grandmother go to Pigalle anyway, and Nicole isn't there to make the save? Nicole's right, Henri—she has to go back, because if she doesn't, and Edmond dies, both you and I will cease to exist. Without Edmond around to eventually father children, there will be no us, *Ton-ton*—it's as simple as that."

Susanne had a point, didn't she? Henri looked over at John, who nodded his acknowledgement that Susanne was indeed correct. "I'm afraid that Nicole and Susanne have won the argument, Henri. If I can figure out how to send Nicole back safely, we should do it, in order to keep the stream of time on its intended course, in a manner of speaking."

Henri was about to object, but John held up his hand to stop him. "My main concern is making sure Edmond doesn't die. The Bruante line depends on it."

"But—" Henri began.

"But," John echoed, continuing his train of thought with an index finger raised, "if I can achieve that without sacrificing Nicole's life, all the better, wouldn't you agree?"

Now that was more like it, Henri thought. "Of course, but how would you propose to do that?"

"I'm open to suggestions. The first thing that comes to my mind is the obituary."

"What about it?" Susanne asked.

"What if we send her back with it?"

"That would terrify her," Henri said.

"Exactly. That's the point." John smiled and patted Nicole's arm. She looked at him with raised brows.

It just might work, Henri thought. "If Nicole saw her own death notice, she would be sure to avoid the scene of the accident. Are you proposing we put a copy of it in her pocket, or something?"

John nodded. "Why not?"

There was only one problem. "When Nicole came through the Time-Tunnel the first time, didn't she lose her clothes on the way?" Henri asked. Granted, he had only heard a cursory summary of Nicole's time travel experience from Susanne, but he knew for a fact that Nicole and her traveling companion had both been naked when they appeared in the gallery after being sucked through, ten days ago.

"I think we ended up nude on this side because we were nude on the other," Nicole said. "You see, he and I had been busy in bed together, when the Time-Tunnel opened."

Had John's face just turned red? Henri thought it had. The scientist cleared his throat. "Nicole's right. I've sent back rodents with identification tags attached to them, and when they ricochet back, the tags are still there. I think it's highly unlikely that the Virtual Hole would somehow cause clothing fibers to disintegrate."

"That might actually be successful." Henri nodded; he would go for that, if Nicole did, and of course Susanne would, too. He gave Susanne a look that said "truce," and she nodded her agreement.

"Getting back, though, to the matter at hand," John said, "there are many problems here, but one that we need to concentrate on first. We have a time deadline. Today is June tenth, correct?"

Susanne looked at the calendar on her watch. "Yes, why?"

"Because that means we have only three days to return Nicole to her Time-Shell in 1877 before the incident at Pigalle occurs."

"How do you mean?" Henri asked. Science had never been his strong suit, so he wouldn't turn down a chance to be tutored by an expert.

"Without getting too technical," John began, "there are certain laws that govern the pairing of Time-Shells, and where a Virtual Hole forms between two points on the Stream, which my Time-Transfer experiments on mice have incontestably established. The Rule of Chronologic Symmetry, for instance, dictates that Time-Shells will always line up predictably, so that the month, day, hour, minute, and second will be exactly the same in both Shells—but the year on the Stream will be different. Another law, called the Rule of Recollection, guarantees that once a Virtual Hole forms between two Time-Shells, those two shells will always find each other again, if a stimulus resulting in the creation of a Virtual Hole happens to occur in either of the Time-Shell pair."

"So this means that time is flowing in parallel here and in 1877," Susanne offered. She was apparently the brighter of John's two impromptu pupils, but Henri wasn't too far behind her.

"Exactly." John looked at his watch. "It's three-sixteen p.m. on June tenth here, so it's three-sixteen p.m. on June tenth there. Now, using the Rule of Recollection, where, exactly, do you think the connection from our Time-Shell to elsewhere would end up, if we created a Virtual Hole beginning on our end right now?"

"In 1877," Henri said; he seemed to be getting it now.

"More specific," John prompted.

"Three-sixteen p.m. on June tenth, 1877," Henri answered.

"Correct."

"You've given us some good news and some bad news," Susanne offered, somewhat sullenly. "The good news is that if you can figure out how to return Nicole to 1877, we can be sure that she'll get back to the right place—"

"But the bad news is that you only have three days to work out a way to do it," Henri finished.

It would be tight—very, very tight—and the worried look on Dr. John Noland's face told Henri that Susanne's American houseguest was thinking the very same thing.

Chapter Seventeen

John's mind raced as he tossed and turned in his guestroom bed. It looked as if he'd actually be able to meet the three-day deadline, but only if overnight mail was really overnight, when overseas was the destination. Who knows, he might even have twelve hours or longer to spare! Talk about cutting it close—this one would definitely nick the skin.

He had to give himself credit. He had played the detective quite well out there in the dining room, and with the proof he was in the process of obtaining, he felt certain that his solution would be the correct one. Nicole had been extremely cooperative, a big plus—answering all of his questions calmly, with thorough descriptions and some particularly well-placed insights.

John had discovered early on that Nicole was something special, a Susanne incarnation with nothing but physical appearance in common with her twin. Nicole was levelheaded, Susanne was mercurial; Susanne was egotistical, Nicole was instinctively kind and reliable. The list went on and on. John's infatuation with picking out the differences was the major cause of his early morning insomnia.

Nicole had surprised him with her insistence on returning home, despite the uncertainties and dangers involved in doing so. Going back meant risking death, both as a result of the process involved in getting there and because of what might very well transpire after she arrived; yet, Nicole was still resolved to do it.

As John thought about it some more, he suddenly realized that Nicole was actually willing to sacrifice herself for Susanne, indirectly. Why? Because by saving her son, Nicole would in turn be saving generations of Bruantes, right down the line, leading eventually to Susanne, the ultimate beneficiary of Nicole's self-sacrifice. John knew that Susanne would never dream of doing the same for Nicole, if the tables were turned. Despite their genetic connection and shared good looks, these two women were very different people. John had quickly become enamored—intellectually, he kept telling himself—with

Susanne's mirror image.

He thought back to his interview with Nicole, whereby he had sensed as much about her as he had learned about her time and space predicament. "Can you describe exactly what you remember, right before you ended up in the gallery?" he had asked her.

"The painting turned into a white, hot empty hole that sucked me in."

"Before that." He was trying to identify the stimulus for the Virtual Hole's creation. If it had happened once on that side, he could make it happen again on this side—but he would have to learn what had produced the connection between the two Time-Shells first.

"I posed for an artist named Guy, that entire week," she explained, "and when the painting was finished, I agreed to take him into my bed. He was very insistent that we needed to celebrate—and, to be very honest, I was lonely."

To his surprise, the image of her celebrating with another man bothered him, more than it should have. He pushed the feeling away, trying hard to remove the sentiment from what was meant to be a purely objective scientific interrogation. "Exactly when did the Time-Tunnel appear during your, um, activities?" He felt embarrassed, which was ridiculous.

"We were going to sleep after a very long night," she explained with a hint of a smile.

Had the Virtual Hole materialized as a result of Nicole's lovemaking, perhaps because of a hormone surge during the sexual encounter? It was certainly possible. After all, chronotonin shared an amino acid backbone with a variety of other sex hormones. Some of John's laboratory experiments suggested that it functioned, at least in mice, as a very potent pheromone. Had Nicole's chronotonin levels peaked with her climax? This would be slightly discomforting to tease out, but it had to be done.

"Can you tell me exactly when the Virtual Hole opened, in relation to your moment of…pleasure?" He felt stupid, but not just because of the idiotic phrase he had chosen to describe an orgasm. Here he was, sitting right next to a stunningly beautiful woman, grilling her about the details of her most recent sexual encounter. This was not an everyday occurrence, so how could he not feel self-conscious? The room had suddenly become very warm, and since he was wearing a t-shirt, he couldn't resort to undoing the top button of his shirt to help mitigate the heat.

"He means *la petite mort*," Susanne had clarified, quite unnecessarily, her lips forming a naughty smirk.

The comment didn't faze Nicole. "Guy was a skilled lover. I had a few of those that night," she had said, looking back at John with unapologetic eyes—brown, blended and tinted with green. One thing was certain: Nicole Bruante wasn't shy. This trait, at least, she shared with her great-great-great-granddaughter.

John looked away, trying to make sense of it all. If Nicole had climaxed several times, why hadn't the Virtual Hole opened with her first orgasm, or the second? Something just didn't add up—there had to be something else. "Was there anything at all unusual about your intimacy that night? Think back. Had you done something out of the ordinary with the artist?" He swallowed hard, but it couldn't be avoided—he had to ask, there was simply no choice. "Perhaps you tried a different position, or a new technique? Anything at all unusual?"

"There was something," she said immediately.

He braced himself for more embarrassment. "What, exactly?"

"We had been drinking—not just wine, but absinthe too."

Absinthe? That just might do it, if— "Was absinthe a beverage that you had ever consumed before?" John asked, excited by this new information.

"Absinthe wasn't easy to get back then," Henri commented.

"That is right," Nicole said. "It was very expensive to buy. I drank it on rare occasions, usually when somebody offered it. Guy promised to bring me some that night, but he almost could not get it. The bottle he came with—the one that he was able to get, at his fourth stop before coming to my apartment—was different than all the others I had tasted before. It was so strong, first of all; but he told me that it was also laced with something else. Laudanum, I think."

Extra-potent absinthe, with opium added? That would definitely do the trick, if Nicole carried the right mutation! What if Nicole had the same transcription-activating chronotonin gene alteration that some of his mice had? If she did, exposure to hallucinogens, like absinthe and laudanum, would accelerate her hormone production by many logs, eventually resulting in sky-high chronotonin levels. That had to be it!

Now John could start to piece together the unique scenario that had resulted in Nicole's once-in-a-lifetime transposition in time. Perhaps the intended script, in a manner of speaking, was for Guy to fail in his attempts to obtain absinthe (laced with laudanum) for his lover. Without it, a Time-Tunnel would never have been produced in Nicole's attic bedroom that night. Nicole would have stayed, as intended, in her native Time-Shell, and two weeks later, she would have died, also as intended—the result of her successful attempt to save Edmond from the oncoming carriage, a two-edged sword that was meant to produce the fatal thrust that had abruptly ended Nicole's life but had saved Edmond's at the same time. But, in a bizarre deviation from fate's plan, Guy had somehow obtained the perfect time-travel aperitif, a unique event that had taken place in only one Time-Shell: namely, this Nicole's Time-Shell of Origin. *Et voilà!* Here she was.

John felt confident now that chronotonin was the stimulus that had produced an electromagnetic deviation over Nicole's bed in her native Time-Shell, which had in turn created a Virtual Hole centered on a Common Object—a painting—connecting Nicole's Time-Shell with theirs. Now it all made sense. This real-life scenario corresponded exactly with all of his experiments in rodents.

"You say the Virtual Hole opened in a painting hanging over your bed?"

"Yes, the one Jean called *The Origin of the World*."

John turned to Susanne. "Were Nicole and her friend found near that particular painting in d'Orsay's exhibit hall?"

Susanne nodded. "Yes, directly across the room from it."

The electromagnetic energy associated with the Time-Transfer must have propelled both Nicole and Guy forcefully through the Virtual Hole, into this Time-Shell—and into the gallery. John rapidly put two and two together in his mind, and Henri noticed.

"It looks as if you've come to some conclusions," the elder Bruante said. "Would you care to fill us in?"

"Yes, sorry." John turned his chair so that he sat face-to-face with Nicole, so close that he was tempted to take her hands in his so that the coldly analytical data would be softened into something more direct and personal. He didn't, though. Why? For reasons that were clear to him then, but somehow not so clear to him now, as he tossed and turned in his bed.

"I'm fairly certain you have a gene mutation that's activated by the ingestion of mind-altering drugs," he had told her, "resulting in the overproduction of a hormone called chronotonin—a peptide that has the ability, under unique conditions, to open up connections between Time-Shells."

The blank look on Nicole's face told John that he was being way too technical. He had to remind himself that the field of genetics was still in its infancy in 1877 and that the discipline of molecular biology wouldn't even be invented for another century. He would have to keep it simple—not because Nicole, an intelligent woman, wouldn't be able to understand it, but because he didn't have the time right now to give her a science lesson.

"Let's just say that I think you've inherited, from either your mother or your father, a unique sensitivity to drugs like absinthe and laudanum. When you over-indulged ten days ago, your body produced an excess amount of a chemical that created a tunnel between your time and ours—with something called a Common Object at both ends." The Common Object, he felt certain, was the painting.

"This Common Object, then, is *The Origin of the World*?" Susanne asked.

"I'm certain of it. Extrapolating from my experiments with mice, we'll have to produce a Virtual Hole beginning at that same Common Object, hanging at this very moment on the wall of the exhibit room at Musée d'Orsay, here in 2011, in order to return Nicole home to a destination ending under that very same painting hanging on the wall over her bed in 1877."

"Do you have any idea why I made it through, while Guy did not?" Nicole asked, her face going white. "He was horribly crushed, while I escaped with just a few bruises. Why did he die?"

"My theory is that he didn't have the gene alteration, while you did. In mutated mice, the excess chronotonin that they produce functions as a shell that protects them from being injured by the excessive pressures that exist within a Virtual Hole. We call the shell a 'halo.' I think you had a chronotonin halo, and he didn't."

Once John believed he knew what had happened, he could begin to act. The first step was to contact one of his graduate students in Chicago to get the ball rolling. He excused himself from the table and went to the living room to make the call. After a few rings, his contact in

Chicago picked up.

"Paul, listen to me carefully," he had said to his student. "How much TMMP do we have on hand in the rodent laboratory?" TMMP was the abbreviation they used for their injectable and ingestible psychotropic solution—a potent combination of thujone, mescaline, morphine, and psilocybin. Thujone was distilled from wormwood, the active psychedelic component of absinthe, while morphine was an opiate, a modern-day version of laudanum. Both of these drugs had worked on Nicole before, in 1877, so theoretically this four-drug concoction—an even more potent hallucinogenic mixture than what Nicole had consumed before—should work even better.

"We have 50 or 60 cc, I think," Paul said, and John did the body weight calculation in his head. That should be just about enough to thoroughly intoxicate a human being if taken by mouth, and to effectively activate Nicole's chronotonin production in the bargain.

"Could you send me all of it, Paul—overnight delivery, in a refrigerated biologics container, to the address that I'll give you in a moment." He would have it delivered to Susanne, at d'Orsay, where a signature at the time of delivery could be provided by any of Susanne's office staff. This would be safer than risking conveyance to her residence, where there might not be someone to accept it; plus, a museum destination, although not a university, shaded John's unusual request with at least a suggestion of the academic.

"Will you need some needles and syringes as well?"

"Yes," John said. "Send ten of each, please." Paul must have thought that John needed the solution for an experiment overseas, perhaps at the University of Paris, where injection of the psychotropic mixture into a rodent's tail vein would be required if John was planning on providing a time-travel demonstration. It was much better for Paul to think so.

"I'll get that out to you right away," Paul said. It was 5:10 p.m. in Paris, so it was 9:10 a.m. in Chicago—perfect timing. The package would probably arrive tomorrow, in the late afternoon, or the following day, June 12th, by mid-morning. "Is that everything?"

"No, there's one more thing. I'll be sending you something, too, by overnight mail—a sample of hair, including attached skin and follicle, from a human subject. I'd like you to run a DNA analysis on the roots using our array of site-specific probes, to find out whether the specimen in question contains a chronotonin mutation—and if so, which one. I'd also like you to measure the levels of chronotonin in the hair fiber. I want to know exactly how much normal chronotonin is in the hair, and whether it contains any altered chronotonin as well." Certain gene mutations resulted in excess production of "wild-type" (normal) chronotonin, while others produced a conformational variant of the hormone that made it a much more potent peptide. "This is a priority, Paul. As soon as you have the results, scan the analysis printouts and email them to me."

By the time the TMMP arrived, the genetic testing would already be in progress. John just wanted to make extra sure that his suspicions about Nicole's genetic make-up were true, before he made the attempt to send her back. It could be a disaster, if she didn't really have a chronotonin halo to protect her.

"I am thankful that you are interested so much in my safety," Nicole had said later, her formal French already laced with an undertone of familiarity. She and he seemed to connect on an unspoken level—a bond perhaps that was more akin to doctor and patient, rather than man and woman? If he kept telling himself that, all would be well, because anything more than a professional relationship between the two of them could lead to serious problems. The last thing he needed right now was another problem to deal with.

It was certainly interesting to contrast Susanne's reaction to the whole genetic mutation thing with Nicole's. For Susanne, it was always about Susanne; this time was no exception.

"Do you mean to tell me that there's a mutant gene in the family?" she had asked with a look akin to repulsion.

"It's not what it sounds like. Mutations are a mechanism by which species change and adapt to an uncertain environment. Many mutations are advantageous, rather than detrimental."

"I need to know whether I have the mutation, too."

"What does it matter?" he had replied, finding it difficult not to feel irritated by Susanne's unrelenting focus on herself. "Unless using LSD is on your list of recreational activities, I hardly think your mutation status is relevant."

"Look, John, I have the right to know. Just send a sample of my hair along with Nicole's tomorrow, okay?"

He shrugged. Why not? Scientifically speaking, the genetic penetrance of a naturally occurring chronotonin mutation would, after all, be interesting to study. So, first thing in the morning, he would send Nicole and Susanne's hair samples for Paul to analyze.

John rolled over and looked at the clock: it read 2:22 a.m., and his mind was still racing. Well, enough was enough, he decided, finally breaking down and digging into his toiletry bag to retrieve a bottle of Ambien. He took the sleeping pill with a glass of water, feeling his thoughts slow down, almost immediately. As he eventually drifted into relaxation, the certain harbinger to sleep, he felt relieved.

There was no more he could do tonight, anyway; and so, he finally let it all go and fell into a deep and solid slumber.

It was funny how rest had radically changed Nicole's perspective on just about everything related to the here and now. Granted, there were other factors besides a good night's sleep in play too, including the squabbling between Henri and Susanne about whether Nicole should stay or go, which clearly identified Henri as a Nicole Bruante advocate, and Susanne as an adversary of sorts. Nicole was reassured by the way John had insisted on the analysis of her hair, to be sure she wouldn't be crushed by the energy of the Time-Tunnel during her return to the past. It was nice to know that some people cared for her; two of her three twenty-first-century companions openly did.

The look Nicole had noticed on John's face indicated that he might be doing his best to hide the real danger involved in this crazy notion of sending her back in time, her trip here repeated but in reverse. The whole thing made her feel as if she were a convicted prisoner en route to Devil's Island. If she only had two days left in this place, it seemed obvious that she should do everything in her power not to waste one second of her remaining time here—and this was the new philosophy that had spawned from the dreamless ten hours she had just spent under the covers. If a death sentence was inevitable, then she was owed, in a figurative sense, her last meal: three courses—three wishes, if she got her way—involving a person, a place, and a thing.

She slid out of bed and pushed aside the curtains to her open window with two fingers, feeling the breeze of a clear, sunny day on her naked skin. Yesterday had been all clouds and rain, perfect weather for a day spent inside—but not today. She picked out a pair of trousers and slipped them on, still not quite used to the feel of fabric so tight about her legs, since women of her time always wore skirts or dresses. She found a turquoise t-shirt, a slightly worn cast-off, most likely from Susanne's past. After slipping it on, she grabbed a comfortable looking pair of green-and-blue shoes that would serve her quite well, she thought, on her days adventure outside.

When she ventured out to the dining room, she found John busy with some strands of hair, which he was carefully placing inside a small black cylinder, no taller than his thumb, with the letters *K-o-d-a-k* printed on the side. Susanne was sitting across from him at the table, rubbing the top of her head with two fingers. "That hurt," she complained.

John shrugged. "You're the one who asked to have your hair sampled." Nicole watched him write Susanne's name in red on a slip of paper and tape it securely to the side of the little black tube.

Nicole pulled out a chair, moving it over so that she could sit right beside him, just as she had yesterday. "You'll want mine next," she stated, tugging at four or five strands at once. She grimaced slightly at the first try, then pulled harder, her scalp holding tight, until finally she held her hair with attached roots between her thumb and index finger. John offered her an empty black bottle, sliding it with the back of his hand over the tabletop toward her, their hands touching—his intention, no doubt. She inserted her hair into it and slid the container back to him. He snapped on a cap and then prepared a label for hers. It didn't take him long to attach the identifying slip of paper to the side of the specimen bottle with transparent tape, placing it next to Susanne's on the table in front of him when he had finished.

Susanne had gone to stand in front of the window that looked out onto the street in front of the building. "The surveillance car is gone," she commented. "They're tailing Henri, now."

"That's good," John said, "because we don't want the police in tow when we attempt the Time-Transfer."

Susanne nodded. "Very true. Henri can be our decoy." She turned away from the window and came back to the table, sitting down again across from Nicole and John. "Speaking of Henri," she continued, "he called a little while ago. The DNA results from our last trip to the museum are in. The hair samples from the four paintings are perfect matches, all of them." She had a big smile on her face, and it was obvious that she felt as if she was only a small step away, now, from her much longed-for recognition as the woman who had proven that Degas was a well-intentioned fraud.

"A match to Nicole's hair?" John's request for clarification was unnecessary. Of course it was her hair; she had modeled, after all, for all of those paintings and many, many more.

"Yes. According to Henri's contact in the DNA lab, the four museum specimens match not only the *Nude Reclining* sample, but with Nicole's hair, as well."

John turned to Nicole with a smile. "You and your mitochondrial DNA are famous, now," he said. "Your genetic imprint and your images have been preserved in those paintings for the entire world to admire, for centuries to come." He paused for a moment. "I'm not sure you realize it, but you've been immortalized. Your youth, your beauty, your spirit, and now your DNA, will live on forever on those canvases."

"Except that she's anonymous," Susanne said harshly. "Nobody will ever know her name."

"Who cares?" he replied with a shrug. "A name is just an arbitrary designation that has no bearing on who a person really is. Nicole is famous, in my book, even if no one ever knows what people called her when she lived and breathed." He turned back to Nicole. "Those paintings are your legacy. The artist left behind his signature, but you've left behind something alive, something that no one will ever forget. People will remember you—your body, your face, and your gestures—long after they return home from their visit to museums all over the world. You're the star in all of these paintings, Nicole—not Courbet, or Degas, or Renoir, or Manet."

Nicole had never thought about it like that before; apparently, neither had Susanne. Before, she had looked elated, but now it was as if the air had been let out of her balloon. Susanne wasn't the type of person who liked being nudged out of the limelight. Yes, her theory might make her famous as an art historian, but she would never be able to take credit for Nicole's role as a direct contributor to art history.

Susanne got up, eyeing Nicole with a touch of jealousy in her eyes. "We'll get you back on the palette soon, if all goes according to plan. You'll have years of nude modeling ahead of you as a nameless celebrity, after you've returned home—as long as you avoid those horse-drawn carriages." She turned to John. "I'll be at work all day. Your time-travel potion should arrive later, and I'll sign for it, as we discussed. Do you want me to bring it back here?"

"If you can store it someplace safe at the museum, it would be better to keep it there, since we'll need it on-site for the Time-Transfer."

"I'll lock it in my desk drawer. Tomorrow night, then?" She picked up her handbag and went to the door.

John nodded and turned to Nicole. "I'll send off the hair samples immediately. Paul should be able to get me confirmation of your chronotonin status by tomorrow afternoon at the latest, as long as he gets your hair sample in the morning. Once we're certain you'll have a protective hormone halo surrounding you, I'll feel much more comfortable about trying to send you back."

So, it would be tomorrow—just after midnight, as they had previously decided. Susanne would take care of the security guard with sleeping pills dissolved in a snifter of fine brandy, offered as a pre-coital aperitif, the actual act aborted long before it could even begin. The nightshift officer's drug-induced stupor would last into the next morning, when his relief shift would find their confused and disoriented colleague just waking up at his desk, slumped over the video monitors that had been shut off hours earlier. Susanne had claimed that she could pull it off, no problem. Nicole hoped that she could.

"Au revoir," Susanne called gaily, back to herself now—no doubt because Nicole wouldn't be around that much longer to be a thorn in her envious side. "I'm off." The door clicked shut behind her, leaving Nicole and John to their own devices. *Perfect.* That meant that it was time now for Nicole to start working on her first wish.

"I will be coming with you, John, to post the specimens," she announced, deciding that it would be best not to give him a choice in the matter. "Afterwards, you and I will take a side-trip. All right?"

His blue eyes gazed back at her, unsure. *This isn't wise,* they seemed to say, but she didn't care. She was a condemned woman, and she was determined to have her way.

"I plan on going on this journey today with you. I need this, John," she explained. "It is very important to me." There was something between them—there had been, even from that first moment their gazes had locked in the hallway when Susanne had shown John to his room. He had understood her then, and he understood her now. There would be no need for any further convincing.

He nodded. "All right. And where will our side trip take us?" He seemed a bit sad, as if he was resigned to what fate had in mind—no, to whatever *she* had in mind.

"To Montmartre. I would like to see it, here and now, before I leave." The place, in her wish list from this morning, was almost certainly hers, now, for the asking—John would never deny her. Later on, she would have the person, and then the thing. She would enjoy that last item the most, the bittersweet conclusion to her final request before her day of reckoning.

It didn't take them long to mail the specimens at a nearby DHL office, with guaranteed next-day delivery to Chicago. John seemed to know all about the awe-inspiring underground rail cars that the people here called *Le Metro*, so she followed him, taking the first opportunity to grab his hand so that he could guide her through the crowds, a convenient excuse for contact that he didn't question—and that he didn't seem to mind at all, either.

On the train, they stood close, a steel pole between them on the crowded car, their fingers and shoulders touching as they steadied themselves against the rocking and swaying motion of the first dozen stops. The car lurched, and he held her, briefly—his hand on the small of her back, his fingers on cotton with heated skin underneath, his hip a perfect fit on the adjacent curve of her waist. At their stop, he held her hand again, and she grasped his fingers tightly as they crossed the threshold from car to platform.

He led again, and she followed. They were inseparable, just as she wanted it, with her palm in his as they navigated the sea of people until they found the train they needed. The car wasn't crowded, so they sat on the bench in front, her thigh against his, both of them willing; her foot, eventually, crossing under his, making gradual headway toward the transition from awkward to perfectly natural. At Station Abysses, their planned destination, they took the stairs, two hands joined now, his behind and hers in front, as they climbed what seemed an endless spiral that twisted up and up from the buried tunnel of underground tracks, through the rock and soil of the highest city hill, to finally emerge at the top and onto a cobblestoned square in Montmartre.

They were both out of breath, so he took her hand again with a touch that hinted at something different evolving now between them, pulling her gently onto a bench next to him, cool and warm at once beneath the shade of a towering tree. They faced a church, its facade a smooth expanse of brown-finished concrete.

"There was no church here, in my time," she said quietly.

"It was a field."

He got up, and she followed, walking together down the stone grade, just two dozen steps or so until they stood arm in arm in front of the church. "Église Saint-Jean-de-Montmartre," he read from a plaque. "Construction began in 1894."

"That was long after my time," she said.

"After your time," he said pensively, "but well before mine." How bizarre, to think that they had been separated by more than a century until a natural occurring anomaly in her physical make-up had caused this unnatural flip-flop, allowing her to be standing here next to him in the far distant future. In two days she might be walking past this very spot again, in a time when it was just an empty field rather than home to a church. It was strange to think about this and stranger still to think that time existed at this very moment behind and ahead of them, an infinite and perpetual stream.

"Did you live around here?" he asked, his voice hushed.

"*Oui,* at the top of this hill," she replied, pointing.

"Come on, then," he said; so they passed through the courtyard and up ten stairs times ten, following the sidewalk around the curving ridge toward Place du Tertre, passing houses and stores and restaurants on their way to another street. Two blocks further, and they were finally there, standing in front of a renovated three-story building with flower-wells in front of each open-shuttered window. The sign on the mailbox read, 25 Rue de Ronsard.

"This is where I lived, in the attic room." A window located below the triangle of the roofline had looked tiny then—and it looked tiny, now.

"Would you like to go in?"

"No. I will be back here, soon enough."

The sun felt warm on her face and chest, just as she imagined his body would feel, lying next to her on those cold and lonely nights, up there below the rafters. This was something they would never have together—at least not up there. She turned to face him, taking his two hands in hers, intending to kiss him. But he stepped back.

"We can't—" he began.

She gazed intently into his eyes. "We already have," she replied.

"But you'll be leaving, soon."

"That is exactly why we should."

Her wish would be granted. The place was hers, and now the person; tonight, she would have the thing.

Chapter Eighteen

Susanne had painted herself into a corner, but it's not as if she had had any real choice in the matter. She had offered René this partnership out of desperation, cutting him a sliver of the pie in order to save the rest of the whole for herself. That was a sacrifice that couldn't be avoided, but one that still left her seething.

The thing that really got to her is that she had only herself to blame. She had been too cocky, settling for shortcuts when a tiny bit of extra effort would have done it, putting her in first place and landing her in the winner's circle alone, rather than tied to a freeloader who would end up taking part of the credit—her credit—for years and years of hard work. But if she hadn't handed René the shared trophy, he would have ruined everything. In fact, she might have been walking at this very minute down a hallway whose walls were decorated with bars and locks instead of oil and watercolor paintings, if she hadn't pulled René off the warpath and into her confidence.

The morning after her close call at the museum, she'd met René as promised at their usual hotel room, a few hours before she would have to drive in the rain to pick up John at Gare du Nord. René had had the authorization paperwork with him, of course, but it was only after his other needs had been met that they'd sat, naked, on the edge of the bed to legitimize her illegal sampling escapade. She had expected to sign two copies, but he had brought only one.

"We'll make an even exchange," he had said. "When you give me the DNA results from the hair extraction, I'll hand over the proof that what you and your uncle did wasn't an act of international vandalism. Until then," he had said while folding the papers neatly and slipping them with finality into the front pocket of his jacket, still draped on the back of the hotel room loveseat, "these papers don't exist. As far as I'm concerned, we never signed them. I'll destroy them and turn you in to the authorities if you don't hold up your end of the bargain."

And she had no reason in the world to doubt him. René was as driven to succeed as she was. He had taken every opportunity, in phone call after phone call, to remind her that he was dead serious. Since their early morning appointment yesterday—all business for her, but business and pleasure for him, the fun and games transpiring both before and after their signatures had dried on the authorization paperwork—René had been nothing less than obsessed with getting the information that Susanne now held in her hand.

Well, here it was, a copy of Henri's faxes of this morning, nine or ten pages at least, filed away nicely in an official-looking folder; and in just a few minutes, the unrelenting René Lauren would have what he wanted—but Susanne would too. Avoiding a prison term would be a very good thing indeed; if she could do that and still enjoy the accolades from the confirmation of her theory, all the better. It had even occurred to her that if she played her cards right, sharing the credit with René might actually pay off with more of a jackpot than if she had succeeded in gambling solo. René's role in uncovering the Degas deception would undoubtedly land him a promotion; with the d'Orsay director's chair empty, she would be perfectly positioned to slide right into it. Susanne might still come out on top, as she usually did—her favorite, and customary, position in both business and pleasure.

René's office was not in the back hallway with all the others, but on the other side of the museum, a three-room suite behind and adjacent to the front lobby, equipped with every convenience, including a very pretty administrative assistant whose job description, Susanne felt fairly certain, included duties that the sexy blonde shared with the assistant director of acquisitions and special exhibits. That didn't matter. It's not as if René actually meant something to Susanne; in fact, it would be better for everyone involved if he had someone else's shoulder to cry on when Susanne eventually put a stop to their late-night and early-morning rendezvous.

As soon as René vacated his office, Susanne would summarily vacate their mutually convenient arrangement. As the new executive director, she'd also send the overly accommodating secretary packing. She couldn't wait.

She had taken a shortcut through the special exhibit galleries, which meant that she had to pass painting after painting of Nicole. She kept telling herself that it didn't really bother her, but it did. She stopped for a moment in the second room, in front of a particularly seductive *After the Bath* piece that depicted Nicole's ass in a way that could only be described as breathtaking. She lay nude, reclining on her right side with her back arched, her right leg bent inward and her left leg stretched out, so that the smooth curve of her round and perfect derrière formed the center point of the highly sensual pose. Susanne had modeled an almost identical scene once, in her freshman year at the University of Paris, but with her arms extended up and over, in a way that accentuated the sexy lines of her curving back much more successfully than Nicole's pose ever could. Susanne had also angled her right leg out rather than in, an ingenious personal touch that had opened her up ever so slightly, so that a soft and delicate fold of pink had become the central focus of her painting—right there, where one thigh met the other. Now that was the way to do it, in her opinion. If it had been Susanne instead of Nicole, all of these paintings would have left their indelible mark on history, not just the solitary Courbet hanging alone, without a pairing, in the first exhibit room, the only truly controversial masterpiece in the whole lot. If it had been Susanne instead of Nicole, everything would have been different. There was no doubt about it, Susanne would have changed the history books, but not as "model unknown." Susanne had never (and would never) settle for anything even remotely associated with remaining nameless.

Susanne couldn't help but think about what John had said this morning about the subject matter of a piece of artwork, and the crucial role the artist's model played in a painting's legacy. She couldn't completely agree with him, but she had to admit that there was a grain or two of truth to his viewpoint. Susanne, for one, had always enjoyed seeing her beauty immortalized—her incomparable body, nude and exposed, captured forever on canvas, her image burning itself into a viewer's memory after being viewed and admired at an art exhibit somewhere…

"Somewhere" was the word that spelled out the problem, she realized. The student artists who had painted Susanne were nobodies; God knows where those paintings of her had ended up—in attics, in basements, or in some flea market, most likely; but not in art museums like d'Orsay. Somewhere was nowhere, and that was the issue. Real artists—men and women with reputations behind them—had painted Nicole, and therefore Nicole's image would be admired by millions of people in places like this, for centuries to come.

Nicole would live on forever, specifically because she was Courbet's model—and Manet's, and Renoir's, and Cassatt's; not because of her aptitude for the nude pose, or the way her flawless body seemed to lend itself so naturally to paint and brush. With the right artist, Susanne could have easily been another Nicole, but better. She shrugged. Out of sight, out of mind—out of my apartment, and out of my life. A misplaced ancestor who belonged in a different time may have outdone Susanne in the nude modeling arena, but if all went well, this particular nineteenth-century beauty queen would be returning to her own pageant after midnight tomorrow. When Nicole was gone, all would be well.

She kept moving, through the largest special exhibit gallery and out to the catwalk, making a right and heading down the hall that overlooked the sunken level of the museum, over to her left, eventually finding herself in the lobby, opposite the security desk on the other side. The museum had just opened, and a thin line of people had already formed along the wall, behind a row of roped-off posts near the door. Susanne headed across the lobby, smiling pleasantly at the guard, a youngish officer with short brown hair and a small silver earring in his left earlobe.

"Bonjour, Rousseau," she said, calling him by his last name and wondering if it would be him on the midnight shift tomorrow, or another one of her many d'Orsay security team admirers. It made no difference, really, since they all wanted her, each and every one. A sway of the hips, a suggestive word or two, a light kiss that promised more, perhaps; and finally, some heavily spiked brandy is all it would take to eliminate the first barrier to Nicole's final departure. No worries, she thought—most men were putty in her hands. After she had finished shaping the security-guard variety, Nicole would be history, literally and figuratively.

Rousseau nodded, watching Susanne lustfully as she passed by, his eyes on her breasts and his thoughts elsewhere, no doubt. She passed through a set of double doors to the right of the security control room, which led her into a back hallway, immediately in front of a sign marked Executive Director. There was no reason to knock, since the first line of defense would be sitting prettily just inside, behind a desk that was intended to field interceptions if need be.

"He's expecting me," Susanne declared, hardly looking at the woman who undoubtedly thought of herself as competition, but wasn't. Jeanine was wearing more make-up than usual, and her coifed hair looked as if it had just been professionally set. She was one of those women who felt compelled to work at her beauty, even though she would still be striking without the lipstick or blush. The girl probably lacked self-confidence, a character trait that seemed completely foreign to the ever-confident Susanne. A touch of color on her lips and cheeks was all

Susanne ever needed to wrap up her package for her next lucky victim, and tomorrow night would be no exception.

Susanne pushed open the door behind Jeanine's post, ignoring the platinum blonde's vocal objections and stepping into the dimly lit sitting room adjacent to René's office. He had left his door wide open, so she walked in. He was sitting at his desk, but started to get up when she came in.

"Don't bother," she said, walking around the desk to half stand and half sit on the edge of the mahogany desk, next to his chair. She made as if to hand him the folder containing the DNA analysis, but then pulled it back with a snap of her wrist when he reached out to take it.

"Not so fast," she chided. "We had a deal, remember? You give me the proof of your authorization, and I'll give you this copy of the matching hair samples."

"No problem," he replied with a shrug, pulling out his middle desk drawer to retrieve a folder of his own. "Here you go."

They made a simultaneous exchange. Now René had what he wanted, and Susanne did too. It was done, for better or for worse; now may the gold and silver rain down on them both.

He opened the folder, thumbing through page after page of matching DNA sequences, followed by a summary sheet explaining that all the hairs—four from the gallery sampling, and one from *Nude Reclining*—were identical. Susanne had of course omitted the papers that detailed the exact same DNA sequence, obtained from Susanne's temporary houseguest.

"Good work, Susanne," he finally said, straightening the edges of the miniature stack of papers on his desk before putting them neatly back into the folder. "Our little discovery will change the face of Impressionist art history forever."

"You're holding my life's work in your hands," she replied. "Handle it with care, René."

"Of course I will." He smiled, and she decided it would be fine; everything would be fine. "We'll announce it together," he added, "sometime next week, as partners. All right?"

"As partners." Although the words almost stuck in her throat, that's exactly what they were. For better or for worse, she and René Lauren were partners, but their marriage of convenience wouldn't last.

She would get her annulment as soon as the announcement was made.

"Partners," she said again, slipping her shoe off and putting her foot directly on his lap, her toes in his hardening groin. *Partners.*

~

By the time they crossed the courtyard behind Susanne's apartment together at the end of the day, John had come to an important realization. Over the course of the past forty-eight hours, he had been able to shake off whatever hold Susanne's memory had had on him, because the memory itself had magically materialized right in front of him.

He had remembered Susanne in a certain way, denying all of her deficiencies and magnifying all of her positives, to the point that his recollection of her, stored away in his head for nearly twenty years, was nothing more than an idyllic fantasy. From the outside, Nicole was Susanne, just as John remembered her; from the inside, she was without a question everything the real Susanne was not—but ironically, everything that John's infatuation had tried, unsuccessfully, to turn Susanne into.

He had wanted this Susanne—this memory that had unbelievably become transformed into a real person named Nicole—desperately, secretly dreaming of the day when he and Susanne might be reunited, and wondering if the image he had created in his mind would turn out to be a perfect match with the real thing. Well, it wasn't; but, to his astonishment, Nicole was. Nicole was the Realist's line-and-brush facsimile, while Susanne was the Impressionist's vague and blurry interpretation of what John had wished his college heartthrob could be. John would happily take the Courbet, then, and toss away the Seurat. Now that he had the real thing, why settle for the Pointillist version?

Strange, how it had taken someone from the past to give John closure on his own past. Nicole was a woman who didn't belong here, a woman who had come from a place and time that no longer existed, a time traveler whose very existence in the here and now had been enough to make John see that he needed to start living in the here and now as well, instead of haunting those days that were long gone, his life consumed by a past memory that wasn't even accurate.

Then, when Nicole had announced that they shouldn't hold back, he had felt ready to soar—yet he wasn't quite ready to throw the door open and let his heart fly out. This was all very confusing, logistically and emotionally speaking. That's why he hadn't kissed her when she had made her move in front of her Montmartre apartment.

He had wanted to kiss her—desperately, in fact; and he should have. Nicole had given her argument, and John had been convinced, but then the perfect moment had somehow passed, and he had decided that he shouldn't push it just yet.

They had strolled together instead, hand-in-hand, up the street from the house where she had lived in 1877, to the top of the winding hill, and finally into the bustling activity of Place du Tertre. The square was lined with artist vendors, some with true talent, sitting quietly next to their displays of nudes, landscapes, or portraits, while others seemed no better than gypsies, loudly soliciting the crowds of tourists in an attempt to sell their worthless wares. They had passed an oriental artist who was sketching a truly mediocre caricature of a little boy, while in the next stall an old Frenchman wearing a black beret sat on a metal folding chair, waiting for someone to buy one of his truly breathtaking nudes.

"It was not like this here, in my time," Nicole said, clearly disappointed. "All of the artists who painted in this square when I lived in this place had a gift."

It was true that Picasso and Utrillo, among others, had painted in Place du Tertre in the late 1800s. "There aren't many artists like that anymore," John replied. "The Impressionist movement produced a surge of talent that hasn't been paralleled since. It must have been amazing to live here back then."

He realized as soon as he said this that he had used the past tense, when he should have used the present. Nicole did live here, and his heart sank when he remembered that she would be returning to this very place in his past—in her present, oddly enough—tomorrow night.

"Come on," he urged, pushing the thought aside in favor of the moment. "There's a famous church up here that I've always wanted to see." They passed together through the square and rounded the corner. There, soaring above them, stood the huge, shell-white domes of one of the most renowned basilicas in the world, the beloved Sacré-Cœur de Paris.

He heard Nicole gasp. "They finished it, then," she murmured. "They had just started construction when I left." She turned toward him. "I would like it very much if we could please go in."

"I must sketch you first," a voice behind them said, "if your husband will allow." They turned to see an older man in the stereotypical black beret of the Parisian artist.

Being called Nicole's husband made John blush; Nicole, on the other hand, didn't seem to mind at all. "Will you let him draw me, husband?" she asked, a twinkle in her eye. He nodded, trying very hard not to look as awkward as he felt. "My husband says yes," she declared, laughing, and John couldn't help but laugh, too.

He watched over the artist's shoulder as the man began sketching Nicole's beautiful face on his drawing pad. She sat perfectly still on a small ledge of stone supporting a wrought iron fence that surrounded the perimeter of Sacré-Cœur, with her legs crossed—a professional herself in the fine art of figure posing. After ten minutes or so, John dug into his front pocket and produced a few bills of paper currency. He handed the money to the surprised artist while at the same time taking the pad and pencil from his hands.

"But I am not finished!" the artist objected.

"I would like to finish it," John stated. "Is the money enough?"

The artist fanned out the bills in his hand, counting quietly to himself. "*Oui,*" he finally concluded, smiling broadly. "Now, we will see what you can do!"

John started sketching; and now the street artist stood behind him, watching with curiosity as John put the charcoal pencil to paper.

"I did not know that you could draw," Nicole said, resuming her pose after stretching her legs for a second or two.

"I was very good, a long time ago," John replied. It was ironic, really, that Nicole was wearing the very same shirt that Susanne had worn, that night when John had sketched her in the coffee shop on their first date, sitting in front of the fireplace with the steam from her cup of cocoa brushing pale and hot on her neck and face. He took his time, just as he had then, looking up at a memory of turquoise, the very image of past become present, no longer fading but bright, Susanne replaced by Nicole; and then back down at the paper, over and over again, until finally, more than half an hour later, he had finished.

The sidewalk artist clapped his hands. "Fantastique!" he said. "Very well done, indeed, monsieur!"

Nicole broke her pose, and John walked over to sit down beside her on the wall, the drawing pad face-down on his lap. She touched his arm. "May I see it?"

He turned the pad face-up to show her the portrait. The outline of her face had been framed by the street artist slightly off center and upwards, which had left John just enough room to drawn in her neck, shoulders and chest, and fill in the details—the rich expressiveness of her eyes, the delicate angle of her nose, the inviting fullness of her lips, and the beauty mark, positioned just so on the highest ridge of her left cheekbone. In place of steam and wisps of smoke and flame, John had substituted ivy, behind and around, climbing softly on Nicole's shoulders. The other picture's fire had burned out, while this drawing teemed with the new growth of spring, offering hope and a new beginning. If only Nicole could stay, and give him the love that he had lost before and had now seemingly regained.

"It's beautiful, John. May I have it?" she asked.

He had kept his sketch of Susanne as a hoarded keepsake that sat at the bottom of a dresser drawer, a painful and unhealthy reminder of his heartbreak. This drawing, he decided, would have a very different fate. "Yes," he replied; yes, it would go with her. Nicole asked him to sign it, and so he did, ripping it off the artist's pad and handing the remaining sheaf of blank paper, along with the charcoal, back to its waiting owner. Then he folded his drawing, again and again, until it was small enough to fit into the back pocket of Nicole's pants. "Perhaps you will remember me, when you see it."

"I will remember," she said, her brown eyes tinged with green gazing into his sad and lonely blue ones. He would remember, too.

They had approached the basilica from the side, by way of Place du Tertre; now they walked around to the front, looking down at the seemingly endless cascade of stairs that began at the foot of Sacré-Cœur and ended at the base of Butte Montmartre. Turning, they climbed the bright white steps of Sacré-Cœur hand-in-hand, after pausing for a moment at the foundation stone, which had been laid in 1875. "A small chapel was consecrated here in 1876," she explained, "for people to use while the church was being built. I came here often."

"Do you believe in God?" he asked.

"Of course I do," she replied. "He brought me to you, did he not?"

Yes, he had; and tomorrow, he would send her away.

They reached the top of the stairs, where a greeter handed them an informational brochure, instructing them in a whisper to respect the sanctity of the vestibule and refrain from taking photographs. Inside, John felt the presence of something unquestionably spiritual, permeating the travertine stone, the glass, and the marble—even the air itself. Nicole lit a candle, so he did too, and with eyes closed, he prayed—for what? Without even thinking, he had prayed for something lasting between them, for something durable and meaningful, for a bond that comes only once in a lifetime. He had prayed for something that could never be, because she was leaving. He had prayed for love.

The narrow stairs leading to the top of the dome were open, so they walked one behind the other up to the observation deck, where they had a view of all of Paris sprawled below them at the foot of the ancient butte. "This is my city," she said quietly. "It does not matter what the year on the calendar says." She turned to view the cityscape from a different angle, when something caught her eye, over to the right. She frowned and pointed. "That was not there, in my time. What is it?"

"It's the symbol of Paris, the Eiffel Tower. It was erected in 1889 as an entrance arch to the World's Fair." John smiled, sadly. That was twelve years after Nicole died. "Do you like it?" he asked.

"No." She made a face. "It is ugly."

"Some people think it is very beautiful—especially at night, when it comes to life with thousands of tiny lights, like stars."

She seemed willing to accept this possibility. "I would like to see it, at night. Perhaps it could be beautiful, with lights."

Yes, it was beautiful; and she was too. He wanted to hold her—to wrap her in his arms and tell her that everything would be fine. But that would be a lie. Yes, he might be able to get her back to 1877 safely, but then she would be gone, and each of them would be alone on either side of forever.

They left the church, hungry, to find a place to eat. It was almost 4:00 by the time they finished eating at an outdoor café halfway down the hill toward the Abysses Metro stop. They shared some cheese, a baguette of bread, and a bottle of wine; then, slightly tipsy, they carefully descended the same stairs they had climbed well before noon and successfully renegotiated the Paris underground back into the heart of the city. It was a short walk from the station to Avenue Georges V. Although Susanne's house was no longer under surveillance, the back entrance still felt safer. He had the key out, poised and ready, but she stopped him, just before metal slid into metal, with her hand on his.

"Thank you, John."

"For what?"

"For today. It was—"

"Incredible," he finished. And now, the time was right. He pulled her toward him, and the kiss was incredible, too—long and lingering, going on and on as if time itself had stopped. He wished it would. This was the answer to his prayer—she was the answer to his prayer. But soon she would be gone, and it would all be over. He tried to pull away, thinking it would be best to stop, but she held him close. Her lips on his spoke a wordless argument that he simply couldn't resist.

"The drawing of me—the one that you gave me," she finally said, her lips still touching on his, "it is not enough."

"What do you mean?"

"You must prepare another one," she insisted.

He didn't understand. "What's wrong with the one from Montmartre?"

"It shows only a part of me," she said. "I am more than just a face and a neck. Come upstairs, and I will show you."

She led, and he followed, up the stairs and into the empty apartment. He found a drawing pad in Susanne's desk drawer and a set of old charcoal pencils. When he had confirmed that he had what he needed, she took his hand again, pulling him with silent understanding, no need for words, down the hallway and into her bedroom. Her bed was unmade, the blanket pulled down, the top end folded over the bottom and resting partly on the floor, the sheets creased and furrowed from last night's sleep, when her naked skin had rested on burgundy silk, a scene that was easy for him to imagine, and one that he would witness again in just a moment.

She slid out of her shoes, the beginnings of nudity drifting from her toes over the smooth arch of her feet, onto elusive ankles and up the swell of calves and the whisper of secret shins. Buttons in front were easily opened, revealing whites, tans, and pinks, gladly uncovered, anything but shy; and then her blouse joined the pants on the floor, turquoise tumbling down on rumpled beige with a sigh, right there at his feet—and it was done.

Nicole climbed onto the sheets, looking into his eyes, brown and green and warm and close. She slid on her back, up and smooth, a reclining nude against a pillow, her right shoulder propped up ever so slightly, arm extended down on that side, pushing urgent and close against her body, right under her breast, lifting it upward, aching and soft and firm. Her right arm reached out across her navel, breathing in and out against skin and muscle and ribs, a hand resting palm-down on the opposite hip, legs bent over to the right and together, dual lines of long and trim desire. At the other end, she had turned her head to the left, pillowed in the crook of the opposite arm, eyes closed, enjoying some private ecstasy that he must capture on paper. And he would—he knew that he would.

Wordless still, he drew, and she posed—artist and model, his past and her present, taking him back in time almost twenty years to the studio in Chicago, where he had painted a similar body, a different person, the wrong one—one that he had mistakenly thought was right. Nicole, this biologic enigma, was the right one, a treasure that he would have to return—soon, too soon. God's gift and fate's curse, both at once. He had found her, only to lose her. How would he survive? How in the world would he survive without her?

When he was done, he tore the paper from its pad, folded it once, then twice, and then again, and placed it on her nightstand.

She opened her eyes. "Can I see it?"

"When you get there," he said. "Take it with you, and look at it then."

He started to get up, but she reached out, taking him by the arm and pulling him toward her, gentle and forceful at the same time. They kissed again; and while they did, she unbuttoned his shirt, pulling it off his shoulders, her breath quickening in his mouth as she undressed him. He helped her open his pants, his fingers on hers down there, her tongue in his mouth and on his lips up here, her hands reaching down to free him with a moan and a palm against his hidden skin. In a moment, quick and pressing, his clothes joined hers on the floor; and then, with her on top, her softness yielded while his hardness strained powerful and intent against her, and inside her.

There was no need for words; their shared voice was primal and transcendent, all at once. Her breath was shallow, and his was panting, as he moved out from under her, and around to behind. Her skin, moist and warm, burned like fever in front of him, his lips in her hair and his mouth on her neck, melting and melding in a blended flame, wick and wax and dripping heat. His cheek touched hers with rough on smooth, her back arching, twisting around to urge him back down, his tensing muscles no longer behind her but alongside and in front. She shifted to face him, her breasts pressed moist against his chest, her leg draped over his, vulnerable and open, her wetness like tears that streamed down onto her cheeks and open lips. Time, like her river, flowed forward and backward—down and down and down, and up and up and up, finally reaching that pinnacle, her moment and his together, more than a shudder and a cry, the past and present and future combined.

"*Mon Dieu*," she whispered, trembling.

My God, he thought, shaking. What had they done? And how would he survive? How in the world would he survive—without her?

Chapter Nineteen

By now, Henri was used to being tailed. For the past two days, a police car had been parked on the street outside of his house twenty-four hours a day, and wherever he went—always on foot, his usual way of getting from one place to another—one of the two assigned officers sitting in the surveillance vehicle would get out and follow, keeping a safe distance back, usually a half-block or so behind, trying to blend in with the other sidewalk pedestrians.

They thought he hadn't noticed them, but he was more perceptive than most people. Although Henri had had no further face-to-face visits from inquiring law enforcement officials, the constant presence of the 36 out there was more than a little disconcerting. He had willingly given his DNA sample to Inspecteur Crossier the day before yesterday; the results, by now, were almost certainly in—along with Claudine's. The able homicide detective would be disappointed on both counts—where would she point her gun next?

It was Henri's job to ensure that he was still the main target, drawing the fire away from Susanne, Nicole, and John while they attempted the Time-Transfer tonight at the museum. It wouldn't do for H.G. Wells and company to have a police escort accompanying them to the final chapter in this bizarre, real-life version of a science fiction novel. Henri had agreed, just a few moments ago up in Susanne's apartment, to serve as an on-going distraction for Crossier, who was probably scratching her head at this very moment as she reviewed the Bruante DNA analysis print-out, sitting at her desk at the 36.

It had been somewhat tense up there, on the *deuxième étage* of 14 Avenue Georges V. Henri had been sitting on the living room couch, sipping the café au lait Susanne had served him. John, mini laptop balanced on his knees, sat on a leather push-back chair, reviewing the DNA and chemical analysis read-outs that his graduate student in Chicago had just scanned and emailed to him. Lost in ultra-focused concentration, John had scrolled up and down the pages of his downloads until he was satisfied (or maybe dissatisfied?) with the answer.

"Well?" Susanne had inquired irritably, navigating around the coffee table and sitting down on the couch next to Henri. Nicole, perched nervously on the edge of a matching loveseat to the left of the sofa, reminded Henri of a wrongly accused defendant awaiting the jury's contentious decision.

"This is a little bit complicated," John began.

"Keep it simple, John," Susanne replied curtly. "Am I a mutant, too?"

Of course it was always about Susanne. Henri couldn't help himself. "We're more interested in Nicole's genetic status at the moment, *ma chére*." Susanne shot him a look that could kill, but Henri didn't care. "What's the verdict, professor? Will Nicole be able to make it through another Virtual Hole leading to the past without getting crushed?" This was the bottom line, after all. Henri wanted to be certain that Nicole could safely reach the other side, a concern that he knew John shared as well—because if Nicole couldn't make it back unharmed, Henri knew exactly where he'd be spending the rest of the day. It wouldn't take that long, really, to convert his attic bedroom in Saint-Germain-des-Prés into an apartment of sorts for an unexpected but permanent houseguest.

"Nicole is something we call a homozygote, and Susanne is a heterozygote."

Henri had heard Nicole's quick intake of breath. "What does that mean?" she had asked, locking gazes with John, but the glance that passed between them seemed far more personal than professional. When it came to matters of the heart, Henri was never wrong; and this time, it didn't take a mind reader to see that John and Nicole had made a connection, probably on more than one level.

Henri, a true romantic, couldn't help but smile to himself. *L'amour* was a beautiful thing, transcending boundaries of every kind, ranging from the social to the geographic, but Henri felt fairly certain that this romance, if that's what he was seeing, would go down in the record books as the first long-distance relationship separated by time.

John looked down at his computer screen, visibly troubled—by what he saw there? No, it wasn't that at all. Susanne was probably oblivious to the emotions that showed so clearly on John's face, but Henri wasn't. Henri was certain now, there was no question about it: John was in love, and what he had to do tonight would result in heartbreak—mutual, it seemed. What a tragedy that two people would find love, only to have to say goodbye before they had a chance to really say hello.

"Well," John began, valiantly all business now, "Nicole inherited one chronotonin mutation from her father and another, completely different one, from her mother. We call an individual with two mutations for a particular gene a homozygote, and individuals with a single gene mutation a heterozygote."

"Does Nicole have the chronotonin mutation that you thought she would have?" Henri inquired.

"Yes, she has the promoter site mutation," John confirmed. "This gene produces normal levels of normal chronotonin, until it is activated by certain psychedelic compounds. When Nicole ingested absinthe and laudanum, her chronotonin levels hit the roof, and that's what opened up the connection between her Time-Shell and ours."

"What about the other mutation?" Susanne inquired, crossing her arms. Henri could see that all she really wanted was for John to cut to the chase.

"That one is called a 'missense mutation.' The altered gene produces a more potent version of chronotonin. The hormone made by this gene differs, in a conformational sense, from the so-called 'wild type' or natural molecule. It has the ability to produce low-level electromagnetic deviations in the Time Stream when present in normal concentrations in the body—enough, in all likelihood, to help protect Nicole from the crushing pressures she experienced when she traveled through the Virtual Hole, but definitely not enough to actually create one."

"So which mutation do I have?" Susanne asked impatiently.

"Let's put it this way," John replied, "there's no genetic reason to think that you and magic mushrooms shouldn't get along famously. You've got the mutation that isn't affected by ingesting psychotropic drugs."

Susanne got up from her seat, visibly satisfied with the result. "It's settled, then," she proclaimed, addressing John. "Nicole should be able to get back to 1877 safely, and if all goes well with our little going away party tonight, we'll be wishing her *bon voyage* shortly."

For a fleeting moment, John looked as if he had been stabbed in his gut with a knife—and Nicole? Her face had turned a shade paler.

"Theoretically, Nicole should be safe," John said, "but we're not talking about a mouse here. What we're proposing has never been tried on a human before. There might be dangers and risks involved in the process that none of us has anticipated."

Was John having second thoughts? If so, the personal was winning the tug-of-war with the professional.

"We have a deadline to consider," Susanne reminded him. "There's no turning back now." The lines of her face had hardened with the determination of self-preservation. Susanne's, and Henri's, very existence, in all likelihood, depended on Nicole's return to the past.

"I know the risks," Nicole spoke, calm and stoic. "I'm going; and I'm going tonight." Nicole was determined, too—Henri knew the look. There was no further discussion.

Henri knew that John's sixties-style psychotropic admixture had arrived yesterday, and that Susanne had signed for it, locking it safely in her desk drawer at the museum. It would be important for Henri to keep the police busy while his niece functioned as master of ceremonies at d'Orsay; that's what he and Susanne had spent some time discussing over a second café au lait, in the relative privacy of Susanne's dining room. It seemed quite unnecessary to pull John and Nicole into this particular dialogue, since it did not involve either of them directly; anyway, they had both seemed quietly grateful for the opportunity to spend some time alone together, just across the foyer on the couch in the living room.

At this very moment, they sat knee-to-knee, conversing in discreet whispers about—what? He knew what: their impending separation, most likely. Susanne, in her usual self-absorbed fashion, seemed to have no clue that her ex-boyfriend and her lookalike ancestor had in all likelihood become romantically involved.

"I'm sure Claudine's DNA results are in," Henri had said, "along with my own. Without objective proof linking either myself or your cousin directly to the body, the inspector might be tempted to abandon her theory."

Judging from Crossier's line of questioning the other day, Henri had deduced that the homicide detective believed that Henri had killed Claudine's pimp, or maybe her drug supplier, in order to protect his wayward niece. So far, Henri had functioned as a very effective decoy, a role that he might not be playing much longer if the crime scene evidence didn't point at least a circumstantial finger his way.

"That would not be good," Susanne said. "We need to keep the police focused on you, at least until tomorrow morning. I don't want them following us to the museum tonight."

"Do you have any ideas?" he had asked her.

She smiled; of course she did. One thing about Susanne is that she always had a plan. "Remember when this place was being renovated, and I stayed in your spare room for a few months?"

He nodded; how could he forget? He loved his niece, but she wasn't the easiest person to live with. Well, that wasn't exactly true, since it wasn't really her that he had had a problem with, but the endless phone calls from hopeful admirers, and her frequent overnight absences to sample the short list. He didn't know how she could keep them all straight in her head, although her smart phone seemed to have a special program to do just that. "Of course I remember," he answered. "In fact, I still think I have some of your clothes in the guest room dresser."

"That's exactly what I was thinking about, *Ton-ton*."

"What, your clothes?" He didn't get it at first, but then it hit him. "The woman that I abandoned in the museum—the one that I killed for—was naked," he rationalized out loud. "I wonder what happened to her clothes?" he asked, keeping in perfect step now with his wily niece.

"You took them, obviously; and now, you're worried that the police might find the evidence you took from the crime scene, if they ever decide to search your house."

"I think it's about time for me to get rid of them, don't you?"

"Absolutely. Remember, there was a struggle," she said, improvising. "Dirty them up a little bit before you toss them away in a dumpster somewhere, in full view of the gendarme who is following you. Try not to pick the pricey stuff, though. There should be plenty of non-designer options in your guest room dresser."

He would go a step further than that. Susanne agreed that it would be a nice touch for Henri to throw in some of his own clothes as well, bloodied here and there by a cut on his leg or his arm, maybe, that he could easily inflict on himself with a pair of scissors or a kitchen knife. And then, the *pièce de résistance* would come in the form of a heavy mallet, one of the many tools of his trade, and one that could have easily caused the right type of head trauma, if applied forcefully, metal end first, against someone's skull.

These finds, hauled out of the trashcan by the excited police officer and wrapped up nicely in plastic bags with twist-tie bows, would keep the 36 busy for at least a day or two and would, in turn, keep Henri in the spotlight until early next week, or later. By then, Nicole would be gone and John would be back in Chicago. It wouldn't matter, then, what the police did; but now, Susanne and her all-star cast needed to keep the authorities out of their business. This drop-and-run piece of play-acting seemed a perfect way to do just that.

So Henri had left, intent on executing his next assignment as soon as possible; and now, after almost losing his on-foot pursuer inadvertently at the last busy intersection, he had arrived back on Rue du Bac, rounding the corner to approach his house—and the parked surveillance car containing one rather than two watchful occupants—visible now, less than half a block away.

After a half jog up the stairs that gave access from the outside to his *premiere étage*, Henri let himself into his upstairs flat through the side door. His tail lingered behind a line of shrubbery for a moment, thinking that Henri was unaware that someone, collecting overtime for the express purpose of being nosey, had been right behind him the entire morning—waiting for his mark to be inside his apartment with the door closed before attempting to rejoin his companion in the unassuming department-issue Mercedes that was idling out in front.

There was no time to lose. Henri picked one of Susanne's outfits from the dresser drawer, tearing the hem of the skirt and the collar of the blouse and soiling them on the tiled kitchen floor before throwing them into a garbage bag with a pair of her shoes. Then he moved on to his own bedroom, choosing some worn pants and a fading denim shirt, along with an old pair of work boots that he had been meaning to throw away for months now, anyway. His arm would bleed more than his leg, especially if he made the slice over one of the lines of blue that tracked up and over his biceps; so, with his eyes closed, he pressed the blade into his skin, letting his blood stain the throwaway clothes that he had placed on the table, right under his arm.

It all looked wonderfully incriminating. When the police actually analyzed the spatter, they would discover that the blood didn't belong to their victim. Rather, they would determine it belonged to a careless art restorer named Henri Bruante, who would explain that he'd accidentally cut himself with a razor-sharp planer while re-surfacing a frame.

He took the inside stairs down to his ground floor workshop, where he picked a large mallet, the perfect crime weapon dissembler, and dropped it with a thud into the bag. Along with the clothes and shoes, it completed his collection. Now he was finally ready for a nonchalant walk past the surveillance car to find a public trash can on the street—not the small one on the corner, which was usually full to overflowing anyway, but another one, a larger dumpster located six blocks down and three blocks over. It would work out perfectly, his guilt magnified by distance—the farther, the better—and by the time he returned to his house, the CSI team would be swarming around the garbage container and picking through the evidence.

He made the trip there and back without a glitch, delivering his package to the dumpster. Now that it was done, mission accomplished, he felt much better. Back in his living room, he poured himself a glass of cognac and settled into his favorite easy chair for a few moments of down time. Remote in hand, he switched on the television, already tuned to France 3, his usual viewing preference. It took a moment or two for the cable box to boot up, but when the screen flashed on to breaking news, he couldn't believe what he saw.

A press conference, televised live, was taking place in front of Musée d'Orsay, of all places. The star of this particular headline piece was none other than Susanne's executive director, René Lauren.

"The results of the hair analysis are definitive," he was saying. "Now, thanks to modern technology, we have DNA evidence that supports my theory that Courbet, not Degas, painted the *After the Bath* masterpieces."

"Monsieur Lauren," a reporter asked, "how did you discover the hair embedded in these paintings? Were you following a lead from historical documentation?"

"I observed the hair in one of the Courbet nudes and also in the side-by-side Degas pairing. That's when the idea came to me, so I authorized an art restorer to retrieve a hair from each of four paintings."

This was bad—very bad. Lauren was trying to pass off Susanne's theory as his own, and he was succeeding. But there was more.

"Our sources tell us that this find has already resulted in your confirmed nomination to the Ministry of Culture. Is this rumor true?"

"I'm not at liberty to say," he replied, but the smile on his face could only mean that he had already signed his contract.

"If you were to speculate," another journalist said, "who would replace you as executive director of Musée d'Orsay, if you happened to receive this appointment?"

"François Bertolette," Lauren replied without hesitation. "He would be my choice, if my position at d'Orsay ever needed to be filled."

Henri sighed. This turn of events would devastate Susanne, whether she admitted it or not. Even the woman of steel might break, once she got wind of René Lauren's betrayal. There would be a confrontation, of course—Susanne was not the type of person to take a beating like this lying down. But what good would it do? Lauren would now be viewed as the mastermind behind this explosive Courbet and Degas discovery, and he would be the one to reap all the benefits, while Susanne stood by with her fists clenched and raised, but with no muscle behind her punches.

What could Susanne do, really? She could threaten to expose him as a cheat and a liar, but it would be her word against his—and whom would the public believe: the executive director of d'Orsay—a man with an impeccable reputation to back him—or a hotheaded assistant director with arguably questionable motives, making wild accusations against a boss whose position she clearly coveted? The train had left the station; in fact, it had already gained enough momentum that it couldn't be stopped, no matter what Susanne threatened to do.

In Henri's opinion, Susanne stood helpless on the tracks. If she didn't get out of the way fast, the oncoming rush of the inexorable would flatten her, once and for all.

Well, somebody had to tell her, so it might as well be him. Henri picked up his cell phone, letting his speed dial call her mobile. It only rang once before she picked up. "Susanne, it's Henri," he announced. He took in a deep breath. "Turn on your television and tune to France 3—and please, don't shoot the messenger."

Chapter Twenty

It was time for the Time-Transfer, and Susanne was furious.

As she pulled her red BMW into the underground parking lot at d'Orsay—with John in the front passenger seat, quiet as can be, and Nicole in the back, equally silent—Susanne just couldn't get a grip on her anger, try as she might. She had confronted René face-to-face, immediately after talking to Henri this afternoon. She had driven directly to the museum, catching him just as the news vans were pulling out of their parking spots.

She had intended to make a scene, but with no one around to see it, her energy would have been wasted; so behind closed doors instead, she had found herself trying to open a hole in a brick wall with a wooden stick. She kept replaying the interchange in her mind, a mostly one-sided rage against the smug René, who barely reacted to her threats and assurances of retaliation. She said she'd expose him; he replied that no one would believe her. She swore she would ruin him; his answer was, "Go ahead and try." She promised to call his wife and tell her about their affair, but he responded by looking back at her with contempt, informing her that his wife, and everyone else, already knew—and had known for months.

Susanne threw the terms "academic plagiarism" and "intellectual property" in his face, but he had only smiled. When she mentioned "sexual discrimination," he had actually laughed out loud. He'd be singing a different tune, she predicted, when a lawsuit instead of an irate and fuming mistress slapped him in the face. She had stormed out of his office with her hand stinging and her indignation seething. The whole thing was outrageous, and she would get her revenge.

Finding an attorney wouldn't be hard, but the fight would be, potentially. The Courbet and Degas theory had been the topic of her master's thesis of course, so at least there was something in print, albeit only a department copy, on file somewhere in the stacks of the University of Paris. Copyright laws might not apply to a student's scholarly research piece, though, which was really just an extra-long essay, submitted in exchange for a lettered degree.

Besides, there hadn't been anything of true substance in those pages. Her thesis was an ingenious hypothesis that in the end had turned out to be true; back then, however, she had had no hard evidence whatsoever supporting the premise in her footnotes, bibliography, or appendices.

And what about the sexual discrimination angle? She wouldn't get far with that one, since François Bertolette was as qualified as she was for the executive directorship (if not more, it pained her to admit), and there were two other women on d'Orsay's staff besides Susanne that also had been passed over as potential candidates for the position. A legal battle wouldn't be easy, but what other option did she have? It's not like she could just pick up and start her life over again somewhere else. She had repeated these agonized thoughts to herself for most of the evening as she sat at her dining room table with a bottle of cognac in front of her, weighing her nonexistent options. Her tentative conclusion was that good things were worth fighting for—and she was a fighter.

She wouldn't be popular, though; she would be earmarked as the troublemaker who had eaten sour grapes and who now was on a mission to bring the grocer to his knees. Could Susanne really stay at d'Orsay and function productively in that kind of environment? She would be a woman scorned, a loser whose own stubbornness would not allow her to step out of the ring gracefully, forced by her very own character makeup to flaunt her rejection for all to see, instead of her body—a foreign concept, and one that she couldn't help but dread. She was strong, though, a woman who always had a plan—and right now, her plan was the better of two—or more—evils.

She drove down through the concrete tunnel, as heavy machinery lowered the curtain of metal behind her with an odd finality, as if to say there was no going back. She had to admit to feeling trapped. The only world Susanne had ever known—back there, up the ramp, and on the other side of the cold aluminum garage door—no longer existed. Adjusting to the new reality that awaited her would be a challenge. But she was up for a challenge; she always was. This Bruante was tough as nails, and she would never change. If that way out, behind her, was blocked, then she would just have to find another exit. The world on the other side of the front door, instead of the back, would be better than her old one. When one door closed, another one opened, as they always said; it's just that she liked what was behind door number one, and it was a shame that she had lost it in the way she had.

Try as she might, Susanne's attempt to think positively was having a meager impact on her anger management problem. She sped erratically through the empty parking lot with squealing tires, pulling into her designated space with a screech. She noticed in the rearview mirror that John and Nicole were exchanging glances as the car jolted to a halt.

Susanne was out of the car before either of them had even unbuckled. She couldn't really care less what either of them thought of her. She had her own issues to deal with and couldn't be bothered with the irrelevant opinions of a pitiful ex-boyfriend and a misplaced distant ancestor. She had people to see and places to go, starting with the security guard waiting for her upstairs in the front lobby. Her two sidekicks would simply have to keep up if they didn't want to be left behind in the dust.

She looked at her watch—1:15 a.m. They had thirteen hours, give or take, before Edmond's fate would be determined one way or the other, in another Time-Shell located in the distant past. John had better be true to his word. He'd said he felt fairly certain that he would be able to open the right connection from this time to the other, using Nicole, her mutated chronotonin gene, and a bottle of his magic potion.

Danger be damned! He worried too much. If Nicole had traveled safely from the past into the future, there was no reason to doubt that the same trip would succeed in reverse. The so-called chronotonin halo would protect her, John had said so; and John, the all-knowing Nobel Prize contender, was the world's authority on this kind of thing, so he would know. The Time-Transfer would work, she knew it would, and this time, a one-way ticket was what Susanne was counting on. Out of sight, out of mind—out of the museum, and out of this world and her life. That's where the lucky time traveler was going tonight, once and for all.

Nicole got out first, waiting for John on the opposite side of the car before walking with him over to the driver's side, where Susanne stood waiting. Something was going on between the two of them, Susanne felt sure, but she didn't really care. The way they looked at each other told Susanne enough, but there were other clues too: the trembling of John's hand when he had folded the copy of Nicole's obituary, slipping it carefully—even intimately—into the back pocket of her jeans; the way Nicole's eyes had glistened with emotion when John had pledged, in almost marriage-vow solemnity, that he would get Nicole back to her own Time-Shell safely; or how he had touched her just so, his arm around her waist, taking her hand in his to help her into the car just a little while ago, when they had left Susanne's apartment together.

All of these things added up to one thing: a problem for them that didn't concern her—unless, of course, their little romance got in the way of tonight's big adventure. Now Susanne had to focus, and she couldn't afford to lose her concentration on a pair of lovebirds who were temporarily sharing the same cage.

Always feeling better when she alone held the reins, she decided it was time to spur on the horse. "We'll take the elevator upstairs," she said, slipping right into action mode, "and you'll wait for me there. After I take care of the security guard and turn off the video cameras and motion alarms, I'll make a detour to my office, on the way back to get you." She had locked up John's elixir, the one that would intoxicate Nicole, in her desk drawer. She hoped the procedure wouldn't take long, because it would be nice to put this all behind her, and quickly.

Nicole and John actually held hands in the elevator—cute, in some people's book, but sickeningly sweet in Susanne's. Apparently they didn't care what she thought of them, either. Well, the feeling was mutual. Let them flaunt their little love affair for the next twenty minutes or so, because by 2:00 a.m., all of this would be nothing more than ancient history—at least in Susanne's book.

The elevator opened a moment later on the far end of the catwalk. Nicole had been here before, but John hadn't. "Wait right here, both of you." Susanne didn't wait for their reply but headed instead down the walkway to the left, retrieving a pint of spiked brandy and some bright red lipstick from her purse as she walked. At the other end, she stopped for a moment to freshen her painted lips, pressing them together to even out the color.

She had dressed specifically for tonight's deception, in spiked black heels and an ultra-short party dress, cut low on top and riding up obscenely high down below. She made a dramatic entrance into the front lobby, giggling as she steadied herself with one hand against the wall, zigzagging on precarious heels to finally arrive at the security desk. This time, the night guard was a guy named André. *Perfect,* she thought; he would make a much easier mark than Pierre had, the other night.

She leaned on the counter, directly across from André. "I'm so drunk," she slurred. "I never get like this!"

"I, uh—well, oh my," he stuttered. He struck her as a poor excuse for an attack dog—one that would be easy to subdue with Susanne's particular cut of meat.

"I'm done here, André," she confided, following her script perfectly. "Finished. My personal life is an absolute mess, my career is over, and I have nothing left to look forward to. What the hell," she declared, raising the bottle in the air. "I might as well drink and be merry." She eyed him knowingly. "There's nothing companionship and a bottle can't fix, they say. Care to try?" She moved toward him but slipped, catching herself by grabbing the edge of the counter, a nicely executed touch. "I'm so clumsy. It must be the heels."

He gulped, and his eyes grew wide. "Perhaps you need to sleep it off, Mademoiselle Bruante," he said, getting up from his chair and moving around the security station to help her. "I can't leave the museum, but I could help you over to your office so you can rest on your couch."

"I'll let you help me to my office, André, but sleep wasn't exactly what I had in mind." He was next to her now, and he jumped when she threw her arms around his neck. "I came here looking for you, and I guess I found you!"

"But Mademoiselle Bruante—"

"Call me Susanne, please." She leaned forward, so that their lips were almost touching. "You're cute. I've always thought so." He glanced down to examine her cleavage, and a few beads of sweat started to form on his brow. It was working; she had known that it would.

"You came here tonight, to—to find me?" he stammered, incredulous, but she noted that he did not back up.

"*Oui.* You're just what I need right now," she cooed. She kissed him, long and sexy and arousing. He put his arms around her, but when he tried to pull her close, she put both hands on his chest and pushed him away with a playful smile.

"First you need a drink. If I'm a little bit tipsy, then you should be too!"

He nodded, ready, it seemed, to agree to anything just to get her in the sack. She still had the flask—more sedative, really, than brandy—in one hand. She held it to his lips, so very helpful—tipping it up just enough to give him the first powerful dose.

"That's strong," he said, swallowing hard and shivering as the tranquilizer in disguise hit his stomach.

"You'll need a bit more to catch up with me," she said.

He nodded again, as docile and compliant as a pet dog, taking the bottle from her hand and swigging almost all of it down.

That should do it, she thought, *but how long will it take for the drugs to do their job?* She might have to show a lot more skin before the sleeping pills finally kicked in. No problem, she thought, turning around and pretending to fumble with the zipper on the back of her dress. "Could you help me with this, André?"

"Yes, sure, come here." His speech already sounded slurred and his eyes looked glassy.

That was fast, Susanne thought. At least now she wouldn't have to bare it all for the sake of science—although she would have been more than willing to.

"I feel…dizzy," he said.

"Because you drank it too fast, silly." She took him by the arm, guiding him around the security island and easing him back into his chair. "Rest here a minute or two, and then we'll go down the hall for some real fun and games."

"Fun…" His smile was drugged, his eyelids heavy.

"And games," she finished, pushing the chair forward on its wheels toward the desk.

"So…sleepy." He folded his arms on the table, laying his head down. "Sleep," he mumbled, and in a matter of seconds he was out.

It was time to get down to serious business. The security panel consisted of a semicircular display of individual video feeds from all of the museum's surveillance cameras, a newly updated system that was controlled by a touch screen panel located directly in front of André, who was dead to the world. His chair was on wheels, luckily, so Susanne was able to roll him out of the way without too much effort.

This must be it, she thought, touching an icon labeled "Master Video Control." Next to it, the On box shimmered a backlit green, while the Off box, unlit, waited patiently for her command. She touched the Off button, and it immediately glowed a soft red. The On button was no longer lit, and the video feeds, like magic, all went dead.

"*Et voilà!*" she proclaimed. Now to deactivate the motion detectors. Each painting was connected to an electronic sensor on the wall, which would alarm if someone attempted to remove it from the wall. With that task complete, her plan would involve three more stops on the way to its final execution. The first stop would be straight to her office, to get John's Time-Transfer concoction; then to the elevator, to gather up the Time-Transfer participants; and finally, to the gallery, for the solemn assembly underneath *The Origin of the World* for the Time-Transfer itself. Well, two out of the three of them would be solemn; she, for one, wouldn't be crying. Tonight would mark the start of a new beginning—the old discarded for the new, the future uncertain but still stretching ahead, a world of challenges she had not asked for but would embrace nevertheless. It would all be better with the Time-Transfer behind her. She couldn't wait.

She crossed the lobby, taking the door behind the ticket counter to access the administrative hallway in back. Her office was down there, close to the other end, just three doors down from the emergency exit—the one that Nicole had triggered when she had been pursued by gendarmes down this same passageway, almost two weeks ago now. Susanne entered her office and used the tiny key, hidden in the pocket of her purse, to open her desk drawer. She retrieved the clear liquid—colorless and bland, looking so deceptively innocuous in its graded glass flask, the meniscus curving upward on either side. Was it odorless and tasteless, or pungent and bitter? Susanne would never know. She had the wrong gene mutation—or the right one, depending on how you looked at it—so she wouldn't be the one to sample John's specially manufactured pick-me-up. Nicole would; it was always Nicole.

A moment later, she pushed open the door to the back of the exhibit galleries, a short cut to the opposite side of the museum, and the elevator where the not-so-happy couple waited for her, undoubtedly dreading what was about to happen next. First room, second, third, fourth and fifth—there she was, hanging on the wall, and there and there and there—Nicole everywhere, and everywhere Nicole.

Susanne could never get away from Nicole, it seemed, but in a few minutes, all that would change. The renowned, anonymous model would be left far behind, in a manner of speaking, thanks to a Time-Tunnel devised by God himself, facilitated by a gene that had been altered by his whim, with the ability to alter time itself. "Renowned model?" Susanne could have done that, too, and much better. Nicole had simply been in the right place at the right time. Given the same opportunity, Susanne would have been more than renowned. "The celebrated and legendary Susanne Bruante"—now that was something to daydream about.

She found John and Nicole waiting exactly where she had left them. Now it was time. Without a word, she handed John the flask and then turned on her heel to lead them back to the gallery. She didn't look back—she would never look back, because everything important to her lay straight ahead.

"How should we do this?" Susanne asked, stopping in front of Courbet's erotic painting—what John had called the Common Object. Susanne looked at the depiction of Nicole's genitalia, most likely indiscernible from her own, where the Virtual Hole would begin and end, an energy tunnel that would take a time traveler in from this side and spit him out at the other. The whole bizarre process reminded Susanne of time's distorted imitation of creation followed by parturition: stimulation and arousal, injection and fertilization, and then a rapid assimilation followed by ejection—a rebirth, really, of an actual person through some kind of futuristic, electromagnetic birth canal.

Would it hurt? How would the tunnel look, and how would it sound inside? Would the journey be rapid or slow? These were questions only a time traveler could answer; at the moment, there was only one person in this room who could qualify as one of those.

John held up the flask, studying it, his sadness undisguised. "Nicole needs to be near the Common Object. After she drinks the TMMP, you and I will need to step back—way back. Otherwise we'll get sucked into the Virtual Hole."

"Should I lie down?" Nicole asked. Susanne saw that the younger version of herself wouldn't meet John's eyes. This would be difficult for her, and for him. *C'est la vie.*

"I would say that you should try to reproduce your positioning from before—if you remember."

"I was on top," Nicole answered quietly. Now this might be awkward. How would the good Dr. Noland handle this kind of ultra-personal information?

"You should squat, then, in front of *The Origin of the World,*" he replied, surprising Susanne by keeping his cool—at least for now.

John gripped the flask tightly, safe and secure within his palm, giving Susanne the impression that in the end, he might actually decide that he would keep it, rather than giving it up for Nicole to drink. "You'll have to take it all, Nicole. The amount of hallucinogen in this bottle should be just enough—" He paused for a moment, and it seemed to Susanne that he was engaged in an inner struggle to rein in his emotions. "Enough…to send you back."

His voice quavered; in a second, so would his will. For the job to get done, Susanne saw that she must do it herself. "I'll handle this," she said, snatching the bottle from her former lover.

"But—"

"Wait over there, John." It was a command, not a request. "I'll join you in a minute, as soon as she drinks it."

Susanne held the bottle, although he had resisted, and now he seemed rooted to the floor. Maybe a gentler approach would be needed to convince him to step back. "Look, I know what's going on here," she said, trying to lend a note of kindness to the hard edge in her voice. "You're too close to this, and even a blind man can see why. You need to let me do it, because you won't be able to."

John stepped toward Nicole, but Susanne stood in his way. "No goodbyes. It will only make things more difficult—for both of you."

"If it works, it will work fast," John warned.

"Don't worry, I'll move away quickly."

He looked past Susanne, over her shoulder, at Nicole. "When you get to the other side, stay away from the painting, or else you might ricochet back. And remember what I put in your back pocket. Don't go to Place Pigalle! Promise me, Nicole, that you'll remember. Promise me?"

"I promise, John." Nicole's voice barely rose above a whisper. "I promise that I'll remember. I could never…never forget…" Her words trailed off, and she looked at John with a deep longing, a depth of feeling that Susanne realized she herself had never known for another person.

The feeling almost got to her—almost. Susanne shook herself loose from the emotion and reminded herself: *This has to be done now!* She simply couldn't—correction, wouldn't—let these star-crossed lovers waste any more time and risk losing the opportunity to send her rival to her rightful place. Susanne handed John her purse, to give him a purpose, and gave him a gentle, one-handed push toward the corridor. "Here, take this and go stand in the doorway over there. I'll join you in a minute."

"If she starts to ricochet back and forth, that would be a disaster," he said in her ear, so Nicole wouldn't hear. "I hope you realize that if that happens, we'll have to destroy the Common Object—Courbet's painting—after Nicole's second trip back to the past. That would be the only way to break the cycle."

Susanne waved him away. It would be a shame to destroy a masterpiece, but it would never come to that. John was just fretting unnecessarily, as usual, and the last thing they needed at this crucial juncture was something else to worry about. "One thing at a time, John." She had to physically turn him toward the main catwalk and give him another gentle shove. "Go stand over there, please."

He listened to her this time. Now that their modern-day Romeo was out of the picture, she would have to deal with Juliette. "On all fours, Mademoiselle," Susanne told her, realizing but not caring that her instructions sounded lewd. "Assume the position."

Nicole squatted in front of the painting, and Susanne handed her the opened flask. "You must drink all of it."

"I know," Nicole said, her voice flat. She raised the flask to her lips, and in one swig, it was gone. This girl knew how to down a shot. Susanne breathed a sigh of relief. It was done. Finally, it was done.

And now it was time for the fireworks. Let the show begin.

Chapter Twenty-One

It tasted more sweet than bitter, in stark contrast to the moment. Nicole knelt on all fours in front of the painting, trying her best to reproduce her positioning from before, in an attempt to minimize the variables involved in opening up another Virtual Hole leading from here to there. John looked on from afar, while Susanne stayed close—right next to her, in fact, which was much too close for comfort.

Make no mistake about it: Susanne had not chosen her role as some kind of self-appointed Time-Travel expeditor out of any love or concern for her relative. There was measurable danger involved in remaining at Nicole's side, but Susanne obviously had concluded that this risk was greatly outweighed by the potential benefit. By hovering over Nicole's shoulder, Susanne could ensure that the soon-to-be time traveler had taken all of her medicine, every single drop; and Nicole had the distinct feeling that if Susanne could have poured the elixir down her throat, causing her to sputter and gag as it went down, she would have done so gladly.

Nicole had decided to save the impatient Susanne the trouble. She had taken it all down, in one gulp—not so difficult to do, really, since there wasn't much liquid in the small container to begin with. The TMMP, as John had called it, burned warm in her throat, seeping quickly into her bloodstream—almost instantaneously, in fact—and the rapid ingestion led to immediate results. Nicole, having been there before, knew exactly what would come next.

In a state of delirium already, Nicole looked down the front of her blouse at her breasts, both of them falling forward, nipples hard and tingling, pushing hot against the fabric, a sensation that rippled outward in electric static to activate every nerve in her body and every pore of her sweltering skin. But that wasn't all. Her breasts were actually glowing, the left one shimmering pink, containing dizzying whirls of spinning blue; the right one pulsing and burning insanely, a deep green touched with patches of black. Her distorted focus, hazed and steamy, moved from her breasts down to the floor; and with odd detachment, she saw herself in duplicate—one version, vaporous and ethereal, floating up above the other, an earthly shadow, crouching, still, on the floor, with Susanne at her side. The paintings, from her new vantage point up here, were all at eye level, including the one directly in front of her—the one that looked so very familiar.

This had happened to her before, hadn't it? It was hard to recall. Her thoughts were scrambled now, racing forward and retreating back; but she remembered a bed, and a man, and a painting—this painting, the surface as indistinct then as it was becoming now. Those were her legs, parted ever so softly, right in front of her; but in between, at the place where pink flesh stared back at her, partially concealed by the curls of hot brunette wildness, she couldn't tell. Something white was happening there, swirling and bright and awful, starting out small but growing in terrifying increments, a slowly expanding consumption of glaring heat.

In a moment the painting would be gone; she remembered now. The hole would start pulling, just as it had before, and she wouldn't be able to stop it. When that happened, all would be lost—she would be lost, falling and falling into nothingness, searing white turning to frigid black, leading God knows where.

Nicole looked down again. Things had changed: she wasn't down there anymore, but up here instead, her body joined with her soul, an inevitable communion filled with meaning, a signal that meant it would happen rapidly now, the first step in the dreaded consummation, the beginning of the end.

Time had slowed, though, just as it had before. Once again, her skin burned and burned, hotter and hotter, as if she herself were some kind of living fire surrounded by a cloud of heat that John's elixir had ignited by its interaction with her unique body chemistry, emanating outward in a protective shell that she now knew would prevent her from being crushed within the Virtual Hole. A split second, once again, could easily last a minute, one heartbeat was more like ten, a single breath was almost half a lifetime—it was all so slow and sluggish, seemingly unstoppable.

Nicole watched the painting of herself, right there in front, gradually become a blur of unfocused flesh and skin, in slow motion—a collage of pale tans, whites, and browns; a disrupted kaleidoscope of melting paint; a cloud of swirling colorful mist; and finally, a bright white maelstrom, spinning with screaming and broiling wind, leading directly into a void of nothingness that pulled and pulled and pulled.

Nicole was slipping forward—she couldn't stop it—and in a moment the white heat would turn to cold black when it sucked her in, just as before.

The hole would consume her—this is what it did, and that was exactly what it was doing, now. Nicole anticipated the slide forward, inching toward the lip. Was there movement, though, off to the side? It was Susanne, she vaguely realized, preparing to flee toward safety, away from Nicole, away from here, away from the sucking power of nothingness, which stretched ahead. But that didn't matter—Susanne didn't matter. Why? Because ahead was Nicole's world, not behind, just as the hole demanded. *Come to me,* the hole seemed to say. *Come to me, I'm straight ahead. Come to me, come to me…*

But then she felt an impact—her shoulder hitting the edge, the side of her chest scraping the brink, perhaps? Had this happened before? Possibly, but maybe not; she couldn't decide. And then, she found herself, suddenly, looking ahead and behind, both at once, an impossible feat made possible—made real—by her psychedelic eye. Was she falling forward or ricocheting back? Was she being pulled in or pushed out? Nicole felt too confused to know.

Her thoughts, and the sights and sounds around her, tangled together in jumbled chaos—deafening, yet muted. It was wrong, yet it was right; it was right, but also wrong—tumbling and spinning, back and back and back, moving forward perhaps; but then again, no. The past was behind her, but the future was too. It all made sense, but none of it did, until she fell onto something hard, her head crashing into dizzying reds and blues and yellows and greens. And whites, explosive whites, burning and searing with pain back there, where her eye couldn't see. Was this real? It had to be, but it wasn't. It was, but it couldn't be. The paradox was in her mind—that was it! *It's all in my mind,* she thought. *It's all in my mind.*

Come back, the hole seemed to scream. *Come back, come back!*

She was back, she realized. She went in, then she came out, she was gone, but now she was back. As everything faded from white to the all-consuming nothingness of black, she realized that it was over, and she was back.

~

When the time for action finally came, Susanne had reacted just perfectly. Finally, it was over.

It hadn't taken long for John's compound to work. Susanne had seen Nicole's face turn very pale, very quickly, which was Susanne's signal to squat on sprint-ready legs and look for the signs in the painting that the Virtual Hole was beginning to form. She warned herself again, for the twentieth time, that she needed to be careful, staying so close; it just wouldn't do to have the wrong Bruante sucked in. That would ruin everything, throwing a wrench into the gears of her plan—the one that she had spent so much time, recently, conceiving.

John kept yelling warnings, over there by the threshold, but Susanne couldn't care less. He wasn't the one whose life depended on a successful Time-Transfer; so he could scream until he was blue in the face, and Susanne would just continue to ignore him. Susanne was staying, there would be no argument, until the moment she could be sure that the right person was precisely where she had to be, at the right time.

She had kept her eye intently focused on the painting, because this is where Nicole had said the Virtual Hole had formed before, back in the past when her mutated gene had been activated by another potent mixture: absinthe and laudanum, then, offered by a one-night stand who had definitely been in the wrong place at the wrong time, with no chronotonin mutation to protect him from the crushing force of the hole. Susanne's vigilance, her shrewdness, her strength of will—her inherent makeup, genetically speaking—would most definitely prevent anything like that from happening to her. She, for one, always ended up on top; and this time especially, she would be extra certain that her perfect timing would put her in the right place at the right time. She was no Guy, Nicole's helpless bed partner who had met his end because he hadn't measured up. She was Susanne Bruante; and Susanne Bruante always won.

It had started between the legs, a minute undulation on the surface of the painting—ever so slight, barely a ripple, but still enough for Susanne to know that it was starting. The agitation grew, a circular whirlpool now, after only a split second; if Susanne didn't move fast, it would be too late.

It all seemed to happen in slow motion. Susanne had been on her feet in less than a heartbeat, but at that same moment the painting disappeared. Just as she had willed her legs to start running, both the painting and the wall where it had been hanging turned to mist. Before her first step had led to a second, Nicole was no longer crouching on the floor by Susanne's side. Moving fast yet slow, Susanne's next step had moved her against the simultaneously levitated Nicole, and closer to success, while the swirling maelstrom, screaming silently behind her, quickly gained strength; but there was still time. As Nicole hovered and began to move forward, helpless and weightless, at the lip of the void, Susanne made the impact, her hands and her full weight behind her, against Nicole's shoulder and chest. The pull of the hole was only just beginning, so the shove—forceful, yes, and admittedly more than was actually required—sent Nicole tumbling and spinning through the air, back and back and back, toward John, landing with a thud on the floor in the middle of the gallery. That had been the first crucial moment—and Susanne had played it just right.

Next came part two: escape. Susanne knew that she had to get out now, because staying here was simply not an option. She knew that she would need to act fast. With Nicole's chronotonin field abruptly disconnected from its Common Object, the hole would close very quickly—or at least this was her theory.

Susanne turned away from John, away from d'Orsay, away from everything old and toward everything new. She belonged in Bohemian Paris, belonged in1877, belonged in an artist's studio, posing for one Impressionist after another, immortalized on canvas, the most unforgettable *Nude Reclining* the world would ever know. What did she have here? What was she leaving behind? Nothing—that's what. On the other side of that Time-Tunnel, she could start her life over again, and it would be glorious.

The vortex was still there, but it was growing smaller, and smaller, and smaller; in just a moment, she wouldn't be able to pass through. Susanne dashed forward—since her new life depended on it—ran into the jump, and with her eyes closed made the leap of faith that would take her far away.

The energy closed in behind her, propelling her forward, pushing her along on the crest of the electromagnetic wave, into and through the empty void—forward and backward, ahead and behind, into the past but toward her future, once and for all. She knew the hole was closing, a black shadow following closely, disaster barely averted. She felt the hole around her, too, but soft, not hard. Susanne had her own chronotonin halo, after all—not as strong as Nicole's, but strong enough to do the job. Without it, she would have certainly been crushed by now; but look at her, she was just fine. Susanne Bruante was always fine.

As she tumbled and fell, down and down, and up and up, she would have patted herself on the back if she could have. When it had finally been time for action, she had reacted just perfectly. In a moment, it would all be over.

Whiteness surrounded her, in front and to the sides, but not behind; then, just as Nicole had described, it turned suddenly and completely black.

Finally, it was over, and she was gone.

It had happened so quickly that John didn't have time to react. The painting, and the wall in a three-foot radius around it, had suddenly turned to swirling mist, and in less time than it had taken for him to blink, Nicole was lifted up and forward by the interaction of her super-charged chronotonin halo with the oppositely charged magnetic field of the Virtual Hole. Susanne, in the meantime, was in the process of doing the unthinkable—namely, removing Nicole physically from her essential position right in front of the Common Object. After the confusing action was over, John realized that the hole had promptly snapped shut, but not before Susanne had dived into the void herself. Nicole lay on the floor in the middle of the gallery, motionless.

John felt fairly certain that Nicole had sustained a blow to the head—he had actually heard the thud, and he prayed that he wouldn't have to deal with a serious concussion on top of everything else. Nicole was still exuding a very potent chronotonin halo, and there were countless other Common Objects hanging on the walls all around them. In her current state, Nicole was a living and breathing super-inducer, a walking stimulus for the formation of Virtual Holes, and she would be for the next twelve hours or so—unless John could get the remaining unabsorbed TMMP out of her system, and fast. The last thing they needed was for Nicole to open a hole underneath a Van Gogh, for instance, that would suck them both in, transporting one living and one dead time traveler directly back to Vincent's back yard in Arles, circa 1888 or 1889.

John's mind raced as he ran to Nicole's side. Susanne had taken a big risk, relying on her own mutated chronotonin to protect her from being crushed by the tremendous pressures created by the magnetic field distortion within a Virtual Hole. Traveling through the Time Tunnel without the ultra-high levels of chronotonin that a promoter site mutant (like Nicole) could produce was dicey, at best. John wondered if Susanne had even been able to make it past the borders of this Time-Shell.

It was sad, really. It seemed hard to believe that Susanne's life here, in 2011, had been bad enough to trigger this kind of extreme measure, but he could certainly understand how devastated she must have felt when her boss took the credit this morning for her life's work. With her career in shambles and no husband or children to offer her emotional support, who wouldn't leap at a chance to start their life over again in a new and exciting place? Granted, most people would choose a fresh geographic start rather than a chronological one, but Susanne had always marched to her own drummer. *Godspeed,* he thought. In the end, if she made it to the other side safely, Susanne would come out on top. She always did.

Now it was time to focus on the problem at hand. He gently turned Nicole over from face-down to face-up, supporting her head and neck as he did so. There was no blood—that was good—and she was breathing, slow and steady. He put a finger on her wrist to check her pulse, which felt strong and even. Another good sign.

"Nicole," he said, bending over with his lips near her ear. "Can you hear me?" Her head moved, almost imperceptibly. Yes, she had heard him! "I'm going to get you out of here, but you're going to have to help me, by holding on to me with your arms around my neck. Do you think you can do that?" He could easily handle one hundred and fifteen pounds of semi-conscious weight, but the same amount, totally unconscious, would have been a different story entirely.

Nicole nodded again, and this time, she even opened her eyes. "I feel…sick," she said, her voice thick and slow.

Perfect, he thought. If she felt nauseated already, he wouldn't have to encourage her to empty her stomach with a finger down her throat. But here was not the right place for that. If she could just hold on until they got to the underground parking garage, a drying puddle of vomit on the concrete floor, off to the side and in the corner somewhere, would attract much less attention than the same kind of thing up here. "When we get downstairs, we'll handle that," he promised. "Can you keep it down for just a few more minutes, until I can get you there?"

"*Oui.*" She closed her eyes again, moving her lips as if she were talking to someone. She was hallucinating—big time, no doubt. The combination of psychedelics she had ingested was enough to produce a soaring trip, and God knows where her mind was right now.

As he lifted her, one arm under both legs and the other around the small of her back, she wrapped her arms around his neck and laid her head on his shoulder—so vulnerable, so grateful, and so completely deserving of his love and protection. It felt wonderful to have her back like this, and he swore that he would never, ever try to send her away again. He decided, at that very moment, that he had no scientific obligation whatsoever to get Nicole back to where she had come from.

Why? Because destiny, he rationalized, had intended to send her here, and that same hand of fate, just a few short minutes ago, had unequivocally prevented him from sending her back. If this wasn't a sign, what was? It felt right; and as far as John was concerned, Nicole had ended up exactly where she belonged—which was right here, in Musée d'Orsay, on the thirteenth of June in the year 2011, at precisely 2:09 a.m., cradled in his arms.

But what about the Bruante line? They would survive—John's intuition told him they would. Susanne had gone back, hadn't she? And like it or not, by choosing that path, she had taken on the role of Nicole's surrogate, the protector of her own bloodline. It was pretty simple, really. Susanne would feel compelled by her own need for self-preservation to save Edmond—because if she didn't, all of his direct descendants, including Susanne, would cease to exist. John wasn't sure how that would work, exactly, but whatever the mechanism, Susanne would not want to be part of that particular demonstration.

With Susanne's purse hooked on an elbow and Nicole reclining across his arms, John made his way carefully down the middle of the exhibit hall, keeping as far away as possible from the paintings on either side. As he exited the room and moved onto the catwalk, he realized that the museum was littered with landmines: not just paintings, but sculptures, and furniture, and antique decor—all of them potential Common Objects by virtue of their age, and all of them prone to the stimulating effect of the intoxicated electromagnetic "deviant" he held in his arms. One false step and it would all be over. But somehow he got past them all safely, at last stepping with his lovely burden into the elevator again, but this time going down.

As it turned out, Nicole didn't need to crouch in a corner to get rid of the remaining TMMP. There was a large trash bin next to the elevator, so John eased her down carefully onto unstable legs for the purging, supporting her with one arm around her waist and the other on her shoulder. After a few successful retches, he lifted her up again, carrying her across the parking lot to where Susanne's red BMW waited, ready to take them home. Inside the car, he tipped his rear view mirror down, choosing just the right angle so that he could see Nicole resting in the back seat while he drove.

He knew where to go—it wasn't far. Twenty minutes later, after navigating the deserted streets of a sleeping Paris, he pulled up at the curb in front of Susanne's condo. When he helped her out of the car, he found that Nicole could walk—kind of, with more than a little bit of assistance. Although there was very little risk of running into neighbors at this early hour, John wasn't worried even if they did. Nicole could easily pass for a drunken Susanne, being helped up the stairs, one tenuous step after another, by her caring American houseguest...and boyfriend.

Inside, it didn't take long to get Nicole out of her clothes and into her bed. She was his beautiful and irreplaceable *Nude Reclining*, a living and breathing legacy from the distant past, a temporary visitor materialized quite by accident in the here and now, whose visa had just been stamped "Permanent" by the official hand of fate. She would sleep off the effects of the TMMP; even now, her blood levels were probably approaching normal as she dozed—his one and only, the one that didn't get away.

He would join her there shortly, lying next to her and wrapping his own naked body gratefully around hers. But first he had a phone call to make—Susanne's last promise to the other involved party in their endeavor, and one that John intended to keep.

"I'll phone you as soon as we get back," Susanne had said, speaking into her cell phone just before the three of them had left for the museum. The absent, elder Bruante was probably sitting at this very moment in his easy chair, waiting for word that all had gone exactly according to plan.

It took a moment to find the number in Susanne's speed dial. Then, when he touched the screen to make the call, a voice at the other end answered after only one ring.

"Henri, it's John," he announced into the phone receiver. "We need to talk. There were...complications."

Chapter Twenty-Two

There had been "complications," John had said.

Henri thought about the phone conversation he had had with John a few hours earlier, as he took his morning walk—the police following closely behind, of course. He had given Nicole and John a few hours to sleep; now, at ten minutes to eight, it was time for them to conference face-to-face, to work out the logistics of their plan.

Yes, it was a problem that Susanne had disappeared, but he and John had come up with an explanation that would satisfy just about everyone. The diligent Inspecteur Crossier wouldn't be happy—too bad. After all, it wasn't as if Susanne was a full-fledged suspect in the case, given the lack of evidence linking her in any way, shape, or form with any kind of wrongdoing. Besides, Susanne hadn't been given any official instructions by the authorities to stay in the city—or even in the country, for that matter—during the ongoing investigation.

The police would just have to deal with Susanne's spur-of-the-moment decision to relocate to the United States with her American boyfriend. It would be their problem, not Henri's or anyone else's, to get Susanne back to Paris if need be—but it would never come to that. There was no doubt about it, the d'Orsay murder would end up as a cold case because no actual homicide had been committed in the special exhibit gallery two weeks ago.

Eventually the authorities would come to the inevitable conclusion that the unidentified victim was most likely a homeless person, especially when more time passed and no concerned family members or friends came forward to report the dead man as missing. The case would die, and all of the nonexistent evidence would be boxed up and shoved into a corner of the storage basement of police headquarters and summarily forgotten. Give it another month or two at the most, and that would be that.

The pressing question, at this particular moment, was whether the police would want to question Susanne today. That all depended, Henri rationalized, on whether the night guard from last night, a fellow named André, had woken up before or after the morning shift came in. If he had regained consciousness before his colleagues clocked in to relieve him, logic dictated that he would have scrambled to reboot all of the museum's surveillance systems—the ones Susanne had disarmed after her smoothly executed charade—and do his best to cover up his several-hour absence from the land of the diligent.

In this scenario, André wouldn't dare mention a word about Susanne, since keeping quiet would mean the difference between gainful employment and waiting in line for *l'allocation chômage*. His recollections of the night's fun and games might be somewhat hazy anyway, since the brandy had been heavily laced with a dizzying dose of sedative. At any rate, accusing the assistant director of anything more than making a friendly stop at André's desk on the way to her own office might land him in more trouble than he was in already. It would be her word against his, so keeping his mouth shut would be the simplest way to make it all go away.

Henri hoped for this outcome, because if the police came knocking on Susanne's door, the striking physical resemblance between his niece and Nicole would not be enough to fool the astute Crossier. Nicole's speech and mannerisms were all her own, so there would be no way, in this world or any other, for Nicole to pass herself off as the absent assistant director in the company of people who had met and actually knew Susanne.

Henri had not been as surprised as John that Susanne had opted for a one-way ticket elsewhere. Yes, the trip from here to there was risky, but if Susanne had made it, Henri had no doubt that she would use what she knew about the future of Impressionism to position herself just so, as the *prèmiere* nude model for all of the big names. He wouldn't be a bit surprised if, a few years from now, a previously undiscovered cache of Renoir or Degas nudes magically surfaced, featuring none other than the famed Susanne Bruante herself. She might even find a way to get her name, along with her naked physique, into the history books. Leave it to Susanne. If there was a way to make her mark on posterity, she would find it.

Henri agreed fully with John that Susanne would make it her first order of business to ensure Edmond's safety. If Edmond died, so would Susanne—theoretically, at least—and so would Henri, for that matter. No one, including John, could say if Edmond's descendants would cease to exist at the very moment that Edmond died, or if the impact of the boy's demise would be delayed the twenty-odd years that it would have taken him to have children of his own.

For Henri, the one and only important moment of truth would occur at 2:20 p.m. today. As long as he made it past the June 13th milestone, just six-and-a-half hours from now, he couldn't care less about the next one, two decades down the road. By then he would be an old man, if he lived that long, and it wouldn't really matter if he existed or disappeared when he had already lived his best years anyway. Susanne, on the other hand, had much more at stake, since she was still young. Rest assured, she would make sure that Edmond made it, because her own life depended on saving the four-year-old version of her great-great-grandfather.

Henri climbed the front steps to Susanne's apartment; the policeman who had been following him stayed back, stationing himself unobtrusively on a sidewalk bench just a few doors down. Yes, Henri was taking a risk by leading the police here, but then again, there was something to be said for making things look normal. The gendarmes had made the trip from Henri's house to Susanne's residence and back more than once over the past three days, so another visit paid by a loving uncle to his niece did not seem out of the ordinary. He wouldn't stay very long this morning anyway—just long enough to work out John and Nicole's escape plan.

John buzzed him in, and a moment later Henri found himself sitting in the living room on the couch, while John paced back and forth.

"How's Nicole?" Henri asked.

"She woke up at five or so, totally lucid. I filled her in, and now she's asleep again. She's drained, but that's to be expected. She'll be fine."

"How did she react when she realized she was still here, and not there?"

"Worried—about Edmond."

"That's understandable," Henri said. "She's a concerned mother. But I think Edmond will be fine, as long as Susanne made it back."

"Or even if she didn't," John added. "Nicole made the arrangements for her visit with Edmond at Place Pigalle; and without Nicole around to coordinate that meeting, there's a good chance that

Edmond and his grandmother won't be anywhere near that horse-drawn carriage today."

We'll see, Henri thought. *In six hours, we'll see.* "Did you tell Nicole about our plan?" he asked, changing the subject. There was no point in belaboring the Edmond quandary, because what would be would be. There was one positive, though, in all of this: if Henri suddenly ceased to exist in a few short hours, it would probably be quick and painless. Here one second, gone the next—who could ask for a cleaner end to it all?

"Yes, I told her what we have planned; she's on board."

Of course she was! Nicole belonged here, and she belonged with John. The two of them were in love—even the self-consumed Susanne had probably noticed it—and this romance definitely wasn't one of those flash-in-the-pan affairs. It never would be. Henri had a knack for spotting the real thing, and this was it.

"Did you find Susanne's passport?" Henri asked.

"Yes," John said with a smile. He walked over to Susanne's desk, pulling open the front drawer to retrieve the document. "It was right where you said it would be." He held up the passport triumphantly. With his free hand, he gathered up Susanne's purse and carried it to the couch. After setting the passport and the purse on the coffee table, he settled down with a satisfied grin next to Henri. "You were right about the drawer key, too. It was in a zippered pocket in her purse."

If nothing else, Henri knew his niece. Just as he had hoped, it looked like the good Uncle Henri would be an invaluable inside contact in their evolving relocation plot.

"Have you booked the flight?"

"Yes, we leave today, just after one o'clock."

John wasn't wasting any time, and Henri agreed completely. It was best to get Nicole out of here, as quickly as possible, before friends, employers, and homicide detectives started making their inquiries. With an early afternoon flight time, they would be gone a full sixty minutes before the witching hour. It was best that way, really. No need upsetting Nicole unduly with the disappearance of a certain family member, if their worst-case scenario came to pass. Nicole might mourn a little for Henri, but her more devastating loss, logically extrapolated from Henri's sudden demise, would have occurred exactly one hundred and thirty four years in the past, to the exact minute and second. A mother should never lose a child, and Henri prayed that Nicole's new life in the modern world would not be saddened by this kind of tragedy.

"I hope Nicole understands that she will need to truly become Susanne," Henri said. "She should use Susanne's credit cards, write checks from her checkbook, and even assume her name. I'll take care of Susanne's bills, from this end; in a year or two, we can sell the condo. I don't think the two of you will be coming back here anytime soon."

"We'll stay in Chicago," John said with a nod. "My life is there, and if things go the way I hope they will, Nicole's new life will be there, too. Anyway, she can't stay here. Too many people know Susanne in Paris, so there's no way Nicole would be able to pull off the masquerade for more than a few days if she stayed."

"Agreed."

"Will you take care of Susanne's resignation?" John asked.

"I already typed the letter and forged her signature. I'll drop it off at the museum as soon as you leave."

"So, I guess that's it. We seem to have the bases covered." John dug in Susanne's purse and retrieved her keys. "You'll need to get in here, every so often, to check on things—and then there's Susanne's car. Instead of hoofing it, you'll finally have some wheels to get you places."

Henri took the keys, looking at them skeptically. "I'll probably sell the damn thing. There's no place my legs can't get me in this city." Henri held out his hand, and John shook it. "You're good for her, John. Keep her safe."

"I will." John looked Henri in the eye. "And you stay safe, too."

"I'll try." These were meaningless words, really, because Henri's safety rested in someone else's hands, and that person didn't even live in this century anymore.

"I'll give you a call when we get to Chicago," John promised.

"I'll be waiting."

God willing, he would be waiting.

It was June 14th, which meant that exactly two weeks had passed since Inspector Michèle Crossier had been assigned the role of principal investigator in the d'Orsay murder. But she was no further along on the road to solving the case than she had been on May 31st.

Every one of her leads had taken her down a path to a dead end, including the promising-looking bag that held clothes and a metal framing mallet, the bag Henri Bruante had planted in a nearby garbage can—intentionally it seemed—for her men to find. The blood they had tested on M. Bruante's work clothes matched with his own DNA sample, not the victim's; some hair they recovered from the woman's blouse and skirt belonged to Susanne, not Claudine; and the art restoration tool came up completely clean of biologics, which meant that it hadn't been used as the murder weapon.

Still, Michèle believed that something vaguely resembling her theory had transpired in d'Orsay's basement; it's just that she didn't have one iota of evidence to prove it. Claudine's DNA didn't match the hair on the victim's genitals, and neither did Susanne's; M. Bruante's DNA was nowhere to be found, except on the decoy clothing; none of the three persons of interest had left their fingerprints in any incriminating locations; and the victim himself still went by the name of John Doe. Perhaps all Michèle needed was to look at things from a different angle. The problem, it seemed, was that all the angles she could think of had already been looked at.

Why had M. Bruante gone to the trouble of packaging up some phony evidence for her crime lab technicians to scrutinize? The elder Bruante had to be involved in this case somehow; otherwise, why would he bother to throw a stick in the wrong direction for the police dogs to fetch?

"Go back and question him again," Deschamps had suggested at their daily lunchtime de-briefing just an hour ago. That's exactly what Michèle Crossier was about to do.

It was drizzling when she pulled up in front of M. Bruante's home workshop, two spaces behind the surveillance car that had been stationed there twenty-four hours a day for the past four days now. She slid out of her Peugeot, umbrella in hand but unopened, walking up to the driver's side of the white Mercedes to get an update from the officer on duty.

"Has he gone anywhere lately?" she asked Foujois, a heavy-set fellow with coffee stains on his shirt. She knew from yesterday's update that M. Bruante had walked to Susanne's house early in the morning, returning home after only a half-hour or so upstairs with his niece. Then he had gone to the museum in the early afternoon, but only briefly.

Michèle had made her own inquiries afterward, discovering that Susanne had resigned her position as assistant director of acquisitions and special exhibits, in a letter that M. Bruante had hand-delivered for her.

Michèle felt certain that Susanne's decision to quit her job stemmed from the executive director's press conference, televised live from the front of Musée d'Orsay just the day before yesterday. It must sting in the most humiliating kind of way, to have your erstwhile boyfriend make a discovery that should have been yours—but the first one there wins, as they say, and René Lauren had definitely gotten there first.

"He hasn't come outside since yesterday's little outings," the other gendarme, a thin and wiry guy named Godessart, answered. Michèle knew, from the phone debriefings, that Godessart had pulled the short straw yesterday, following M. Bruante back and forth, and back and forth again, on both his morning and afternoon constitutionals. For a man in his sixties, M. Bruante's legs, and his stamina, never seemed to tire.

"He's inside right now, I assume?" From where she stood, everything looked dark and quiet through the windows, both upstairs and down.

Foujois shrugged. "He went in yesterday at around two fifteen, right after his walk back from the museum. Those two doors are the only way out." He nodded toward the front and side entrances. "Unless he magically made himself disappear, he's in there."

It was raining steadily now, so she opened her umbrella. "Good work, boys. Keep it up."

Michèle crossed the street, stepping carefully on the wet pavement, arriving a few seconds later at the business entrance, the one that gave access to M. Bruante's art restoration workshop. She peered in through the adjacent picture-glass window, under the sign that said Closed—odd for a weekday. She made note of a covered painting sitting on an easel off to the side, a long table cluttered with frames and tools, and an alcove in back that the elder Bruante apparently used for drawing and painting, judging from the handful of partly finished canvases there. The place looked dead, with no sign of its owner.

She decided to ring the bell anyway. After three tries, all of them resulting in no response, she made her way from the front of the house to the side, climbing the stairs that led to the *premier étage*. There was no bell up here to ring, so she knocked—a few light taps to begin with, but then louder. She tried again, and again; she was starting to think that maybe he wasn't there after all.

She looked over her shoulder, which gave her a perfect view of the unmarked police car, to glare meaningfully at Foujois. Henri Bruante had probably slipped out unnoticed. If she found out that the surveillance officers had either left their post or had fallen asleep on the job, she would have both of their badges. She turned to leave, her temper well on the way to boiling; that's when M. Bruante opened the door.

"Hello, inspector." His greeting was pleasant and unstrained. He didn't seem at all surprised to see her—his all-too-familiar reaction to all of their dealings so far. "I'm sorry to keep you waiting, out here in the rain. I was sleeping. You see, I have been very busy, these past few days."

She nodded. "I'm sorry to disturb your day of rest—"

"But you have some questions for me, I'm sure, or else you wouldn't have," he finished with a smile. "That's fine. Come in out of the rain, and we'll talk." He stepped politely to one side and let her in.

She closed her umbrella and leaned it against the wall by the door as she stepped into a small dining room, where she saw a table cluttered with papers. "Pardon the bachelor's mess," he said, leading her through the first room and into a second. He motioned toward a couch and an easy chair—he was a most accommodating host. "Take your pick. Could I get you something to drink?" He acted as if he had nothing to hide, which made her wonder what, exactly, he was hiding.

"Thank you, monsieur, but no. This shouldn't take long."

She took a seat on the couch, while he sat across from her on the chair. "How may I help you?"

"You dropped off an interesting bag of goodies for us a couple of days ago. Would you mind telling me why you felt the need to dispose of some ripped and bloodied clothes, along with a perfectly good framing mallet, in a garbage bin six or seven blocks from here?"

"So that's where my mallet ended up!" His tone of voice sounded convincingly surprised. "It must have gotten mixed in with the clothes when I put them down on my workbench to sort."

"So, you didn't mean to throw it out?" She didn't believe him for a second, but she played along with his ruse anyway.

"Of course not. That was one of my better ones. I was just about to order another. If you still have it, would you mind returning it to me?"

She ignored the request. "Why did you dump the bag so far from your house, Monsieur Bruante?"

"The small can on the corner was full, so I took it to a bigger one a few blocks away. It's not that far; anyway, I enjoyed the walk."

Enjoying the walking part was true, at least. Henri Bruante went everywhere on foot, as her surveillance officers could attest. "We found your own blood on the work clothes," she said.

"Of course. I cut myself with a sharp planer, resurfacing a frame." He shrugged. "I could have tried washing them, but the clothes were old anyway, so it was simpler to throw them away."

He seemed to have an answer for everything. The last question she had for him might be more difficult to explain. "We found Susanne's hair on the women's clothes. Why did you throw away one of your niece's outfits?"

"She stayed with me for a few months when her condo was being renovated, and she left some clothes here. She took everything back to her apartment a few weeks ago, except for those."

"They looked pretty ragged," Michèle said, raising her eyebrows. "Normal wear and tear?"

"Not exactly." He smiled. "What Susanne and her friends enjoy behind closed doors is none of my business; let's just say she likes it rough. That's not my idea of a good time, but, to each his—or her—own."

Michèle gazed at Henri with undisguised skepticism. "And you expect me to believe all of this?"

"Why wouldn't you? It's all true." He leaned forward in his chair. "You police always try to look for hidden meaning in everything. It was just a bag of throwaway clothing—nothing more, nothing less."

"So when I question Susanne about her clothes and her sexual idiosyncrasies—when I pay her a visit later today—she'll tell me the same story?"

"She would, if she were still in Paris for you to question."

Had Susanne taken a little vacation to re-think her washed-up career? "I know about Susanne's resignation," Michèle countered, "and I don't blame her for wanting to get away for a few days to get her head together. Where is she, and when will she be back?"

"She's in Chicago with her fiancé, probably picking out her wedding ring as we speak."

"Fiancé?" Michèle stared at Henri, who was grinning at her, as if daring her to think of a snappy comeback.

"Yes, Dr. John Noland. I think you met him, *n'est ce pas*?"

"Well, yes, but I had no idea they were engaged." Could this part of Henri's story possibly be true? "It just seems rather—sudden."

"Not at all, inspector. She and John have had a long-distance relationship for quite some time, now. In fact, they've been discussing marriage for years. I guess they just didn't include you in this particular conversation."

"But what about Susanne's other boyfriend?"

"Do you mean René Lauren, Musée d'Orsay's executive director? Susanne's boss?" Henri laughed. "Yes, they were involved, but never seriously—for either of them, I believe. Susanne's special arrangement with her employer meant nothing to Susanne or to John, if he even knew about it. Susanne is very open-minded when it comes to this kind of thing. John is, also. As I said before, to each his own."

What could Michèle do? Absolutely nothing. Susanne had not been ordered to stay in Paris. She had never been arrested, and she wasn't even under police surveillance anymore.

Henri got up and wrote two phone numbers on a piece of paper. He handed it to Michèle from across the coffee table with a pleasant smile and then sat down again. "You can reach her on her cell phone—or John's, if you'd like. I'm sure she'd be more than happy to talk to you."

Michèle sighed. There was nothing more to say. The guiltless Susanne had skipped town; the virtuous Claudine would get off scot-free; and the eager-to-help and ever-truthful Henri would go on restoring paintings and disposing of bloodstained clothing to his heart's delight. Michèle was finished here, it seemed, but as she got up to leave, she decided to give it one more try.

"What really happened at Musée d'Orsay two weeks ago?" she asked. It was worth a shot. Maybe a head-on approach would make him talk.

He gazed back at her thoughtfully, as if quietly weighing the pros and cons of leveling with her. Finally, he seemed to come to a conclusion, so she sat back down. The question was whether truth or lies had just won the silent debate.

"You won't believe this," Henri stated soberly, "but your victim was a time traveler—and her companion was too. He died on the way here, but she survived."

She was surprised only by the absurdity of his lie. She should have known. Next, he would be telling her that the woman was Courbet's mistress, or Degas' nude model; or maybe that the victim was Courbet or Degas himself.

"Thank you, monsieur," Michèle replied with cold sarcasm. "Maybe this time traveler of yours would be willing to answer some questions? I'm sure she'd be able to clear up everything—and then I'd finally be able to close my case."

"I'm afraid you just missed her," he responded, deadpan. "You see, she's gone back—to the time in which she belongs."

Enough was enough; she was finished here. Michèle got up, brushing past Henri on her way to the door. When she got there, he called after her.

"Inspector Crossier?"

With her hand on the doorknob, she looked over her shoulder, across the dining room to where Henri stood on the threshold of his sitting room.

"What is it, Monsieur Bruante?"

"Nothing, mademoiselle," he said, after a split second of hesitation. Whatever he was going to say, he didn't. "I wish you *bonne chance*, is all," he added, with a sincere look on his face that gave the distinct impression of genuine concern.

She nodded curtly. Then she turned away and, retrieving her umbrella, walked out the door.

—La fin—

The Art Institute of Chicago

Upcoming Exhibits

Renoir's Model:

The Jeremy Maguire Collection, on Tour

Opening December 5th, 2021

This spectacular private collection of nudes, previously unavailable for public viewing, will run through March 1. Tickets will be available on-line or by calling the Special Exhibits office 1-312-555-0100, beginning November 15th. Same day tickets will also be available at the door.

Epilogue

Susanne Noland sat on a bench inside the first room of the special exhibit at the Art Institute of Chicago, waiting patiently for her husband to arrive. She had already viewed the special exhibit, including the audio tour, but she would walk through again with him, just to see his reaction.

It had been more than ten years now, since she had moved to Chicago from Paris. She liked it here, much better than where she had come from. It hadn't taken her very long at all to adjust. She spoke, thought, and dreamt in English now, but a subtle accent remained, a constant nostalgic reminder of the past that she had left far behind.

There were things she missed, of course—Montmartre, for instance (the nineteenth-century version); Henri, who still kept busy with his art restoration business in Paris, even though he was well past seventy years old; and Edmond, especially Edmond, who she hoped and prayed was alive and well in a distant world that she would never see again.

It had been easy enough to assume Susanne's identity. They looked alike, and no one questioned her as they embarked on a plane to the U.S. shortly after her delirium had cleared. It didn't take her long to win the acceptance of John's friends and family—Nicole no longer, but now Susanne, his long-lost college sweetheart. Less than three months later, they were married. Although she would never forget her Edmond, another child had come into her life two years after their marriage, a blessing that she and John had shared together for just over eight years.

As she waited for John to arrive at the special exhibit, she could truly say she had never been happier.

The advertisement for this special exhibit had caught her eye a few months ago, and she had been one of the first to order her ticket online. She had posed for Renoir twice, in the early 1870s; she was curious to see whether those two paintings would be included in this showing of Renoir's nudes, most of them previously unseen. In at least one of them, the birthmark on her left cheek had been clearly visible, and she remembered the pose she had assumed for both, so it would be easy enough, she had postulated, to identify herself in those two nudes.

Sure enough, they were there among the other paintings, but this was not the reason she had called John and insisted that he come to see the exhibit himself.

He entered, finally, through the glass doors, giving her a warm kiss. “Come on,” she said, taking him by the hand and leading him to the first wall. “That’s me—see the birthmark?” she said in French, so that no one but John could understand what she was saying.

He smiled, responding in French as well, “Yes, my dear, that’s definitely you.”

She leaned close to his ear, pointing to another painting on the adjacent wall. “Go and look at that one, and tell me what you think.”

They walked together to the other painting, and he examined it for a brief moment. “This is you, too,” he said, “isn’t it?”

“Is it?” she countered playfully. She placed her audio tour headset over his ears and pushed the number on the plaque next to the painting to start the recorded explanation. “Pay attention to the commentary,” she said, “and you’ll see.”

He listened for a moment; then his eyes widened in disbelief, and he looked over at Nicole for confirmation.

She nodded; it was…

About Charles J. Schneider

“My most treasured memories of childhood involve books: riding my bicycle to the bookstore in sixth grade to buy Dickens, London, Dumas, and Poe; sitting under my favorite tree in the summertime reading Tolkien, Lewis, Asimov, and Heinlein; and lying awake at night, the bedside lamp on, enjoying just one more chapter of Fowles, Barth, Conrad, and Verne.

My love of the written word extended well beyond childhood. I received a well-rounded education with a focus on Literature, History and the Classics while studying at Phillips Academy in Andover,

Massachusetts; followed by a comprehensive Liberal Arts experience at Wesleyan University in Middletown, Connecticut. I discovered my love for Science during those years; and although I eventually pursued a Medical Degree from The University of Chicago rather than a writing career, I recall with nostalgia my passion for Literature and the Arts in high school and in college. At Andover, my favorite courses involved novels, poems and drama; and at Wesleyan, my electives were always literary. Shakespeare, Marlow, O'Neill, Williams, and Ibsen took the slots that were not occupied by Darwin, Watson, and Crick—and so, I graduated with a Major in Biology and a Minor in Literature in 1984.

I never took a course in creative writing; but the years of medical writing and publishing, along with a continued interest in reading fiction in my spare time, eventually evolved into something that has admittedly become more than just a hobby."

Dr. Schneider is a practicing oncologist at Medical Oncology Hematology Consultants at the Helen F. Graham Center (Christiana Care Medical Center) in Newark, Delaware. He lives with his family in Landenberg, PA.

http://www.charlesjschneider.com

CPSIA information can be obtained at www.ICGtesting.com
Printed in the USA
LVOW08s1222220114

370488LV00001B/121/P